None Shall Sleep

by Laura Giebfried

Also by Laura Giebfried

Song to the Moon (book 2)
When I am Laid in Earth (book 3)
Beating Heart Cadavers
The Victim's Game

For Tom Frisk,

Cult leader,
partner in crime,
and foul-weather friend.

Nessun dorma! Nessun dorma! Tu pure, o Principessa,
nella tua fredda stanza,
guardi le stelle
che tremano d'amore, e di speranza!
Ma il mio mistero chiuso in me;
il nome mio nessun sapra!
No, No! Sulla tua bocca lo dir quando la luce splende!
Ed il mio bacio sciogliera il silenzio
che ti fa mia!
Il nome suo nessun sapr,
E noi dovrem, ahim, morir, morir!
Dilegua, o notte! Tramontate, stelle!
Tramontate, stelle! All'alba vincero! Vincero! Vincero!

- from *Turandot* by Giacomo Puccini

Translation:
None shall sleep! None shall sleep! Even you, O Princess,
in your cold bedroom,
watch the stars
that tremble with love and with hope!
But my secret is hidden within me;
none will know my name!
No, no! On your mouth I will say it when the light shines!
And my kiss will dissolve the silence
that makes you mine!
No one will know his name,
and we will have to, alas, die, die!
Vanish, o night! Set, stars!
Set, stars! At dawn, I will win! I will win! I will win!

NONE SHALL SLEEP

Ch. 1

She died on a Friday, right in time to ruin the holiday plans for the students who had hoped to take the ferry to the mainland for the long weekend. The boys stood on the shore even still, watching as the police pulled the water-logged body from the ocean with mixtures of excitement and anticipation on their faces. Several more students joined the crowd once word got out, but by the time she had been zipped out of sight into a plastic-bag, Barker had gotten wind of the situation and sent someone down to chase them away. I watched them idly from the window of the residence building, the phone in my hand slipping down to my shoulder as I did so, until Karl's sharp tone alerted me back to the conversation.

"It's the third one this year, Enim," he said. "You can't keep failing exams, especially in the year before college. What would people think?"

"Right," I said absently, still squinting to see the students whispering feverishly about what they had seen. "What would they think."

"I know this comes down to Jack's influence – there's no other explanation. I rather thought that you would have reevaluated your friendship with him by now, especially given the trouble that he got you into last year."

"True."

"You were very nearly expelled," Karl went on without acknowledging the flatness in my tone. "Anyone else would have been. You're lucky that Mr. Barker was compassionate enough to let you stay on –"

"I'm lucky that my father paid Barker off, you mean."

I wrapped the phone cord around my fingers as I gave the blunt response, reveling in the sound of static as Karl struggled to respond. He would undoubtedly run his hands through his hair before smoothing it down again as he thought of a way to counter my claim, but even the image of him so frazzled in his neatly pressed suit and straight tie couldn't lighten the mood brought on by his phone call.

"I – he – that's not true, Enim. He didn't pay the headmaster off."

"He bought the lacrosse team another stadium," I said. "They're very pleased about it."

"That was a completely separate event. He donated the money so that you could have a better lacrosse team."

"I don't play lacrosse. I don't even go to the games. The only reason he wanted Bickerby to have a better sporting field was so that I could stay in school."

"That's not true, Enim. If anything, he did it in the hopes that you might start playing a sport – we all agree that it would be good for you."

I rolled my eyes to the ceiling, grateful that he couldn't see my expression. Despite the fact that he was a lawyer, he had never been a very good liar: Barker had only consented not to expel me in return for a signed check.

"I'm not playing a sport," I said.

"You really should though, Enim. It would do you good to spend some time outdoors, and you'd make friends with your teammates, and it would look good on your college applications –"

"I'm not playing a sport."

"Well, alright then, what about another extracurricular activity? Something that you can do with your free time ... What about joining the book club? Or the chess team?"

"Definitely not."

"I – well, all right. But there has to be something that you'd enjoy. What about the Latin Club? You like Latin."

I didn't bother to respond. The fact that Karl knew so little about me was hardly a surprise, but it irritated me even so. The only reason that anyone took Latin was because it looked good to colleges, and the only reason that I had taken it was because my father had made me.

"No?" Karl said when I failed to answer. "Come on, Enim. There must be something you'd enjoy doing besides for spending time with Jack."

"Not really."

"But you have to do something this semester – you can't just *not* have an extracurricular activity."

"Of course I can. It's not in the rules that I need one."

"You know what I mean, Enim," Karl said tiredly. "Listen, your father understands if you don't want to play the piano anymore, but he really thinks that you need to fill that time with another hobby."

"Does he?"

"Yes, he does. He doesn't like you having so much unused time – it can't be healthy."

My father spent so much time planning my every move that it was a wonder he had time to do anything else at all. He wasn't comfortable unless he could rest assured that he knew every part of my life was laid out and waiting to happen according to plan – a mission which, so far, had gone all but accordingly. I rather thought that he'd have an easier time accomplishing anything if he stopped dictating the strategies to his younger brother and just came home, but he was evidently confident enough to believe otherwise.

"He's just worried about you, Enim. He doesn't want you to fall into the wrong ... *activities* because of all this extra time that you have now."

I could only imagine what activities my father feared I would fall into, because Bickerby Academy was undoubtedly one of the most difficult places to find trouble – or much of anything – in. It was located in what was, perhaps, the most desolate, forsaken place on earth: an island off the coast of Maine. The summers there were apparently quite beautiful, evidenced by the fact that there were a few dozen vacation homes lining the cliffs that overlooked the water, but I had hardly ever seen more than a few weeks of it. For the majority of the school year, Bickerby was shrouded in a bitter cold that seeped in through the cracks in the windows and up through the floors. Once winter hit, normally in a storm that changed the landscape into a blank expanse of white, the air became so frozen that it was hard to breathe.

Of course, nothing of such weather was mentioned on the

brochures for the school. Bickerby Academy was marketed, quite rightly, as an all-boys boarding school that offered over sixty college credit courses, seven languages, several sports, and dozens of extracurricular activities to prepare students for success in college. Pictures of the campus had all been taken during the warm season, possibly at a time when school hadn't even been in session, and were inviting enough so that concerned parents overlooked the short blurb about the dangerously cold winters. My father, however, undoubtedly welcomed the idea of the school being enclosed in a circle of snowdrifts for the good part of the year. Though he maintained that he had selected Bickerby solely based on its merits, I knew the real reason that he had chosen it for me over all of the other preparatory schools: it was located in a place with no cellphone coverage, no cable television, no internet service, and could only be reached by a ferry that didn't run often enough. It was, in short, inescapable.

"If he's so worried, why hasn't he called in seven months?"

The sound of the phone clattering against wood indicated that Karl had dropped it on the desk, and it took him a moment of fumbling with it before he pressed it back to his ear.

"He's ... well, you know how difficult it is, Enim. He's working very hard, and the time difference makes it near to impossible to call ..."

"Right. But he talks to you about me every other day."

"Not ... not every other day," Karl protested poorly.

"Whatever. I don't want to talk to him anyway."

Karl gave no answer. It was impossible to say which one of us was the worse liar, though I rather hoped that it was him. At the very least I hoped that he thought the reason I wanted my father to come home was so that I didn't have to spend another moment with him.

We had been doomed to not get along from the moment that he took over guardianship of me. Having never had children of his own, he had no idea how to handle me and so his role only involved passing along orders from my father and chauffeuring me to and from school on holidays. Despite my attempts to be insolent enough to warrant him insisting that my father had to come back, he was always too weak to make such a request.

"It's hard for him, Enim," Karl said after a long moment. "Your mother was ... It's hard."

I kept my eyes on the blur of dark green trees outside the window. In the distance, Julian Wynne was making his way towards the residence building. Despite my desire to end the conversation before he had the chance to eavesdrop on it, I said, "No, it's not."

Karl sighed. Inwardly I wondered if he agreed that my father was the least affected of anyone involved in what had happened to my mother. He, at least, had had the opportunity to move away and get on with his life. I had been stuck in the midst of it far longer than I could stand, and Karl had somehow been dragged into it in his older brother's wake.

Claiming that I had assignments to get done, I hung up the phone and hurried away from the office, but had barely circled to the stairs when Julian Wynne called after me.

"Enim!"

His voice echoed with such resonance around the stairwell that I could hardly pretend not to have heard him. Pausing on the landing to the second floor, I waited for him to catch up with me.

"Glad I caught you alone," he said with a smile that didn't match our acquaintance. "Seems like you're never without Jack these days."

He sidled up to stand alongside me as we made our way to the fourth floor, walking at a much slower pace than I would have liked. Julian was, without a doubt, one of the friendliest people at Bickerby. There was something in the way he laughed that made the other boys want to be in on the joke, and something about the way he spoke that made them wish they knew what he was saying. And though I knew him well enough to know that all he truly cared about was getting information to spread around the campus about anything and everything of interest to him, regardless of how high the cost was to the person he had gathered it about, it was impossible to know if it was worse to be his enemy or his friend.

"You know," he said with a thoughtful look playing on his face, "if you wanted to come hang out with Kyle and me sometime, that would be fine. We haven't seen much of you since …"

He chuckled into the uncomfortable silence that the sentence led into as though the inferred situation was even remotely humorous.

"Right. Well, I've been busy."

"Right – busy with Jack," he said. He said the name with a roll of his eyes and bitter tone as though unconcerned that he was criticizing my best friend. "So why aren't you doing orchestra this semester?"

I studied him carefully as I considered my response. Julian and I had never been friends to begin with, having only known one another from living in the same building and being a part of Bickerby's music program, and our association had only diminished further in recent months. I could tell that he was looking for something hidden beneath my well-pressed blue sweater and khakis about the events that had taken place the previous year, and I was none too eager to give anything away.

"Too many classes," I said.

"Oh. Well, that's too bad – we're missing our only piano player."

We reached the fourth floor landing and I hastily pulled open the door. Our rooms were across the hallway from one another, but once I was inside mine with Jack, Julian would hardly think to bother me.

"Right. Well, thanks, Julian, but I've really got to get some things done …"

As I made to move towards the door, though, he reached out and latched onto my arm.

"Wait." His smile faltered and he had to work to keep it plastered to his face, but he gave a nervous laugh and relaxed his grip on my arm. "I was just wondering, did you see what happened down at the beaches today?"

"Not really."

"Right, but you were on that side of campus before, right? So you know what's going on?"

"I heard there might've been an accident."

"Yeah." His piqued interest lit up his face in eagerness. "Did you hear anything? Or see anything?"

"Like what?"

"Like anything," he said impatiently. "I heard they found a body – *a body*. Can you believe it?"

"No."

"Yeah, it was some local girl's," he continued. "Apparently she'd gone missing a few days ago, and now her body's floated up on Bickerby's shores. I went down as soon as I saw the crowd and police swarming the place, but they had already chased everyone away before I got to see anything."

"Shame," I said, but Julian was too preoccupied with the news to notice my derisive tone. A part of me thought that he somehow knew my aversion to the topic of drowning and had singled me out specifically, but I pushed the idea away at the thought of what Beringer would say if he knew how mistrustful I was becoming.

"Well, it's too bad you didn't see anything," he said, shaking me off now that he knew I had nothing to share. "We probably won't know anything for a while, since it's impossible to get any information around here ... The daily might say something tomorrow if we're lucky, though the whole paper might just shut down – I doubt they know what to do when actual news comes up around here."

He waved me off and shut his door on me, and I turned to unlock my own before any more thoughts of the dead girl in the water could press against my mind. When I entered the dorm room, I paused in the doorway to survey it. It was seemingly just how I had left it: small and cramped, a dent in the plaster where Jack had kicked his foot through the wall, and the window cracked open several inches. My side of the room was neatly organized: the bed was made up nicely, the side table was clear, and my books were neatly ordered by subject on the shelf beneath. It was the focus of many snickers from the other students, none who had been burdened with the concern for tidiness. If only they could see how immaculate Karl kept his things, then perhaps they wouldn't be so harsh on me.

I maintained that I wasn't really a neat person anyhow, the room just looked even tidier than it was because it was juxtaposed with Jack's side. His clothes, both clean and dirty, were strewn over every surface as though the furniture and floor were the same to him as hangers. They littered the bedposts and end table, stuck out from his mess of sheets and covers, came out of drawers that were meant for school supplies, and created a second carpet on the floor around his bed. The furniture and molding on his side were also covered in little burn holes from where he stubbed his cigarettes out at random; at first glance, the walls appeared to be polka-dotted.

Even though it looked the same as when I had left for classes that morning, I knew that Sanders had been there. As the monitor for our building, he had a key to all of the students' rooms for security purposes. I doubted that he had ever used his ability to check in on us for our safety, though. Sanders' idea of fun was catching another student breaking the rules. He reveled in handing out detention slips and was always looking for an act severe enough to warrant a trip to the headmaster. When he had first acquired the position, he had been somewhat terrifying given the seriousness that he took it with, but now it was more of an annoyance than anything.

He had undoubtedly been searching for a pack of Jack's cigarettes or any other substances that were against school rules. Yet the problem with sifting through Jack's things was that, even if he put them back in the relative spots he had found them, the months' worth of dust that had cultivated over his untouched books and lost articles of clothing would be upset and give the rifling away. I smiled at the thought of Sanders pawing through Jack's array of dirty clothes and the questionable debris that had missed the trashcan only to come up with nothing. Jack was far better at hiding things than Sanders was at finding them.

"Room search?" I asked, coming into the room and dropping my bag on the end of my bed.

Jack swiveled around in the desk chair, a cigarette hanging lazily between two fingers, and an impish smile playing on his lips. With his dark hair, twice-broken nose and complete disregard for the school dress code, it was no wonder that both Karl and my father yearned for me to stop my association with him. He stubbed the cigarette out on the wood and tossed it in the direction of the trashcan before answering.

"Yep. By the looks of it, he took the opportunity after classes ended. Mind you, he didn't find anything, but this is why we shouldn't leave the room unattended. I'm stocking up on Parliaments while it's still warm enough to walk to town, and if he finds the stash it'll be a long winter."

"It's always a long winter."

"You're missing the point, Nim. The last thing we need is Sanders in here looking through our stuff."

"Right, sorry: Karl called. Where were you, talking to Miss Mercier?"

"No, detention. And for the record, I'd take the detention any day over chatting with Uncle Karl."

"Who wouldn't?"

I took a seat on my bed and pulled my boat shoes off, arranging them neatly by the dresser before unpacking my bag. There were a dozen or so assignments that needed to be done over the weekend, but I had no desire to do any of them.

"You were really talking to Karl all that time? Hard to believe, seeing as both of you are in competition for who can say the least."

"He talks when there's a lecture to be given," I said. "But I ran into Julian in the hall, and he stopped me for a while, too, so ..."

"Wynne? What's he want?"

"Information."

"Obviously, but what's he think he'll get out of you? We

haven't been up to anything in months."

Ignoring his irritated tone, I flipped open my Physics book and tried to remember what chapter Volkov had gone over in class that day. Every series of equations looked the same.

"He's just completely enthralled with the local news, here."

"So he really is bored with life."

"Not exactly. Apparently some girl was found in the water earlier today. Dead."

Jack raised his eyebrows.

"Weird," he said. "I mean, exciting, sure, but weird."

"How's it weird?" I said, again feeling as though I was the only one reacting properly so such disturbing news.

He shrugged.

"You just don't expect murders to happen on the island, do you? Usually small towns weed out psychos fairly quickly."

"I didn't say that she was murdered," I said. "Just that she was found in the water. It could've been an accident."

"Could've been. But women don't really die of accidents, do they?"

"Of course they do."

"No, they don't: men die of accidents."

"Women can die of accidents, too, Jack," I said. "It's not like prostate cancer, you know."

"Ah, but it is," Jack countered, his mischievous love of conspiracies alighted. "You see, men weren't built to last. We were made to hunt, kill, and be killed. Look back at our male ancestors and see how they died, and I bet none of them died of old age or whatever. Cave men were either killed in the wild or else by another guy who wanted his wife and cave, you know?"

I rolled my eyes and continued to look for my assignment, attempting not to look entertained by another of his ridiculous theories.

"No, really, Nim, it's true," he continued. "I took Social Anthropology – I know this stuff."

"You took Social Anthropology with me," I said incredulously. "And *you* failed."

"Whatever, I got the gist," he said, waving me off. "The point is, men are the ones who cut off their arms with power tools and walk through glass doors, right? But women, they don't end up in the emergency room with weird injuries unless someone else inflicted them, you know what I mean?"

"No."

Jack sighed.

"Women don't die of accidents: they either live to see old age, or they get killed. It's as simple as that." He leaned back in his seat and crossed his arms as though the point had any validity whatsoever. "I mean, think of the last three women you know who've died, and I bet they fall into one of those categories, right?"

It only took a moment of the statement hanging in the air before its inference sunk in. Jack's nonchalance turned to guilt at the realization of what he had said, but I bit the side of my mouth and feigned ignorance to keep the conversation away from the subject of my mother.

"Probably."

Jack shifted awkwardly and cleared his throat.

"Anyway, we've got more interesting things to think about than Wynne's newest obsession," he said, shrugging the subject off. "I was talking to Miss Mercier after class today —"

I rolled my eyes and turned back to my assignment once again. Jack spoke to his French teacher, Miss Mercier, so often that it was almost tedious to hear him relay the conversations. Though he was far from being the only student who had taken a liking to her, he was certainly the most candid in his preoccupation with her, often waiting after class to speak with her or else joining her in her room during his study halls. He was also the only one who had become set on the idea of visiting the French Riviera solely because it was the region of France that she was from, and while I was just as eager to get as far away from Bickerby as possible, I wasn't quite sure that the place would have seemed so spectacular if it wasn't Miss Mercier who had told him as much.

"—and she explained the whole visa thing, and it doesn't

look like we'll need one so long as we don't stay too long. So now all we need is for you to turn eighteen and we can go."

"And a few thousand dollars, and to graduate, and to think of a way to convince Karl," I said, carefully copying down an equation from the textbook, "but, yeah, we can go."

"Ah, don't worry about Karl," Jack said with a wave of his hand. "He'll be so sick of you by March that he'll offer to drive you to the airport. And we don't need to graduate, despite what you think."

"We do if you don't want my father sending the *policia* after me."

"*Gendarmerie*, Nim, and I'm not talking about your father: I'm talking about Karl. You could easily pull one over on him without him ever seeing it coming. If it was me, I would've upped and left right when he showed up at your front door."

"Right, but this *is* me," I said, "and I would never do that."

"True. You avoid confrontation at all costs."

"I avoid speaking at all costs."

Jack cackled.

"Good thing you took a dead language," he said. "Though it won't do you much good when we go to France. You know, if you would just come to the Foreign Language meetings with me, you'd pick up some French."

"I can't go to those – Latin's hardly a spoken language."

"So? It doesn't matter. We speak in English, after all. Mainly we just talk about international cultures."

"Sounds like dinner with my father."

"Hardly. Come on, Nim, it's fun – we all just ask questions to the international students and talk about other countries we've visited or want to visit. You'd like it."

"We have international students at Bickerby?"

I couldn't imagine what would attract someone from another country to come all the way to America just to live at the edge of the earth on a snow-laden island. Jack seemed to know what I was thinking.

"Well, we have three," he admitted. "And they're Canadian … but that's not the point, Nim. The point is that the meetings are a good time, and you need to go somewhere besides for the library. It can't be good for you."

"It's good for my grades."

"Apparently not. Come on, Nim – they're fun. Miss Mercier runs them, after all. Just come to one, and if you don't like it, I'll never drag you again."

He grinned in his infectious way, and I pushed aside my homework with the realization that it would never get done that night.

"All right, I might come," I said. "Is it tonight?"

"No, Thursday."

"Oh. I have to see Beringer on Thursdays."

"Ugh."

He made a face at the mention of the psychiatrist, undoubtedly considering a way to convince me that Beringer had purposefully scheduled our sessions on the same day as the Foreign Language meetings just to prevent me from going.

"He's doing this on purpose. It's what they do, Nim, those doctors," he had said, as though there was scientific evidence to back up his theory. "You can't trust them."

"I can't skip the session, Jack. You know he'd freak."

I kept my voice low even though we were alone. I went through quite a bit of trouble to keep the other students from knowing about Beringer, going out of my way to sneak into the sessions and pick up the medication he prescribed when no one was around, and I didn't want my efforts to be ruined by Jack's loud voice. Dropping my eyes back to the textbook, I chewed the inside of my mouth apprehensively.

"Yeah, he would. He'd probably send a search party for you," Jack said drearily.

"Probably."

"Of course, he might just go find you by himself," he said, his voice once-again taking on its maniacal enthusiasm. "Stalk you down in the woods when you're alone … offer to walk you back to your dorm and tuck you into bed –"

I gave him a disgusted look.

"Stop," I said.

"I will," he said. "But Beringer might not …"

I rolled my eyes.

"Please," I added, though I knew it wouldn't do me any good. Jack loved having the opportunity to discuss his negatively-lit views of Beringer. Whether his dislike of the man whom he had never met stemmed from an aversion to authority figures in general or just displeasure that my father was convinced there was something so wrong with me that it needed medical attention was unclear. Or perhaps he was simply trying to make light of the entire situation for my sake, assuming that I must have hated Beringer and everything that went with the weekly meetings, and I had just never bothered to correct him.

"Do you know why people want to become psychiatrists?" he said.

"To help people."

"Right, you keep telling yourself that. It's because they're crazy. Really, Nim, who wants to be around lunatics all day?"

He was fishing for a response and I obliged by answering, "No one."

"Exactly: no one sane. But crazy people love to be around their own kind. It makes them feel more normal, I think. Gives them an opportunity to not be the weirdest person in the room for once."

"Right," I said, barely paying attention.

"Now, you know why people want to become child psychiatrists?"

"To help children?"

Jack ignored me.

"Because they're crazy … about children."

"Oh, God," I muttered.

"Do you ever wonder why Beringer's so keen to come all the way down here just to see you, late at night, all alone?"

Though I did often wonder why Beringer would consent to make the trip all the way out the island just for one session, I felt confident that the reason could at least in part be explained by a generous salary from my father rather than any of Jack's insane theories.

"Please stop," I said again, shaking my head.

He cackled and stood to go to dinner, but I opted not to join him with the excuse that I had to finish my homework. He didn't bother to ask if he should bring anything back for me; I was never quite hungry enough to eat the food at Bickerby.

When he had gone, I shut my textbook and slid off the mattress to go to the window. The campus was dark and silent below, and in the distance the glimmer of the dark ocean was just visible through the trees. Unwillingly my mind returned to the dead girl that Julian had spoken of, and though I knew nothing about her, I pictured her body floating in the water, face-up but faceless, blonde hair billowing out around her head like a halo as the strands rippled in the water, and wondered how it would feel to sink below the surface until the water became black and the air was squeezed from my lungs.

I took a step back and shook the thought from my head. It would do no good to think of such things now, especially given how much time and energy I had put into pushing the thoughts to the back of my mind. But as the silence in the room weighed down around me, images of the fair-haired woman who was somewhere between life and death, with eyes half-open but incapable of seeing, continued to burn against my skull. In my mind I imagined stepping away from her and running away from the beach, leaving her alone on the shore to fade away. I didn't want to think of her anymore.

But I wondered if she ever thought of me.

Ch. 2

Apart from constant chattering about the dead girl, the weekend had brought with it an intense cold spell that fell over the campus, and by the time that Tuesday arrived I was glad that the Columbus Day holiday had passed despite having failed to complete half of my assignments. With the realization that I was too tired from another fitful night's sleep to get any more of it done before classes began, I accompanied Jack to the dining hall, our heads bent low to block out the wind as we crossed the grass. When a particularly harsh gust finally eased up, Jack poked his face back out from his sweatshirt and looked over at me.

"And you really want to wait this out until graduation?" he said in exasperation. "Think about it, Nim: it's sunny and warm in the French Riviera right now."

I was too cold to take my face out of my jacket and didn't reply until we were inside the dining hall. Getting onto the back of the line, I grabbed a tray and quickly slid it down the counter.

"If you can think of a good way to get me there without my father noticing, please let me know. If not, then you'll have to be patient until I'm eighteen."

"Nah, I got nothing," Jack said, unhurriedly filling his tray with everything in reach. "Not even I'm crazy enough to think that there's a way to slip past your father. I just thought you might've found a way to convince him to let you go."

I gave him an incredulous look, but he was too busy collecting the last of the bacon from its tray and adding it to his plate to notice.

"I could never convince my father to do anything," I said.

"I know that, but he obviously has hope that you'll become argumentative. He's sending you to law school, after all."

"We both know that's not going to happen."

"True. Though really, he should've figured it out himself by now. You can't even win an argument with yourself, does he really think you'd be able to become a lawyer?"

"He likes a challenge."

"Evidently." Jack smirked. He finished filling his plate and waited for me to pour myself some coffee before we found a place to sit down. The majority of the tables in the room were empty by now, a telltale sign that we were running late, though Jack seemed none too concerned as he began to eat at his usual pace. I gulped down my coffee quickly in comparison even though it was too hot: Volkov wouldn't hesitate to demerit me for showing up to his class even a minute after the final bell.

"But you do live with a lawyer," Jack continued halfway through a forkful of food, "so you at least have some idea how to lie."

"Karl's not a real lawyer," I reminded him. "He's a tax lawyer – it's like a glorified accountant. I don't think he's ever stepped inside a court in his life."

"Well, there goes that plan, then," Jack replied with a shrug. "I guess we really will have to stick around until March. Shame we can't switch birthdays – no one would care if I was gone."

"Miss Mercier might," I said.

"Good point. She'd probably notice if I stopped coming to class – God knows I'm the only one who pays attention."

"I thought everyone paid attention during her class?"

"I meant that I'm the only one who pays attention to what she's teaching," Jack corrected. "They pay attention to her, all right."

He made a face and finished his breakfast in silence and we broke off to go to our separate classes. I turned in the direction of the Science Department, intent on making it in time and avoiding a lecture from Volkov, but I had only reached the front door and stepped inside the building when the bell rang. The artificial lights overhead flickered as I jogged towards his classroom and sent my shadow scampering across the wall. I reached the door to Volkov's room and gently pulled it open.

Even though the door only made the slightest of sounds when it closed, Volkov immediately took notice of me. He was a white-haired, thin man with sharp features and a hand that always held a metal pointer that gave the impression that it was more likely to be used to hit someone than to point to his slides. His eyes followed me as I slipped into the back row and took a seat next to Cabail Ibbot. I kept my head low as I took out my notebook and pen in the hopes that he would let my tardiness slide for once.

"Mr. Lund," he called back to me. "Perhaps you can solve the equation on the board."

I glanced up to squint at the board. It was a fairly straightforward example, not unlike the ones I had done for practice a few nights before out of the book, but I had no intention of standing up in front of the class and writing out the answer with everyone watching me. Volkov was staring at me expectedly. I shook my head.

"I assume that means that you don't know the answer, as well as not knowing how to tell time?" Volkov asked, and then turned to address the entirety of the class. "If you don't know how to solve problems such as this one by now, you should not bother to take the next exam."

I kept my eyes down on my paper. Beside me, Cabail was sneaking a glance at me. I knew that he knew the answer to the problem on the board as well. He was nearly three years younger than me, overtly odd, with round, thick glasses that magnified his eyes to an unprecedented size, and had never spoken aloud that I had heard. The seat next to him was almost always empty. No one wanted to sit by someone both far younger and far smarter than they were. I didn't mind so much, though, because despite being more intelligent than me, Cabail was also decisively stranger than I was. At least I knew that when people glanced back to where we were sitting, they were whispering about him, not me.

Knowing that Volkov wouldn't waste valuable class time giving me multiple reprimands, I took out my copy of *The Aeneid* so that I could produce at least part of the translation to hand in for Latin. I was so engrossed with finishing the last sentence that I didn't hear the bell ring until Cabail's magnified eyes rotated around in his head and settled on me. He looked like a huge, spindly bug trapped within a glass jar, peering at me in a silent request to be let out. I stiffened and looked up at him. To my surprise, he opened his mouth and spoke.

His voice was a young, twisted sort of sound. It sounded as though he was being strangled by some invisible force deep inside a tunnel.

"What are you doing here?"

I turned my head ever slightly, wondering what he meant by such a question.

"What do you mean?" I said. "I have class."

"I know," Cabail said. His huge eyes stared unblinkingly at me. "So why are you still here? Physics ended six minutes ago."

I jumped and looked around. Surely enough, the seats in front of me were empty. I couldn't fathom how the class had filed out of the room without me noticing, but I didn't have a moment to spare to think about it. Jumping up, I gathered my notes and book from the desk and slid them into my bag before making a dash for the door. Cabail watched me all the while. I let the door swing shut on his blank face.

The campus was clear again, indicating that I was indeed as late as I feared, and I shot across the grounds and through the central gardens at a run in order to get to the Foreign Language Building as quickly as I could. I ran the length of the hall, slowing only when I saw the door to Albertson's room, and took a moment to take a few huge breaths and regain a normal breathing pattern before opening the door.

Albertson's room, unlike Volkov's, was not based in a large lecture hall but rather a small classroom. There were less than two dozen students who sparsely filled up the seats, heads bent low over their translations, with Albertson seated at a desk at the front of the room. It was, essentially, an impossible room to enter without detection. Albertson glanced up at me.

"Sorry, Mr. Albertson," I said, my breath still heaving. I sat down quickly and reached for my book. Albertson gave me a faint smile but said nothing. I blew out a breath of relief at my evident reprieve, glad that I wouldn't be called out twice in a row in front of the class by the teacher, and shakily took out my homework. It was considerably wrinkled from how I had shoved it into my bag and looked like a poor excuse for a graded assignment; I hesitantly smoothed it out with my arm, but the paper remained wrinkled and the ink smudged. I sighed in discontent.

As we set to work on a practice translation that was written on the board, Albertson rose from his chair and came to stand by my desk. I looked up as his shadow fell over me, and he slid the paper onto my desk.

"Your exam from last week," he said in explanation.

"Thank you, Mr. Albertson."

When he turned away, I flipped over the exam and did a double-take. The paper was filled with so many red marks that it would have been easier to point out which parts were correct rather than incorrect. Noticing the number written across the top of the page, I wondered for a fleeting, desperate moment if it had been graded out of something other than the standard hundred points. I bit my tongue and laid the exam back down on my desk, face down. Another low grade. I seemed to have received more in the past two semesters than I had in all the other semesters at Bickerby combined. I wished that there was a way I could disappear across the ocean with Jack after all.

When the bell sounded at the end of class, I hurriedly picked up my things and slid them into my bag to leave, but had only just turned to the door when Albertson called me back.

"Mr. Lund."

I paused and waited for the rest of the class to file from the room. A heavy silence fell around us that I in no way wanted to fill.

"Yes, Mr. Albertson?"

I tried to act oblivious as to why he had stopped me despite knowing that my exam grade was quite possibly the lowest that Albertson had ever graded. I turned back to face him but didn't approach his desk, hoping to remain as close to the door as possible.

"Mr. Lund, I thought you might want to discuss your exam with me," Albertson said.

I kept my face impassive. Albertson studied me with flickering eyes.

"I'm sure you have some questions," he continued kindly.

I squinted and glanced towards the door, anxious to leave, and then looked back at Albertson. I should have liked him, I supposed, with his kind nature and heavily-wrinkled smile. He had continued teaching long after he was due to retire solely because he enjoyed the subject, and not even the fact that his class numbers dropped lower and lower with every year could discourage him.

"No, I don't have questions," I said. I could hear my voice was flat and cold but couldn't think of how to fix it. Albertson frowned slightly at me.

"None?"

"None."

He looked at me for a long while, surveying my face in a way that I didn't like at all – as though he could read every thought just by tracing the circles beneath my eyes – before finally speaking again.

"Enim," he said, with an odd emphasis on my given name, "I understand that you're going through a ... difficult time right now. I was sorry to hear about your mother."

I dropped my gaze to the floor and bore my vision into the white linoleum. The artificial lights overhead sent a horrifying gleam glaring back at me; the light hit me in the eyes painfully, but I dared not look away. I didn't want to see Albertson's expression. He had no right to go looking into my life; he was trespassing where he didn't belong.

"I'm willing to let you retake the exam," he said at last.

My face twitched and my untendered energy boiled down into my legs, making them restless. I wanted to run from the room or jump through the window, but I couldn't. Albertson was waiting for me to say something.

"Thank you, Mr. Albertson," I said quietly.

He nodded slowly.

"I just want to see you do well, Enim; I hope that you know that."

"Of course."

I turned and fled from the room before he could continue the conversation. It was hard to decide which was worse: Volkov's irritated ridicule of me or Albertson's gentle compassion for my wellbeing. I wished that I could sink into invisibility and not have to worry about either of them anymore, but it was evidently too much to ask to be left alone.

I made my way to the dining hall and crossly waited in the long line just to get a cup of coffee. Holding it carefully by the rim, I set it down at an empty table and watched the steam rise off of it.

"That's not all you're eating, is it?"

I looked up at the friendly voice that masked an accusation and found Julian standing in front of me. He was holding a lunch tray and his roommate, Kyle Trask, was at his side. I eyed him skeptically, wondering why he felt it was any of his concern if I was skipping a meal, when they sat down across from me. I instinctively leaned back, unaccustomed to sitting with anyone other than Jack at any given time.

Trask took a large bite of his sandwich and, halfway through chewing it, addressed me.

"So, Enim, you heard about that girl in town?" he asked from Julian's side. I moved my eyes over him. He put the emphasis on the wrong part of my name, unaccustomed to using it. I wondered what he normally called me behind my back.

"I heard."

"Exciting, right? We were all talking about what happened to her. We're taking bets, if you want to put something in."

I raised my eyes to his carefully. Sometimes I wondered if he could hear himself speaking. Other times I simply wondered how Julian could insult my friendship with Jack when Trask was clearly a worse choice.

"What'd you mean, what happened to her?" I said. "She died, didn't she?"

"Well, yeah. We're just wondering how."

"I assume she drowned."

"No, Enim –" Julian laughed and glanced at Trask. "We mean, *how'd* she die? It's not like she went for a swim in these temperatures and cramped up."

I eyed them carefully as they waited for my response.

"She might've," I said noncommittally. I raised my coffee to my mouth and blew on it to cool it down faster. If Julian kept talking, I was going to need an extra cup or so to ward off a headache.

"Oh, come on, Enim – it's got to be something more exciting than that. Kyle thinks she jumped."

I sucked in the coffee unintentionally and burned my lips and tongue. Spluttering out the hot liquid, I coughed violently. It had already scorched the back of my throat.

"I know, right?" he continued, taking my surprise as something entirely different. "I mean, I don't really think so, but it would at least make a better story than what they're saying now. Something about her toppling off the cliffs after a run ..."

The image of her falling into the water and plunging down beneath the surface, never to come up again, came to my mind. I sucked in my breath and was unable to let it out again as though I was drowning as well.

"Are you all right?" Julian asked.

"Fine," I said, but my tone said otherwise.

Julian's eyes moved off of me to look over my shoulder. I followed his gaze and saw that Jack was heading towards us.

"God, does he ever go away?" Julian muttered in irritation, but then, realizing that I could hear him, added, "Well, we're going to meet up with some of the other guys, but ... I'll see you around, Enim."

The two of them picked up their trays to find another table and I waved my hand vaguely in a farewell. I wished that Julian would let the subject of the dead girl drop; the more I heard about it, the less interested in the details I became. I certainly didn't want to hear that she might have killed herself.

"You look like you're in severe pain – you didn't have to reenact Caesar's assassination in Latin, did you?"

I glanced up, torn from my thoughts. Jack had arrived at the table and taken the seat that Julian had just vacated.

"What?" I said distractedly, only half-wondering why he would think that we would reenact something from the first century BC when *The Aeneid* took place in the twelfth.

"Nothing, Nim, it's a joke," Jack said. "What happened to you?"

I pressed my fingers against my temples as the headache that had been threatening to form behind my eyes finally arrived.

"Nothing, just listening to Julian," I said.

"Yeah, I suppose Wynne would have that effect," Jack agreed. "What'd he want, anyhow? Or is he just so bored with his own life that he thought he'd check in on yours?"

"He's just still going on about that dead girl."

"Right, him and everyone else," he said distractedly. "Listen, I was going to take my lunch up to Miss Mercier's – I had a few things to ask her."

"Right, sure. Have fun."

I had barely gotten the words out when he bolted off again, and I finished my coffee and left the dining hall before Julian could think to rejoin me. I had been hoping that Jack would give an entertaining monologue during the meal that would take my mind off of the conversation with Albertson, and without it my headache only worsened as the day went on.

By the time that classes had ended for the day, I had received another reprimand from Donovan for failing to hand in a history essay, and Doyle had interrogated me with questions about chapters from the book that we were supposed to have finished over the weekend, both of which successfully heightened my sour mood. Since Jack would be in class for another hour, I paused in the Center Garden and considered going to the library to begin my homework before my mind flickered to another idea. Without thinking of the consequences, I turned and wandered in the direction of the woods instead.

Bypassing the front gates adorned with the newly-made

Bickerby shield, complete with a thick varnish to protect the figure of the opossum and school motto, CURRE, ANTE URSOS MANDUCARE VOBIS, I approached the place where the grass met the trees and ducked beneath a branch to enter the woods. Though the air was colder without the sunlight and the ground beneath my boat shoes was hard and frozen, there was something in the way that the trees circled about me and blocked out the noises and view of Bickerby that eased my mind.

I walked deeper and deeper into the woods until every side of me was a sight of a thick expanse of brown tree trunks. With the way that the pine needles fell upon the path and the sky looked peeking through the diamond-shaped cutout in the branches above, it looked remarkably like the woods in Connecticut that had lined the backyard of my childhood home. I wished that I could pretend I was there instead.

A chill swept over the spot and compelled me to keep walking. My hands were stiff in the cold and my sweater was much too thin to keep me warm, but I continued walking until I caught sight of the slab of rocky clearing ahead of me. With another few hesitant steps I left the dirt ground and approached the cliffs that overlooked the water.

My mother had always loved the water. The majority of my memories of her were located on the beach, her blond hair turning wavy as it dampened and her white dress catching in the wind. She would clutch her light sweater to her as she crossed barefoot across the sand, too impractical to ever wear a proper coat or shoes.

I inched forward and took a seat on the edge of the cliffs. From there the land plummeted straight down into the ocean in one long, ugly drop. Regardless, I swung my legs a bit to ward off the cold, my shoes dangling over the deep blue pit below, and stared off into the distance. A few years back Jack had managed to convince me to dive off the cliffs for a thrill, assuring me that as long as we jumped out far enough there was no danger in it. I couldn't imagine ever doing such a thing now.

My eyes darted down to the rocky beach that was a part of the Bickerby campus. If what Trask said was true, that was where the dead girl had washed ashore. With its gray stones and the murky hue of the water, it looked solemn regardless. I tried to picture my mother in her white dress and loose sweater capering across it, but the image of her was marred: I could see her stumbling as her bare feet hit the sharp rocks, and the way her face would pale in the cold, and how her eyes would reflect the graying skies and look hollow and chilled as well. She wouldn't be happy here. But she wouldn't be anything anymore, I reminded myself firmly.

I shook my head to dispel the thoughts. I shouldn't have been thinking of her, especially not there on the cliffs. I had spent months learning to keep away from her memory, and yet the traces of her that were most detrimental could still not be cleared out. Her memory floated back to me with every glance at the ocean and every note coming from the Arts Building that I hurried past at a rapid pace, and despite the months that stretched between the moment when she had gone and the present, the memories were just as present as ever and they would not leave me alone.

When the sun sank down on the horizon, looking like an egg that had broken against the surface of the water and pooled down below the depths, I stood and wandered through the darkness back to the campus. In the night Bickerby was as forsaken in appearance as ever, and I hurried through the Center Garden and onto the poorly lit path before anything could make its way out of the darkness.

"You have pine needles in your hair," Jack commented as I sat down across from him at dinner.

I futilely tried to rake them out, but my arms felt heavy and numb with cold. After a moment of watching me struggle, he reached over and pulled them out for me.

"Thanks," I said lowly, more grateful that he hadn't asked me where I had been than I was to have my hair clean.

"No problem."

Leaving my bag next to the seat, I stood and went to get

some coffee. There was a hollow burning beneath my ribcage as I passed the line of food, and I selected a roll from the bread basket in the hopes of impeding it. By the time that I sat down Jack was nearly finished.

"Can't wait for this semester to be over," he said, observing a spoonful of jelled-dessert with boredom before eating it. "Wish we were in France right now."

I tore a piece of bread and put it in my mouth, but my hope that it would dissolve on my tongue ended when I tasted how stale it was. I took a gulp of coffee and waited for it to grow soggy before swallowing.

"Me too," I said tiredly.

Jack glanced up at my tone, but before he could comment on it something behind my back caught his eye. He slouched in his seat and averted his eyes.

"Ugh – Nim, quick: pretend like we're deep in conversation."

"What? Why?"

I half-turned to see what had distracted him, but he grabbed my arm to hold me still with a warning look.

"It's Porker," he said. "Trust me, Nim, you do not want to –"

"Enim?"

He was cut off by a timid, unfamiliar voice behind me. I slowly turned in my seat to face whoever had spoken and was surprised to find that the voice – which had sounded so small – came from someone very large. He stood next to the table awkwardly, hands clasped together in front of his stomach nervously, as his eyes darted between me and Jack. There was a light misting of sweat on his face as he waited for me to speak.

"Hi," I offered uncertainly. Though Jack had uttered a name just a moment before, I hadn't registered what it was. I shifted uneasily as I considered that I should have known him if he knew me, but he didn't look at all familiar.

"I meant to catch you after class," he said, "but you ran out too quickly."

"Right, yeah, I was ..." I faltered as I tried to come up with a proper excuse; without knowing what class we had together, it was too difficult to decide what to say. "I was ..."

Behind me, Jack chuckled. I ignored him.

"I was wondering, since there's an exam coming up, if you wanted to study together," the boy continued. "I mean, I was pretty confused at the last part of the lecture, and I thought that maybe you knew what it meant."

"Ah ... right, the lecture," I said, frantically trying to think of which class he could be referring to. "Right, so that was ...?"

"Hi, Thomas," Jack said, leaning forward in his seat as he finally chose to save me from my discomfort. "Fancy seeing you here, in the dining hall."

"Jack," the boy said, barely taking notice of the insult as though too accustomed to them to give it much thought. He turned back to me with a much friendlier tone. "Yeah, I mean, normally I wouldn't ask, but Mrs. Beake said that this one would be more difficult, so ..."

"Right, Calculus," I said with relief. "Yeah, her exams can be difficult."

"Great – so you'd want to study with me, then?"

I gave a tight smile as I faltered for an answer. Regardless of the fact that I hadn't even known his name, I couldn't imagine why he would want to study with me: I certainly didn't want to study with him.

"Ah ... I already studied for it, actually," I said.

"Even how to derive logarithms from class today?"

"Well, not ... not that, I guess."

"Great, so we can go over it together! How about we meet on Thursday?"

I had barely inclined my head when he beamed and hurried away. As I turned back around in my seat, I found Jack glaring at me with a deadened expression.

"Nim, why did you agree to that?"

"I couldn't say no."

"So you said *yes?* Do you realize what you just got yourself into?"

I shrugged.

"It won't be so bad."

"Are you kidding? It's *Porker*, Nim."

"What's that mean?"

Jack rolled his eyes.

"Do you know why he asked you to help him study? Because no one else in their right mind would do it – it's not like he has any friends." He pushed away his empty tray to put his elbows on the table. "Trust me: there's a reason that no one likes him, and it's not just because he's a complete joke. I had two classes with him last year. All he did was sidle up to people and beg for answers, then once he found someone to latch onto he wouldn't let go. If I didn't hate everyone at this school, I might've even felt sorry for them."

He gave me a pointed look and leaned back in his chair.

"Do you know that his mother still sends him care-packages, too?" he added, as though the thought was worse than bidding for answers.

"So?"

"She sends them every week!" Jack shook his head. "He cries about how much he misses her – it's pathetic."

"Alright, so he misses his mother. That's not the worst thing."

"It is when you're the one stuck listening to him." He gave me a dark look. "If anyone has a right to cry over their mother, it's you – and I've never heard you complain."

I dropped my gaze to avoid answering and rotated in my seat to scan the dining hall. Surely enough, in the far back corner at an otherwise empty table, Thomas was sitting alone. He looked to be reading something whilst eating and accidentally spilled his food onto the page. I watched as he futilely tried to wipe it off, even dabbing his napkin into his milk to do so, before letting his shoulders slump in defeat. I turned back to Jack.

"It won't be so bad," I repeated.

Jack shook his head and tossed his napkin on top of his tray. He stood to leave, but I waved him ahead without me under the pretense that I wanted another cup of coffee. When he had gone, however, I stood to leave as well, ducking in the opposite direction to take the long route back to the residence building.

The campus was pitch-black and silent except for the sound of my shoes on the frost-covered ground. I shivered and pulled my jacket tighter around me, wondering what it was that was pulling at the back of my mind and filling me with unease, when the light on the side of the nearby building flickered and went off. I stood in the dark in the hopes that it would turn back on again, but the bulb appeared to have burnt out for good.

As the breeze caught and drifted over to where I stood, it brought with it the distant sound of music from afar. I strained to hear it, sure that I recognized the song, when it occurred to me that I was much too far from the Arts Building to hear anything of the sort. What was more, the classical notes were coming from a piano, and even if it wasn't too late for any of the students to be practicing, I was certain that I was the only one who played that instrument.

Fumbling through the darkness, I hurried up the path to where it grew lit again and scrambled inside the residence building. My heart was pounding painfully against my ribs and the newfound silence in my ears was hollow and cold. I shook myself and reasoned that the music could have easily come from somewhere rather than the emptiness all around, but no amount of rationalizing could take away the numbness that had set in over my legs. No one at Bickerby knew that song but me: it had been taught to me by my mother.

Ch. 3

When classes came to an end on Thursday, I had nearly forgotten about the promised study-session with Thomas until I found him waiting for me at the back of Mrs. Beake's room. Groaning inwardly, I forced a polite smile while hoping that he didn't want to study for too long; I had numerous other assignments that were more important than studying for the exam.

We walked in silence across the campus to the library, a large building with ornately placed bricks decorating its façade. I frequented the library so often that it felt more familiar than the student lounge in my building, though it felt rather odd to walk in with Thomas in tow. I found a vacant table and set my calculus book out to the chapter we had discussed in class, but had no idea where to begin.

"So ... was there a particular part you wanted to study?" I asked.

Thomas scratched the back of his ear.

"Sort of ... all of it," he admitted lowly.

"Right."

I flipped to the beginning of the chapter and made a few comments about it, but it was clear that he wasn't following what I was saying. After a few more minutes of struggling to go over it with him, the realization that Jack might have been right came over me.

"Do you want to just ... look at my notes for a while?" I asked after another half-hour had passed without getting much further than the first example in the chapter. He nodded eagerly and took my notebook, scrambling to copy down everything that I had written. I gave him a wary glance before deciding to do my Latin assignment while I waited.

"Does it make more sense now?" I asked when he passed my paper back a while later.

"Not really," he said. "Hopefully it will tomorrow, though."

"Right."

I looked back down at my translation, which was just

missing the last line, and squinted as I tried to recall the declension of one of the nouns.

"How do you do it?"

I looked up at his statement and found him staring at my pile of assignments with an expression of awe.

"Calculus, you mean?" I gave a noncommittal shrug. "Math's kind of easy for me, so ..."

"Yeah, but what about the rest of it?" Thomas persisted. "How do you keep from falling behind?"

I looked at my paper and sighed.

"I don't."

"But you have to," Thomas said. "They'll take away your scholarship if you don't keep your grades up."

I looked up at him uncertainly as the tip of my pen continued to press down onto the page, leaving a horrible dark spot in the middle of the line.

"I'm not on scholarship," I said.

"What?" he said. "But ... Only I thought you were, too, since you study all the time and ..."

He trailed off with a look of perplexity on his face, and I finally realized why he had singled me out to study with him.

"So you're just like everyone else, then," he said.

"What?"

"Smart, rich, good-looking. You've got everything."

"I – that's not true."

I gave him an odd look as his tone turned cold. His offended tone didn't match the fact that I had just spent the last hour allowing him to copy all of my notes.

"So why do you bother to study at all? It doesn't matter if you fail a class."

"Yes it does. Just as much is at stake if I fail a class, Thomas."

He scoffed.

"Yeah, right. Your parents can just pay Barker off – I'd get kicked out of school."

"My parents don't pay Barker off. I just study."

"Of course they do. What about what you and Jack did last

year? Why didn't you get expelled for that?"

I looked back down at my nearly-finished Latin translation futilely, not wanting to discuss the incident from the previous semester in the least.

"I didn't believe it when everyone said you took the blame for Jack, and Barker let you off because your parents paid him off – but I guess it's really true," Thomas ridiculed.

"What?" I said, regardless that the statement was very close to the truth. "Who said that?"

"Everyone says it. Everyone knows it. Jack's been in way too much trouble to have gotten off without so much as a detention, but you've never been in trouble before, so ..."

"It's not true," I said suddenly. The smugness in his tone irked me almost as much as the idea that everyone was still talking about what had happened did. I quickly tried to draw up another explanation in my head, but nothing was coming fast enough.

"Yes it is."

"It's not – that's not why we weren't expelled."

For a split-second Thomas looked unsure.

"Then how'd you get off?"

"Barker just ... decided to let me off," I said.

"Out of the goodness of his heart? Come on, Enim – you're lying."

"Not out of the goodness of his heart," I said. My heart skipped several beats. "It's because my mother had just died."

The library, which was already quite quiet, grew more so at my words. Thomas' mouth had opened a bit and he stared at me in silent shock.

"I ... I didn't know," he said at last.

I shrugged in what I hoped appeared to be a careless way.

"Now you do," I said expressionlessly. Before he could offer the standard sympathies that I had grown all too use to, I collected my things and muttered a hurried goodbye. Once I had escaped into the cold air outside the building, I let out the breath that I had been holding upon telling the lie. My heart continued to beat irregularly all the way back to my dorm room.

"So how'd your date with Porker go?" Jack asked as I stepped into the room. "Do you think it's love? Should I draw up engagement invitations?"

I sighed loudly and dropped my bag next to my bed, already mourning the loss of what might have been a productive afternoon.

"No," I said heavily. I glanced over at him before adding in a low voice, "You were right."

"Sorry? I didn't quite catch that," he said mockingly.

"You were right," I repeated. "He's ..."

"Annoying? Pathetic? An incredible waste of space?"

"Problematic," I countered.

"What do you mean?"

I ran my hands through my hair and rubbed at my eyes.

"Nothing, he just ... he went on and on about how unfair it is that my father pays Barker off to let me stay in school."

"He should meet your father – then he wouldn't be jealous."

"Yeah, well ... I don't know. I didn't know what to say."

"Don't tell me that you told him you'd help him study again," Jack said incredulously. "Nim, nothing he told you could be sympathetic enough to waste your time with him."

"No, I didn't tell him that."

"Good."

"I told him that my mother died and that was why Barker let me off the hook last year," I said tonelessly.

"Ah, Nim," Jack said, shaking his head at me. "What'd you go and lie for? Who cares if your dad bought Barker off?"

"I know – I don't know why I said it."

He looked at me closely for a moment and I was afraid that he might say something more about my mother, but then he simply gave a shrug.

"Oh well, nothing you can do about it now," he said. "Though next time you want to elicit sympathy, just say that you have a heart murmur or something."

"Will do."

He stood and stretched with a loud yawn and I felt myself growing more tiredly simply by looking at him.

"Want to go to dinner?"

I glanced at the clock.

"You go," I told him. "I have to meet Beringer soon, so ..."

"Right, Beringer." Jack rolled his eyes. "Have fun. If you decide to skip it, though, the Foreign Language meeting goes until eight."

I nodded irresolutely and he donned his sweatshirt and left. With the realization that I wouldn't complete any of my assignments on time, I pulled on my jacket and headed down to the Health Center, wishing futilely that Beringer could write me a note out of doing them.

Beringer's office was at the far back of the Health Center in what had once been a filing room. The cabinets had been pushed to one side of the wall, lining it in harsh metal, to make room for a desk and chairs for the weekly sessions. Though cramped, it was warmly lit by a desk lamp rather than strewn beneath fluorescent lights, and it was as secretive as I could have hoped for.

"Hello, Enim," Beringer said as I entered. "How are you?"

He smiled over at me across the desk where his hands were neatly folded over an open file. He was about the same age as Karl, though looked younger due to the lack of lines around his eyes and mouth that had drawn across Karl's face in recent months; and though he wore the standard dress shirt, slacks, and tie that Karl did, there was something far more relaxed in his appearance than the other man could ever hope to have. It was the type of nature that my mother had had that could always put me at ease.

"You seem distracted."

I blinked and shook my head at his voice, aware that I had been staring blankly and had failed to answer his question.

"Sorry, Dr. Beringer. I was ... thinking."

"Oh? About what?"

"Just ... classes."

He waited a moment to see if I would go on, but I dug my

eyes into the hem of my sweater to avoid doing so. Though I liked Beringer, I was always careful about the content of our sessions. I knew the subject that he had been hired to get me to talk about, and the knowledge that he was waiting for me to say something about it only made me less inclined to speak of it.

"How are they going?" he asked.

"They're ... all right. I'm falling a bit behind."

"I see." He nodded understandably. "Are you still having trouble concentrating?"

"Yes."

"Because your mind is elsewhere."

He said it gently, but it pressed against my chest uncomfortably all the same. I turned to stare at the one of the filing cabinets and waited for him to ask the question that he always did.

"What do you think about when your mind is ... in another place?"

I kept my eyes on the metal so that I wouldn't have to look at him when I lied.

"I don't know."

"I see. And are your thoughts still making it difficult to sleep?"

"Yes."

"Is the medication helping? Because if it's not, I can adjust the dosage or we can switch to something else altogether."

"No, it's fine."

His expression had barely flickered over my face, but he seemed to know that I was lying just as though he had peeled back the skin stretching over my skull to peer inside of my head.

"Well, that's good, then," he said, making a note in my chart. "But if you ever find that it's not working quite right, let me know. It's only there to benefit you."

He set the pen down and leaned back in his chair before continuing.

"Was there anything in particular you wanted to talk about

today?"

"Not really."

"Apart from classes, how are things at school?"

"They're fine."

"And Jack?"

"Fine."

He gave the slightest of smiles at the response.

"Is there anything that's not fine going on?"

I stared at my hands as I searched for a response. As difficult as it was to hold a conversation by saying so little, it would be much harder to say anything more.

"A girl in town died. Her body washed up on the beach earlier in the week."

Beringer leaned his head against his hand and furrowed his brow.

"Well, that's certainly far from fine," he said. "Have you given it much thought?"

"A bit," I admitted. "It's hard not to with everyone talking about it."

"Oh? What do they say?"

"All sorts of things," I said, my face twitching at the thought of Jack's ridiculous theory. "But nothing serious. They're just excited when something interesting actually happens around here."

"And do you find it interesting?"

"No. Why would I?"

He made no response, but only because he didn't need to. The air in the room seemed suddenly much too stuffy and the compact space felt too tight with all of the filing cabinets and bookshelves piled up against the walls. I tugged at my collar and stole a glance out the small window behind Beringer's chair, but the sky outside was so dark that it only made the room feel more barred. I turned back to him and cleared my throat.

"She's just some girl who died," I said. "There's nothing exciting about that."

"No, certainly not," he agreed. "I only wondered if it was

bringing up some other thoughts that you might have, given the ... similarities it shares with an event in your own life."

"I don't see any similarities."

"No?" He turned his head slightly, but his voice was un-accusatory despite my blatant lie. "Her death hasn't brought up any thoughts on your mother?"

"No."

The flat note in my voice seemed to drop through the floor and create a crater between us. Beringer stared over it as he observed me, willing me to say more but knowing that I wouldn't. He waited for as long as he could in the hopes of drawing out just a word from me about my mother, but I was resilient in my resolution not to do so.

"Well, I'm glad that it hasn't been bothering you," he said. "But if it was, I would hope that we could talk about it."

I gave a short shrug, still unwilling to speak, and allowed him to turn the subject to my lack of ambition about schoolwork only so that we could fill the room with something other than heavy silence.

"Well, we're just about out of time," he said sometime later, glancing at the clock as another bout of quiet stretched between us. "I'll write a refill for your prescription."

He reached into the top drawer and pulled out a yellow pad of paper to jot down the usual prescription. He smiled as he handed it to me as though the last hour had been something other than a complete waste of his time, and I had the sudden urge to apologize to him for being so difficult, or at least to admit that I had never taken the medication, but the words faltered before they could come: apologizing would require an explanation that I was not willing to give.

"Thank you, Dr. Beringer."

I pocketed it and wandered down the hallway away from his office at an aimless pace. By then nearly all the staff at the Health Center had left for the night apart from a custodian mopping the floors and a lone secretary. Overhead, the fluorescent lamps were so bright against my skin that it felt as though they were leaving me transparent.

The campus was too dark at that time of night. The path was barely lit by a few lamps on the sides of buildings and the moon was hidden under clouds that threatened rain or snow. In the darkness I kept losing my footing and stumbling. At one point, heading through the garden, I tripped over a stone bench and slammed into the ground. The sudden impact of my hands against the solid, frost-filled ground made my elbows buckle and the side of my face hit the frozen dirt, and when I slowly lifted my head back up, my ears were ringing painfully. After they stopped, I found that the silence in the air had been replaced by the soft sound of music in the distance. This time I could hear it more clearly: it was the same song that I had heard before, *Nessun Dorma*.

Hurrying to my feet, I sprinted back to my building and up the stairs to my dorm room before I could even register why I was afraid. When I slammed the door behind me to crush out the remains of the lingering song, I expected to see Jack jump up from his bed in a spray of sheets and blankets to see what the matter was, but his bed was empty. As I leaned up against the door to catch my breath, I decided that he must have stayed after the Foreign Language to talk with Miss Mercier.

My limbs were shaking as I undressed and got into bed. I curled my legs up to my chest beneath the blankets to cut down on the shivering despite knowing that it had nothing to do with the cold. Though I tried to think of something apart from the dead girl or the music that I had heard, it was difficult given the conversation with Beringer. I kept returning to the unspoken similarities between the two women that I had hoped no one else would draw while the distant sound of the ocean sounded in the background.

I waited up for a long while for Jack to get back. He was so late in returning that I thought he might have gotten stopped by Sanders for missing curfew, but even Sanders wouldn't hold him hostage with a lecture for so long. I sat up and peered over at his bed to see if he had somehow snuck in without me noticing, but his bed was still empty. When the clock read that it was past one in the morning, I grabbed my jacket to go look for him, but no sooner had I pulled it on over my pajamas than the door opened. Jack quietly entered the room and tiptoed over to his bed. I sighed loudly.

"Sorry – did I wake you up?"

His nonchalant voice dispelled any worry that I might have harbored for his wellbeing. I took off my jacket and sat back on my bed.

"I wasn't asleep," I said. "I was just about to go find you."

"Why? What's wrong?"

I rolled my eyes in the darkness.

"It's one-thirty – I thought something happened to you."

Jack cackled as he took off his sweatshirt and sat down on the edge of his bed to remove his shoes. Pulling the laces out of a knotted mess, I could see the outline of his face change as his cheekbones rose in a grin.

"Like what? I was eaten by a bear?"

"You might have been."

"Actually, that was what I was trying to prevent from happening."

"Sorry?"

"I offered to walk Miss Mercier back to her house."

"Oh." I raised an eyebrow to the ceiling in a silent question. After a brief but heavy pause, I said, "And?"

"And then I walked her back to her house."

"Where does she live, Canada?" It didn't take that many hours to walk clear across the island and back multiple times. I had a strange sense that Jack was hiding something from me and an even stranger one that I didn't want to know what it was.

He didn't answer even though I waited several minutes for him to go on; I could tell that he wouldn't even if I flat-out asked him.

"Well, I'm glad you weren't mauled, at any rate," I said when the silence became uncomfortable.

"I appreciate the sentiment."

"Goodnight."

"Or good morning."

He climbed into bed and fell asleep immediately, but I stared up at the ceiling for a good while longer mulling over what he wasn't telling me. I wanted to think that he had simply badgered her with questions about France, but that didn't explain why he wouldn't come right out and say so. After sidling through the other possibilities, though, I decided that I really didn't want to know.

In the brief moments when I was able to drift off to sleep, my dreams were filled with images of a dead girl floating in the water. She would sit up on the waves as though it were solid ground and point at me accusingly for lying to her. I jolted awake as she did so, shaking so much that I didn't want to go back to sleep, and my eyes were still open when the sun cut in through the windows and scattered light across my bed. I rolled over and groaned as my head pounded in protest and the room lurched as I stood to dress: I wasn't sure how much longer I could go without sleep.

I didn't feel nearly as bad as Jack looked, however. The dark had hidden him from my sight when he had come into the room hours before, but now I could see that the majority of his face was a bruising of blues and purples. The entire left side looked as though it had been beaten with a heavy, blunt object: the eye was rimmed in thin blue skin, the cheekbone was raw and red with fresh marks, and his lips were bloodied with ripped skin. There was also a long gash through his eyebrow which drew a white line of skin through the dark hair.

It certainly wasn't the worst that I had seen him, and I hardly recoiled when I laid eyes on the impressive wounds, merely raising my eyebrows in response and giving him a weary look as I reached for my shoes. Jack seemed wholly unfazed by his appearance, or perhaps unaware of how bad he looked, and instead commented on my own.

"You don't look so good."

"Thanks, Jack."

I pulled my sweater on over my collared shirt and smoothed out a wrinkle that had formed in my khakis from folding them incorrectly, but no amount of straightening of my clothes could help the fact that my eyes were sunk beneath dark circles and my blond hair had faded and thinned. As Jack pulled on his sweatshirt without bothering to change out of his clothes from the previous day, I squinted at my reflection in the mirror. Even my once-blue eyes seemed to have faded to gray.

"And what happened to you?" I asked as we made our way down the hall to go to breakfast.

"Peters and I had a bit of a dispute."

"I'd say. Some night."

"That it was."

Sometimes I thought that Jack got into fights solely because he was bored. I couldn't imagine – even with back-to-back classes in which my teachers droned on endlessly, mountains of homework, and absolutely nothing to do for fun – ever being so bored that I would want to get my face punched in over and over again by a lacrosse player, but I supposed that Jack had a much lower tolerance for the uninteresting and a much higher one for pain. I raised my eyebrows at him shortly as we reached the campus and set off in the direction of the dining hall.

"Was this before or after the meeting?" I asked as we crossed through the Center Garden, half-heartedly attempting to place the events of his night in some order.

"Sometime during, actually."

"I thought you were looking forward to the meeting – why would you want to ruin it by getting into a fight?"

"For the record, Nim, I didn't start this one. Peters had his own agenda."

"Why was Peters even there? I took English with him last year: he could barely speak that. I can't imagine he'd be taking a foreign language."

"You're right on that account – he's taking basic French for the third year in a row."

"And he hasn't considered giving up by now?"

"Well, he's not really interested in the language, is he? None of them are."

Jack rolled his eyes as we trampled over some low shrubs to get through the gardens quicker. Of course Peters, like most of the French students, was just taking the class because of Miss Mercier. Jack seemed more annoyed about the idea than usual. The nagging inkling that there was something he wasn't saying came back to me.

"Bet Miss Mercier wasn't too happy that you two were fighting," I commented.

Jack shrugged.

"She was upset."

"Did she write you up?"

"No, she wouldn't do that," he said. "She gave me a lecture – *en français*, of course, which kind of negates the disappointment of it all. Everything sounds good in French."

"Right."

"She knew it was Peters' fault anyhow. I was simply defending myself."

"You didn't do a very good job," I said, looking over the state of his face again.

"It wasn't my best fight, no," he agreed.

We steered around a group of students coming down the path and then hurried towards the dining hall. The wind had picked up again and the air was too cold for my light sweater and jacket. Jack pulled his sweatshirt further about him, evidently thinking the same thing.

"And then you walked her home."

I slid the point into the conversation as seamlessly as I could, hoping that Jack would divulge more information on the matter.

"Yep."

He reached forward to pull the door to the dining hall open and stood back to let me in. An out-coming student eyed us unpleasantly.

"Stop being such a faggot, Hadler," he said as he passed us by.

Jack rolled his eyes and ducked inside, shivering as the warmth in the air returned. I almost applauded him for not taking the opportunity to pick another fight, but then I reminded myself that he was probably in too much discomfort from his current injuries to consider getting any more. It couldn't have been very pleasant to be constantly black-eyed and sore-ribbed, even though he continually allowed himself to be so.

"And why did you walk her home, again?" I asked as we stood in line, finally giving into my curiosity.

"Why wouldn't I?"

"Why would you?" I countered.

"Ah, come on, Nim. By the time she'd finished breaking up the fight, lecturing Peters and me, and cleaning up the meeting room, it was already late. I wasn't about to let her walk home alone."

"Is she frightened of the dark?"

"She should be – nothing good happens when women walk home late at night."

"Meaning?"

"Meaning that it's not safe, Nim."

"I hardly think Bardom Island is crawling with crime," I droned, watching him spear several pieces of bacon and add them to his tray. I looked at it fleetingly, trying to muster up the appetite to take some, before passing it by. Perhaps there was something more appealing further down the line.

"It doesn't need to be crawling with anything – all it takes is one lunatic who crosses her path and she could be in trouble."

"I never knew you were so chivalrous."

Jack turned and gave me an impish smile.

"I'm plenty chivalrous, Nim. I'd walk you home in the dark, too."

"What would the point in that be? You just said that only women are in danger."

"Wrong – I just said that women *were* in danger. You'd be in trouble, too. Look at the way you dress."

"Sorry?"

"Between the shoes and the sweater alone, Nim, you're screaming to be mugged."

"I'll inform the school – maybe they'll change the dress code."

"They might. Your father won't change his, though."

When we reached the end of the line my tray was still decisively empty. I looked down at the last items being offered that morning in the bread-basket: the bagels looked questionable, the muffins horrid, and the pastries sickeningly sweet. I eyed the whole-grain bread mistrustfully before giving in and dumping two slices onto the toaster rack. By the time I had returned from getting myself coffee, the toast was charred with black. I sighed and put them on my tray regardless.

The coffee eased my headache considerably and I was able to think again. As I crunched on the burnt toast, I got the nagging feeling that I was forgetting something. After pulling my Latin translation out of my bag to complete the line that Thomas had prevented me from finishing the afternoon before, the feeling didn't disappear, but I considered that it had to do with the numerous assignments for other classes that I had failed to complete.

When the bell rang two hours later and signaled the end of Latin class, however, it suddenly occurred to me what I had forgotten. As I was sliding my books into my bag, Albertson approached my desk. I sat back up and faced him. He had a paper clutched in his old hands; it was bright white with a smooth finish that was highlighted in his wrinkled, blue-spotted fingers.

"Enim, are you still prepared to take the make-up exam today?"

My mouth instantly dried and my stomach squirmed uncomfortably. Having completely forgotten about the make-up exam, I hadn't studied for it any more than I had the first one.

"Oh, yes – I'm prepared."

He gave me a smile and returned to his desk. Looking over the first page of questions, I realized that he had given me the same exam as the previous one: the questions had not even been reworded or reordered. Had I just looked over the one that I had failed, I would have been able to complete it again easily. I dropped my head into my hand miserably.

I filled in answers that I knew were incorrect with a feeling of annoyance, and when I had completed the poorly-written translation on the last page, I stood and dropped the test on Albertson's desk and fled from the room before he could ask me how it went. As I hurried across the campus, I vaguely wondered what another failed exam would do to my grade.

My mood only worsened as the day went on. I had forgotten to do my reading for English and Doyle, sensing as much, bombarded me with questions that I could only give stuttered responses to, much to the amusement of my classmates; Donovan returned the History essay that I had all but failed; and Calculus, normally an easy enough class for me to disappear in, was made uncomfortable by the fact that Thomas had moved his seat to sit next to me. By the time the day was over, I was ready to lock myself in the dorm room for the rest of the semester.

Jack was leaning up against the door to our room when I returned to the residence building, wearing a miserable expression that rivaled mine and made his bruised features look, if possible, worse.

"You look about as happy as I feel," I commented.

"Yeah? What happened to you?"

I unlocked the door and stepped inside before answering. He rolled lazily into the room behind me.

"Nothing, just classes," I said, not in the mood to relive the day's events. "What are you doing out in the hallway?"

"Forgot my keys."

He glanced around the room for a moment in search of them before getting down on the floor to look beneath the bed. I watched him shake out a few shirts and turn out the pockets on a pair of pants before he turned back to me.

"Did you see where I left them?"

"No," I said. I glanced about at the mess on his side of the room and shook my head in wonder. "Are you sure you didn't lose them?"

"I might've."

I was hardly surprised: he was constantly misplacing them. At least once a semester he would rely on me to let him in and out of locked buildings around campus as well as our residence building and dorm room. Sometimes the keys would turn up in a random, completely illogical location; other times he would have to break down and buy a new set.

"When did you last see them?"

"Hard to say for sure."

"Today?"

Jack leaned back on his heels from his crouched position on the floor and thought for a moment.

"No ... I didn't need them until now."

"So they're probably somewhere in here," I said. "You used them to get it last night, after all."

Jack thought about it and then frowned.

"No, you left the door unlocked last night." He ran his hand through his hair and sighed. "Which means that I probably dropped them when Peters attacked me."

"Check the lost and found, then."

"Who actually brings things to the lost and found?"

"I don't know – the custodian might've."

"Right," Jack said skeptically. "Let's face it, whoever found them probably tossed them in the trash."

He stood and shrugged, evidently resigned about the prospect of paying for a new set.

"So that's my room key, building key, student card, and campus card," he ticked off solemnly, "which means I'll have to shell out the full sixty for replacements. Great."

"Use Karl's account," I said, pulling out the bank card that Karl gave me and tossing it over to him.

"He lets you use this?"

"Yeah. It makes him feel like he's doing something."

Jack looked down at the card and mockingly admired the glossy silver plastic with an impish smirk.

"In that case, thank you Uncle Karl," he said. "I'll be sure to send him a letter of my appreciation – right after I charge a few more things to the account."

"Go to town."

"I will – literally."

He stopped and looked more closely at the card, viewing it as though seeing something of interest that he hadn't noticed before. The silver caught in the lamplight as he moved it slowly in his hands. Glancing back up at me, he said, "You know, I'd bet we could pretty far on this alone. We could drain it, get to Europe, and set up some place. By the time Karl noticed, it would be too late."

"Too late for what?"

"To find us."

He looked at me enticingly, daring me to consider his idea for just a moment.

"Come on, Nim. We could leave right now."

It the dim light, his eyes were darker than the lightless sky outside. He was looking at me earnestly with an excitement that I couldn't get up the nerve to muster. I rubbed the bridge of my nose tiredly.

"No, we couldn't," I said.

"You really want to graduate?"

"No, but my father would hunt us down if I left now."

"He might never find us," Jack said. "If you think about it, we've been training our entire lives how to disappear."

"I have to wait until I'm eighteen," I said. I toyed with a thread on the comforter as I spoke, wondering if Jack could tell that I wasn't being completely honest. "You know he'll send anyone he can to find me as long as I'm a minor."

Jack blew out a heavy breath that sent his dark hair up from his forehead and then shrugged.

"Yeah, you're probably right," he said, pocketing the card. "I guess we can wait it out."

"Why are you in such a rush to leave, anyhow?" I asked, pulling off my boat shoes and sitting down on the mattress. "Was Miss Mercier giving you more ideas about leaving?"

"I wish," Jack said. "She wasn't here today."

"Why not?"

"Her friend's sick or something, so she went to visit her."

His tone was duller than the situation called for.

"That's too bad," I said. "For her friend, I mean."

"Yeah, but it's weird, isn't it?"

I pulled out my notebooks and ordered the assignments from most to least important, though I still had no energy to begin any of them.

"Which part?" I asked, dropping the Physics book back down.

"That she was suddenly called out of town for a sick friend. I've told a lot of excuses in my life, Nim, and that sure sounds like one."

"Why would it be an excuse, though?"

"That's what I want to know. But you'd think that she would have mentioned it in class yesterday."

"Or when you walked her home," I said offhandedly.

"Yeah, or then. What are the chances that she got a call between then and now?"

"I don't know. When did you actually get back to her house? Midnight or something?"

"Yeah. So what does that leave, a five-hour window or something for the morning ferry? You took statistics last semester – what's the likelihood of it happening?"

"I don't think there's a formula for something like that, Jack," I said, rolling my eyes as he skipped over what he had been doing out so late the night before once again. "We only ever calculated completely useless data, and then did some more calculations to figure out how wrong we were about our initial findings."

"What a waste."

"You're telling me."

He looked across the room with a discouraged expression.

"Come on, Jack," I said. "It's not the end of the world. She's coming back."

"Yeah, I know. It's just that I was looking forward to talking to her this weekend."

"You can talk to her when she gets back."

As I said it, I was suddenly struck by a bitterness that I couldn't quite place. His dejected tone seemed like a plea to get me to spend the weekend going in and out of town or venturing through the Bickerby woods, and the idea that he was trying to sway me into doing so despite knowing that it would mean I wouldn't finish my assignments bothered me more than it should have. Somehow, his disappointment that he wouldn't get to speak to Miss Mercier for a mere number of days seemed unqualified knowing that I had been waiting for months to speak to someone who, I knew, would never speak again.

Ch. 4

Just as he had predicted, the weekend was spent in relative boredom. A drizzling rain began sometime during the morning on Saturday and continued well into Sunday night, preventing anyone from doing anything other than holing up in their rooms. Even though I had thought that spending so much time inside would ensure that I finished my homework, by the time we went to sleep on Sunday night there were still several undone assignments in my bag.

Jack fell asleep almost immediately after lying down. I wished that I could do the same, especially given that I had slept so little in the past four nights, but my eyes stayed decisively open. After an hour or so of staring at the ceiling, tiredness finally began to seep into my bones, but no sooner had my eyes begun to flicker shut than a strange pattern of lights danced in front of the lids. I reopened them and stared across the dark room. After a moment, the room lit up with speckled lights once again.

The window was on Jack's side of the room and was hard to see out of properly without being on his bed. Throwing off my covers, I crossed to his bed and cautiously raised one leg to step over him. Grabbing the window frame and heaving myself over so that I was crouching on the sill, I peered down to the grounds to see what the source of the light was.

Surely enough, several rays of light were crossing the campus. It took me a moment to realize that there were various people with flashlights walking about below: the campus was alit with pinpricks and beams of light, painting the darkness with dots and slashes. I frowned and pressed my face closer to the window, wondering what was going on.

"Nim, if you wanted to cuddle, you could have just said so."

Jack had awoken and turned on his side to face me. Though tired, he was clearly amused.

"Stop," I said, rolling my eyes. Since he was already awake, I took the opportunity to step off the windowsill and onto the mattress. My legs were cramped from how I had been sitting. "Look at this – what'd you think's going on down there?"

Jack sat up and knelt beside me to observe the grounds. He squinted through the darkness.

"Looks like a search party," he said. Just as I had done, he pressed his face closer to the window to try and make out more of the scene without the distracting glare from the moonlight on the glass.

"A search party?" I repeated. "For who?"

He shrugged.

"Missing student?" he suggested. "One who hasn't figured out to sneak out past their building monitor yet, evidently."

"Seems like a lot of trouble for a student out of bed."

"What else could it be?"

"Some sort of prank?" I suggested. It wasn't entirely uncommon for sports teams or clubs to initiate new members by inviting them to do something stupid or reckless, though it was usually to a lesser degree of trouble that ensured that, if caught, the highest punishment would be a suspension.

"No … those are police flashlights."

I didn't have to ask how Jack could tell the difference between a regular flashlight and a police-issued one. Instead, I said, "So a prank gone wrong? What do you think – vandalism?"

"Nah … look what we did last year: *that* was vandalism, and Barker didn't call the police on us."

"No, he called my father. That was worse."

"True, but it turned out better: you didn't even get a detention."

"No, I got a psychiatrist."

"Good point. I'd take the detention any day."

"But why would they be here?" I said. "Barker wouldn't send the entire police force out for a student out of bed."

"True."

He sat back from the window and was silent for so long that I thought he might have fallen asleep again, but then a clicking noise sounded between us and a light appeared. He had flipped open his lighter and was lighting a cigarette. His expression was thoughtful.

"You know what I think?" he said with a hint of deviousness in his voice. "I think this has to do with that girl who washed up on shore on Columbus Day."

I glanced over at him warily.

"They found her," I reminded him skeptically, "so why would they need a search party?"

His grin glowed red behind his cigarette.

"They found her, sure," he said. "But they didn't find whoever *threw* her."

I rolled my eyes.

"On that note," I said briskly as I made to climb off of his bed, but he grabbed my arm and pulled me back.

"Ah, come on, Nim," he implored. "– just think about it: nothing ever happens on this island, and then what? A girl goes missing, is found dead, and the police are on Bickerby's front steps."

The flame from the lighter went out and drenched us in darkness. Jack sighed before shutting it, shaking it roughly, and flipping it back open so that we were bathed in light once more.

"Why would a killer choose to hide at Bickerby?" I said. "That doesn't even make sense."

"Nim, you're so naïve. He's not hiding here, he *lives* here."

"What?"

"He's a student."

I paused, mouth still open from the negating response that I had been about to give, and then frowned.

"Why would someone here throw a local girl off the cliffs?"

Jack rolled his eyes in exasperation.

"Why does anyone do anything, Nim?" he asked incredulously. "Besides, does it matter?"

"If someone down the hall from us killed someone? I think so."

"No, I meant that it doesn't matter if one of us did it at all," Jack countered. "Think about it: a local girl shows up dead, and where do the police start looking? Here."

He gave me a blunt look and I sighed in agreement. Whenever something was to go wrong on the island, whether it was turned over trashcans littering the streets or an excess of noise coming from the campus during sporting events, the locals didn't hesitate to draw up formal complaints against Bickerby students. They blamed us for anything and everything that they could, going so far as to say that we were the reason their tourist season had been severely depleted. Their complaints were, perhaps, a large part as to why the rules for the students were so harsh.

"Good point," I said.

"Thank you." He stubbed his cigarette out against the window sill and kicked his covers back so that he could crawl beneath them again. "Now, you're welcome to stay and keep vigil, but I've got to get some sleep."

I threw one last glance out the window at the flashing lights before climbing off of his bed and returning to my own. The sheets were cold and uninviting, and I couldn't seem to get my mind off of the girl in the water and how she had gotten there; I wondered if she had died before hitting the surface or struggled uselessly while she drowned.

I was awoken far too early by the door to the room opening loudly and a sharp sweep of cold air coming into the room. Instinctively curling up beneath the covers, I half-raised my head to see who had opened it. Jack was still asleep across the room.

"Boys."

I looked up at the familiar unpleasant voice. Sanders was standing in the threshold looking stern, his thin face holding its ever-present look of disapproval that ran from his eyes and down his nose.

"Lund, Hadler," he said curtly, "get up."

Sanders wasn't a very threatening person in appearance. He was of average height and had the build of a student who lived off of nutrient-lacking school food and whose only recreation was walking back and forth to the library. It was only his expression and tone that made him so reproachable, and only his quickness in handing out warnings and reporting students to staff members that made him intimidating. He had single-handedly reported Jack to the administrators forty-six times and succeeded in warranting him probation on a few occasions. He had almost gotten him suspended, as well, for smoking and drinking on campus, but was unable to retrieve proper evidence that Jack had actually been doing either.

"Sanders," Jack said at last, rolling over on his bed to peer at the other boy. "Fancy seeing you here."

"You need to get up, boys," Sanders said somberly. He waved his hand as though he was a traffic monitor inviting a line of cars to come through a construction zone. Jack and I looked at one another warily before complying.

"Right, good," Sanders said once we had stood. "Now, I'm here to inform you that students have orders to stay in their rooms for the morning until further notice."

"What?" Jack said. "You woke us up to tell us to stay in bed?"

"You should have been up hours ago, Hadler," Sanders countered. "It's no wonder you're always in trouble – you have no self-discipline."

Jack rolled his eyes.

"So what's the deal, Sanders? Why can't we leave the room? You didn't put us on house arrest, did you – what'd we do this time?"

Sanders raised his eyebrows at Jack's words.

"I don't know, Hadler, what *have* you done?" he asked.

Jack turned his head to look my way.

"Quick, Nim – hide the evidence," he said tonelessly.

"Hadler," Sanders warned.

"Sanders," Jack countered. "Come on – you wake us up to tell us to stay in and then you don't tell us why?"

"What about classes?" I said.

"What about breakfast?" Jack asked.

"I – official orders are to stay in for the morning, boys, just until further notice –"

"Right – meaning that you have no idea what the reason is," Jack said.

"No. No, I know what the reason is, but it's not my place to divulge –"

"Yeah right. They didn't tell you, did they Sanders? You're not important enough to know the goings-on around here, are you?"

Sanders stuttered in response, grasping for something to say to counter Jack's accusation, but was saved from doing so by a voice from the door.

"*I* know what's going on."

The three of us turned to see Julian Wynne leaning up against the doorframe, arms crossed as he observed the conversation taking place between Jack and the building monitor.

"How would you know?" Sanders demanded.

Julian gave us his most convincing smile and shrugged.

"You don't need to know that. I just know."

"Well, don't go spreading anything around, Wynne. It's official business, not just some gossip –"

"It's more than that, though, isn't it?" Julian said. "It's news. And I think everyone has a right to know the local news, don't you?"

Sanders didn't reply. Jack raised an eyebrow at the exchange.

"Well either tell us or get out, Wynne," he said. "I'd like to get another hour of sleep if there aren't any morning classes."

Julian gave him a dark look before sidling into the room.

"What'll you do for me if I tell you, Jack?" he asked. "Specifically, mind you. Information isn't free."

"I'll tell you what I *won't* do to you," Jack replied. "Specifically, to your face."

"Watch it, Hadler," Sanders said. "And you, too, Wynne. You can't go making deals and threatening one another – I'm standing right here, after all."

Neither Jack nor Julian looked very worried by Sanders' supposed authority.

"All right, Jack." Julian shrugged in a careless way. "I'll tell you for nothing, then. It's not like you have anything I'd want."

"I should hope not," Sanders said.

"The police were here last night searching the grounds," Julian continued, ignoring Sanders' remark.

"That's all you know? Nim and I could've told you that much."

"Sure. But do you know who they're looking for?"

"Enlighten me."

"A girl who went missing."

Jack and I looked at one another, each raising an eyebrow in turn.

"Didn't they already find that girl?" Jack said. "You know, washed up on shore? What happened – did they misplace the body?"

"Hardly. I'm not talking about that girl. I'm talking about a different one."

Jack didn't seem to have an answer to that, though he did a good job of keeping the surprise from his expression.

"Two girls go missing in the same week?" he said casually. "What are the chances?"

"Wait a minute," Sanders cut in irritably. "Where did you hear that, Wynne? That's not what I was told."

"What'd you hear, then?"

"I – I told you, I'm not at liberty to discuss ..."

"You want to know what I think, Sanders?" Julian asked disparagingly. "I think you don't really know why we're all in for the morning, do you?"

"You know what *I* think?" Jack said. "I think neither of you do, so would you mind leaving us alone? Nim and I'd like to enjoy our morning, and it'd be impossible to do so with you two hanging around."

"Whatever that means, Hadler," Julian said, throwing us an odd look.

Jack appeared unfazed.

"Yeah, why don't you start that rumor up again, Wynne? I

haven't heard it in a while."

He shepherded the two other students from the room and shut the door firmly behind them before turning back to me with a shaking head.

"I swear, next time Sanders uses his administrative key to get into our room, I'm going to make sure that it accidentally falls down the drain in the bathroom ..."

He sighed and plopped back down on his bed.

"Do you think Julian's right?" I asked after a moment. "About the police looking for another missing girl?"

"No. He probably just made that up hoping that Sanders would tell him the real reason – but obviously neither of them knows anything."

"Right," I said, oddly disconcerted all the same.

"I mean, it's like I said last night: if a girl went missing, why would the police be searching the Bickerby campus? They'd do better hanging out by the beach, wouldn't they?" He reached over to his bedside table to get a cigarette in lieu of breakfast. "Besides, why would they conduct a search party at night, anyhow?"

"To find the girl before it's too late?"

"Nah. Like Barker cares about a local girl who went missing. I'm telling you, Nim, he had that search party out there to look for whichever of us threw the girl, and he did it at night so it wouldn't draw any negative attention to the school."

I scratched my hairline absently as I considered what he had said.

"You really think someone killed her?" I asked him at last.

"I know. Of course, it's probably something completely dull and unexciting ... Next week we're going to hear that some guy attacked her and threw her body off the cliffs, and no one will be surprised. That's what happens when you lock hundreds of teenagers inside an all-boys school and tell them to behave."

"I wonder how Barker will talk his way out of that one," I mused.

"Easily. Who do you think would care about some no-name

local girl over the son of an important, rich stockbroker?"

"The locals might."

"Yeah, they might. Or they might be perfectly happy to forget the whole thing when Barker writes them a check for more money than they've earned in a lifetime."

He gave me a look before finishing his cigarette and going back to bed. I wanted to do the same, but a nagging voice in my head reminded me that I still had homework to finish for class that afternoon. Pulling up my bag, I set to work despite the tiredness dragging down my eyelids.

Sanders came to inform us that we were free to leave the building midway through the morning. I stirred Jack from his sleep with my foot and we both donned our warmer jackets and scarves before heading outside. The sunless gray sky would do nothing to keep the cold away.

Outside, the weather had only worsened. The rain had brought with it the end of the autumn season: the nipping chill in the air was a sure sign of winter. Beside me, Jack was pressing his hands to his ears to ward off the cold. I looked down at my hands to see that they had turned a blotchy red and that the fingertips were a purplish-blue. I clenched them to keep warm.

When we reached the dining hall, I learned with frustration that no coffee had been made that morning. Tipping the thermoses over my cup in a futile attempt to get a drop of coffee from the previous night out, I finally gave up and joined Jack at an empty table.

"So what do you think?" he asked me as I sat down.

"About?"

"About the murder."

"I think I'm going to murder someone if I don't get some coffee soon."

"Hopefully it's Sanders or Wynne," Jack said with a cackle. "But what about the dead girl? Who do you think killed her?"

The pounding in my skull was louder than his voice; I paused to press my head into my hands.

"How would I know?"

"You wouldn't, I just wanted your best guess."

"I don't have a guess," I told him. I hadn't liked hearing about the girl in the first place and wanted no reason to talk about her more. "Why would you want to think about something like that?"

He shrugged and took a bite of his English muffin.

"I can't help it, Nim – I love a good mystery."

His eyes were alight and mischievous. I could almost see the conspiracies forming in his mind behind the dark irises, undoubtedly searching for alternatives to the mundane theory we had settled on just hours before.

"I know you do," I said. "But check one out of the library – don't go looking for them."

"Like I'd ever go to the library," he said. "But it does have me thinking ..."

"What?" I asked warily.

"We should go to the boathouse."

"What? How do those two thoughts even go together?"

"Think about it, Nim: it's the perfect time to break the rules."

"How is it the perfect time? The police are swarming the place."

"Hardly," he said. "Did you see even one officer on campus this morning? They've all cleared out."

"Only because Barker's hoping that no one will know what's going on," I countered. "I bet they'll be back tonight after we're all in our rooms."

"Alright, forget the police, Nim – it'll be fun."

Even his most earnest of expressions couldn't convince me to sneak out to the boat house and steal one of the rowing boats again. We had done it a few times in the past, of course, to feed his insane idea that it was possible to row all the way to the mainland and escape Bickerby, but we had certainly never achieved the feat.

"No."

"Why not?" he pestered. "We haven't done anything fun all semester."

"We haven't been in trouble all semester, either," I said. "And I'd like to keep it that way."

"Why? It's not like we've ever gotten caught before. Besides, I hear Barker's in the market for a new stadium to match that nice sporting field he had installed ..."

"Karl will kill me. Besides, it's too cold to go out to the ocean. We'll freeze to death."

"Better than dying of boredom," Jack muttered, but he let the idea drop all the same.

The week passed in a constant drone, broken only by the occasion reprimand or reminder of how poorly I was doing that semester. Upon entering Latin on Thursday morning, Albertson slid the make-up exam from the previous week onto my desk. I didn't have to turn it over to know that I had failed: the red ink from his pen showed through the back of the page, circling and underling my numerous mistakes.

To make matters worse, Thomas had resumed his seat next to me in Calculus and had taken to glancing at me repeatedly during class. I wished that Mrs. Beake would tell him to go back to the other side of them room, though since he wasn't technically doing anything wrong there was no reason for her to do so. I wasn't certain what to make of his silence, but I didn't want to break it to ask. When the final bell rang for the day and I stood to leave, however, he stopped me.

"Enim, wait up," he said breathlessly.

I paused as he spoke and the rest of the boys went around us to the door. I watched them go with the fleeting wish that I had left a little quicker. Thomas toed the ground with his shoe as he thought of what to say.

"You know, I was really sorry to hear about your mom," he said suddenly.

I looked at him uncertainly, suddenly glad that the rest of the students had left.

"Right. Thanks."

"I didn't know," he went on, "you know, that she died and all."

"Right ... and all."

He nodded absently and I pulled at my collar uncomfortably.

"So what happened?" he asked after another drawn out pause.

"Sorry?"

"To your mom. How'd she die?"

I ran my tongue over my teeth as I debated my answer.

"It was ... cancer," I said.

"Oh, that's horrible." He looked thoughtfully down at his hands. "So is that why you were gone a few weeks after the holidays last year?"

"Yes."

"Oh ... I thought you were just on vacation or something."

"Nope. Not on vacation."

"Right ..."

He paused again and I glanced at the door, anxious to leave and end the conversation.

"So she died right around Christmas? That must be awful."

"Pretty awful," I responded expressionlessly.

"But at least you knew it was coming."

"No, it was pretty sudden."

He gave me an odd look.

"I thought you said she had cancer," he asked. "So ... didn't you expect it?"

My tongue felt heavy from the lie and I struggled to find a way to cover myself.

"Right, well ... we thought she had longer," I said unconvincingly.

"Oh. Of course." He looked as though he was going to say something more, but I quickly cut him off.

"Actually, I've got to get back to my dorm," I said. "But it was ... nice talking to you."

As I turned to go, he got up the nerve to speak again.

"Say, Enim ... would you maybe want to study with me tomorrow? There's that Calculus test on Friday, and I didn't really get that thing that Mrs. Beake said about the integral logarithms ..."

He watched me expectantly as I failed to answer. Despite the pleading in his tone, though, the thought of spending any more time crammed at a table with him locked in a conversation about matters that ought to have been private was too much to bear.

"Actually ... I don't think so, Thomas," I said. "I'm kind of busy right now."

His stare turned cold.

"Oh. Right."

"But ... I'll see you around," I concluded awkwardly as I stepped towards the door.

"Yeah. You will."

His glare seemed to follow me all the way down the hallway and to the door, and once I stepped outside I broke into a brisk walk just to put some distance between us. His wavering moods were highly unsettling, and I wasn't sure if it was worse to be his friend or his enemy.

"His friend, definitely," Jack resolved when I relayed the conversation to him an hour later. "I mean, what are you afraid he'll do if he doesn't like you? Sit on you?"

"That, or kill me in my sleep," I said, taking a seat on my bed.

Jack swiveled around in the desk chair with a cigarette clenched between his teeth.

"Ah, come on, Nim – that won't happen. I have tons of enemies, it's never hurt me."

I gave him a disbelieving look.

"Says the guy who looks like that," I said blatantly, indicating to his massively bruised face.

"Right – good point. But this is *Porker*," he said, waving off my concern. "He's more likely to just mope about you and eat his feelings. Don't worry."

"All right," I agreed halfheartedly. "But you didn't see him ... He looked pretty upset."

"That's because you worry too much," Jack said. He took another drag from the cigarette before letting his arm drop down to the desk, but his expression was far from unconcerned, as well.

"How was your day, then?" I asked.

"Dull as usual."

"Even French?"

"Especially French," he said. "Miss Mercier's still out. It's been nearly a week – can you believe that? And the Foreign Language meeting was supposed to be tonight."

"Well, I guess her friend's pretty sick," I reasoned. "It's not like she'd go see someone if they just had a cold."

"Ugh, great," Jack said exasperatedly. "What if they're on their deathbed? She might not be back for a month. Some people take forever to die."

I slowly lowered my bag to the ground; Jack looked horrified at his word choice.

"I mean –" he began apologetically.

"Forget it."

We sat in silence for a long moment. The room was simultaneously chilly and stuffy and I couldn't decide whether or not to take my jacket off. Jack looked down at his hands, a guilty look mixed in with the worry on his face.

"Maybe we *should* do something," I said suddenly.

"What?"

I chewed the side of my mouth as I stared out into the distance. Across the campus, just visible through the tree line, was the darkly glistening water. It looked so silent and unassuming from my spot behind the window, and it hardly seemed possible that it had drowned the girl from town. I imagined her being pulled under over and over again, her lungs filling with fluid instead of air as she struggled to breathe, before her body finally grew too weak to fight and sank beneath the surface. It seemed like an easy way to die – and yet, not quite easy enough.

"Maybe we should get out of the room for a bit," I suggested. "You know, do something fun."

"Really?" Jack asked skeptically. "Fun as in go to the library and watch you study, or fun as in go to the boathouse?"

I tore my gaze from the window.

"Fun as in boathouse." As his face lit up spectacularly, I glanced at the clock with the sudden reminder of my appointment with Beringer that night. "Only, we'll have to go after eight or so."

"That's great – it's better to wait until it's late anyhow, so no one will see us leaving."

With his mood restored, he spent the good part of the next few hours chattering on about something he had read in history about the founding of Bickerby which had added to his belief that the place had once served as a jail. Though entertaining, I once again found my assignments were left completely undone for the next day.

After filling up on multiple cups of coffee at dinner, we left the dining hall and broke off to go our separate ways. I headed over to the Health Center in the already-dark sky, half-heartedly wishing that I had one of the police flashlights to light my way rather than the failing lights on the sides of the buildings. The secretary waved me past her desk upon entering and I wandered down the hallway to Beringer's office. After a light knock on the door, he called me in.

"How are you, Enim?"

"Fine."

I eased myself down into the chair across from him, readying myself to deflect his questions and come up with lies to cover my untold truths, and both feeling very certain that it was all for the best but particularly guilty about it all the same.

"Is there anything in particular you'd like to talk about today?" Beringer asked.

I shook my head as I always did and gave a weak smile, wishing that I could just tell him something that would ease his mind and make him think that the sessions were at all worthwhile. The idea that he came so far out of his way just to see me made me feel worse for always avoiding important subjects.

"How has your week been so far?"

"It's been ... fine."

"And classes?"

"Fine."

He smiled a bit as he paused, so used to hearing the response and yet not at all accustomed to it, and looked down at the file lying open on the desk in front of him. After a moment he folded his hands over it and looked back up at me.

"Why do you think you're here, Enim?"

"Here with you, you mean? Or in general?"

"Here with me."

I moved my eyes to the darkening view outside the window.

"Because my father wants you to fix me."

"Oh?" Beringer said. "What makes you think that?"

"I don't think it, I know it."

"How do you know? Has he told you?"

I scraped my tongue over my teeth as I waited to respond. My father and I had had few conversations that consisted of more than formal pleasantries or outright arguments, and he had certainly never opened up enough to tell me his reasoning behind any of his decisions, but I had known exactly what he meant when he hired Beringer to come out to the island to see me: he wanted to put me back into place and to right me before I could commit any further wrongs.

"Why else would you be here?" I said.

"Do you think that that's why I'm here, Enim? Because I want to fix you?"

I made no motion to respond. Beringer gave me a contemplative look beneath a frown.

"I have no desire to 'fix' you," he said, pausing in thought. "Do you want to be fixed?"

"No."

"Do you think that you need to be?"

"Isn't that the same question?"

"Does it have the same answer?" When I failed to respond, he said, "I know that you don't take your medicine, Enim."

I looked back over to him quickly.

"What? No, that's ... I ... I take it."

He wasn't convinced of the lie. Giving me a slight smile, he said, "You forgot to pick up the prescription last week."

I sighed and looked down at my hands. Though Beringer had begun prescribing me medication months before, I had never so much as opened a bottle. The pills were stockpiled beneath my mattress, all lined up in orange rows: sometimes I could hear them rattle as I tossed and turned in the night.

"Believe me when I say this, Enim," Beringer said quietly, "I only prescribe it to you to help you, not to change you in any way."

"I know, I just ... I just don't know, Dr. Beringer."

"It's only to help you sleep and increase your appetite. I think that if you were to take it, you might feel considerably better."

"Right. Or at least my father would feel better."

"What do you mean by that?"

"Nothing, just that he ... he's afraid that I'm ..."

"Go on."

"He's afraid that there's something wrong with me. Because of what happened."

"I see." Beringer peered at me more closely. "And ... what *did* happen, Enim?"

I turned to face him again, wary that he might be trying to trick me with his words, but his expression was as straightforward as the question had been.

"You know," I said. "It's written in my file, isn't it?"

"Your file says what happened to your mother; it says nothing about what happened to you."

"Well, nothing happened to me. That's why."

"Perhaps not, though it says in your file that you refused to talk about the events that led up to the incident, and I rather wonder why that is."

I shrugged despite the sudden stiffness in my shoulders, but it was hardly worth the effort to pretend that I didn't know what he was talking about.

"There was nothing to say," I said.

"I see. And what about now? Is there anything to say?"

I swallowed and looked at the clock, but the session was

barely half over. I sucked in my cheeks as I debated what to tell him.

"I don't ... I don't want to talk about my mother, Dr. Beringer."

"I know you don't, Enim. But I think that we should."

He waited for me to respond, but I could not. The room seemed to have dropped several degrees and I had to press my hands beneath my legs to keep them from shaking. Beringer eyed me cautiously.

"I wonder, Enim, if you don't want to talk about what happened because you feel guilty about it."

I clamped my teeth down on the insides of my cheeks to keep my expression neutral; my throat was too tight to swallow.

"Why would I feel guilty?" I said.

"I wouldn't know; I had hoped that you could tell me."

I shook my head too quickly to warrant innocence and kept my eyes on the ground to avoid Beringer's gaze. After several minutes of silence, he quietly suggested that I could think about it and allowed me to leave. I hurried from the office without another word.

"Back so soon?" Jack asked as I entered the dorm room. "Beringer's cutting the sessions short?"

"Yeah," I said distractedly.

"What a cheapskate. Not that I'm complaining, mind you – I'm all for having him waste your dad's money rather than your time."

He grinned and flipped off his bed, hurriedly pulling his sweatshirt and shoes on and collecting something from the bedside table. It took me a moment to remember that I had said we would go down to the boathouse. For a fleeting moment I considered telling him that I was too exhausted, but then I changed my mind: I needed the distraction.

Flashlight in hand and pocketknife in the other, Jack paused in the hallway to make sure that we hadn't alerted Sanders to what we were doing. It would soon be after-hours and our building was silent except for the occasional snippets of conversations and muted sound of music coming from a set of blaring headphones that hadn't been turned off. Sanders' door was decisively shut against a silent room and we crept past it without incident. Hurrying down the stairs, Jack glanced over his shoulder to give me an energized look. After a brief pause, we opened the main door and slipped out onto the grounds.

The campus was dark and silent in the night, and only a few lights on the sides of buildings lit the way for us to sneak out across the grass and through the garden in the direction of the woods. The air was a crisp cold that scratched at the skin beneath my sweater and coat and hastened our stride.

"Here – I think it's through here."

We had reached the fence that circled around Bickerby's campus. It was chain-link and mostly covered by some spindly plant, though the branches had been plowed back in one section to reveal where the metal wire had been cut. Jack swept away some of the dead leaves and tugged at the fence to enlarge the hole. With a quick grin, he pulled himself through the opening. I stooped and followed him. The wires yanked at my clothing as I went, momentarily preventing me from going through, but with a firm tug I stumbled out onto the other side. In the moonlight, the hoarfrost spreading across the dirt shone white like marble on the ground. I stood and wiped it from my hands before we continued.

The boathouse was visible in the distance. It was a small wooden building off to the side of the woods that sat amongst the rocks on the shoreline with large double doors chained shut for the winter. Jack pressed his forehead against one of the frost-covered windows to ensure that the boats were there before crossing to the doors. Taking out his pocket knife, he proceeded to slip the blade between a slight gap in one of the links and pried it apart. With the chain broken, he easily slid it off the door without touching the lock. I crossed my arms as I waited for him to get the doors open, too used to seeing him breaking and entering with such ease to be impressed.

"Here we go," he said, shining the flashlight inside.

The place had an old, rotting smell that I could never get

used to. The salt water that had either flooded the place after heavy rains or dripped onto the floor when the boats were brought in filled the space with the distinctly foul smell of mildew. It was a wonder that Barker hadn't had the place redone as he had the majority of the other buildings. Jack grabbed the end of one of the boats and indicated for me to take the other. Walking backwards, I maneuvered out the door and onto the rocky shore. Jack trailed behind me carefully, but neither of us could help as the boat hit the doorframe at a sharp angle: the sound of cracking wood filled the air and we both stopped and listened as the air around us rang out. Nothing around us stirred to indicate that we had been heard, though: we were too far out from campus for anyone to hear us.

"Let's just drop it and drag it," Jack said, releasing his end of the boat and clutching his back.

"No – it'll be too loud."

"It won't. Besides, no one will hear. Think about it, Nim – we're in the middle of nowhere *in the middle of nowhere*."

I glanced around at the empty shore and chewed my lip, still worried about being caught. The beach looked more forsaken than ever beneath the dark sky, and the bluish hue of the rocks highlighted their jaggedness. Behind them, the ocean looked more uninviting than ever.

"Fine," I said, and dropped my side of the boat as well. As we shoved the boat towards the water, the plastic squelched against the rocks with a horrific sound. When it finally slapped against the water I climbed into it and Jack gave it a final shove forward before jumping in after me.

It only took a moment for us to get into the rhythm of rowing the oars in synchronization. The boat was intended for eight rather than two, and it took us a while longer to get out into the ocean than it would have for two members of the rowing team, but we were able to maneuver it in the direction we wanted and succeeded in propelling out against the steadfastness of the waves. When we were a good deal away from the shore we eased up on the oars and let the boat rest against the waves. The blackness of the water slapped the sides of the boat as we paused in an attempt to gain entry.

Jack leaned back and stretched his legs out, staring up at the sky. His face was white with moonlight.

"You ever think about what it'll be like to leave here, Nim?"

"All the time."

The stars were reflected in his eyes as he tilted his head back. The white light highlighted the damage on his face more clearly: the skin beneath both eyes had turned a sickly red-purple and one lid was black; his lower lip had cracked and was hardened with blood. I had begun to forget how Jack looked without the characteristic injuries, or perhaps I had never known him without them. Even when I had met him he had sported a bruised face, though back then he didn't have the bend in his nose from having it broken so often. There was a distinct white scar going across the bridge of it from where he had been hit in the face with a glass maple-syrup bottle a few years back, and the other more recent one running through his eyebrow from the fight with Peters. And yet, as far as I could tell, there didn't seem to be anything wrong with him: it was only me who harbored something ugly beneath the neatly-ironed dress shirt and sweater.

"Imagine what it'll be like to get up and do whatever we'd like," he said. "Get up at any hour, dress however I want, smoke my morning cigarette, and go about my day the way I choose."

"You already do three out of the four of those," I pointed out.

He tore his eyes from the sky to look back at me.

"Way to be a downer, Nim."

"Right, sorry."

"Isn't there anything you want to do when we leave here? Drink real coffee? Wear something other than khakis and blue sweaters? Read a book that's not for English class?"

"I don't know. Not really."

"There must be something," he persisted.

72

I shrugged.

"I guess ... I haven't really thought about it."

He rolled over so that his head was resting on the side of the boat and looked at me carefully.

"Nothing? Really?"

The idea must have been entirely foreign to him given that he had been waiting to escape to France for years now. I wished that I could think of something that I would enjoy even a fraction as much, but nothing crossed my mind. The blankness was oddly disturbing.

"What about once you're eighteen?" Jack said. "You've got to be looking forward to being free from your father."

"I'm pretty free from him already," I said. "It's Karl I've got to get away from, now."

"Right. And that house."

I stared into the black all around us, training my mind away from the image of the place where Karl and I resided in my father's absence.

"Yeah, that'll be good."

"But there's got to be something else you're looking forward to," he said. "Isn't there something you've always wanted to do? Jump out of an airplane or something?"

"Definitely not."

"Right, didn't think so," he said with a grin. "But there has to be something."

He was undoubtedly right, though I had to strain to think of what it was. Years before, my mother had insisted that one day we would see *Turandot* together, the opera that her favorite song, *Nessun Dorma*, was from. As the boat rocked back and forth with the waves, I thought of how she had sat next to me on the piano bench and taught me the notes to the aria that she had converted to sheet music, and how she would hum the song even on the days when she refused to leave her room.

"I guess I thought about seeing *Turandot*," I said reluctantly.

"Seeing a tornado? Wicked," Jack said.

"No, *Turandot* – it's an opera."

"Oh. That makes more sense. Well, from you, anyway."

He smirked through the dark at me and I smiled weakly in return, my thoughts still faraway on the moments that I could never get back again.

"Well, we could go see that," he said with a shrug.

"Jack, it's an opera," I said.

"So?"

"So it's an *opera*," I repeated. "You'd hate it."

"I might not."

"You would – it's not even in English."

"Ugh – don't tell me it's in Latin or something."

"It's in Italian."

"Oh, that's not so bad." He sat up and considered it for a moment. "Even better – we can see it in Italy. It's just a train-ride away from France."

He scooted closer to the middle of the boat at the idea.

"Yeah, let's do it," he continued. "We'll go see Tornado, take a look around Italy, send your dad a postcard or two – it'll be great."

He grinned over at me in his infectious way, but for once my expression didn't flicker to mirror his. Something about the thought of going to see the opera without my mother gnawed at my insides and my heart burned against my ribcage. All at once, looking out over the dark expanse of black that was the surrounding ocean, it finally occurred to me that no matter how much hope I harbored inside, she would never stand on the beach with her back to the shore again, or play the piano in the parlor of the house we had once shared, or dream of seeing the opera that she had loved so well again, because she was gone – and I would never get her back again.

Ch. 5

Something clattered behind Jack and broke me from my thoughts.

"What was that?" I said.

He squinted through the darkness and patted his hands along the side of the boat before groaning.

"The oar just fell."

"What? In the water?"

"Yep."

He brushed his dark hair from his eyes and peered over the side of the boat to see where it had gone.

"Do you see it?"

"I think so – here –"

He grabbed my arm so that he wouldn't fall and leaned over the boat to snatch it back up. The moonlight was just bright enough to make out the hint of white plastic that was floating a few feet away.

"Almost –" he said, fingers outstretched over the water.

He had only leaned the slightest bit further, but it was enough to throw us off balance: the boat rocked horribly before flipping onto its side and throwing us into the water. I hit the surface with an impact that felt as though I had slammed headfirst into a sheet of glass that shattered and dragged me down through its shards.

My mind went black as I plummeted downwards and my limbs turned to stone in the cold, preventing me from kicking my way back to the surface. Above me, the moon was just a glimmer of white as I sank; it wavered up through the water, waving in its place in the sky in a silent farewell, and then disappeared as the world faded to black.

Though my lungs compressed and body sank, my mind stayed as active as ever. I was certain that I was seeing exactly what the local girl had as she drowned, and the dismal sky was so desolate that I found I didn't mind sinking lower and lower if only to get away from it, and a strange part of me felt very calm as I descended towards the ocean floor.

Something clamped around my wrists and kept me from sinking down further: Jack had found me and was tugging me up. He dragged me past the surface and I choked out a breath before he flung me back into the righted boat and heaved himself in after me. I couldn't hear his chattering teeth over the sound of my own, but he appeared to be shaking just as badly as I was.

"I thought you knew how to swim," he said , gasping in the cold air.

I only shook in response, too cold to answer properly. When my jaw had stilled enough to speak, I asked, "Did you get the oar?"

"No."

"What?"

"Sorry, Nim, I was a bit busy getting *you*," he said.

"Right."

I slowly sat up from my curled spot and looked out over the water: the black surface was smooth and silent now, and all trace of the oar and my desire to sink down with it was gone.

"At least we still have the other one," I said.

"Think again: it went over with us."

"So we lost both of them?"

"That's what it looks like."

We fell into silence again. It was only after several minutes that I realized I had lost my shoes as well; my feet were so cold and stiff that it was hard to tell.

"So what do we do?"

"I don't know, shout for help?"

"No one would hear us."

"Good point." He gave a violent shiver and then looked around. "Well, then I guess we'd better find the oars."

"They're probably at the bottom of the ocean by now," I said.

"No they're not. Oars float."

"Yeah?"

He nodded and rotated around to see if he could catch sight of either of them, but was careful not to lean over the edge of the boat again.

"There's one," he said after a long moment. He gave me a look. "Stay here ... I'll see if I can get it."

He eased over the side and back into the water, swearing at the painful cold as he went, and then swam in the direction of the oar. After a minute he shouted that he had it and made his way back, dropping the retrieved item into the boat before climbing in himself.

"Just one?" I said, but hurriedly bit my tongue as he sprawled on the floor in a fit of shivers.

I took up the oar and did my best to steer us back to shore. It was a much longer, more difficult journey back: it seemed to take an eternity just to reach the halfway mark, and at one point I wasn't even sure that we were going in the right direction. My arms were so stiff with cold that I could hardly move them, but halfway there Jack regained some of his energy and took over. After another seemingly endless amount of time, the boat bumped to a stop and scratched against the rocky shore.

We climbed onto the beach with languid, heavy steps and had barely gotten away from the edge of the water before we collapsed again with cold. It felt as though my hands were being compressed under smoldering weights – the bones crushed to powder as the skin shriveled and died. My feet protested in pain as I stood up again, but it was impossible to know if they hurt more from the cold or sharp rocks below them.

Jack didn't seem to be fairing much better. I could see him stumbling across the beach in repeated attempts to walk before he finally gave up and crawled towards the woods. His soaked clothing weighed him down as he went.

"What about the boat?" I said, looking in vain at the distance between it and the boathouse.

"Just leave it."

"But then Barker will know we broke in and stole it," I protested, though I didn't think I would be able to drag the boat back to the boathouse regardless.

"No, Barker will know that *someone* broke in and stole it. He won't trace it back to us."

I gave the boat one final glance before agreeing then, hugging myself to keep warm, I followed Jack as he fumbled through the trees and broken fence back onto Bickerby grounds. The grass was cold and frozen under my feet as we stumbled along, silent except for rattling breaths and Jack's occasional swear as he collided with things in the dark.

"Finally," he said, thumping to a stop against the door to our residence building. "Do you have your key?"

"No," I said. "Do you have *your* key?"

He had had it in his pocket when we left the room and had used it to lock the door behind us; I had seen him slip it into his pocket before switching on the flashlight. His lack of response, however, was an answer enough to my question.

"Jack – don't tell me you lost your keys *again*."

"Here's the thing, Nim. I had the keys, they just aren't in my pocket *anymore*."

"What do you mean? Where are they?"

"Possibly at the bottom of the ocean."

"Possibly?"

"More than likely, really."

I sighed heavily. I should have known better than to trust Jack with a set of keys, but I hadn't thought that even he could lose them so shortly after getting a new set. The night was unbearably cold and all I wanted was to bury myself beneath every blanket in the dorm room and lay there until I stopped shaking.

"But you can pick the lock," I said.

"Sure," Jack replied. "Do you have a hairpin?"

"Of course I don't!"

"Then I can't pick the lock – these ones are tricky."

Refusing to accept that we were locked out of the building until someone opened the door on their way out to breakfast the next morning, I searched for a solution.

"Come on – I've seen you break in teachers' offices with a stick of gum," I said.

"Right, but I used the gum to stop the door from locking, not to unlock it. Besides, we don't have any gum, either."

"What do we have?" I asked, wondering how many of our belongings were currently floating to the bottom of the ocean as we spoke.

"Not much. Well — I might be able to use one of the laces from your shoes to pick it," he said.

"Too bad. My shoes are gone."

"What? You lost your shoes?"

"Don't remind me," I said wearily. "Karl's going to kill me when he finds out."

"Just tell him they got dirty — he won't be able to stand that."

I nodded, thinking that he had a point, when something rustled behind us and a large shape came into view in the corner of our vision. We both saw it at the same time and jumped back.

"I might be able to help," said a tentative voice.

Squinting over at it, I tried to make out who was there. The voice sounded vaguely familiar, though I didn't want to believe who it belonged to. My stomach squirmed uncomfortably.

"Nice of you to join us, Porker," Jack said, crossing his arms.

Thomas edged forward towards us from the shrubbery. I felt my heart sink all the way down into my stomach. He was looking at us with utmost pleasure that could have only meant he was reveling in the idea of having something to hold over our heads.

"Jack," he said curtly. "Enim. Having a nice night?"

"Lovely," Jack replied darkly.

Thomas eyed Jack coldly. For a moment he fumbled in his pocket, breaking his gaze on us, and I stole a glance at Jack. His fingers had curled around the handle of his pocket knife. I reached over to grab his forearm: threatening Thomas wasn't going to help us.

"Here," Thomas muttered to himself, finally pulling out what he had been looking for. I could see a flash of metal in the starlight and heard a jingling sound, but it took a moment to realize what he was showing us. "Looking for these?"

I squinted, barely able to recognize the keys through the dark.

"Hand them over, Porter," Jack said.

"I don't think so," Thomas replied, pulling the keys back behind his back. He seemed to be under the impression that if he hid them from view, Jack wouldn't able to get them from him.

"Where'd you get those?"

"You dropped them coming out of here."

"When we were coming out of here?" Jack repeated. "What, you've been spying on us?"

Thomas didn't answer. I could see him fumbling with the keys behind his back, undoubtedly searching for what to say.

"Thanks, Thomas," I said, finally breaking into the conversation. "You're a real lifesaver."

I reached forward for the keys, hoping that he would simply give them back, but he snatched them back and shook his head at me.

"Not so fast," he said. "I – I'm not just going to give them to you."

"Oh, please," Jack said, taking a step forward. "You can hand them over, or I can take them from you. Which do you prefer?"

"You're not taking them," Thomas said. "I – I'll give them to you, but I want something in return!"

The keys jangled in his hands. I glanced up at our building, glad that Sanders' room was on the opposite side and that he wouldn't be able to look down if he heard the ruckus.

"How about I just take them from you and let you walk away, Porter?" Jack said, taking another step forward. His face glowed white in the night lighting and his expression was hard. Thomas took another step back.

"No," he said shakily, fingers grasping the keys to ensure Jack didn't grab them away. "I – I'm not afraid of you, Jack. Even – even if you beat me up, I can still tell Mr. Barker that you were out."

"So are you," I reminded him.

"It doesn't matter!" Thomas said angrily. "You and Jack have been in too much trouble – you'll get a two week suspension, minimum, for another offense! You won't graduate!"

He looked between us as he gave his threat, but it didn't have the effect he had been hoping for. Jack rolled his eyes.

"You won't graduate, either, Porker," he said, taking another step forward, "so I'll take my chances."

Thomas swallowed.

"It doesn't matter if I get caught or not; I'll be booted out of here regardless for my GPA."

Jack gave him a scathingly mocking look.

"Oh, poor Porter," he cooed. "Too stupid to stay in school. What a shame."

Thomas looked as though he wanted nothing more than to shove Jack's keys down his throat and watch him struggle for breath, but Jack was far too irritable from the cold to heed the warning look that I gave him.

"Fine," Thomas said after a moment. "You might not care, Jack, but Enim does."

"Nim doesn't care if you tell on him: Barker will let him off."

"Not about that," Thomas countered. "I know something else about him."

Jack raised his eyebrow and gave me a look.

"What, about my mother?" I said, trying to think of what he thought he could do with that information. I shook my head. "So what?"

"Not about her, no. About your ... confidant."

"My what?" I said bewilderedly as Jack mirrored my expression.

"You know, your little secret over at the Health Center," Thomas said maliciously. "That *doctor* who you have to see every week."

The coldness that had pierced my skin gave way as a wave

of heat came over me instead. I stared at Thomas uncomprehendingly.

"How do you know about that?" I said.

"I saw you."

"You mean you *followed* me?"

I narrowed my eyes in irritation, but my voice was shaking with the cold.

"Maybe," he confirmed. "It wasn't easy ... you're very secretive about it. What's the matter, Enim? Don't want anyone to know that you're not so perfect?"

I couldn't find the words to respond. My face felt so hot that I was sure I was burning with a fever.

"I wonder how long it would take the school to find out about it," Thomas mused. "An hour? Two?"

"I'll break your jaw if you do," Jack responded harshly, but even though Thomas looked nervous at the threat, I made up my mind and stepped between them. My heart rate quickened.

"All right, what do you want, Thomas?" I said. "I'll do it."

He was licking his lips anxiously as he glanced back and forth between Jack's threatening stance and my own apprehensive one; it was hard to know which of us was shaking the most.

"I – I want the answers to Mrs. Beake's homework and exams," he said. "For the rest of the year. You write down the answers and give them to me."

I looked at him, completely astounded.

"We're in the same class, that won't help you," I told him. I found it hard to believe that he would go through so much trouble to get me to do his work for him. I wasn't sure if I should be annoyed or feel sorry for him.

"I dropped chemistry so that I could change my schedule around," he said.

His request wasn't spur-of-the-moment; he had obviously been planning on having me get the answers for him for some time now. Perhaps he had thought that I would do so out of friendliness, and then when that hadn't panned out he had resorted to blackmail.

I ran my hair through my half-frozen hair.

"Fine," I said. "I'll give you the answers. Now ... hand over the keys."

He hesitated. Swallowing, he said, "If you don't give me the answers, Enim, I will tell everyone. Don't think I won't."

He dropped the keys into my hand. When we had stepped far enough back, he turned and scurried through the darkness back to his residence building. Jack glanced at me uncertainly before we unlocked the door and snuck back up to our room.

We stripped off our wet clothes and replaced them with dry ones before collapsing into bed silently. I could hear Jack's jagged breathing turn heavy after just a moment and knew that he had succeeded in falling asleep, but I laid awake for the remainder of the night. Worse than the thought of getting caught cheating for him or the one of him telling everyone about Beringer was that, if it was so easy to find out about the latter, it might be just as simple for him to find out the truth about my mother.

After a sleepless night, I pulled myself out of bed the following morning to find Jack awake and half-dressed. My head was pounding and I was certain that I was getting sick from nearly freezing to death the night before. Before I could look at the clock to see what time it was, though, there was a quick knock on the door and it opened. Sanders stood in the doorway.

"Ever heard of waiting for an answer before entering someone else's room?" Jack said irritably, wearing only his pants and an annoyed look. Sanders surveyed him with a squinted gaze.

"What's the problem, Hadler? Are you doing something you'd rather me not see?"

"Yeah – getting dressed," he answered. "Do you want to follow me into the shower to finish our conversation?"

"Actually, we're not having a conversation," Sanders replied. "I'm here for Lund."

I looked over at them quickly.

"Why?" I said.

"You have a message to go up to the main offices," Sanders said. "Mr. Barker wants to see you."

My heart stopped momentarily. It was unheard of to be called to Barker's office for anything but the most serious offenses – even Jack, who had seen more trouble than most of the school combined, had only had to see Barker once: the rest of the time, other teachers had always been the ones to berate him and give him his punishments. Porter must have been caught sneaking back into his residence building and elected to turn me in as well.

"Why? What'd I do?"

"I don't know, Lund," Sanders said. "I'm just bringing you the message."

Sanders was observing me with interest. I could tell that he was just waiting to hear what I had done to warrant a visit to the headmaster's office: his face lit up excitedly as though he hoped that I might allow him to escort me there like a prisoner. Jack glared at him openly.

"Sanders, have you ever heard the phrase, 'shoot the messenger'?" he asked casually.

"Yes, I have."

"Have you ever *experienced* it?"

Taking the hint, Sanders chewed his tongue and backed from the room. The door closed loudly behind him. As soon as he was gone, I turned wildly to Jack.

"What do I do?" I said. "Thomas must've gotten caught outside last night and turned me in!"

"Hold on, you don't know that," Jack said calmly. He was so used to being in trouble that the idea of it hardly fazed him. "If he had been caught then he would've turned me in, too."

"Then why do I have to see Barker?"

Jack shrugged.

"Maybe he wants to have tea with you," he said. "You know, catch up. Talk about your dad, the weather, politics – the works."

"Don't be sarcastic."

"I'm serious, Nim – what else could it be? It's not like you could've done anything bad enough to be called to his office, so it must be some social call. Just go and come back – and don't worry about it. If you look guilty, he's going to know something's up."

"How do I not look guilty?" I wondered aloud, but Jack only smirked without a response.

I dressed in my cleanest pants and selected an unwrinkled sweater from the closet, but since I had lost my boat shoes I was forced to wear a pair of loafers instead. I sighed as I realized that I would have to call Karl and ask him to send another pair; I would never get through the winter without them.

"Good luck," Jack called after me as I left the room.

Barker's office was located in the Welcoming Hall, a large brick building located at the top of the hill past the sporting fields. As far as I knew, it didn't serve any real purpose other than to showcase his innate egotism in every aspect of his life. The walls were lined with evidence of students that he had supposedly shepherded to success: there were cabinets filled with trophies, yearbooks dating back decades on full display, and numerous awards hung up on the walls.

At the very back of the building was his ornate, overly large office. It was a wonder as to why he needed such a large office considering his notable absence at the school – he divided his time between his summer house in town that overlooked the water and his winter home in a warmer state – and when he was at Bickerby, he certainly didn't have a role beyond keeping up appearances. Unless there was severe trouble, he left the duty of handing out punishments to the other administrators. I swallowed again as I wondered what I had done.

I dug my hands down into my pockets as I walked up the hill to the building. I had left my soaked jacket behind and the chill in the air quickly seeped beneath my sweater. I stepped into the main hallway, wrinkling my nose at the sight of the multitude of framed pictures and certificates lining the walls, and hesitantly stepped down towards Barker's office. I ran my hand through my hair nervously before I knocked.

LAURA GIEBFRIED

"Come in."

His secretary called me into the outer office; his private one was located behind thick oak doors. I approached her desk and cleared my throat.

"I was called to Mr. Barker's office."

She glanced up at my quickly as though I was annoying her. "Name?"

"Enim Lund."

"Looned," she repeated. "Looned ... Looned. Yes, they're waiting for you. Knock before you enter."

I forced myself to approach the door and gave the softest of knocks. Barker called me inside. Though I had only met him on a few occasions, his gruff voice was easily recognizable: it always sounded as though he had just downed a shot of whiskey and it was still burning his throat.

"Enim, Enim, there you are."

Barker was a huge man. I had either forgotten quite how large he was, or he had put on more weight since I had last seen him several months ago. He was standing behind the desk wearing one of his customary three-piece suits in a shade of forest green, looking rather like one of the mounds of grass outside the window behind him. When I hesitated in the doorway, he ushered me inside with a wave of his hand. The tone of his voice was friendly enough, and for a moment I thought that Jack might have been right in thinking that there was nothing to worry about. No sooner had I let out a sigh of relief, though, than I noticed who else was in the room: Karl.

My knees jerked beneath me.

"Why don't you have a seat, Enim, and we can get started?"

I looked back at Barker with a fearful expression. My legs were heavy beneath me and I had to yank them from the floor in order to get over to the chair. Once I had reached it, I nearly collapsed upon it.

"Do you know why you're here, Enim?" Barker asked.

I swallowed as I contemplated if it would be better to admit what I had done or feign ignorance. Throwing another glance in Karl's direction, I decided on the latter and shook my head stiffly.

"You have ... no idea?" Barker asked.

My heart was pummeling against my ribcage and I was sure that my expression gave away my guilt, but I shook my head again regardless. Barker sighed.

"You mean to tell me that you have no idea that your grades are severely low?"

"What?"

Having expected him to say something entirely different, I couldn't hide my surprise. Barker's eyebrows knotted at my tone.

"Your grades, Enim," he said, his voice rising impatiently.

"This – this is about my grades?"

"Yes, it's about your grades. You're failing every class, young man."

He pulled out the chair to his desk, which was the same shade of forest green as his suit, and took a seat. I licked my lips anxiously as I debated how to respond.

"All of them?" I managed at last. Barker gave me an astounded look.

"Yes, all of them!" he said irritably, as though I had hoped that the punishment to be different if I was still passing just one. "Your GPA is below a *one* – I'm sure that I don't have to tell you that that means you're on academic probation."

I looked at my hands without responding; the brief relief that I had felt from learning that I had not been reported by Thomas had quickly been replaced by a sense of foreboding. From the corner of my eye, I could see Karl shifting in place.

"This late in the semester, when there's no chance of your grades lifting, the course of action is immediate and indefinite suspension," Barker imparted.

I shut my eyes at his words. Karl had come up to the school to take me back to Connecticut. As the realization came, a feeling of illness came over me: I couldn't go back there. I wrapped my hands around the arms of the chair thinking that he would have to pry them off before I would consent to go.

"What do you have to say for yourself, young man?"

I looked up at Barker's voice. He was looking at me expectantly, though I had no idea what he hoped that I would say.

"I ... I mean, I thought I was passing Calculus," I said at last.

Barker looked far from impressed.

"He's not very on top of things, is he?" he said, looking over at Karl. Karl gave me a stern look to stay silent before responding.

"No, I assure you that he is, Charles. He's just been ... distracted lately."

"Yes, yes ... so you've said." The headmaster's eyes traveled over me suspiciously as though expecting to see some sign of disturbance written along my face. From his side, Karl gave me an impatient nod to compel me to speak.

"Right. I've been distracted," I said, bowing my head to convey what my toneless voice could not. "I'm sorry, Mr. Barker."

"Good, good – so long as you understand the situation," Barker said, shuffling some papers on his desk to the side to clear a spot for his arms. "Well, even though you're doing so poorly with little chance of scraping by, I'm willing to hold off on your suspension given the ... circumstances. I've spoken to your uncle and he assures me that your grades are a reflection of the ... most tragic situation with your mother."

My eyes flickered over to Karl and narrowed. I could only imagine what he had invented to tell Barker in order to smooth things over.

"As one of Bickerby's finest young men, Enim, I'm willing to give you the proper needed amount of time to grieve," Barker continued, drawing my eyes back to him. "I understand how trying this must be for you. Your father informed me that your mother had been sick for a long time ... I often wondered why we never saw her at school events. Even so, it must have been quite a shock ... a most difficult situation ..."

The heat in Barker's office was much too high and it was

quickly becoming difficult to breathe. I swallowed repeatedly to keep from retching as my neck swelled in my collar.

"I'm going to give you some leeway, here, Enim. I've spoken with your teachers and they've agreed, given the circumstances, to give you the chance to raise your grades, granted that you put in the effort. If you do exceptionally well for the rest of the semester – which at this point normally wouldn't change anything – then they'll raise your grades to passing ones."

Barker watched me with bulging eyes as he waited for me to respond, but my voice was still stuck in my throat. The wooden arms of the chair beneath my hands grew damp with sweat.

"Of course, I also expect that you'll be on your best behavior," he said. "I'm doing you a favor, here. I don't want any trouble out of you. No more incidents like last year –"

"That's past us." Karl interjected the headmaster in mid-breath. As their eyes met briefly from across the room, Barker waited to exhale. The subject was clearly still a sore one. "There's no need to revisit it."

"I just don't want anything repeating itself," Barker said cautiously. "After all, I gave him a chance last year to get his act together, and here we are again."

"With a completely different situation," Karl said. His voice was firm; he appeared to have taken on the role he was accustomed to personating as a lawyer.

"But a situation nonetheless, Karl."

"One which I am just as willing to pay you for, Charles."

Barker's face twitched with a smile; the price of letting me stay was unmistakably worthwhile.

"Yes, you're right, Karl, of course," Barker said. "Forgive me, it's just ... that little stunt that Enim pulled last year was quite upsetting for all of us here at Bickerby."

"I'm sure that it was," Karl said, though he sounded dubious of Barker's claimed upset. "But, really, Enim was just going along with what was obviously Jack Hadler's idea."

"That may be, Karl, but it was *your* nephew who admitted

to lighting the thing on fire, not Hadler –"

"And it was *me* who compensated the school for its – loss – as well."

Karl raised his voice ever slightly as he spoke. As they bickered, I took the opportunity to wipe my palms on my pants. The deal that they had already made was of no concern. As I waited for papers to be signed and hands to be shaken, I sank down in my seat and wished that I could disappear.

"And Bickerby benefited greatly from it, Karl, as you can see."

Barker slid his chair back and indicated to the view from his window. His office overlooked the sporting fields which had grown more expansive over the summer.

"Beautiful, isn't it?"

"Yes," Karl agreed, though his tone was peppered with cold. Barker smiled regardless.

"Well, now that we're all on the same page," he said, picking up his pen to jot something down on a piece of paper, "we can move forward from this little mess."

He turned his smile to me in the ugliest of expressions.

"Here's a late pass, Enim," he said, finishing the note and clicking his pen closed. "Now, run off to class before you miss too much more."

His condescending tone was worse than any stern or displeased one, but I stood and mutely stepped forward to take the pass anyhow. I needed to get outside before I suffocated.

"There's a good lad," he said. "Now, make sure that you keep those grades up. I know that you're upset about your mother, but she wouldn't have wanted you to neglect your schoolwork."

My heart went cold. Halfway through reaching for the late pass, I lifted my eyes to Barker's and stared straight through him, no longer able to keep the words at bay.

"You don't know what my mother wanted," I said quietly.

Barker's smile slid downwards until his mouth was a thin line. He eyed me with venom.

"Well, perhaps not, Enim," he said, "but I know that no

one in their right mind would want their son to fall on academic probation."

A cold breeze went through the room like a chill. It picked up the late pass and slid it off the desk and onto the floor, but no one seemed to notice. My hand dropped back to my side and clenched into a fist.

"She wasn't *in* her right mind," I said just as quietly. "But maybe no one told you that."

As soon as I had said it, I wished that I could take it back. Barker's eyes went to Karl in silent confusion and the younger man shook his head in dread, but neither of them knew how to proceed. Barker was at a complete loss: he must have had been under the impression that my mother had passed away from some terrible disease. He kept glancing at Karl to try to make sense of what I had said, but Karl was firmly avoiding his gaze. The matter that none of us ever discussed had escaped into the room to suffocate us.

Finally Karl spoke.

"Enim, why don't you go to class."

It wasn't a question. He was directing me from the room so that he could smooth things over with Barker before it was too late. I wondered what wild fabrication he would invent to explain what I had said – anything other than the truth.

"Why don't you go to hell?" I returned.

Karl made no response. He was as composed and reserved as ever; it was as though I had said nothing at all. I stared at him with every bit of contempt and hatred that I had ever felt towards him, willing him to shrivel and die from the look alone. He was just like my father: playing what had happened to my mother as a means of getting what he wanted and eliciting pity that he didn't deserve.

"You know what happened to her."

"I don't know what you're talking about, Enim," Karl responded quietly.

"Oh, that's right," I said formally, "because you weren't *there.*"

The jab seemed to strike him physically and he recoiled. As

he took a step back from me, Barker looked between us. Despite his confusion, he was well aware that there was something unsightly in the conversation that he had been blinded to.

"Enim," Karl repeated, "go to class."

I turned and fled from the room, but it was only because I couldn't stand to be near him for a moment longer. Doing my best to look normal, I hurried past the secretary and slipped out into the hallway. When I reached the grounds I didn't bother to look at the clock to see what time it was; I wasn't going to attend classes that day.

I crossed to the edge of the campus without caring if anyone could see me. Slipping beneath the low branches, I made my way through the trees until I came to the cliffs. The water was the brightest of blues beneath me, like a blanket that had been laid out to fall asleep on. Compared to the jagged rocks beneath my feet, it looked soft from where it waved below – inviting, even. I closed my eyes before the thought could fully come and tried to clear my head. I wished that I could will myself away.

It wouldn't take Karl long to smooth things over with Barker: only a half-hour of his time or an extra figure scrawled in his checkbook. He and my father were well-trained in how to fix things, after all. The thought left a bitter taste on my tongue.

I sat down on the edge of the cliffs and stared down into the blue. My mother had never felt so far away. And yet, if I strained hard enough, I could hear the song that we had played together on the piano in the distance over the waves; and if I imagined harder still, I could see her standing on the rocky beaches below with her white dress billowing out behind her. And I wasn't afraid to admit that I wished that she was there with me, because she was the only person in the world that had ever understood me, but I could never admit that I also wished the unthinkable – that she *wasn't* there and that she would leave me completely, and that her memory would finally fade away.

Even beneath such a miserable sky, the water was such a

deep, thoughtful blue. When I thought of returning to Connecticut for Christmas, and of what it would be like now that everything had gone wrong, I would have given anything to prevent it. I tried to shut my mind on the memory from ten months ago but it burned against my eyes. For a moment, as I watched the water waving up at me, I wished that it would surround me as it had the night before and drag me down. I could feel it sinking into me, grasping me, saturating me, suffocating me, and for a moment it felt very right, very welcoming, even –

The wind smacked my face and I stumbled backwards and fell to the ground. My hands broke my fall and the skin was torn on jagged rocks and broken twigs. I clutched them to me, grimacing in pain, and curled up as the cold began to seep in through my clothes. I sniffed at the wind and buried my face in my arms. The fall had knocked the sense back into me and I suddenly felt sick for what I had been thinking. I didn't want to drown, after all, and I didn't want to die. I just wanted to feel better – but when would that happen?

I stood from my spot and hurried back through the trees towards Bickerby. At the edge of the woods, I slowed to catch my breath and smoothed my hair and sweater down in an idle attempt to compose myself. The grounds were empty and still as though they had been frozen in place.

I returned to my residence building quickly, head bent low to cover my face from the wind or any passersby who might have noticed my expression, and slipped inside just as the sky lost its last touch of blue and turned fully to gray. Heaving myself up the stairs to the fourth floor, I shut the door to the dorm room behind me and collapsed on top of my mattress. The dozens of prescription bottles hidden beneath it rattled as I did so. For a moment I considered reaching down and opening one; Beringer had said that they would make me feel better. But he didn't know what thoughts I was trying to force away.

"There you are." Jack's relieved voice sounded from the door sometime later. "Where have you been? I've been looking for you everywhere."

I lifted my head slowly.

"Nowhere."

"But – were you in Barker's office this whole time? I looked in all your classes, plus here, plus the library, plus the dining hall. Sanders keeps coming by the room, too, asking where you are – he says he's got a message for us or something – what's that all about? Did Barker suspend you?"

"No, I ... no."

"But what happened?"

"With what?"

"With – with *Barker*, Nim," Jack said incredulously. He crossed to sit beside me on the bed. "Did Porter get caught last night? Did he rat you out? Because I saw him on campus, and I swear I'll –"

"No, it wasn't that."

Jack eyed my expression uneasily.

"Then ... what is it?"

"It's nothing; I'm just on academic probation."

"You're what?"

"On academic probation," I repeated. "I'm failing every subject."

"So he suspended you?"

"No. He and Karl worked it out, like usual."

Jack gave a relieved sigh and leaned his head back against the wall.

"Oh – well, that's good. I mean, it's not *good*, but it could definitely be worse." He gave me another odd look and added, "Right?"

"Sure," I said.

"Was there something else? You look ... weird."

I instinctively smoothed down the front of my sweater and shook my head.

"No. I'm fine."

He opened his mouth to counter the claim, but was stopped by a quick knock sounding on the door. It opened to reveal Sanders standing in the doorway for the second time that day.

"Hadler, Lund," he said curtly. "What are you doing?"

"What does it look like we're doing?" Jack asked from beside me.

"I'd ... rather not know, I think," the building monitor replied, glancing between us uncertainly.

Jack rolled his eyes.

"If you came to see if Nim's been suspended, you're out of luck," he said flatly. "Sorry to disappoint you."

"No, no, that's ... that's not why I came by." He looked flustered and had lost a bit of his usual solidity, failing to address Jack's comment or add any remarks about my whereabouts as he normally would have, and stood in the doorway as though too anxious to step over the threshold. "You two missed the student meeting in the residence lounge."

"Right, well, we never go to those," Jack said. "What'd you discuss this time? How residence life is? What channel to keep the TV on in the student lounge? Or was it a petition to get rid of 'quiet hours' again?"

"No, it was nothing like that, Hadler."

"Oh good," Jack deadpanned, "because I wouldn't want you to take a poll without counting my vote."

"This isn't a joke, Hadler."

"Believe me, Sanders, I know. It's not like you have a sense of humor."

The other student sucked in a breath and stared at Jack with a hollowed expression.

"This is serious. Something's happened." He looked between us oddly, and his eyes rested a moment too long on mine in a pleading manner. "Someone's ... someone's died."

"Oh." Jack made a face and glanced over to me. "Like another local girl or something?"

"No. No, not a local."

"Someone in our year?" He pulled his legs up to his chest as he considered it. "Was it that guy on the third floor with the weird eyes? He always looked sickly to me ..."

"No, it was ... it was one of the staff."

"Right," Jack said with a nod. "Well, that's understandable. Some of the teachers here are pushing eighty, at least –"

"It's not that – it had nothing to do with age," Sanders said quickly. "It was ... it was one of the younger teachers." He paused and looked between us again, his uncomfortableness clear. "It was ... it was one of your teachers, actually, Hadler. Your ... your French teacher, I believe. Miss Mercier."

A ringing silence met his words. For a moment I thought that I might have misheard him, or that he had made the tale up to get back at Jack for years' worth of insults, but his expression was too miserable to be anything but truthful.

I looked around at Jack to see his response. His form had gone very still as though frozen in place and he was staring blankly at Sanders without seeing him. His eyes appeared overcast and his mouth had gone dry, and for a long moment he didn't move.

"Wait," he said at last, giving a slight shake of his head and a slim smile. "Wait, that's – that's not true. She's not dead."

"I ... I'm afraid that she is, Hadler."

Jack shook his head again as though hoping to dislodge the words that Sanders had planted there.

"No, she's – she's not dead. She was just out of town. She'll be back." His tone had gone from disbelief to certainty, and his frown held every conviction that his version of events was truer than Sanders'. "She's just out of town visiting a friend – she can't be dead."

"I ... She is, Hadler. I know that it's a shock, but ..."

"No."

Jack tossed his bag off the end of the bed to clear the space around him; it clattered to the ground and spilled textbooks onto the floor. As he stared at Sanders, daring him to refute him again, the other boy backed up a bit against the wall. Jack stood to face him properly.

"She was just visiting a friend," he repeated. "That's what they said. So how could she – how'd she –? What happened?"

Sanders could only shake his head. Jack ran his hand through his hair without taking notice of him.

"How did it happen? Was it a car accident or something? Did she – was it –?"

"I don't know, Hadler," Sanders said, his voice uncharacteristically quiet. "They didn't tell us anything other than that she had ... passed."

"That can't be it – there has to be something else!" Jack said angrily. "She didn't just walk out of here to see a friend and die, did she?"

"She never actually left to see a friend."

"What?"

The three of us turned as another voice sounded from the doorway. Julian Wynne was leaning up against the frame. Though his expression was of well-feigned sorrow, he couldn't keep the excited gleam from his eyes.

"There was no friend," he repeated. "Barker made that up to cover the whole thing up."

"What 'whole thing'?"

"Her disappearance," Julian continued, gazing down at his nail-beds as he spoke. "She just never showed up to school one day, and when someone went to look for her, they found her house was empty. Front door was left open and everything. Barker didn't want it to get out, so he said she'd gone away."

"Wait, so did she just disappeared?" Jack asked. "She didn't die?"

"No, she disappeared *and* died."

"In that order?"

Julian shrugged.

"Hard to say. She died, and the police found the body sometime later."

"So that's what the search party was for?"

Jack's voice had lost its edge. Without it, he sounded much younger and slighter than he was, as though he had withered away to something small and weak.

"Yep." Julian smirked a bit without seeming to realize it. Whether he found the idea of another strange happening or Jack's upset more entertaining, it was hard to tell.

"What else do you know?" Jack said. "What happened?

Where'd they find her?"

"In the woods," he said. "Halfway between Bickerby and the town, apparently. Right on the path, in plain sight." His face was twitching as he divulged the details, and he seemed to be in no hurry despite Jack's insistence to know what had happened. "They said that she was dragged out there."

"But the search party was ages ago," Jack said. "If she was right – right there – why didn't they find her before then?"

"Oh, they found her alright," Julian said, switching to lean up against the other side of the doorframe. "Only, they weren't sure that it was ... her."

"What's that supposed to mean? Why didn't they know it was her?"

Julian's pupils had dilated in the dim lighting to such an extent that his eyes appeared to be black holes.

"Because," he said quietly, "they found her in *pieces*."

Ch. 6

Ice crunched beneath my feet as I hurried through the cold to the residence building. Though it was barely two weeks into November, the sky above was threatening snow again and my hands had turned a sickly shade of blotched blue and red from forgetting my gloves. I had intended to spend the afternoon at the library finishing up my Latin assignment for Albertson, but upon looking through my folder I had found that it wasn't there. As I made my way to the stairs to search my room for it, someone called me back.

"Hey – wait a second –"

The voice sounded from my right and I backtracked to see who it was. Josh Brody, the building's student secretary, had opened the glass window fronting the office and was beckoning me over. I stepped away from the stairwell door and approached him instead.

"Enim, right?" he asked, smiling as though we were friends. He pronounced my name with the emphasis on the wrong syllable, though; he must have read it off a piece of paper. "Come on around: you've got a message."

I gave a fleeting look at the stairwell door before wordlessly going around the side of the office and stepping inside. Brody had already begun to flip through a stack of notecards to find the message intended for me.

"Here we are," he said after a moment, finding my name amongst the stack. "Eenim … Luhnd?"

"Lund."

"Looned, right." He smiled friendlily. "Is that Dutch?"

"Swedish."

"Oh, only I *thought* it might be Dutch," he continued conversationally, "because you got a call from the Netherlands. Your dad works over there? What's he do?"

I was momentarily too shocked to respond. Taking the notecard from Brody's hands, I stared at the message in disbelief that my father had called the school. He hadn't done so since my birthday in March and, considering how poorly the conversation had gone, I hadn't thought that he would call again. My heart skipped several beats as I reread the message several times, but it only gave instructions to call him back.

"The number looks pretty long," Brody said, leaning over to take another look at the card. "I can try to dial it out for you, if you'd like. Sometimes those extensions can be tricky –"

He leaned over as he made to take a better look. Apart from being the building's secretary, Brody was also captain of the lacrosse team, vice president of Bickerby's student council, and the third topmost student in the school. I stared at him as he took the paper from my hands again to see if he could discern how to dial the number and a sudden agitation came over me. I tugged the message back away from him.

"No, thanks, though, Josh," I said. "I can dial it myself."

I picked up the communal phone and pulled it as far from the office as it would go. The receiver would only stretch four feet away from the office desk, though, and I resignedly punched the number in still within earshot of Brody. The phone gave a screeching beep to inform me that the number was not valid. I punched it in again only to receive the same message. Chewing the side of my mouth unhappily, I returned to Brody and asked him to do it for me.

He smiled.

"Sure," he said, pulling the phone back to him and taking the message from my hand. He dialed the number easily and got it on the first try. "It's ringing," he said, handing it to me.

I pulled it away from him again and stepped over to the wall, but knew that he could still hear me from the glass cubicle. Before I could fret over the fact that the first conversation I would have with my father in months would be less-than private, though, the phone clicked and a garbled voice came over the line.

"Goedenavond, met Jansen."

I paused without trying to decipher the words, instead wondering if I was speaking to a secretary or colleague of my father's, or perhaps someone at a desk in his hotel. Clearing my throat, I said, "Hello, I'm calling for Daniel Lund."

"Ik begrijp niet wat U zegt – wacht even." There was a clattering of noise as the phone was put down, and a moment later someone else had picked it up.

"Hello, how may I help you?" said the woman in a high, pleasant accent.

"I'm calling for Daniel Lund," I repeated.

"Yes, okay. Are you a client?"

"No, I'm his son."

"His son? I will go retrieve him for you. One moment, very please."

As the phone was put down again, I could hear the clicking of heels as she walked away from it. An uncomfortable silence stretched on in her absence. I dug my free hand into my pocket as Brody pretended to look through an assortment of papers, but his eyes were fixed in place.

"Enim."

My father's voice cut through the phone so suddenly and sharply that I nearly dropped it in surprise. Turning my back on Brody fully, I pressed the receiver as close to my face as it could go before answering in a low tone.

"Hi, Dad."

"Enim, I've just spoken with Karl," he said, bypassing a formal greeting. "You're on academic probation?"

I should have realized that that was why he had called, but in all that had gone on in the weeks following the visit to Barker's office, I had assumed that Karl had simply neglected to tell him.

"Right. Yes, I am."

"How can that be possible? You were in the top ten of your class the last time I checked – what's happened? Is it that roommate of yours again?"

I rubbed my forehead tiredly. I hadn't been in the top ten of my class since two semesters ago, though I was hardly surprised that my father had not realized it until now. His quickness to blame Jack for my failure was at least reassuring that not everything had changed, though.

"No, I just fell behind."

"Fell behind? Enim, you're failing every subject!"

"I know, Dad."

He gave an irritated sigh that came over the line as a harsh stream of static. I pulled the phone back from my ear to keep from promoting a headache.

"This is ridiculous, Enim. I can't even believe it – you know better than this!"

"I know."

"Karl tells me that the headmaster is allowing you to stay on," he continued as though he had not heard me. "I want your grades back up in record time, do you understand? I won't have you failing out of school."

"I know."

"Good." There was a prolonged pause as he seemed to consider saying something else, and I pulled in my breath as I both waited for him to ask me how I was doing and thought of how I would answer. Before I could decide, however, he said, "Right, well, I've got to get going."

"Wait, but Dad –" I said, cutting in before he could hang up. My voice faltered even though the question that I had been agonizing over was so simple. "Are you coming home, soon?"

He waited so long to respond that I wondered if he had hung up already.

"Enim, I can't talk about this now. I'm very busy. If you need something, ask your uncle."

"But I don't want to talk him. I –"

"That's what he's there for."

"But I don't want to," I repeated, thinking again of Karl's ease in filling Barker with lies about my mother. My father would have at least told Barker that the matter was private and of no bearing on my academic standing. "I want to know when you're coming home."

He sighed in agitation.

"I'm very busy right now, Enim. Things are just getting started here with the company."

"So what does that mean? You're not coming home? Not – not even for Christmas?"

The question was met with silence. If not for the sound of his breathing on the other end, I would have thought that the line had been disconnected.

"No. I won't be there for Christmas."

"You –?"

"I'm very busy right now, Enim, and it's very late here. I'm tired, I have a headache, and I have a very important meeting first thing in the morning that I'm supposed to be prepping for. This is something that you can discuss with Karl."

"But Dad, I can't spend the break with him – not in that house, not with –"

"*Goodnight*, Enim."

He slammed the phone down before I could begin to explain it to him. The sound of the dial tone blaring from the other end rang in my ears for a long moment before I replaced the receiver. Brody stole a glance at me as I returned the phone to his desk and I turned away as quickly as possible. I was sure that even if he hadn't overheard the conversation, my expression would give it away.

Hurrying up the stairs, I plowed down the hall and into my room before I could come into contact with anyone else and slammed the door behind me. Jack, who was slumped on his bed with a newspaper at his side and a cigarette in his hand, didn't bother to acknowledge me. I gave him an annoyed look before going to the bedside table to search for my Latin assignment.

He had been oddly distant since the news of Miss Mercier's death had broken, choosing to fill his time by taking long walks into town for refills of cigarettes to chain-smoke and endless supplies of newspapers that never held any interest. I prodded a stray piece of laundry back over the imaginary line dividing our sides of the room with my foot, both annoyed at the whiff of whiskey that wasn't quite concealed by the cracked window and that my lost assignment was probably buried beneath the mess he had made.

Though the students tried, Barker refused to give details concerning Miss Mercier's death. The local paper had a few blurbs about what was deemed 'a horrific tragedy,' but only gave as much information as Julian had. Her obituary was short and focused on her life rather than death, and after it had appeared in the paper the week following her death, her name had all but disappeared from the headlines.

Barker had not yet managed to procure a long-term substitute for her French class. It was hardly unbelievable seeing as the island had been overturned by such a forceful amount of snow. At times the buildings would shake and send avalanches of it crashing to the ground, taking huge icicles with it. Sometimes they would shatter like glass against the iced-over pavement, other times they would spear the ground dangerously. Whenever a potential teacher came to review the position, the weather seemed to drive them away before they could get off the ferry. Winter on the island was even more brutal than usual.

Though Senora Marín had offered to teach the class in lieu of another teacher, she quickly become overwhelmed with it – undoubtedly due to the fact that she didn't speak the language in question – and a series of other teachers began taking turns with it instead. Even Volkov had taken the time to teach one of them, and from what Jack relayed, he had been one of the better French speakers, Russian accent and all. Yet they all cycled through so unregularly that it was unquestionable as to why the course had come to a standstill: homework assignments assigned by one teacher were graded by another, lessons were forgotten or repeated but never in order, and quizzes and tests were out of the question.

Occasionally, after one of those confusing French classes, someone would mention Miss Mercier, but it was only ever in passing. Her name was uttered with a type of quick whisper that was reserved for the dead. There was a memorial for her on the bulletin board inside the Foreign Language Building. Pictures of her smiling and waving from various class activities over the years, or from between happy-looking students in the graduation gowns, or lined up with the other teachers in yearbook pictures gazed down at me whenever I crossed through the building to Latin. Seeing her there so blissful and full of life when she was anything else perturbed me. More than once as I passed the photo-covered board, I had the urge to yank the entire thing down. She was dead – they should leave the thought of her life alone.

When the Latin assignment didn't turn up in any of my other notebooks, I dumped my bag out on my bed and searched through the contents a second time, swearing and running my hands through my hair in frustration when it didn't show up. The translation was the largest project of the semester. I had been working on it painstakingly in an attempt to show Albertson that I was repentant for how poorly I had done all semester; if I lost it, there would be no time to redo it before it was due the next day.

"Have you seen my translation of the *Aeneid*?" I asked Jack as I stooped to search beneath the bed. I patted the dark ground and pulled open every book piled on the shelf as I searched for it, turning my side of the room into a state that rivaled Jack's untidiness.

"What?" His reply was slow and his eyes unfocused as he tried to distinguish me from a heap of clothing on the carpet.

"My translation," I repeated. "It's a blue notebook, it says 'Latin' on the front – it has my homework in it –"

Jack only shook his head, clearly unconcerned with what I was saying. I sighed angrily at him before snatching up my jacket and hurrying from the room.

Jogging down the stairs and out onto the grounds, I pulled my scarf around my face to ward off the harsh chill that bit at my skin. It occurred to me that I might have left the notebook in Albertson's room and that someone had turned it into him. I reached the Foreign Language Building and ran inside, skidding to a stop outside of his room and going in. The room was empty and dark. I switched the lights on and combed every inch if it in search of the notebook, but it wasn't there.

My stomach dropped and left a hollow pit in my abdomen. The assignment was worth thirty-percent of my already low grade, and if I didn't turn it in then I wouldn't pass the course.

The realization that I wouldn't get off academic probation and would be suspended indefinitely at the end of the semester shook me. I felt sick to think that I would have to return to the house in Connecticut with Karl, and worse so with the knowledge that my father wouldn't make an appearance at all during the weeks that I would be there. I leaned up against an empty desk and swallowed hard. The room buzzed all around me.

I retreated back outside numbly, halfheartedly trying to come up with a way to recreate the lost translation before class the next day or else come up with a good excuse to present to Albertson as to why I didn't have it, but my thoughts were decisively blank. I was halfway across the campus when my shoes caught the ice and I slipped: my feet flew out from under me and I crashed onto my back, and when my head struck against the frozen ground with a deafening impact my vision ducked in and out of black.

A group of students snickered as they passed me on the path and my face grew hot in the cold. I moved to get up but nearly immediately slipped again and fell back to the ground. I threw out my arm to break my fall and my elbow bent backwards as I did so. I groaned in discomfort and curled up in the snow, irritated and cold, as I waited for the shooting pain to die down.

"Are you all right?"

Julian appeared next to me on the path. As he stared down at me with a concerned frown, I scrambled to stand back up again.

"Fine," I responded shortly. My loafers slid on the ground and I moved to get off the icy patch that I had hit before I could fall for a third time.

"Are you sure?"

"Yes."

Julian observed me with an uncertain nod.

"Right, you just looked a little ... off."

I straightened and ran a hand through my hair. My clothes were wet from the snow, but I righted them regardless in an attempt to appear less rattled.

"No, I'm fine." Both my arm and head were throbbing painfully, but I refused to admit as much to Julian. He was staring at me as though waiting to pinpoint something wrong with me; I averted my eyes quickly, but I couldn't hide the fact that the skin beneath them was thin and dark from dozens of sleepless nights.

"You should probably get some better winter shoes," he advised, looking down at my loafers. "Those ones aren't good for the ice."

"Wow, thanks Julian," I said angrily. "Great idea."

He gave me an odd look before biting down on his tongue.

"I'm just trying to help," he responded coolly. "Jesus, it's no wonder you don't have any friends."

He shook his head and turned away down the path. I watched him disappear around the bend before taking another cautious step forward; my loafer caught the ice again and I fell back to the ground. I swore loudly at the blank white sky.

When I finally made my way back up to the dorm room, still at a loss as to what to do about the missing assignment, Jack was still lying on his bed. After eying him to ensure that he was still conscious, I gave him an irritated look and dropped my bag down with a thundering sound that made him clutch his head in discomfort.

"What are you doing?" I said reproachfully, coming into the room and kicking off my shoes. He was staring at the newspaper intently. "Crossword puzzles?"

"Maybe. Not like there's much else to do." His head lolled to the side as he spoke, but his blurred vision caused him to look at the wall rather than me. "Foreign Language meetings are cancelled, obviously."

"Right. So are Thursday nights drinking nights now?" I asked, but before he could answer, I registered the day of the week. "Wait, it's Thursday?"

The missing assignment had thrown me off and I had completely forgotten about the meeting with Beringer. I looked at the clock and saw that I was nearly twenty minutes late. Not waiting for Jack to answer, I pulled my loafers back on and rushed out of the room to the Health Center as quickly as I could.

Beringer made no mention of the delay when I entered the office. Taking his reading glasses off and smiling in greeting, he indicated that I should sit down. I crossed to the chair and collapsed into it. My legs felt heavy and dead beneath me, and my shoulder throbbed even harder from the fall earlier that afternoon.

"How have you been, Enim?" he asked quietly.

"I ..." I shook my head without finishing the sentence; the usual answer of 'fine' wouldn't come. "I guess I've been ... I mean, I haven't been great."

"No?"

"No."

Beringer nodded and folded his hands together over my file. I vaguely wondered what was written in it.

"Is there anything in particular that you've been feeling?"

Thinking past the conversation with my father, Jack, and Julian, my thoughts returned to the moment that I had stood on the cliffs and considered jumping off. I pushed the thought away before it could fully come, though: it wouldn't do any good to tell Beringer such a thing.

"Just ... not great."

"And have you thought about why you might be feeling this way?" he asked.

I shrugged and looked at my hands. Beringer watched me carefully.

"Do you think that it's because the Christmas holidays are approaching?"

"I ... I don't want to talk about my mother, Dr. Beringer."

"I know you don't, Enim. But I think that we should."

He looked at me carefully as he waited for me to answer. In the lamplight the surrounding objects cast shadows onto his face that flickered and swayed without him moving.

"I just ... it's just not that easy," I said.

"What's not easy?"

"Talking about her."

"Talking about her, or what happened to her?"

I chewed the side of my mouth and fidgeted in my seat. He was making it sound so simple, as though the two matters could be separated when they were really the same. If I could have plucked out the memories of her without associating them with who she had been or who she had become, then I wouldn't have had to lie awake every night. I could have thought of her peacefully, easily, instead of being tormented by the things that she had done.

"Both."

"I see."

He gave me a thoughtful look as he waited for me to go on, but when I didn't he dropped his voice and continued, "Enim, I know that you don't want to talk about this. I understand that. My only fear is that in a month's time you'll be going home for the winter break, and all of the things that you would rather not discuss will become ... overwhelming."

"I could just not go home."

"Do you think that avoiding this will be any help in the long run?" he asked, giving me a look that compelled me to understand his point, and I slowly shook my head. "Have you and your father discussed how you'll spend the holidays this year?"

"My father's not coming home. It's just going to be me and Karl."

"I see." He looked back down at the file, perhaps searching for an idea as to why that would be, before continuing. "And how do you feel about that?"

"It doesn't matter; I don't care." I paused to play with a loose thread on the seat cushion before adding, "He wasn't there last year, either."

"No?"

I stared at the chair leg as the memory came back and used every ounce of willpower to push the thought away.

"No. It was just ... my mother and me."

Beringer's eyes flickered over me; the shadow across his

109

face cut his expression in two.

"And then it was just you," he said after a moment.

"Yes."

"Enim," Beringer said quietly, "I can't help you unless I understand, and I can't understand unless you tell me what happened."

"You know what happened."

"I know the outcome, but no one knows what happened in that brief window of time except for you."

I swallowed and turned my head away from him, not daring to look him in the eye for a moment longer. The memory of that night was expanding in my mind, but my head didn't have the capacity to contain it. In a moment it would burst and split my skull into two.

"I can't ... I can't tell you."

"Why's that?"

"Because," I said, but my voice broke and it sounded more like a noise than a word. I shielded my face with my hand before Beringer could see my expression of guilt until I could compose it again.

"Enim," he said quietly, leaning forward across the desk towards me, "whatever happened between you and your mother was *not* your fault."

His voice was compelling, but my heart had gone cold.

"You don't know that."

It was too much for him to ask what had happened, just as it was too much for everyone to want to know. I couldn't imagine what they all thought, though every now and again I got a glimpse of it as they looked me up and down. All that I knew was that, no matter how horrible the scenarios were that they had drawn up in their heads, they had to have been better than the truth.

"I just can't tell you, Dr. Beringer."

He looked at me for a long moment before nodding.

"All right, Enim." He paused as he considered where to go from there. "Though I wonder, do you ever talk to anyone about your mother? Your father? Your uncle?"

"No."

"What about Jack?" he asked, glancing down at the file to recall the name. "Do you ever mention her to him?"

"I might bring her up in passing," I said. "But Jack knows that I don't really like talking about it."

"I see. Though, I wonder, what do you think he would say if you told him?"

The idea had never occurred to me, though I could imagine the way that his face would twitch as he said the usual declaration, *Ah, Nim,* before launching into an explanation of why I shouldn't feel badly about it. Regardless that his reasoning would be untrue, the corner of my mouth rose very slightly at the thought that he wouldn't care. Yet with the way he had been so distant in the past few weeks it was hard to imagine telling him anything.

"I don't know. Probably nothing."

"You think he would be silent? Why's that?" Beringer asked, leaning forward towards me a bit.

"He's just ... He hasn't been very much like himself lately."

"No?"

"No."

"And have you given any thought as to why?"

"I know why: his favorite teacher died. It's just ..."

"Just what?"

"It's just ... I don't get why he – I don't understand how he could –"

The question was either too difficult or too demeaning to state, and I withdrew into silence. The idea that Jack had fallen into some distant reverie after learning of Miss Mercier's death seemed almost offensive: it wasn't fair that he was able to so easily admit his loss, or to miserably search the papers for any mention of her name, or to wear the defeated expression of grief that so easily came to his features when I had worked so long and so hard to maintain my composure over an event that I couldn't even admit had happened.

"Grief looks different for all of us, Enim," Beringer said quietly. "There's no right or wrong way to miss someone."

When the session had concluded and I stepped outside, the cold night air immediately sank beneath my collar and chilled my neck. I shivered as I pulled my jacket up to cover it, but without my scarf the fabric was just as cold against my skin. As I stood in the heavy darkness, the familiar sound of music floated over to me from the distant trees. I quickly pulled myself away and hurried back to the residence building.

When I reached the dorm room, Jack had already turned out the lights and gone to sleep. His breathing wasn't quite as deep as usual. I undressed and got into bed silently. Lying beneath the covers and facing the wall, however, my eyes stayed open for the remainder of the night. Whenever tiredness overcame me and they started to flicker shut, thoughts of a dying woman crept into my mind and jolted me awake again.

I was so exhausted the next day that I could barely keep my eyes open in Physics. My arm was still throbbing from falling the night before, and my skull felt as though it had been hollowed and frozen over in ice. Halfway through class, when my eyelids began to droop, Cabail Ibbot leaned over to stir me.

"You might want to pay attention. This is probably going to be on the exam."

His strange voice cut through the dull tones in the room and my eyes opened widely. I looked over at him briefly before glancing around the room to see if anyone had heard us talking, but his voice had gone unnoticed by the rest of the class. I shot him a look to warn him not to speak to me anymore: I would be in enough trouble that day without an added reprimand from Volkov.

Despite straightening up and attempting to pay attention to what was written on the board, my mind was still far from Volkov's lecture. It bounced from one problem to the next slowly enough to cause me to fret but too quickly to draw any conclusions as to what I should do about them. My main concern was what I could tell Albertson in twenty minutes when I didn't hand in my translation, but every time that I tried to form a reasonable excuse my thoughts would wander back to my mother and Miss Mercier. It felt rather as though I was pinning them against one another to decide which had suffered the greater tragedy.

"Good luck on Monday," Cabail said when the bell rang and everyone stood to leave.

"Right," I replied. The boy in front of me turned halfway around as I spoke, perhaps thinking that I was speaking to him, before frowning and going on his way.

By the time I reached the Latin classroom, the room was nearly filled. I took a seat and resigned to speak to Albertson about the homework assignment after class ended.

"Oh, Mr. Lund," he said as I shuffled up to his desk an hour later. "Did you have a question about the ablative absolute?"

He indicated to the board where he had been going over the grammatical usage of a noun phrase during class, but rather than look at where he pointed I dropped my eyes to the floor.

"No, I ... I'm here about the homework."

"Oh, of course," he said, shuffling through the notebooks on his desk that the rest of the class had turned in. "Here, let me just find yours and we can discuss ..."

"No, it's – mine's not there, Mr. Albertson," I said.

He paused midway through the pile and pinched his lips together in a frown.

"No?"

"No."

He waited for my explanation, but I still hadn't thought of one to give him.

"And why isn't yours here, Enim?" he finally asked.

"I ..." I toed the ground with my shoe as I stumbled over the untruthful-sounding truth. "I lost it, Mr. Albertson."

"You lost it?"

It sounded worse out loud than it had in my head, but I couldn't backtrack and think of a more honest-sounding lie to give him now that I had said it.

"Yes. I did."

I couldn't meet his eyes, though I could feel them digging into my expression even so. I wished that I had just let him discover the missing notebook for himself after I had left: it would have been less humiliating.

"I see," Albertson mused. He exhaled heavily as he thought of how to proceed. "Well, that's rather unfortunate, Enim."

"Yes."

"That assignment is worth a very large percentage of your grade."

"I know."

"A zero would mean, for you, failing the course."

I swallowed, no longer able to answer, and gave a stiff nod instead. Albertson sighed again.

"And seeing as neither of us wants that to happen, I'm sure that we can come up with an alternate solution," he said gently.

My eyes rose to his face as my heart hammered within my chest, hardly believing what he was about to say.

"How about I give you a passing grade for the semester, and next term we ... start afresh?" he said. "Does that sound fair?"

It was more than generous, though I didn't know how to express as much gratitude as I had for him. He smiled at my silence.

"I know that this is a ... difficult time of year for you, Enim," he continued softly, "and I know that you've been struggling. I'd much rather have you focus on yourself than on this class."

It occurred to me that he didn't believe that I had lost the translation, and the guilt from having him think that I was counting on his kindness to pull me through the course left me feeling drained. I thanked him and left the room, pulling my scarf around my neck as I went to hide the lower half of my face from view.

The day moved endlessly forward. After the final bell finally rang at the end of Calculus, I heaved myself from my desk and made my way back to the residence building. When I stepped into the dorm room, Jack was already there.

"Don't you have class?" I asked.

"I had French, but ..." He shrugged. "Not much point in

going."

"Right."

I stood by the door for a long moment as I considered him. Though he was just sitting a few feet from me, he seemed much farther. For a long moment I wondered if it was possible to reach him at all. The idea that I could not was far too unsettling: without him, I would have no one.

"So, are you ... dropping French?"

"Probably," he replied. "Je pense que je l'ai appris assez."

"Right."

We looked at one another with the odd unfamiliarity that we had upon meeting each other years beforehand. At that time, he had stood by the desk with his hands in his pockets and chewing his lip as he waited for me to speak, and I had stared at my boat shoes. After a long moment he had commented on my name, to which I had explained that my mother had selected without my father's consent. I could still hear the way he cackled as he considered it.

"So the paper really hasn't said anything?" I asked, pulling my scarf from my neck and indicating to the article in his hands. "Do they give any explanation?"

"No, they haven't even mentioned that she was murdered," he replied. "I think they're trying to pass the whole thing off as something completely normal – like she was killed by a bear or something."

"Right, because that happens all the time around here."

His face split with a grin.

"Hence the school motto."

I kicked off my shoes and climbed up beside him on the mattress, carefully flicking a cigarette butt onto the ground as I went, and leaned over to skim the article.

"But that can't be it," I said. "People don't just fall over and die and lose limbs in the process. Something obviously happened to her."

"Something *did* happen to her, just not what everyone believes."

"They really think she was eaten by a bear?"

"Something like that." He gave a shrug. "Let's put it this way: it's been four weeks since it happened, and the police aren't even pretending to look for whoever did it. They don't even mention it in the paper anymore – and it's not like there's loads of other exciting news going on. You'd think that this would be the top priority."

"Maybe Barker's got people on the case," I said. "You know, like someone better than the local police force. He must care. He was her boss, after all."

"Right – *Barker* cares." Jack rolled his eyes. "You saw how he conducted that search party, Nim: in the middle of the night. He didn't even want to admit that she was missing. And when they found her dead, he definitely didn't want us to know anything about it. I wouldn't be surprised if the reason the police aren't looking for a killer is all because Barker doesn't want to draw any negative attention to the school."

"But what about the other teachers, then? Her colleagues must care."

"Maybe, or maybe they'd rather not think about it, either. People don't like to have their lives interrupted by things like this – they'd rather just forget her and move on."

I was drawn back to the conversation with my father the previous day. His insistence that it was work that kept him away from home was growing more and more unbelievable as the time passed and his excuses piled up.

"So what's going to happen, do you think?" I said. "They just won't even bother to look for the killer?"

Jack shrugged.

"Probably."

"But then no one will ever know who did it."

"Not necessarily." He stubbed his cigarette out on the window pane, crushing it until a dark smear like a dead moth appeared on the white.

"What do you mean?"

"I'm going to figure it out on my own."

"What, like track down her killer?"

He shrugged noncommittally, but it was evident from his

expression that he had made the decision some time ago. I turned my head to the window and stared into the glass at the image of myself, mulling over my own unyielding resolve to search for something without an answer despite the way that it ate at my mind, and had the urge to warn him of what the un-discovery could do to a person. And yet the possibility that his question might have an answer was just enough to be compelling, and the thought of a distraction from the memories that seeped into my dreams was even more so, and I let the warning quiet without coming.

"Well, you're never going to find it on your own," I said. He looked over at me stubbornly and opened his mouth to argue, but I cut him off before he could do so. "You're going to need my help."

Ch. 7

The campus was a long stretch of white, barren and cold as a wasteland, and the sound of the distant wind screamed from somewhere far off. Since the rest of the students and staff were spending the weekend inside, Jack and I had taken the opportunity to sneak out unnoticed. As I walked behind him and tried to shield my face from the cold, I tried to decipher where we were going; any chance of asking him was denied by the sheer cold that struck my face whenever I pulled it from my scarf.

Jack bypassed the edge of the empty sporting fields and made his way to the woods before disappearing past the line of snow-covered trees that created the boundary between the Bickerby campus and the town. Only the knowledge that no one else was out in the sub-zero temperatures kept me from protesting that we would get caught, and I followed him beneath the branches.

The cold was painful. My feet were hard and stiff in my loafers and snow immediately slipped down into them and drenched my socks; my hands felt nearly as cold curled up in my pockets; and every time I tried to breathe through my nose, the air got stuck in frozen nostrils. I was well beyond shivering, and looking at Jack in his sweatshirt and light coat was only making me colder. Only his eagerness seemed to drive him on.

The town was not much warmer, though we stumbled out into it in relief all the same. I hadn't seen much of it apart from the route that I took from the ferry to the front gate of the school, and everything around me looked unfamiliar and uninviting. With the heavy coatings of snow covering all the small houses and shops and the dimly-lit street lights, the place looked rather like the ceramic display that my grandmother used to set up at Christmastime, though the sight in front of me was much more forlorn.

"Where is everyone?"

Jack shrugged.

"School, work," he supposed. "Wrapped up in blankets

next to their electric heaters, shivering violently."

"Or already frozen to death."

"Could be. But don't worry, it's not much further. We'll be there soon."

He stopped outside our destination a short time later: a small house down a back street on the far side of the island. It was hard to tell if it was white or gray, for it had been a dark blue-green originally and the newer layer of paint had all but chipped away. The poor structure looked ready to collapse under the weight of all the snow that had built up on top of it and the short driveway hadn't been plowed since the first snowfall of the winter.

"Very nice," I commented.

"Yeah, well, it used to be," Jack said. He wrinkled his nose as he looked over the worn façade. "It was Miss Mercier's house."

The evident abandonment of the place suddenly made sense, and my eyes lingered on the pathway leading up to the front door that hadn't been touched by footsteps. A breeze shook a dead tree nearby and its branches rattled like death. The entirety of the place was forsaken.

Jack put his hands on the picket fence and hopped over it: the gate was frozen shut. He trudged towards the porch before realizing that I wasn't following him.

"Well? Come on," he said.

"Come where?"

I looked at the house of the dead woman and subconsciously took a step backwards. I didn't even like looking at it; I certainly didn't want to go closer.

"Inside."

"Jack, we can't just go *in*."

I looked around, half expecting to see a police barricade barring us from entering, but the house appeared untouched by the authorities.

"Sure we can."

We looked at one another over the fence, Jack looking confident, me dubious, before another gust of wind came over us and drenched me in cold. I conceded and climbed over the fence after him.

He jimmied the lock with his pocket knife and the door gave away easily as though the house had been waiting for someone to enter it again. I stepped carefully over the threshold. The inside was almost as cold as the outside: I could see my breath in white gusts against the dark wallpaper.

It was a quaint house, hardly anything to admire, but I supposed that it had been much nicer when Miss Mercier had still lived in it. The cold had seeped into the wood and created an air of deterrent all around, and there was a musty smell that made it unpleasant to breathe. I followed Jack into the small kitchen and saw that the table and chair set had not been removed yet. Glancing around, I realized that the entire house was still furnished even though no one had lived it in for over a month. There were dishes in the sink and a plate on the counter that had been left out for a meal that had never been eaten. My stomach twisted uncomfortably, but it had nothing to do with the sight of the rotting food. I quickly turned away.

"This place is a wreck," Jack commented from the other side of the room.

For someone who had no sense of tidiness himself, the statement seemed a bit unprecedented until I saw what he was talking about. The area behind the kitchen had been used as a storage room of sorts. The walls were lined with shelves that had once been stocked with pantry items, though now the contents of them had been pulled down and strewn about the floor. Cereal boxes were ripped open, cans had been dented and ripped of their labels, and canisters were opened and cracked. Yet despite the mess covering every inch of floor space, there was no food in sight apart from a box of dry pasta that scattered the ground. Every other container had been licked clean.

"Where's the food?"

"Rats?" Jack guessed. I immediately took a step backwards. He smiled wryly at me. "Don't worry, Nim, they only come out at night."

"That's *bats*. Rats come out whenever they choose."

"Right. Let's go upstairs."

He turned and went back out into the hall, but I remained where I was on the threshold. The eeriness of the house had not let up in the few minutes that we had been there; if anything, it had only grown stronger. I didn't like the idea of sneaking around the house at all. It seemed like more of an intrusion because the owner was dead. A flickering part of me wondered if she was somehow watching us.

"Jack, what are we doing here?" I said hesitantly.

He stopped midway up the stairs and looked down at me.

"Having a look around," he said with a shrug. "You know, see if we can find any evidence or whatever."

"Evidence?" All at once the idea that we were looking for Miss Mercier's murderer seemed ridiculous, as though Jack and I had been caught playing a game that we were much too old to partake in. "I thought she died in the woods – why would there be anything here?"

"She was *found* in the woods, but she came home first, so something happened between the time she got here and was dragged there."

The steps creaked on their own accord; the wood was groaning from the cold weather. Jack eyed them warily.

"We just have to figure out what that was," he said slowly. Turning from me, he hurried up the stairs before they could make any more noise. I watched him retreat into the dark hallway, but I was still hesitant to follow. It felt as though the house would shatter at any moment from the cold and bury us beneath it. I ran my eyes over the walls again, almost expecting to see the cracks confirming my fears, and then I ran after him. At least in his presence, the feeling that I was not entirely alone could be explained.

Apart from a small bathroom, the only other room upstairs was Miss Mercier's bedroom. The feeling of sheer intrusiveness increased as I looked at it. It was bad enough that we had broken into her house: it was downright wrong to go through her bedroom. But the hallway was very narrow and dark, and the silence of the house was creeping up on me, so I stepped over the threshold regardless of how my conscience protested.

It took me a moment to find Jack. The door was partially closed and I edged around it, first only seeing the dresser and end of a neatly made bed. When I nudged the door with my foot, Jack's form came into my view next to a small table covered in picture frames and keepsakes.

"Find anything?"

"Not yet."

He moved back and sat down on the dusted-rose-colored bedspread. When I saw him sitting there, his shoes leaving snow on the carpet, his dark clothing contrasting severely with the pastel trimmings, and the hood of his sweatshirt falling down over his narrowed, devious eyes, it struck me how out of place he was in Miss Mercier's home.

The room was furnished in a gentle sort of way: there was an antique bureau between two small windows, each with ruffled curtains that matched the bed-skirt, a few paintings up on the walls, and a bookshelf lined with both English and French titles. Near the closet there was a pair of shoes that had toppled over from being kicked off, perhaps intended to be put away properly at a later time. On a chair by the far wall there was a light dress that had been laid out to be ironed. I stared at it for a long while. The light fabric and pale blue color seemed so incongruous given the amount of snow outside. She had picked it out to wear long before snow had come to the island. Though it was only a season ago, it felt like a lifetime.

"What do you think?" Jack said. "See anything that might identify a murderer?"

"Hardly," I said. My legs were cold and aching but I didn't want to move the dress from the chair to sit down. I fidgeted in place instead, hoping that we would be out in the open air again soon. "I doubt we'll see anything the police haven't already gotten."

Jack hummed quietly.

"It doesn't really look like they've been here, does it?"

I glanced around the room again. From what I could tell, he

certainly seemed right. Even so, I said, "Well, they're not supposed to touch anything, are they? They just take pictures and whatnot."

"I guess."

I moved over to the table that he had been standing at before and looked at the photos.

"That's her sister," Jack said, coming to stand behind me. The woman in the picture was a few years older than Miss Mercier had been. She was standing and pointing excitedly at a sign. "Those are her parents, and then that's the whole family on holiday in Düsseldorf … Her brother-in-law and nieces, and that's the college she went to in Rhode Island …"

He pointed to the pictures easily as though he was quite accustomed to seeing them, and all at once I remembered how much time he had used to spend with her, waiting after classes and visiting her during study-halls. I had always known that he had liked Miss Mercier, but I hadn't quite realized the extent of his association with her. I replaced the picture frame back down on the table. My hands were too cold to hold it any longer.

"How do you know all this?" I asked as he finished relaying a story about a visit that Miss Mercier had taken to Quebec.

"She told me," Jack said with a shrug.

"She told you about her family?" I asked. "While you were …?"

I trailed off, hoping that he would finish my sentence for me. When he didn't, I was forced to complete it with a harsh-sounding allegation.

"…in her room?"

"Yes."

I couldn't tell if he was baiting me. His response was easy and nonchalant, and all I could think was that he was either incredibly innocent or incredibly guilty. He had to have known how unfounded his suggestion sounded, though he was certainly acting otherwise. I rubbed my thumb over the jagged nail of my forefinger as I surveyed him.

"Jack," I said, deciding to simply ask him rather than

wonder about it any longer, "were you …?"

Yet before I could finish the question, a dark shape moved behind him. I leapt back and crashed into the table, sending the photos to the floor. The frames clattered against the wood.

"What's that?"

Jack spun around as well, standing in front of me as he searched the room for what I had seen. Sure enough, a dark-gray creature had bounded across the room. Its claws scratched the hardwood with a coarse scraping sound as it propelled across the room, and then it ran to the wall and bounded off of it again to come back towards us. I could hear the rough sound of its hissing.

"Fuck – what is that?" Jack said, jumping back as I had done. We backed up against the wall in alarm. The creature was blocking our path to the door and I dug my fingers into the wallpaper in the hopes that the wall would collapse to give us another escape route. For a moment we stood tensed in place, but then Jack leaned forward with squinted eyes to peer at the thing on the floor in front of us.

He visibly relaxed and sighed.

"It's a *cat*."

Surely enough, it was. Its exterior was a bit off due to a large amount of loose, matted fur that hung from its form. It was emaciated to the point of death and appeared to be more of a ghostly skeleton that was wearing another animal's flesh in an attempt to masquerade as a living creature.

Jack looked over at me with a pointed expression, and as I let go of the wall and crossed my arms with a nod, we both silently agreed to never tell anyone that we had been so afraid of a house-pet.

"Miss Mercier had a cat?"

"Not exactly," Jack said. "It's a stray, but she used to feed it and would let it in for the night sometimes. She was afraid a fox might get it."

The cat hissed at me and raised its body in an arching position as though preparing to attack. Its pale yellow eyes were fixed on my face.

"She should have let the fox get it," I muttered.

"Nim!" Jack said, giving me a look. He stepped forward and knelt down in front of the strange creature, holding his hand out to it. I rolled my eyes.

"It's not going to shake your hand, Jack."

"I don't expect it to. I'm letting it sniff me."

"Why?"

"To get acquainted."

When the cat came closer, he reached over and picked it up. I made a revolted face.

"Jack, that thing is probably crawling with diseases," I said. "Just chuck it outside and wash your hands."

"I'm not going to *chuck it* outside, Nim."

"Whatever, place it nicely outside, then," I said. "Just so long as you get rid of it."

"I'm not getting rid of it," Jack said. He gazed down at the cat in his arms and rubbed its neck affectionately. "Look at it, Nim, its hungry."

"What do you want me to do? Buy it lunch?"

"We have to feed it," he said.

"No, we don't."

"Nim," Jack said, looking at me sternly. "This thing's been locked inside the house for over a month. It must be starving – you saw the pantry downstairs. It's eaten everything it could get its hands on."

"Paws."

"Paws, sorry," Jack said, rolling his eyes. "Come on, have a heart. How would you like it if you hadn't eaten for a month?"

I hadn't eaten for nearly a year, but I thought that it wasn't the moment to inform Jack. There was no point in arguing with him, anyhow.

"All right … I'll see what's in the fridge."

I trudged down the stairs and back into the kitchen, feeling even odder now that I was snooping through a dead person's kitchen looking for ingredients to make a meal. My eyes fell again on the empty plate on the counter. I wondered if Miss Mercier had eaten her meal before she had been killed or if there hadn't been time. Perhaps the cat had mewed at the closed door as it waited for her to come back before finally hopping up on the counter and eating it itself.

Shaking myself from my thoughts, I crossed to the refrigerator to return to the task at hand. No sooner had I opened the door, however, than I immediately turned my face away. The contents of it were horribly gone by: sour milk, old eggs, and a selection of cheese reeked from their shelves. I pulled my sweater up over my nose and pushed a few leftover containers filled with potatoes and vegetables to the side before determining that there was nothing remotely edible there and shutting the door.

"Find anything?" Jack said from the doorway. The cat was mewing softly in his arms.

"Not unless you want to poison it," I said. "Which might be for the best …"

"Nim – what's with you and this cat?"

"It's not this cat," I said. "It's cats in general. I don't like them, and I'm fairly certain that I'm allergic to them."

"You're not."

"I could be."

"We're not poisoning the cat," Jack said.

"I'm just trying to be humane," I said. "It's either food poisoning or hypothermia – either way the thing's going to die."

Jack looked down at the creature with a frown, suddenly consumed by the idea that Miss Mercier's cat was going to starve to death.

"I have to take it back to school," he said.

"No. Jack – no."

"Come on, Nim … It needs food."

"No – where would we put it?"

"In our room."

"Jack, we can't have pets at Bickerby. It's against the rules."

Jack rolled his eyes.

"Right, so is smoking and drinking, and yet we've been doing pretty good with that for seven years."

"Only because you threaten Sanders regularly," I argued.

"So this will be no different," Jack replied. He cocked his head to the side and gave me a look. "Come on, Nim … please? It'll starve …"

I shook my head at his theatrics, knowing that he was purposefully playing off of my inability to see him whine. He continued to make a face at me over the scruffy head of the ugly creature and I averted my gaze. The room gave another causeless creak and I shivered. The house was too haunting: I had to get out of it. Looking at Jack and realizing that he was not going to be the one to cave, I sighed and muttered, "Fine."

He smiled gloatingly.

"I'll make it up to you," he said.

"I doubt that."

I pulled my coat further around me as a chill came through the glass of the window. Jack could keep the cat so long as we left the house before anymore unexpected visitors popped up.

"Can we get out of here now?" I said. "There's nothing to find."

"Yeah, sure."

He tucked the cat beneath his sweatshirt to keep it warm before stepping out into the hallway. I followed him quickly, glad to be getting out of the house. The horrid weather outside was far more inviting than any of the rooms inside the dead woman's residence. When we stepped out onto the front steps and shut the door behind us, I instinctively reached for my keys to lock it as though we were leaving our dorm room. When my hand slipped into my pocket, however, there was nothing there.

"What?" Jack asked me, turning back to face me when I didn't follow him down the steps.

"I don't have my keys," I said.

He shook his head.

"You're getting as bad as me," he commented.

I patted down my pockets even though I knew that they had been in the right side of my pants. Swearing into the cold, I looked back at Jack imploringly.

"Do you still have yours?"

"Yeah, on my bedside table."

"Jack! Why'd you leave them there?"

He shrugged guiltlessly.

"I figured you had yours," he said. "How was I supposed to know you'd lose them?"

I sighed and searched my pockets again, but the keys were gone.

"Well, you had them when you left, right?" Jack said, noticing the distress on my face. "So you must have dropped them somewhere between here and Bickerby. We'll just take the same path back."

"We'll never find them in the snow."

"We might." He sighed and patted the cat's head absentmindedly. "It's not like you to lose things."

"I know. I don't know how I could've ..."

I stopped midsentence as it occurred to me that I would have noticed if I had dropped the keys on our walk into town because I had had my hands in my pockets to keep them warm. The cat stared at me with its pale eyes and I narrowed my own at it. I must have dropped them up in Miss Mercier's room when I had jumped back and crashed into the table.

I turned back to the door and went inside. Jack followed me, and together we went back up the creaking wooden stairs and into the delicately decorated bedroom. Crouching on the floor, I began to pick up the picture frames that had toppled over and replaced them in the general order that they had been on the table. A few of the frames had cracked, and one had completely shattered. I carefully swept the glass shards into a pile, feeling guilty at the destruction even though Miss Mercier would never know that it had happened.

"Find them?" Jack asked from behind me.

"Yeah, they're right ..."

I reached out to grab the key ring that was near the back leg of the table when something else caught my eye. Frowning, I stopped and picked it up instead.

"Is this yours?"

"No. What is it?"

He stooped next to me and peered at what I was holding. It was a folded piece of standard printer paper that appeared to have something written on it. It must have been tucked behind the photograph that's frame had broken.

"I'll just put it back, then," I said, but Jack reached forward and grabbed my wrist.

"No, what if it's something important?"

"What if it's something private?" I countered. "You know, seeing as it was hidden and all."

"I don't think she'd mind," Jack said. "Just take a look. If it looks private, we'll put it back."

I sighed and looked down at the paper, grinding my teeth subconsciously as I did so. It didn't sit well with me to go through Miss Mercier's things, but Jack was looking at me expectantly and I was reminded of the reason that we had come all the way out to the house in the first place, so I gently unfolded it. I wasn't quite sure what I had expected – perhaps something as provoking as an old letter or as dull as receipt for the frame – but I was surprised when I saw what was written inside. It was a list, neatly printed in dark ink, of names.

"What …?" I murmured as I read through them. Looking sideways at Jack, I raised my eyebrow. "What is this? Friends of hers?"

"Why would she keep a list of her friends' names hidden?" Jack said.

"I don't know," I said. I held the paper up to his face. "Do you recognize any of them?"

He shook his head slowly.

"Could they be students of hers?"

"No," Jack said. "Look – they're all girls' names."

"Oh," I said. "Well … could it be …" I didn't finish, for my train of thought ended. I couldn't think of any plausible explanation as to why Miss Mercier would hide a list of names – or why anyone would, for that matter. "Why would someone hide something like this?"

"I don't know," he said. "Maybe … I mean, a guy might

have a list of girlfriends, but not a woman."

"It doesn't really make sense for her to have it, then," I said.

"Unless it's not her list."

I looked up at him warily.

"What are you saying?" I said. "That Miss Mercier was blackmailing someone?"

Jack's gaze shifted. Staring at the wall, he became engrossed in his thoughts. The cat mewed and wriggled under his jacket, but he appeared not to notice.

"Maybe she was," he said.

Even without knowing Miss Mercier, I could hardly believe that she would do anything of the sort.

"Come on, why would she do that? I mean, apart from wanting money."

"She must've had a reason … I mean, a good reason."

"Such as?"

He hesitated.

"I don't know," he said, scratching the back of his head uneasily. "But, I mean, it makes some sense, doesn't it?"

"Not really."

"Think about it, Nim: obviously someone killed her, right? What we have to figure out is why."

"Maybe she was mugged, or raped, or ..."

"But she wasn't. She was hacked to pieces."

"All right, so someone really hated her."

"But this was Miss Mercier," he protested. "*Everyone* loved her. Everyone."

I ran a hand through my hair as I debated what to think. On the one hand, what he was suggesting made sense with what we knew; yet on the other, his explanation was even ludicrous compared with some of the other theories he had invented over the years.

"So what do you think?" I asked. "That she was singled out? For what reason?"

He plucked the paper from my hand and waved it in the air between us.

"I think it has to do with this."

"We don't even know what that is," I protested.

"Not yet, but we will."

"But ..."

My voice petered out; the sound was overtaken by the crashing of wind against the windows. It had begun to snow again.

We wandered back out of the house and through the town beneath the snow. The sky was white above us and echoed the sound of the cat's mews from Jack's arms. The strained sound of it was horrible to listen to: the desperation cut through the air worse than the cold did.

When we had returned to the room, Jack laid it gently upon his bed. It blinked slowly at the wall and turned away from us. Jack sat beside it and pulled out the list of girls' names again.

"Amy Davis," he said aloud, "Rebecca King. Megan Cook. Take a look at this again, Nim: any of them sound familiar?"

"They all sound familiar," I said, glancing down at the list as he held it out to me. "They're generic enough names. Well, except maybe Katie DuPont."

"*DuPont*, Nim."

"Right."

I gave him a look to indicate that I could care less how it was pronounced, but he had already returned to studying the names and didn't notice.

"Allison Hall," he murmured. "Why does that sound familiar?"

"There was an Alan Hall who graduated last year. He lived in our building."

I sat down on my bed and pulled my loafers off gingerly; my feet were caked with ice from the walk to town and throbbed from the cold. I reminded myself to ask Karl for another pair of boat shoes before remembering how angry I was with him; I resigned to wait out the winter in discomfort.

"No, *Allison* Hall sounds familiar, I'm positive," Jack said. "I just read it somewhere."

"Maybe in a book."

"A book? When was the last time I read a book?"

I glanced up at him and shook my head. It was a wonder that I was the one on academic probation.

"Alright, a newspaper article, then," I said, eyeing the ones that he had clipped and pinned up next to his bed distastefully. "It's a common name – it's bound to sound familiar. You've probably heard of someone called Allison Hall before."

"Where? At my grandmother's bridge game? It's not like there's a surplus of women around here."

"But that's here," I said. "Miss Mercier didn't spend all her time at Bickerby; she must've known people in town – and they were probably women."

Jack raised an eyebrow.

"But she *did* spend all her time here," he said. "It's not like she had a knitting circle or something that she went to weekly, or a bunch of friends in town. All her friends were back home."

"She must have had some friends here," I protested. "This was Miss Mercier – she got along with everyone."

"Getting along with people is different than having friends. She wasn't close to anyone here – she was lonely."

I eyed him carefully, wondering how he knew something so private, before deciding to let it go.

"Well, maybe that's a list of people one of her colleagues gave her of people she might like to hang out with."

"And she hid it behind a picture of her family?"

"Maybe she was embarrassed ... She couldn't have wanted everyone to know that she was lonely."

Jack wasn't convinced. Admittedly, I wasn't either, but I was anxious to go over the questions that Volkov had shown us in class the other day that would be on the exam. Looking down at them, I realized that I should have taken Cabail's advice and paid attention to how they were solved. I half-wished that I could find him so that he could show me how to do them, but he was never in library and I didn't know which residence building was his.

"I know I've heard it before," Jack repeated.

He continued to mutter to himself for the next hour. Realizing that I would never get any studying done as long as he was awake, I set my book down and decided to get some coffee while the dining hall was still open.

"Want to go to dinner?"

"You go. I'm not hungry."

"Really?" I asked in disbelief. "That's a first."

I gingerly shuffled over to the door in the soaked loafers.

"Hey, Nim – can you bring back some fish?"

"I thought you weren't hungry," I said.

"Not for me, for Dictionary."

"For what?"

"For Dictionary," he repeated, pointing to the cat.

I eyed it warily before looking back at him.

"Jack, you can't name the cat Dictionary," I said.

"Why not? This way whenever we're talking about her, no one will think anything of it."

"Yes, they will," I argued, wondering what Sanders would think if he heard me say that I was getting food for a reference book. "And you can't name it, because we're not keeping it."

"Chicken's fine, too," he said. "Whatever looks best."

I sighed and shut the door with the realization that he wouldn't change his mind and made my way to the dining hall alone. The selection of food looked worse than ever, and I carefully wrapped what I could only assume was meat in a napkin before slipping it in my pocket and going to get my coffee.

I hovered beneath one of the lights outside of a building and took a sip, afraid that I would spill it if I tried to walk all the way back to the residence building. The light on the building went off after a moment of inactivity and I had to wave my arm to get it to turn on again. The darkness made me all the more aware of the sound of the ocean in the distance. It sounded like death.

"You shouldn't think about it."

A movement in the corner of my eye made me jump and I dropped the styrofoam cup: the hot coffee hit the icy path and

133

melted a thin circle away.

Cabail Ibbot watched me carelessly from the other side of the path, seemingly oblivious to the fact that he had startled me.

"What are you doing?" I said irritably, shaking my hand where the liquid had burned it.

"Nothing."

He was even odder there than he was in Physics. He peered over at me through his huge round glasses, and I felt rather like a specimen stuck in a slide under his microscope. It was a wonder that I had ever considered studying with him.

"You and Jack are up to no good," he said.

"What do you mean?"

He could have been referring to a number of things, though I had the sinking suspicion that he, at least, had noticed us sneaking into town that morning. I glanced around us cautiously to ensure that we were alone.

"You should really leave it alone," he said.

"Leave what alone?"

He turned his head slowly to the side.

"What you're doing."

"I'm not doing anything," I said. "But maybe *you* should leave me alone, Cabail – you shouldn't sneak up on people in the dark."

I turned and hurried back to my residence building before he could get the chance to outright accuse me of breaking Bickerby rules. Though I didn't think that he was after the answers to exams, his warning disconcerted me just as much as Thomas' threat had.

I fumbled with the keys as I tried to get back inside the residence building. Apart from being cold to the point of frostbite, one of my hands was now scalded from the hot coffee as well. As I stood trying to open the door, the sound of piano music was just audible over the howling wind. I banged on the door as it grew louder in the distance, and Josh Brody hurried over to let me in.

"Thanks," I said, rushing past him to the stairwell before he could ask me what my hurry was. The music faded away halfway up the staircase, but my unease stayed put. It wasn't until I was back in the room that I realized I was shaking all over. Edging towards the bed, I leaned against the mattress as my legs went numb beneath me.

"You know, you might be right: I could have read the name in the paper," Jack was saying from across the room, "though I can't figure out why I would've been reading local news before this happened ..."

My stomach heaved and I dropped to the floor, retching onto the carpet before I could think to run down the hallway to the bathroom. The room was spinning hazily about me and my head was incomprehensibly heavy. As it fell forward from the weight, Jack hopped up from his bed to grab my shoulders and keep me from slumping forward into the vomit.

"Are you all right?" he asked as I leaned my head against the edge of the mattress instead. It was pounding harder than ever and my vision was blotched with black. I couldn't think to answer him.

He heaved me up onto the bed and I flopped across it sideways. As a chill came over the room, I tucked my legs up and shivered against the cold comforter. Jack pulled the one from his own bed over to lay across me. It was thick with the smell of cigarette smoke and heavily wrinkled, but substantially warmer than mine was. I pulled it further around me and waited for the room to stop moving.

"Want me to run down to the Health Center?" he asked.

I jerked my head to the side in a reply. Though it was much too early, he flicked off the lights to let me sleep, though the cat's yellow eyes glowered at me through the darkness. I pulled the comforter over my head to shield them from view.

When the chill finally lifted from my skin and my breathing became calmer, I relaxed a bit beneath the covers. My jaw was sore from how harshly my teeth had been chattering, but the headache had dulled enough to allow me to think again. I exhaled against the mattress and let my eyes flicker shut.

I awoke the next morning when Jack came back into the

room. He set a cup of coffee and a bagel down on the bedside table before crouching down to see if I was awake.

"Rise and shine, Nim," he said cheerfully. I looked at the clock and saw that it was well past ten. "Sleep well?"

I slurred a response as I sat up, careful to do so slowly so as to keep myself from being sick again.

"Thanks," I mumbled out at last.

"No problem. I figure I owe you, and all, seeing as you've been cleaning up after me puking for five or so years ..."

I reached for the coffee with a heavy, clumsy hand and managed to wrap my fingers around it after a moment or so. When I brought it to my mouth to take a sip, however, I saw that he had brought me tea instead.

I groaned.

"Trust me, Nim: you don't want to drink a cup of coffee on an empty stomach. You'll just puke again." When I only stared down into the cup with distaste, he added, "Just drink it: it's caffeinated."

I knew that it wasn't. The tea was the familiar smell of sweet-peppermint that my mother used to drink. She had put her mug on the top of the piano to cool so often that there had been a permanent ring on the polished black. I took a sip of it as I thought of her, but the taste was acrid on my tongue. I put the cup back on the bedside table.

"Feeling any better from last night?" Jack asked.

"Yeah, I'm fine," I said. "It's probably just ... something I ate."

"Could be. I was going to see if I could figure this list out some more," he said, waving the paper in his hands. "I thought I'd run down to Miss Mercier's office – she might have something in there, too."

I nodded without registering what he had said.

"All right, so I'll see you in a bit, then," he said. "Don't let Dictionary out while I'm gone."

The cat mewed up at me from beneath the desk. I narrowed my eyes at it in return.

When Jack had gone, I curled up against the headboard and

wrapped the comforter around me again, slowly munching on the bagel in the silence. The wind had died down considerably from the day before, but still shook over the ocean in the distance. I stood and pulled my damp clothes from the day before off and dressed despite having no intention of leaving the room for the rest of the weekend. The cat's eyes followed me all the while.

For a long while I debated what to do. The music from the opera that had been following me was too persistent and haunting to ignore, but the thought of admitting it to anyone was worse. I wondered what Jack would think if he knew that I was hearing things, or worse – what Beringer would do if he found out.

I brought the comforter over to Jack's bed and sat upon it so that I could look out of the window. Over the tree-line in the distance, the ocean was glistening in a deep, royal blue. I watched it waving at me from afar and leaned my head up against the glass. Beneath the scent of cigarettes, I could smell the salt in the air as clearly as if I was standing on the shore. In my tiredness I allowed the memory to come rather than forcing it away, and the image of my mother standing on the beach with her back to me as she stared out across the ocean molded in front of my mind. I wondered what she saw in it that was so enticing, and I wished that I could pull her away.

Be a good boy, Enim, and don't tell your father on me.

"I shouldn't have let her go," I said into the window, my breath fogging up the glass. From beside me, Dictionary mewed disapprovingly. I tore my eyes from the water to look at her before returning to my bed. As I shut my eyes decisively to sleep, it was with the hope that when I woke up, I would feel better.

Ch. 8

By the time that I had trudged across the campus to the library midway through December, the snow had soaked my pants from the knees down. The leather on my already-worn loafers, which seemed to be permanently soaked with snow, finally gave way and ripped along the sole. I took note of the damage just inside the library door before sighing and making my way to an empty table.

There were so many assignments and exams to study for in the week before the holiday break that I had barely gone a moment without sitting hunched over my books, and my back had developed a crick that no amount of straightening would fix. As I pulled my Physics book closer to me from across the table to check an equation, a shadow fell across me from the side.

"Hi, Enim."

Porter gave his usual polite greeting as he approached the table. I glowered at him before quickly pulling out the copy of the assignment that I had done for him, eager to give it to him so that he would leave me in peace. Upon pocketing it, however, he sat down next to me.

"Studying hard for the Calculus exam?" he asked.

"Yes."

"Oh, good ... Because, you know, I've had such a good semester since our little deal, and I'd hate for anything to mess up my grade now."

"Right."

He had already given me a run down about the exam several times over the past month, going over how I would write down both the questions and the step-by-step answers for him in detail before dropping off the pages before his exam began, and I was in no mood to hear it once again.

"And I know that *you'd* hate it if I accidentally mentioned that you see a ..."

"You'll get the answers, Porter," I said angrily. "Now stop talking."

He gave me a surly look before getting up and shuffling away. As I watched him go, I had the sudden urge to throw my textbook at his retreating form.

No sooner had I returned to my work than I was interrupted again, this time by Julian Wynne, who sat down on my other side with his roommate, Kyle Trask.

"Hey, Enim," he said. His usual friendly tone was somewhat lessened as though he was still upset about the conversation we had had weeks before, but seemingly not enough to warrant being left alone. "What are you up to?"

"Studying."

"Yeah, I could see." Julian eyed my Physics homework with an unpleasant expression. "Glad I took Chemistry."

I paused halfway through the equation that I was working on, too distracted to think of the next step. Julian put his elbows on the table and leaned closer.

"Say, Enim, are you and Porter friends or something?"

"What? No, definitely not."

"Oh, good," Julian said. "Only, I saw him over here talking to you before, and I thought that maybe ..."

"Thought what?" I asked.

"I don't know. It looked like you two were having a pretty interesting conversation."

I glared at Julian out of the corner of my eye. Between him, Thomas, and Cabail, I was being to feel as if everyone was watching me.

"Well, we weren't," I said. "Why would I have anything to do with Porter anyway?"

"It's not like you have great taste in friends," Trask scoffed.

I narrowed my eyes at him. Julian gave a nervous laugh.

"Right, well, we were just wondering," he said. "It sort of looked like he was ... bothering you about something."

I chewed the inside of my mouth as I debated what Julian might have overheard. His mouth was curled in a pleasant smile, but his eyes were darting over my expression.

"I just helped him study a couple of times," I said nonchalantly. "Now he thinks we're friends or something."

"Right."

He nodded without believing me, and I returned to my work in the hopes that he had lost interest and would leave. Just as I picked up my pen to finish the equation, however, he began to speak again.

"So what's Jack been up to lately?"

"What?"

"Jack," Julian repeated. "I haven't seen much of him lately. What's he been up to?"

"Nothing." I gave Julian a wary look before pulling my eyes away again. I could imagine the look of mocking hilarity on his face if he knew that Jack was trying to solve a murder.

"Jack's never up to nothing," Julian said.

"Well, now he is," I said.

Trask scoffed again.

"Yeah right," he said. "He's been weird since Miss Mercier died."

Julian nodded in agreement.

"I heard him asking Senora Marín about her a few weeks ago – practically pleading with her for information. It was weird enough that he was so obsessed with her when she was alive, but now he's obsessed with her death, too."

I gave them each a disapproving look.

"So? You two were pretty interested in that local girl who washed up on shore in October," I said.

Julian's smile twitched.

"Right, but ... that was different, Enim."

"How so?"

"Because, that girl was ... that was just a bit of excitement. I mean, we didn't know her. But Miss Mercier ..."

"Everyone knows Jack liked her," Trask said.

"Everyone liked Miss Mercier," I said.

"Not like Jack liked her."

I threw another cold look their way before shaking my head and packing up my belongings; it was obvious that I would never get anything done in the library.

"Come on, Enim," Julian said. "You have to admit that it's

weird. Kyle and I are just worried about you being stuck in the dorm with him all the time. What if he goes all weird or something?"

"I'll take my chances," I said.

"He's up to no good, Enim," Julian said flatly as I stood to leave. "And if he does something stupid, he's going to drag you down with him."

I moved to step around the table but Julian caught my arm and held me back.

"Don't forget what he did last year," he said lowly. "He pulled that stunt and then let you take all the blame."

"I took the blame because I was the one who did it," I said.

"Brainwashed him, too," Trask muttered.

I yanked my arm free and strode away from the table before the conversation could go on a moment longer. When I returned to the dorm room, Jack was sitting on his bed with Dictionary in his lap. Though she wasn't quite as skeletal as she had been when we found her, she was just as eerie to look at. I put my bag next to the bed before sitting down.

"You're back soon," Jack said. "Finally realize that it's not worth it to study?"

"Hardly."

"Then why're you here? Miss me that much?"

He gave me a devious smile and I rolled my eyes.

"Library's a bit too crowded," I said. "Thomas and Julian wouldn't leave me alone."

"Porter and Wynne? Are they friends now?"

"No; they came over separately. Thomas wanted to harass me about math, and Julian just wanted to remind me how much he hates you."

"How sweet of him. I'll remember that the next time I pass him in the hallway."

He looked back down at the paper he was reading while absentmindedly petting Dictionary with his other hand.

"What are you up to?" I asked.

"Just reading something about Miss Mercier."

"Right." I paused as I watched him, a frown forming on my

face. "Say, Jack, you don't ... I mean, you don't tell people that you're interested in her murder, do you?"

"Who would I tell? You're the only person I can stand talking to." He glanced up and caught my expression. "Why?"

"Nothing, just something Julian said."

"About me and Miss Mercier's murder? What's that?"

"Just ... just that you were interested in it." When Jack looked taken aback, I quickly went on. "I told him that you weren't, plus I reminded him how interested he and Trask were about the dead girl earlier this semester, and that seemed to shut him up."

"Right, exactly," Jack said, still looking a bit unsettled. "They talked about her for weeks. Trask used to sit next to me in History and go on and on about it ... 'What do you think she did? Think she jumped?' It was like he's never heard of someone dying before."

He shook his head and returned to the paper again, and I took the opportunity to pull my textbook back out of my bag. When I opened it back to the page I had been studying, though, I noticed that Jack's eyebrows had turned downwards in a frown.

"Wait a minute ..."

"What?" I said.

"That girl," he said, rubbing his forehead as he tried to remember. "The one who drowned. What was her name?"

"I don't know."

"I think it started with an 'S' ..."

"That'll narrow it down."

"Samantha? No, Sarah," he said. "Sarah someone."

"Why does it matter?" I said. I hadn't like discussing the girl months ago, and now that it was so close to the holidays my aversion to the subject had only increased. I regretted having brought her up at all. "She died months ago."

I tried to turn his attention elsewhere, but he had already jumped up from the bed and paid me no mind. As he began to sift through the pile of mess on his side of the room in search of something, I eyed him questionably.

"What are you doing?"

"Looking for the article."

"What article? The one about the dead girl?" I said exasperatedly. "Jack, that was months ago. You'll never find –"

"Here!"

He had overturned an enormous pile of textbooks and short-sleeved shirts to reveal the newspaper lying flattened beneath them. I faltered midsentence and shook my head.

Still standing in the middle of the room, he began to read through the headline quickly. His eyes swept over the sentences at record speed, and when the article was cut off, he flipped through the pages to find the rest of it in another section.

"Sarah Hayes," he said. "Nim, her name's Sarah Hayes."

"So?"

He ran his hand through his hair fervently, his eyes seemingly glued to the page.

"*Sarah Hayes*. That's one of the names on Miss Mercier's list!"

When I only stared at him in bewilderment, he brought the hand-written list over for me to see. As I read down to find the name at the bottom, he flipped through the newspaper pages again to reread the article.

"Did they ever figure out how she died?" he asked. "This one only talks about how she was found."

"She drowned."

"Right. Drowned. But how?"

"Toppled off the cliffs jogging."

He was too busy studying the article to notice the deadened sound of my voice. I swallowed as I thought again of the dead girl that had crept into my thoughts at night months ago and turned my head so that I didn't look out the window at the ocean. Though distant, the sound of it had grown louder in the quiet.

"So Miss Mercier has a list of girls' names, and one of the names is of the dead girl who fell off the cliffs," Jack said. "But why?"

"Maybe she was petitioning for a fence to be put up."

"But what's with the other girls' names?"

"Maybe they're friends of Sarah's."

"I'm not sure that that makes any sense."

"I'm not sure that any of this makes any sense, Jack," I said, but he had busied himself with lighting a cigarette and appeared not to have heard me.

He had not gotten any further in his reasoning by midweek, and I was too concerned with passing my exams to be of much help to him. What was more, I was reluctant to give any of my attention to the unexplained dead girl. I could still hear the sound of the ocean too loudly from the distance, and my thoughts had formed the distorted image of her falling from the cliffs and plummeting into the water. It repeated over and over again in my head until it morphed into one of a woman with blond hair and a white dress plunging into the water, only she wasn't falling from the cliffs, but rather jumping from a bridge ...

"Are you all right, Enim?"

I looked up from the floor as Beringer noticed my preoccupation. He considered me carefully from across the desk, a small frown pulling at his face. I nodded quickly before straightening in my seat and smoothing down my sweater to reassure him.

"I'm fine," I said.

"Of course. Only ... you looked a bit far away."

He studied me as I gave him a polite smile in the way that made me wonder if he could tell what I was thinking. If nothing else, I was sure that he knew that I wasn't being honest.

"Is there anything you wanted to talk about today in particular, Enim?"

The subject that I had been trying to avoid thinking of for so many months pressed down against my eyes, and I shut them to block the images out. I kept my teeth clenched on my tongue and shook my head. Beringer's brow fell a bit into a frown.

"You know, Enim, you can tell me anything," he said. "You always can. No matter what you say, I won't judge you. Do you know that?"

My expression twitched and I nodded unconvincingly. Beringer's frown deepened.

"Is there anything you'd like to say, Enim?" he asked patiently. "Anything at all?"

I shook my head.

"Maybe something that's been on your mind?" he suggested. "Or something that's been bothering you? It can be anything."

"No, there's ... there's nothing."

"Nothing at all?"

He was waiting for me to change my mind, just as he had been doing since we had begun the sessions months before. The hopefulness that he had had then had faded ever slightly, and I wondered how long it would take before I had worn him out, just as I had done to Karl and my father and anyone who had ever associated with me at Bickerby.

As I struggled to find something to say that would placate his concerns, he leaned forward into his hands and pressed them to his mouth to hide a frown. His sleeves were rolled back and his reading glasses were tucked over his shirt in lieu of a tie, and the light that the desk lamp sent over his eyes and skin made them glow in warmth. He seemed to be the only thing on the island that had not succumbed to the harshness of the winter. For a moment, as I stared at him, I wondered what it would be like to talk to him because he wanted to talk to me and not because he was paid to, and I wished that he was there because we were friends rather than because of the horrific tragedy that I refused to speak to him about.

"I ..."

The familiar music from the opera had begun again. It came over the distant trees and around the cracks in the window to splinter against my ear, and I jerked away from the sound with a sudden shake of my head.

"What is it, Enim?" Beringer asked, mistaking the reason

for my movement. "What were you going to say?"

"No, it's nothing. I ... I was just thinking of something, but it's not important."

"What were you thinking of?"

I put my hand over my eyes and shut them tightly as I tried to think. The idea that I dragged Beringer out to the island only to make him sit in uncomfortable silences with me only worsened my ability to think up anything to say to him, and the music that had twisted its way back into my head was clouding every thought that I had.

"Turandot."

"Sorry?" Beringer shook his head as though he hadn't heard me correctly. "What's that?"

"Turandot," I repeated, though I already dreaded bringing it up. "It's an opera."

"Oh, I see. Is that something for school?"

"No, it's ... just an interest."

He raised his eyebrows.

"Really?" he said. "Forgive me, I've just ... never heard of a teenage boy who enjoys opera. How did that interest arise?"

I shifted carefully in place.

"I ... It was my mother's favorite. She used to play one of the arias on the piano, and she would tell me the story at night."

"I see," Beringer said delicately. "And she taught you to play it, too?"

I nodded.

"And what brought those memories up today?"

I ran my finger over the jagged edge of my nail as I considered how to answer. I knew that I couldn't tell him about how the aria crept into my mind late at night and toyed with my memories unrelentingly. His reaction would be far from welcoming, especially given what was written in the file-folder lying between us.

"Nothing, I just ... sometimes I just like to think about it."

"For any particular reason?"

I sighed as he persisted with the topic as I ought to have

known he would. From the way that his eyebrows curved downwards over his eyes, I knew that he was waiting for me to tell him something about my mother that would explain my behavior over the past twelve months.

"I just ... I mean, I guess I just wonder how it ends."

"What do you mean by that?"

"It was never finished, so I just ... I wonder how it ends." When he continued to look perplexed, I went on. "The writer died before he completed it, and someone else added another ending but ... it doesn't seem to fit."

"I see." He leaned onto his hands as he considered what I had said, and I had just been brooding over the idea that he was finding a way to bring the subject back to my mother when he asked, "What is the story?"

"What?"

"The story – Turandot. What's it about?"

"I ..." I shook my head. "It's not ... I mean, I wouldn't do a good job of explaining it."

"I'm sure that you will. I'd like to hear about it – unless there's something else you hoped to discuss?"

I quickly shook my head. Running a hand through my hair, I tried to recall how my mother had told the story to me when I was younger. She had an eloquence about her that I had never possessed, and the story was entertaining each time regardless of how often I had heard it before.

"Well, it's ..." I cleared my throat and sat up a bit in my chair. "It's about a guy – a prince – and it takes place in China. So he ... he comes to the palace of a foreign land, and he ... he meets his long-lost father, the king of a different place, who's sort of been in hiding since his kingdom was overthrown. And ... and just as he's arriving, an execution is beginning for another prince."

I paused again, aware that I had already left out a dozen important details and that the story was near-to-impossible to understand. Beringer smiled across the desk at me, however, and indicated for me to continue.

"So the unnamed prince finds out that the princess of the

land is unwed, and that she makes her suitors answer three riddles. If they answer correctly, she'll marry them. If they don't, she beheads them. The last suitor who's tried gets executed even though he's well-liked by everyone which, you know, sort of shows what type of princess Turandot is, but despite knowing all of that, the prince falls in love with her when he sees how beautiful she is.

"So ... the prince says that he's going to try and answer Turandot's riddles, and his father and his father's servant try to stop him. And ... and the servant is especially adamant, since she's really in love with the prince, but the prince has already made up his mind so he goes after Turandot."

I paused again to see if I was making any sense to Beringer who, in return, looked to be at least impressed at hearing me speak more than a few words at a time. I cleared my throat again before going on.

"So Turandot gives the prince the riddles and he somehow manages to figure all three of them out. She's pretty unhappy at the idea of marrying him and – seeing how upset she is – he offers to give her another chance to get out of the marriage. He says that if she can answer one of his riddles, she can still behead him, but if she doesn't guess, she'll still have to marry him."

"And what's the riddle?" Beringer asked as I paused.

"He asks her what his name is," I said. The music from the aria that would have begun to play at that point in the opera was somehow sounding in my ears, and I could see my mother shaking by the window as she listened to it, distressed that she would never know the answer. "And she ... she tells everyone that no one is to sleep until someone finds out his name, and that if they don't she'll execute the entire kingdom. And ... and she finds the prince's father and servant girl and threatens to torture them until one of them says his name, but the servant girl insists that she alone knows, and she kills herself without saying what it is."

Beringer waited a moment before speaking.

"And then what happens?"

"That's it," I said. "That's how it ends."

"I see."

He said it with certainty even though I doubted he understood what it had meant to my mother. He didn't know the way that the final riddle – the ending of the opera – had tormented her with its answer. He hadn't seen the way she would stand at the window and stare into the nothingness while it played throughout the house at full volume until my father came home and shut it off. He didn't know how she had come to my room every night and asked if I had figured it out yet, silently begging me to think up the answer that she would never know. And he didn't know how that answer was all that was still clinging on of her, and how it followed me with its relentless sound as it haunted me with the guilt that if I had just known, she would have found some peace.

I could feel Beringer's eyes on me and purposefully pulled away, turning in my chair until I faced the wall instead of his desk. I looked at the clock and implored it to pick up speed so that I could leave, but the session was going slower than ever.

"And you think about how it would have ended," Beringer stated slowly. "What are your ideas?"

I swallowed as I stared at the side of the filing cabinet. The faintest image was reflected in the dark metal. Though I knew that it was a reflection of myself, I imagined instead that it was her staring back at me.

"I think that the princess knew she had lost, and she didn't want to marry the prince, and so she killed herself."

Beringer's eyes flickered over me.

"That sounds like a terrible ending," he said quietly. When I didn't respond, he leaned forward on the desk and continued in a low voice, "I know that we've spoken in the past, briefly, about the holidays, and I think that it's important to discuss them today, as this will be our last chance before you go home."

"Right."

"Are you having any thoughts about the break? How you'll spend it?"

I chewed the inside of my mouth and gave a half-hearted shrug, neither confirming nor denying that I had spent the last few weeks agonizing over the two-week period that I would spend stuck in the house in Connecticut.

"I'd like to at least go over how you feel about the holidays, Enim," Beringer continued. "I am worried, given your aversion to the subject, that you may become ... distressed as Christmas approaches. Could you tell me your thoughts about it?"

"I ... I don't really think about it, Dr. Beringer."

"You don't think about what?" he asked. "How you'll feel, or the anniversary itself?"

"I ... neither. I don't think about either of them."

"Not at all?"

"No. I mean, sometimes. But I ... I'd rather not think about it. I'd rather just ... just wait for it all to pass."

Beringer exhaled slowly and pressed his mouth to his hands. Even without looking at him directly, I knew that his brow was furrowed in concern.

"And if it passes," he said, "what will happen then? How do you think you'll feel the day after Christmas?"

I shook my head. My thoughts had grown too heavy with thoughts of the opera and it was difficult to think.

"Enim," Beringer said, "what happened on Christmas last year?"

"You know."

"I don't know," he said. "I don't know what happened. I need you to tell me."

"Well, there's – there's nothing to say."

"No? Nothing happened? It was just a normal, everyday holiday?"

His voice was soft but it was digging under my flesh: I could feel it peeling back the skin over my skull as he tried to see further inside my head.

"No, you –" I looked back at him as I tried to explain something with no answer. "I don't know what you want me to say: you know what happened. Do you just want me to repeat it? I'll just echo whatever's written in my file – is that what you want me to do?"

"I just want to hear what happened, Enim. There's no specific answer. Just what happened that night."

"She jumped off a bridge," I said, my arms shaking as I clutched the chair. I was aware that it was the first time I had said it aloud. The words sounded unforgiving in the air.

"What else happened?" he said calmly.

"Nothing – nothing else happened! Why does everyone think that? Why does everyone keep asking? You're waiting for me to say something, but there's nothing to say!"

There was a crack in my voice as I finished and I turned my face away, swallowing to make it smooth again.

"What happened before she left for the bridge?" Beringer said. "Did you see her before she went?"

"Yes. Yes, but nothing happened. She was ... There was nothing different."

"What do you mean? What was happening?"

"I ... I don't know. We were – she made me dinner. She was – she was listening to the soundtrack from the opera. It was – everything was normal. Nothing happened; she was fine."

Beringer ran his hands together as he sorted through my disjointed statements.

"So you had dinner, and you were listening to a favorite song of hers, and then ...? What happened next, Enim?"

"Nothing. I mean – you know. She ... she left. She went to the bridge. She jumped."

"Did she say anything to you?"

"No." The lie came out as automatically as always, firmer and more defiant than the rest of my shaky words. "No, she just left. I – I didn't even know she was gone until ... until later."

"And that's when you called Karl?"

I ran my tongue over my teeth as I tried to recall the details without thinking of the actual memory. It was so hard with the music blaring in my ears. Beringer waited as I fidgeted with my hands.

"I called my father," I said. "He didn't pick up."

"I see," Beringer said. "And when he didn't answer, you called your uncle?"

"Yes."

"And he did what?"

I bit down on my tongue until the pain tore me from the memory.

"Nothing," I said. "He did ... nothing."

Beringer waited through the silence, but I couldn't think of anything more to say. I had told him all that I could, and the rest was well-worded and written down in the papers lying between us. I refused to paraphrase them just to prove that I wasn't in denial of what had happened.

"I don't want to talk about this anymore, Dr. Beringer. I don't ... I don't see how restating all of this will make anything any different – or any better."

He stared at me for a long moment with a sorrowful expression, and when he spoke his voice was just a murmur over the loudness in my head.

"I know that you don't want to talk about it, Enim. I know. But something about that night is upsetting you, and I'd like to know what it is."

"My mother jumped off a bridge," I said. "That's what upsets me."

"And I understand that, but I don't think that this is grief. Not now, not after twelve months. I think that this is guilt."

I was silent for so long that an eternity seemed to pass between us, pushing us away from one another until I couldn't see him sitting there anymore. He was so distant in the room, just a fragmented piece that didn't fit into the images around me from my memories, and I couldn't think to understand why he was there watching me. I felt the room collapse and rebuild into the kitchen where she had last stood, her light sweater covering her white dress, her feet bare against the floor as she tiptoed around to the aria playing in the background, her face calmer than I had seen it in so long, and she looked more like herself than she had in so long: so clear, so at ease, so content.

"Enim? What is it that you feel badly about? What don't

you want to say?"

His voice broke through the thoughts and the shattered picture faded away. As the room reemerged, a coldness came down on my skin that left me feeling ill. Before I could give in and speak the words pressing against my mouth, I stood and circled around the chair and wrenched the door open. Stumbling out of the room, I ran down the hallway and out the front door away from the answer that I couldn't give to him.

The air was cold and biting, and the ground beneath my feet was hardened with frozen snow. I staggered my way down the path and into the Center Garden, not sure where I was going but certain that I had to get away from him before the truth rose up between us, sinking us, drowning us –

"Enim!"

I heard Beringer's voice in the darkness before I could see him, and had barely begun to turn in surprise when his hands closed around my forearms. He held me as I fought to get away from him, trying to escape even when then was nowhere to go, and his grip was firm but not harsh. When I finally stopped struggling, he loosened his hands and placed them on my shoulders instead.

"It's all right, Enim. It's all right."

"It's not."

The words were wrecked by a sob, and I turned my face away to try and hide any tears that the darkness did not.

His hand was warm on my shoulder, and the feeling was reminiscent of the way my father used to take hold of me to pull me into an embrace, and of how my mother would pull me close and tell me that she loved me. It was a touch that I hadn't felt in so long. I wished that he was someone else, or that I was someone else, because his ability to understand me was halted by the file that sat between us in the office, and his compassion was something manufactured from a diploma hanging on a wall.

"It will be," he said, but I couldn't bring myself to believe him.

Ch. 9

"You need a haircut."

It was the first thing that Karl had thought to say to me in the four hours that we had been driving, but I didn't feel obligated to respond. He looked over at me as he waited for me to speak, his light hair as smooth as ever and his blue eyes muddled beneath a frown, and sighed in discontent when I turned away towards the window instead. If we were going to coexist for the two-week holiday break, then I rather thought that we would have to get accustomed to ignoring one another.

The light misting of snow that had followed us from the port in Maine had turned into rain, and the back-and-forth motion of the windshield wipers was making me drowsy. As Karl continued to pinpoint flaws in my outward appearance, I leaned my head against the window and drifted off to sleep.

The sound of the car door slamming woke me up sometime later, and I could just make out the blurred shape that was his form as he hurried through the rain before he disappeared into the house. Karl had become accustomed to living in the residence that belonged to neither of us, but I was still wary of what it held. Shrinking back against the seat, I ran my eyes over the place as I waited out the time before I would have to go inside.

It was a standard house that had belonged to my maternal grandparents before their deaths. I had a few neutral memories of visiting them there when I was younger, but those had been largely ruined by the time that I had had to spend there over the past year. My father had moved us in with my grandmother after selling my childhood home, though I wasn't sure that he had ever intended to live there himself: he had coincidentally gotten a job overseas before his living arrangements had been discussed.

My grandmother had never particularly liked my father and would often tell me so during the weeks that followed his departure. It was only she who seemed to share my thoughts that he had abandoned his family, and I had held a certain amount of regard for her for that alone. A large part of me thought that she had died purposefully to force him to come home again, but her plans had been thwarted: he had not returned upon learning of her death, but had sent Karl to take her place in the house instead.

I opened the car door but remained seated. Even the damp chill and soft pattering of rain couldn't hasten me inside. A huge puddle had formed outside of the house that flooded the remains of my grandmother's peony garden and front path; if it didn't stop raining soon, it might rise up to flood the place. Then we would all drown properly.

I grabbed my bag from the backseat and went inside. I could hear the heat hissing from the radiator, but the cold seeped in through the old wood and chilled the house regardless. I shivered and hurried upstairs.

"Oh, Enim, I didn't hear you come in."

I paused on the landing as the caregiver spoke to me but didn't turn to face her. The trail of light leading down the hallway indicated that the door to the room at the end of the hallway was still open, and I had no desire to see inside. I could never be quite certain what laid there out of sight. She hummed to herself as she closed the door and made her way down to where I stood. Only when I was certain that the door was closed did I relax and turn to her.

"Hello, Mrs. Quincy," I said politely.

"Hello, dear," she said, reaching over to pat my arm. "I was just going downstairs to put on a pot of coffee, if you wanted to ..."

She indicated to the room that she had just left, but I averted my gaze.

"Right." I said. "Thank you, Mrs. Quincy."

She nodded solemnly at me and turned to go downstairs. When her footsteps had died away into the kitchen, I hurried into the room at the opposite end of the hallway and shut myself inside. Mrs. Quincy had been coming to the house as long as I had lived there. With her warm tone and little laced-up shoes, she appeared more compatible in the antiquated house than either Karl or I did, and she was certainly more comfortable there.

The faint sound of beeping that came from down the hall was only slightly audible from my room, but I took a pillow from the bed and shoved it into the crack beneath the door even so. The room had been converted to a small bedroom for me by my grandmother when I had moved in. Though she had decorated it in shades of blue, the floral-patterned bedspread and curtains negated the attempt at masculinity. I dropped my bag at the end of the bed and perched on the edge of the mattress. The place was both too familiar and overly foreign all at once.

The only assignment that I had over the holidays was to read *Jane Eyre* for English. Though I was desperate for something to do to pass the time, I couldn't get past the first few pages. Throwing the book back down, I pulled my bag up to the bed and began to unpack my clothes instead. I took my time lining up the multiple pairs of khaki pants and light-blue sweaters, smoothing the unwrinkled fabric down as I went, and moved them into the empty dresser drawers. As I picked up my bag to store it in the closet, something rattled within it. I reached my hand inside to see what I had forgotten and was surprised to find a bottle of the medication that Beringer prescribed. I stared at the orange plastic with a frown, wondering how it had gotten there: as far as I knew, I had stored all of them beneath my bed at Bickerby.

"Enim –"

Karl barely knocked on the door before opening it. In the split second that the pillow prevented it from opening, I shoved the bottle into my pocket and sat back on the bed. He stepped into the room suspiciously.

"What are you doing in here?"

"Nothing."

"I can see that."

"Then why did you ask?"

He opened his mouth to retort before thinking better of it.

"Dinner's almost ready. Come downstairs."

"I'm not really hungry."

"Well, come down and see how much you can eat anyhow."

"I don't want to."

"Well, you have to."

"No, I don't."

He clenched his jaw at my defiant tone.

"Enim, I don't want to argue with you about this."

"Then don't."

I glared at him from my place on the bed. He looked more tired than I had ever seen him, though it had nothing to do with the long drive up to Bickerby and back. We had only been with each other for less than a day, and already I was wearing him thin. It would be a wonder if either of us got through the holiday break at all.

"Enim," he said wearily, "please come downstairs. Please."

After a long moment of no response, he sighed and left the room.

I listened to the sound of his footsteps on the floor below as he paced through the kitchen, and though the sounds of clinking and scrubbing were barely audible I knew that he was doing dishes and washing the counters. Karl had the annoying habit of cleaning when he didn't know what else to do. It was hardly a surprise that my grandmother's dusty house was so immaculate.

I fell into a fitful sleep hours later, turning back and forth on the old mattress as I tried to find a comfortable way to lie, while pressing the pillow over my head to drown out the sound of beeping from down the hallway. It sounded louder in the dark; I didn't know how Karl could stand to sleep in the room next to it. I had only just drifted into a deeper sleep during the early hours of the morning when a loud knock sounded on the door and woke me back up.

"Enim?" Karl stepped into the room and looked around. "Are you still asleep?"

"Obviously."

"It's nine in the morning," he said. "You don't sleep this

late at school, do you?"

I pushed the comforters off of me and made no response. Getting groggily to my feet, I fished around for something warmer to put on as Karl watched me.

"Well, come down and have breakfast. It's ice-cold by now, but ..."

"I'll go down later," I said.

"No, you should come down now. You didn't have dinner last night, you must be ... starving."

He lingered on the last word as he stared at my bare arms, and I quickly pulled a sweater over my short-sleeved shirt before he realized how thin they were.

"I'll go down later," I repeated.

"Why don't you come down now?"

"I have to go to the bathroom."

"I ... all right. Come down in a minute, then."

I twisted past him and went down the hallway, quickly shutting the bathroom door as the beeping from the next room grew louder. I took my time so that he wouldn't wait for me to come back out, and when I was certain that he had gone back downstairs I crept back to my room and shut myself inside.

"Enim," Karl said ten minutes later, knocking on the door. "Come on – come downstairs."

The doorknob rattled and twisted as he tried to get the door open again, but the lock prevented him from doing so. After a few minutes of useless pleading he gave up and went back downstairs. I stared at the painted wood unfeelingly.

He came back periodically throughout the day and attempted to coax me out, but I had already resigned not to leave the room. The cold light from the window was an indication that it would snow again before the week was out, and the room had a chill despite the sound of heat hissing through the antiquated radiator. I backed up into the corner of the room with the comforter over me and sat stilly until my limbs went numb. When he came back up the stairs that night, I barely flinched as his hand slammed against the door.

"Dammit, Enim!" he said. "This is ridiculous! Open the

door!"

I shut my eyes and tuned out his voice. A dull discomfort had settled in over my head and I was exhausted despite doing nothing all day. As I stared at the peeling wallpaper and waited for him to withdraw and leave me in silence again, my throat burned. In his anger he finally bore some resemblance to his older brother, and the familiarity of the angry voice coming through the door was just another reminder of things that I wished I could forget.

He gave one last failed attempt to stir me the next morning before he left for work. His voice was heavy and tired as it came through the wood, and he sighed without waiting long for a response. When I listened to the sound of his car pulling away, it was with a mixture of satisfaction that he was gone and unease with the silence that he left; the house was much too empty, and yet not empty enough.

The beeping sounded more loudly from down the hall and I sat up in alarm. Pushing the covers off of me, I crossed the room to the door and peeked out into the hallway. Someone had left the door open to the guestroom. The horrible noise sounded louder in the otherwise silent house. It pounded against my skull and threatened to split it open.

"Oh, Enim –" Mrs. Quincy came out of the bathroom and paused upon seeing me. "Did you want to go in? I can wait downstairs, if you'd like –"

"No," I said quickly. I withdrew into my room before she could ask me again, shutting the door firmly in the hopes of blocking out the sound of the machines in the room. As I leaned my head up against the wood, I tried not think of what was hidden just out of sight behind the habitually-closed door, but the memories that constantly lingered on the edge of my mind were beginning to break through.

I crossed the room and went to the window to look outside. It had begun to snow again, just as it had the night that she had gone. I squirmed in place and teetered back and forth as I watched it fall. Even inside, my covered feet were cold against the carpet. I wondered what could have possibly driven her on long enough to walk all the way to the bridge barefoot.

I shivered and went downstairs to get a cup of coffee. If not for Mrs. Quincy, there wouldn't be any in the house. As I sat on the counter and looked around the spotless kitchen, I found that I rather missed the messiness of the dorm room that I shared with Jack. Had he been there, he would have toppled over the neatly-lined boxes in the cabinets or rearranged the contents of the refrigerator just to irritate Karl.

To distract myself I tried to imagine what he was doing, but even though I knew that he was searching for more connections between Miss Mercier and the list of names that she had written, it all felt very far away. It was as though she had never died, and there was no list of names, and it was all just a blurred dream from the night before that was peculiar but meaningless. The events from twelve months ago felt much closer than anything recent did, and for all I knew, the entirety of the last year had not happened at all.

I stood up and dumped my cup in the sink before scouring the kitchen for something to eat. Apart from a fruit basket that someone from Karl's office had sent over and a plate of gingerbread that Mrs. Quincy had baked, the cabinets were quite empty. I looked through the shelves and opened up an unmarked tin in the hopes of finding something more appetizing but only found dried leaves inside. Sniffing it cautiously, I realized that it was Karl's tea. The scent was the familiar one of sweet-peppermint, just like my mother used to drink. I replaced the lid and shoved it to the back of the cabinet.

I returned to my room and laid down on the bed rigidly. My back ached against the cold mattress and my stomach felt hollow as though it had been burned with acid. I shut my eyes as the beeping from down the hall persisted to drum against the walls, making the room pulse all around me, but couldn't fall back to sleep.

"What are you doing?"

Karl arrived home hours later and peered into the room at

me. I didn't move from my spot. He sighed and rubbed the bridge of his nose.

"Well, it doesn't matter. Come down and have some dinner."

"I'm not hungry."

"You must be. You haven't eaten all day."

"I might've," I said. "How would you know?"

"You didn't."

"How do you know?" I repeated. "You were at work."

"Don't be difficult, Enim. I know you haven't eaten – Mrs. Quincy said so."

"Did she? Do you pay her extra to spy on me?"

"Stop it. She said that you were holed up in here all day and she was worried about you – that hardly constitutes as spying."

"Right."

"So come down and have dinner."

"I'm not hungry."

"Enim, just come downstairs. I don't want to have this conversation every night."

"Neither do I. I'm not hungry, and I'm not coming downstairs."

Karl ran his hand through his hair in frustration.

"Enim, I've had enough of this. Come downstairs."

"No."

"Enim –"

"I'm not going downstairs."

"You have to."

"Why?"

"Because!"

His tone was much too similar to my father's, and in the dimly-lit room their appearances didn't seem so different. I straightened a bit in my spot and momentarily considered doing as he said, but then the light hit his blue eyes and fair hair and I changed my mind. He wasn't my father and I felt no obligation to listen to him.

"Because why?"

"You know why, Enim – so come downstairs. Now."

"No. Why do you care if I eat or not, or if I stay in my room all day? Why can't you just leave me alone?"

"Because!" he said again, his exterior finally cracking to give way to his anger. He raked his hands through his hair as his bright eyes flashed in anger, and I pressed my back into the wall in the hopes of putting more space between us. "Because your mother stopped eating in the end! Now come downstairs, for Christ's sake!"

The silence that rang throughout the room after his outburst was broken almost immediately by the sound of increased beeping from down the hall. He turned towards it as it grew louder and pulled away from the door to go to the guestroom. As he checked to make sure that everything was fine, I stood to lock myself inside the bedroom. He returned a moment later and halted upon seeing the closed door.

"Enim –" he began exasperatedly, but then he sighed. "Dammit, Enim. This is ridiculous."

He retreated downstairs without another word. I sat in the dark for hours as I waited for him to return, certain that he would appear at the door any moment and bang on it for me to let him in. As the numbers on the clock shifted by, however, the house stayed silent but for the beeping down the hall. Finally I eased my shoulders and relaxed enough to fall asleep.

When I rolled out of bed the next morning, his car had already gone from the driveway. I made my way down the hall to the bathroom, rubbing my shoulder as I went to dispel some of the soreness, and quickly stepped inside and shut the door. The beeping pounding through the wall echoed off of the tiles and I turned the faucet on to drown out the sound. Under the harsh lighting, my reflection peered back at me from the mirror with a ghostly, deadened expression and I turned away from it before I could recognize any more similarities to my mother than Karl had already drawn.

"Oh, Enim – there you are." Mrs. Quincy poked her head out of the guestroom as I made my way back down the hall and offered me a friendly smile that I couldn't return. "How are you this morning?"

Her eyes traveled over me knowingly and I smoothed down my sweater to appear less disheveled. I wondered if she could tell that I was still wearing the same clothes that I had been the day I arrived.

"Fine," I said stiffly. Then, remembering what Karl had said the night before, I added, "I was just going downstairs. To eat."

"Oh, that's good ..."

She seemed to want to say something more, but I had already turned from her and started down the hallway. I couldn't focus on a conversation as long as the door to the guestroom was open, even if it was only open a crack. As I hurried down the stairs, it occurred to me that she might mention my behavior to Karl when he got home. I wondered how long she had been giving him reports on my daily activities.

I went to the kitchen and poured myself some coffee. Then, going to the plate of gingerbread men that she had brought over a few days before, I successively bit the heads off each one and lined the bodies back up on the plate. I was sure that the two of them could draw some conclusions as to what it meant.

I returned to my room and attempted to get further in *Jane Eyre*, but after rereading the same page numerous times I threw it back down in defeat. The thought of Doyle ridiculing me loudly when I returned to school was a much more welcome thought than listening to the beeping down the hall for another fourteen endless days. More than once, I had the strong desire to go down to the guestroom and pull out the plugs to all the machines if only to end the noise, but then immediately regretted the thought. I put my pillow over my head and laid in stillness for the rest of the day instead.

"Enim," Karl said when he came home to find me lying in such a way, "what are you doing?"

I didn't bother to respond; nothing I said would make any difference to him, anyhow.

"Should I bother to ask you to come down for dinner?"

"I'm not hungry."

"Of course you're not," he said bitterly. "I can see why, of course – given the state of the gingerbread in the kitchen."

I smiled into the pillow, glad that he had found them already.

"Mrs. Quincy was quite upset," he went on irritably. "It's bad enough that you look sick – you don't have to act like it, as well."

"And how am I *supposed* to act, Karl?" I said, sitting up and letting the pillow fall to my lap. "What do you want me to do – celebrate the holidays happily? Be overjoyed that Christmas is coming?"

"No, of course not. That's not what I meant."

"Yes it is," I countered. "That's what you all want – to just pretend that everything's all right and go on normally."

"No, we just – we just want you to get out a bit more, and eat something once in a while, and make some friends –"

"I have friends."

"You have *a* friend, and he hardly counts. A few more would be more normal for your age."

"I have others."

"Like who?" Karl snapped at my defiance.

I searched my brain rapidly.

"Cabail Ibbot."

"Who?"

"He's in my Physics class."

"You've never mentioned him before."

"Not to you."

Karl gave an exasperated sigh.

"To who then? Beringer?"

"Maybe. At least he listens to me."

"He's paid to listen to you!" Karl said angrily. "He's paid to like you, and to put up with you – I do it by choice!"

"And not very well."

"Do you just enjoy being difficult? Are you doing this to torture me because I'm here and not your father?"

"Don't flatter yourself," I said scathingly. "It has nothing to do with you."

I turned my head to the window only so that I didn't have to look at him. I hardly expected Karl to understand why I had had so much trouble eating and sleeping for the past year; if I wasn't able to tell either Jack or Beringer, then I certainly wouldn't be able to explain it to him.

"Then what is it? Why are you doing this? Why are you acting this way?"

"Because my mother *jumped off a bridge* last year," I said. "Which – apparently – everyone else would rather just forget about."

"No one's forgotten, Enim!"

"Of course they have."

"Who? Who's forgotten?"

"Everyone!" I repeated. "All her friends, all her family – you, Dad –"

"*I've* forgotten?" Karl interrupted angrily. "I have? I'm the one who's here every day, Enim – I'm the one who lives here and stays here! I've hardly forgotten!"

"You're here because you have to be," I said, standing and tossing the pillow to the side. His accusation that the time I spent at Bickerby was some sort of reprieve from the painful memories of what had happened to her was worse than anything else he could have suggested. He didn't know what it was like to lie awake every night going over the events in his mind, thinking that he could have done something differently, wishing that he could have stopped it –

"I'm here because I choose to be!"

"That's not true – you're here because my father makes you!"

"He – I – who told you that?" Karl said, clearly flustered. "Is that what he said?"

Though my father had said little on the subject altogether, I knew that Karl was a replacement for the role my grandmother had left upon dying; he couldn't fool me into thinking that he was there for any other reason than compliance.

Karl straightened and exhaled deeply in an effort to subdue

his exasperation.

"It's not true, Enim," he said. "I'm here because I want to be. Because I ..."

"Don't," I cut in derisively. "Don't say it's because you care. You don't."

"How can you say that? I've been here – dealing with all of this – for months. I've put up with you, I've taken care of –"

"Taking care of? Is that what you call this? Taking care of someone? We hate each other!"

"That's – that's not –"

"That *is* true!"

"No, it's not! I'm doing my best here, Enim –"

"Because my father makes you!" I shouted, my voice hoarse as I did so. "He *makes* you stay here, he *makes* you take care of me –"

"That's not true; I do it willingly –"

"No you don't!" I shouted hoarsely. "You do it because he's angry at you – because you feel guilty!"

He looked struck as I said it, shaking his head in confusion at what he had heard, but I didn't pause to let him speak. The guilt that I had been harboring for months now had reached its limit, and all that I wanted to do was shove it off of myself and onto him before it suffocated me.

"You feel guilty because you could have stopped her!" I said wretchedly. "It's your fault – it's your fault that she jumped!"

Karl cheeks hollowed in a way that I had never seen before and his expression changed to one that I couldn't begin to explain. And it happened so quickly that, had I not been staring right at him, I would not have believed it: he stepped forward, raised his hand, and struck me across the face. I stumbled backwards and onto the floor, more out of surprise than hurt, as my face and eyes burned.

For a long moment neither of us spoke. My chest rose and fell as I sat curled beside the bed, my hand pressed against my face, and his own breathing was ragged where he stood above me.

"Enim, I –" He was at a loss for words. His rage had gone and he stared in shock at what he had done, his expression horrified as he looked down to where I was sprawled on the floor. His jaw quivered as he tried to rectify his mistake. "Enim – I'm sorry."

I slowly turned my head to look up at him.

"No you're not."

I stood and pushed past him before he could think to grab me and hurried down the stairs, pulling my coat and shoes on as quickly as I could, and ran outside. I swerved in and out of streets to ensure that he could not follow me, putting as much distance between us as I could. I imagined him running out the door after me, perhaps calling my name, before slinking back inside to avoid the questioning stares of the neighbors. Only when I was certain that he was not there did I finally slow down and try to find where I wanted to go. Everything looked different in the snow. Time seemed to drag on endlessly as I made my way.

The bridge stretched over the river unassumingly, frozen beneath layers of snow and ice, and looked nearly as forsaken as it was. I approached it cautiously and stepped onto the side walkway. No cars were in sight. I wondered if it had been just as empty a year ago when she had come down to it, or if someone had seen her as they passed on their way home from a holiday party. She had to have looked out of place in her sundress and bare feet.

With the resolve to not think of her dwindling, I clutched at the cold railing with an aching expression and all the feeling from the chill on my skin and tiredness of my feet withdrew to make room for the pain that had set in over my lungs. I shook as I leaned over the edge to stare down to where she had fallen. Chunks of ice floated below. She had hit one on the way down and snapped her neck.

I bit down on my lip and the view of the water blurred behind tears. Despite seeing her huddled in her room in the dark most days and listening to my father tell me that she was sick, I had never really thought that she would do it. I couldn't understand what she had seen waiting for her down in the fragmented water that was more inviting than the life that she had had with me.

And it wasn't enough to regret it all. It wasn't enough to feel badly that I had let her go that night, or to make excuses as to why I hadn't reached out and grabbed her arm to hold her back. I couldn't be happy to blame Karl for whatever his part in the mess of it all was, because Karl wasn't the one who had let her walk out the door. The walk to the bridge, the police at the door, the muffled sound of my father's sobs through the floorboards, the pain wrapping itself around all of our necks and cutting off the connection between our heads and our hearts – they weren't Karl's fault. They were mine. I had done that. I had caused that pain. It was no wonder that my father couldn't look at me or speak to me. I had made the error. I had let her go.

As my fingers burned against the cold metal, I let go of the railing and shoved them into my pockets instead. The fabric was stiff in the freezing temperatures and it took me a moment to realize that there was something there. I removed it to see the medication bottle that I had hidden from Karl. The orange plastic was barely visible in the dark, but the pills rattled inside to break the thick silence all around. And it occurred to me that Beringer was undoubtedly right – that I would feel better if I just took them like he prescribed – but I also knew that I didn't deserve to feel differently or better: I had ruined everything. I had let her go.

And as the memories tried again to push their way to the forefront of my mind, I pressed my head to the bridge and let the frozen metal sear against my skin to keep them from coming. The pain ripped at my flesh and burned against my brain, but my throat was too dry to sob and my jaw was too stiff to scream. When the cold had worked its way into the center of my head and numbed every thought away, I dropped down to my knees and knelt desperately in the remains of snow and rain. My head throbbed with a pain so severe that it threatened to split my skull into two, but it was worth it to keep the images away. For I knew that if I let them come to remind me of what I had done, I wouldn't be able to live with myself for a moment longer.

Ch. 10

When the slush seeped into my clothes and saturated the fabric, I pulled myself from the ground and stumbled back to the main road. Warmth spread over my tongue from how hard I had bitten down on my lip and I dabbed at the blood with my sleeve. My hands were too raw from cold to move. Pulling my coat further around me, I turned and heaved myself up the dark streets. My head was in such a fog that I took a wrong turn and then another, and by the time I made it back to the house the air was a dense black ahead of me. I stumbled up the front steps, weighted with cold and exhaustion.

Karl was in the hallway before I could cross over the threshold. In the dark it was hard to make out his form, but his clothes appeared wrinkled and his face was heavily lined; though several years younger, he looked as old as my father.

"Where have you been?"

"Out."

"Out where?"

"*Outside.*"

He looked over me as though he wasn't certain of who I was. Though his voice was low, there was a definite quiver in it.

"Outside doing what?"

I didn't have the strength to argue with him, nor did I have the mindset to think up a proper lie. I looked away from him and sidled towards the staircase.

"Enim," he said, hurrying around the banister to follow me. "Where did you go? You've been gone for hours – you look half-frozen."

I turned my back on his well-feigned concern and started up the stairs. My cheek still throbbed from where he had struck it.

"Enim," Karl repeated. He caught up to me and took my arm to stop me, but then immediately let go again. He moved his eyes from my face to stare down at the steps as he spoke. "Enim, I – Where did you go? Where have you been for all of this time?"

"It doesn't matter."

"It – it does matter. Something might've happened to you!"

"It didn't."

He looked at me as though he wasn't quite certain that that was true, but couldn't think to dispute it. I pulled away from him and crossed the hallway to my bedroom. As I shut the door, it was with the intention to stay inside for the remainder of the holidays and never speak to him again. When my hand went to turn the lock, however, I found nothing there. I stared at the bare patch of wood with horror. He had taken the lock off my door.

I slowly exited the room and went back to the stairs. He was still poised halfway up the steps, though he had turned to face the wall with his head in his hand.

"I had to, Enim," he said quietly. "You can't stay in there."

I only shook my head; my throat was too dry to speak.

"I had to," he repeated. "You can't do this. I've spoken to your father and Beringer, and they're both concerned as well. You're acting just like her – you're *becoming* her."

I shook my head again, unbelieving of what he had done. Every resolve that I had made to protect myself had been broken, and he was oblivious to it all. I needed that room: I needed the self-inflicted solitude and the silence, I needed the sleepless nights to keep me from dreaming of what I had done, I needed the discomfort in the pit of my stomach that gnawed at my insides as a constant retelling of why I deserved to be empty. I needed a moment of privacy without his lack of understanding about what I was feeling or how I looked, or who or who not I had become.

"You can't ... you can't ..."

"I had to," he said again. "You can't end up like her, Enim. You don't want that."

"You don't know what I want," I said wretchedly.

I turned and moved back into the hallway in a panic. The house had closed in on me further without the comfort of the closed-off room, and I turned in place as I sought where to go.

Coldness crept down from the walls, and with it came the feint sounds of music from the aria that played in repeat just as it had the night she had gone.

And as I clapped my hands over my ears to block it out, I knew that there was no longer a place to go to escape her, but that there was one where I could escape him. I stumbled down the hallway to the opposite end, ignoring the sound of his voice as he called me back in surprise, and my bare feet were cold against the carpet as the walls pressed me from either side. The door to the guestroom was firmly closed in a barrier of bright white, and for a moment my hand was unyielding on the doorknob, but then it twisted to reveal what I had been avoiding at all costs for the past twelve months. I closed the door and locked myself inside before he could think to stop me.

The room looked exactly as I remembered it, though I hadn't been inside of it in years: the walls, ceiling, and furniture were bright white, as were the embroidered bedspread and curtains. Only the hardwood floor was a reminder that the room was a part of the old house: the rest appeared to be another place, frozen in ice and time, sitting under the winter sky. Light from the windows pooled into the room and over the floors as the sun gently rose and, as I cautiously stepped inside, my cold skin was warmed.

The only thing different about the room were the machines that had been set up by the bed. They were too large and unsightly where they sat creating a horrid focal point, and the beeping and whirring noises that they made stung my ears from so close a distance. I stared at the wires that ran from them and up onto the bed, disappearing beneath the covers, and then allowed my eyes to travel up to the person lying on the mattress. Her once-blond hair had faded to something dull and white, and her sea-green eyes were closed behind wrinkled lids. If I hadn't known that it was my mother, I would have never recognized her.

I slowly took a step towards her; my breathing was ragged and cold.

I hadn't seen her since the accident. My father had prevented me from going into the hospital room after it had happened; with the last bit of sentiment that he had ever possessed, he had assured me that I didn't want to remember her that way. When she lived through the night and the next day, however, I had still declined to see her. The image of her in her white dress and light sweater, barefoot and smiling as she spoke softly to me, was so strong in my memory that I couldn't imagine seeing her any differently.

But there she was, no longer hidden behind the closed door in the room at the end of the hallway, her smile gone and mouth agape behind an oxygen mask, her body thinned and breakable beneath the light sheets, covered in wires and tubes that ran to various parts of her body to keep her chest rising and falling and her heart beating despite the fact that she was all but lifeless. The fall had left her brain-dead and paralyzed; she would never be any more than she had been the night she went to the bridge and jumped.

I pressed my hand against my chest as a pain shot through my ribs and had to shut my eyes tightly until it passed. The sound of the beeping had quieted, but only because the music from the aria was rising all around me. It filled my head before I could think to stop it, and though my hands were clamped over my ears, the volume of it didn't lessen.

I pulled myself over to the bed and fell to my knees beside it. My arms trembled as they clutched the edge and my chest ached as though it had been compressed by an unknown weight. The image of her lying there burned against my mind and intertwined with the memories that I had spent so long trying to push away.

Be a good boy, Enim, and don't tell your father on me.

I shook as her voice cut into the music and I swiped at the side of my head to get it away, but my hand only raked through air. She hadn't spoken. She couldn't speak. And I had done that.

I had done it.

The thought came and I pushed it violently away before it

could settle, afraid that if I admitted it to myself that it might slip out into the air to be heard. No one could know what had happened, and no one could know what I had done. The prince's words from *Turandot* rang in fervent tones in my ears along with the music – *my secret is hidden within me* – but the sound of them only added to the crushing pain on my chest.

And if I had known the answer to the riddle – if I had just thought up an ending that had fit – then she would have been appeased. She would have settled down with the answer, and pulled herself from the dark bedroom and out into the rest of the house, content to stay there with us forever instead of set on going to the bridge.

Be a good boy, Enim, and don't tell your father on me.

I could see her clearly standing in the kitchen at our house, her gray sweater pulled loosely over the white dress and her feet bare against the floor. She was smiling as she listened to the song from the opera even though it had been playing in a loop for hours, and her expression was calmer than it had been in so long. And if they knew what I had done, then they wouldn't have been worried about me becoming like her. They would have understood that I deserved to be where I was, alone with the tormenting music and inescapable blame.

Because I had known what she had meant when she told me that she had finally figured out how it was supposed to end, and I had known where she was really going when she kissed my head and told me that she was just running out to the car, and yet I didn't stop her as she went to the door without so much as a jacket or pair of shoes: I only watched her wordlessly as she stepped out into the snow and disappeared into the darkness.

And it would have been so easy to raise my hands and clasp my fingers around her wrists to make her stay, or to follow her out into the streets and pull her home again. And even after letting her go, I could have called my father and told him what she had done, but instead I sat on the steps and stared at the front door, wishing that it was a mistake and that she would come back through it again.

And I couldn't blame my father for not picking up the phone when I called an hour later, because he had trusted me to stay with her while he went to dinner with his colleagues. And I couldn't blame Karl for not getting there quickly enough when I called him next – though I wanted to, and my father undoubtedly did – because I knew that by the time I had dialed his number, she had already jumped. And I wished that I could rip the guilt from my chest and push it onto him so that I didn't have to feel it pressing down on me anymore, but I couldn't when I knew that it wasn't his fault: it was my fault, and mine alone.

I suppressed a sob by clapping my hand over my mouth and shut my eyes to keep the tears from streaming down my face, and I pressed my head into the side of the bed and silently screamed into the mattress. I wished that she would reach over and stroke my head, and soothingly tell me that it was alright and that it hadn't been my fault, but her eyes were closed and her body was still and she wouldn't – she couldn't – ever speak a word to me again.

And when I lifted my head, my chest was burning with a pain more intense than any I had felt there before, and all I needed was for it to go away. It was acid at the base of my throat, scorching the skin inside, and melting away whatever lay beneath the ribs. And the pain wasn't sadness or grief or denial – I knew that now. It was guilt. Pure, unheeded, massacring guilt. It stretched out within me and consumed everything else inside. And I deserved it – I deserved to feel that way – but I didn't want to anymore.

I wriggled my hand into my pocket and took the prescription bottle from it, uncapping it and tipping its contents into my palm before bringing the pills to my mouth. My tongue and throat were so dry that it was near to impossible to swallow them, and I gagged as I choked them down. I no longer cared what they did to me – if they changed me, or distorted me, or ruined me – because nothing could be worse than who I already was.

I placed the bottle back on the bedside table alongside the

metal box that contained all of the wires. It was so orange and out of place in the monochromatic room, like a sunrise over the ocean.

My already full head began to get heavier, though now with emptiness rather than thoughts. It kept lulling onto my shoulder though I tried to keep it upright, and my vision kept fading in and out of black in the white room. I put my hands on the bed and tried to stand but my legs had turned to sand beneath me and I kept sinking further and further down into the floor, into the water, into the ocean that was rising up all around me ...

And my vision flitted over to my mother, lying as motionlessly as ever, and the song from *Turandot* continued in my ears. I squinted my eyes very firmly as I gazed upon her until the image of her changed: she was no longer the broken, emaciated woman in a white gown, but rather the sunlit, shimmering-skinned woman who had laid her head back on gray rocks and light sand, her blond hair fanned out behind her like a halo, and who had looked over at me with blue-green eyes and beckoned me to join her, to watch the water come closer as the tide came in and skimmed our feet ...

And that was how I saw her in that moment, and every moment, and how I wanted to see her forever. I wanted that to be the only image resting on my eyes and warming my hands. I stumbled forward, barely able to keep myself upright for a moment longer, and pulled myself up onto the bed to lie down beside her. I lifted her arm to wrap around my shoulder and imagined that she had done so herself, that she had known that I was there and wanted me to be there with her, and that she, more than anything, forgave me for what I had done.

"I'm just going to the car, Enim."

No, you're not. My jaw wouldn't move to allow me to speak, and the words were lost somewhere within me. I tried to raise my arms to hold her there with me, but she was already at the door and turning to leave.

"I'll just be a minute. You stay right here and wait for me. And be a good boy, Enim, and don't tell your father on me."

And the door opened and icy air blew in to make us colder, and the water from the beach rose to come around us and drown us, and I was stuck somewhere in between the white room and the dark-blue ocean, held in place and not knowing which way to go –

And the light in the room grew very bright above my head – whiter than anything I had ever seen before – and it fell upon me like a bending, never-breaking mirror. It came over me and wrapped around me, reflecting everything I had ever seen and would never see again, and then lifted me from my side and raised me into the sky, up past the old forsaken house and cold winter sky, and over the sparsely strewn clouds and into the nothingness, and I felt my eyes drop down, the lids covering the shining blue, and I finally felt it, the long-forgotten sense in my head – content.

"Enim."

The voice moved into the blankness sometime later, but it was far away and unrecognizable. I tried to shift to hear it more clearly, but my skull was a weight too heavy to move.

"Enim. Enim. Enim."

The mattress had turned to lead beneath me and pressed into my face sharply. My limbs throbbed uncomfortably and the pain in my head was so sharp and relentless that it pushed against my eyes and threatened to disgorge them from their sockets.

"Enim, Enim, wake up. Wake up, Enim, please. Please."

It was so dark and cold that I had lost track of time, and my eyes couldn't open enough to distinguish if it was day or night. I tried to remember what day of the week it was and how many more hours there were until Christmas would come and pass, but holes had filled in my mind and sand poured through them to obscure my thoughts.

"Enim!"

My body jolted without my trying to move, and my head flopped over on my neck and threatened to snap off. Someone was shaking my shoulders. The rough, rapid movements were unsettling my insides. As I opened my mouth to tell him to stop, the contents of my stomach upturned and I heaved forward, retching violently onto him.

"Here. Here."

Karl wiped at my mouth and leaned my head against him to keep it from falling over again. The warmth of his form was offset by the rapid beating of his heart and the hammering in his lungs.

"It's all right. It's all right."

He scooped me up and lifted me from the bed. As he carried me to the door, the figure in white that lay broken beneath the wires became smaller and smaller over his shoulder. He laid me gently on the bed in the room with the floral blue comforter but only put a sheet over me. As it graced my skin, it saturated with sweat.

He murmured something and backed from the room. The sound of beeping grew fainter from down the hall as he closed the door to the guestroom again. Before his footsteps had sounded on the wood to return, though, my eyes drooped shut and I drifted back to sleep.

The sun came through the window sometime later and warmed my skin. Though I had slept, the grogginess hadn't worn off my limbs and the exhaustion remained in my head. I slowly sat up and looked around the room. Books and furniture were overturned and clothes were strewn throughout the room, though I couldn't remember how they had gotten that way. I detached myself from the sheets and stood up shakily: my head was reeling painfully.

There was an empty glass of water beside the bed and a partially eaten bowl of oatmeal. I shifted them to read the time on the clock. My eyes were having trouble focusing, though, and it only blurred in red before me.

My legs felt like pillars of sand beneath me and my footsteps were heavy and clumsy as I made my way to the door. When I reached it, it took several moments for my fingers to grasp the knob and twist it, and another to gain the strength to pull it open. I was aware that my head seemed to have expanded inside of my skull.

In the bathroom I turned on the faucet and stuck my head beneath it to gulp down some water. A stale taste was on my tongue and wouldn't wash away. I wiped at my face with my sleeve and stared into the mirror for a long moment before I recognized myself in the reflection: my eyes and hair had faded against white skin, and the circles beneath bloodshot eyes had deepened. I leaned heavily against the sink to keep myself from falling to the floor as I remembered what I had done. The thought left a tainted feeling in my bones.

Halfway back to my room, the muted sound of voices rose through the floor. My already erratic heartbeat sped up at the thought that Karl had told someone what I had done. I turned towards the stairs but only managed to get down a few steps before fatigue caused me to sit down. I didn't want to imagine what would ensue if my father or Beringer knew what had happened.

"...on such short notice."

I slid down a few more steps to listen better. Through the spaces in the railing I could see two pairs of dress shoes at the kitchen table. Karl's were as spotless as ever, but the other man's were covered in dirty snow from the front walkway.

"Don't get me wrong, Karl – I think that it's good for you to take some time off. I was just concerned when you called … Is everything all right here?"

"It's fine."

"Of course, it's just … in all the time we've worked together, I don't think you've ever taken a sick day. I was worried something might have happened."

"No, everything's fine."

"Of course." The other lawyer leaned back a bit in his seat; I rather thought that he didn't believe the lie. "How's your nephew? Is here?"

"He's … upstairs."

"He's certainly quiet – I wish my teenagers had been like that."

"Well, he's … he has the flu."

"All through Christmas? That's terrible – though, I suppose

the holiday isn't really a celebratory one anymore." He dropped his voice to a graver tone. "Is everything else all right? How's your sister-in-law?"

"Evelyn? She's ..."

Karl's feet tapped the ground anxiously as he sought for a way to respond; his colleague folded his hands in front of him.

"Are you and your brother still fighting about her?"

"Well, he ... he still thinks that it would be best to take her off life-support, but he's agreed to keep her on. So long as ..."

"So long as you're the one dealing with her, not him."

"It's not like that, Sam."

"Yes it is."

When Karl made no response, the man named Sam sighed and continued in a quieter voice.

"Karl, I know your thoughts on this matter, and I wouldn't say anything if I thought that there was nothing wrong, but I think that it's gone on long enough. I know that you want to do the right thing by your brother and his son, but this situation isn't helping anyone."

"I'm not letting her die."

"I'm not saying that – you don't have to. But maybe there's another alternative ... Maybe it's time to put her in another place. They have plenty of facilities close by –"

"No."

"I – all right, all right, Karl. I just thought ... It might be good to step away for a little bit."

There was another pause. Karl's feet had stopped tapping. He now appeared quite numb.

"Do you agree with anything that I'm saying?" Sam asked a moment later. "I think you could use some time to yourself. By yourself."

Karl made an indiscriminate noise but gave no further response.

"You could take some time; maybe visit that place upstate where your parents were from. The nurse could take care of Daniel's wife for the time –"

"No, I can't leave."

"You could. Once your nephew's back in school, I mean. You could certainly take the time off work – I would cover for you –"

"No, I couldn't."

"Why not?"

"Because," Karl said. "It's my fault."

His voice was wrecked with devastation. Sam cleared his throat hesitantly.

"I ... I rather doubt that, Karl," he said after a minute. "These things happen. They're never anyone's fault –"

"No, it was my fault."

"Karl, don't be ridiculous. What happened – everything that happened – was just a tragedy. People make mistakes. There was nothing malicious about it, despite what Daniel would have you believe."

"It's not just Daniel. It's Enim, too."

"What? But he doesn't know about what happened, does he?"

Karl didn't answer; his head was in his hands.

"How would he know?" Sam said. "Did Daniel tell him?"

"I don't know, but ... He outright accused me of killing her."

"But that's preposterous, Karl: you can't believe that. This wasn't your fault. She had a serious mental illness."

"But I should have been there ... I shouldn't have ..."

"You didn't know that she was ill."

"I knew about the depression."

"You didn't know about the rest. No one did – not until long after you had put an end to it."

There was silence. Sam uncrossed his leg and leaned forward.

"She jumped because of a choice that she made herself, not because of you. Not because of the affair."

My hand slipped on the railing and I stumbled. The step below me creaked and it was all that I could do to hold my weight against the banister to keep it from alerting the two men to my presence.

"You know that, Karl, don't you? You know that it wasn't your fault?"

"What does it matter?" Karl replied tonelessly. "Everyone else thinks it was."

The chair screeched against the wood as Karl stood up. Sam eyed him prudently before doing the same.

"Whatever they think, Karl, it doesn't change the fact that what you're doing here is admirable. They're lucky to have you."

"I'm not doing it for them."

Sam sighed heavily.

"That I don't like to hear," he said worryingly. He hesitated on the threshold, torn between speaking and silence. "Don't do this for her, Karl. She won't know any differently – she can't. It's not worth it."

"It is to me."

When the front door opened, a gust of cold air came into the hall that filled the house with a damp, dank feeling and wiped away the warmth that had been struggling to remain. Karl shut it after his colleague's departure and leaned his head against the wood, looking as wretched as I felt.

And it struck me quite bluntly rather than sharply, my head pounding and pulsating as I tried to get the thoughts to filter through, that the reason that Karl had stayed in the house for all those months had not been because my father had threatened him to take up the place of my guardian in my grandmother's absence: it was because he cared for my mother, and her alone.

As he shifted by the door, I quickly scampered up the steps back to my room. I shut the door before remembering that he had taken the lock off: the hole where it had been gaped through the wood like a watchful eye staring in at me. I took a sweater and draped it over the doorknob to cover it. His footsteps creaked on the stairs a moment later.

"Enim, you're ... awake."

He opened the door and looked in at me with a strange mixture of surprise and unease. My heart was still beating too quickly; I wished that I had had more time to compose myself.

"How long was I ...?"

"You were in and out for a few days," he said. "Through Christmas. Do you remember any of it?"

My eyes went to the half-eaten food on the bedside table and the strewn books and clothing around the room, but I neither remembered him feeding me nor how I had managed to make such a mess.

"No."

"Do you remember anything from ... before?"

The conversation was even more strained than usual. I was waiting for the sound of his exasperated sigh, or the hard tone of his voice as he gave way to his irritation, but he seemed to have detached himself from anything resembling emotion. Perhaps he was waiting for me to apologize for the trouble that I had caused him or to explain what I had done; he still didn't know me well enough to realize that I would never do either.

"No."

He took the sweater off of the doorknob, folded it, and returned it to the drawer. The frown on his face made him look a bit too much like my father.

"Is there any more?" he asked.

"Any more what?"

No sooner had I asked than it dawned on me that he had been the one to tear the room apart in search of the medication. I shook my head without mentioning the pills stockpiled beneath the mattress at Bickerby; as Beringer had stopped prescribing it months ago, there was no reason to concern him that there was more.

"Good."

"Did you ... did you tell my father?"

"No."

"Will you?"

"No."

He didn't need to say why. My unwarranted decision would be buried deeply along with the rest of the unsightly events of the holidays. He was not failing to report it to my father out of compassion, but rather to prevent the trouble he would be in for allowing me to do something so reckless. Regardless, I was relieved. If my father ever found out, he would be disappointed with me in the same way that he was with my mother: partially for attempting something so damaging, and partially for failing.

"Things have to change, Enim," Karl said. "*You* have to change. Because I can't do this anymore. I just can't."

"Alright."

"There will be new rules that I expect you to follow. You have to start eating properly and you can't spend all your time in your room. Once you go back to Bickerby, you have to start engaging in some activities. *Normal* activities, not whatever you and Jack get up to."

"Alright."

"And I'll be checking up on you to make sure that you're doing well. I've already made arrangements with Barker. Someone will be checking in on you at meal times to ensure that you're eating properly, and if you and Jack get into any more trouble, he'll be expelled."

I bit the insides of my cheeks to keep from retorting and nodded compliantly. I was certain that my frown matched his exactly, and to anyone staring at us we might have looked quite the same. Yet we were alike only in that we were so different – like looking into a mirror only to realize that the images were conflicting. We were parallel lines moving along separate courses, doomed to run alongside one another without ever meeting.

He left the room and I laid back on my bed in defeat. The weeks leading up to that point had eaten away everything that I had ever been, and I didn't recognize anything below my flesh. Yet as I went over it all in my head, one thought flickered encouragingly with the rest: Christmas was over. Everything would be all right.

Ch. 11

The overwhelming smell of cigarette smoke alerted me to Jack's presence before he had even reached the door of the dorm room, made all the more apparent by the lack of it over the past two weeks, but his impish smile was just the same as always as he leaned against the wall and waited for me to unlock the door, and in a moment the scent grew familiar again.

"Glad to see you and Karl didn't kill each other," he said. "Or did you try?"

"What?" I nearly dropped my keys at the question. He indicated to my bruised cheekbone. "Oh, that – I slipped on the ice."

"Figures. It's those shoes."

I nodded wordlessly for fear that my tone might give away the lie. Luckily, Jack was so preoccupied that he hardly seemed to notice my apprehension at all. He tapped his foot as I shifted my keys in my hands.

"Hurry up, will you?" Jack said. "I want to let the cat out of my bag."

"You want to *what*, Hadler?"

Sanders had come out of his room at Jack's loud voice. He crossed his arms and looked at the two of us as he pondered how we could possibly be up to something so soon after returning to school. Jack rolled his eyes.

"I said I want to let the cat out of the bag," he said.

"You have a *cat* in your bag?" Sanders asked disbelievingly.

"What did you think I said?"

"I thought maybe a bat ... a weapon of some sort ..."

Sanders tried to get a better look at his backpack, but Jack shifted it from his view. As I stared at it, I could see Dictionary squirming a bit inside.

"Relax, Sanders. It's an expression. You know what that is, don't you?"

"Of course I know what an expression is!"

"Right. Good, then – so you know that what I meant was

that I wanted to tell Nim something. You know, 'let the cat out of the bag.'"

He rolled his eyes in a well-feigned ridicule of Sanders' logic. Sanders, however, didn't look convinced.

"I think I ought to check your bag, just to make sure," he said.

"That's definitely not necessary, but thanks anyhow, Sanders."

"I think it is – for the safety of everyone on this floor."

"Safety? What's unsafe about a figure of speech?"

"Nothing – but if you actually have a cat in your bag –"

"Why *would* I have a cat in my bag?"

"Don't ask me, Hadler! I'm not the one who has a sick fascination with dead animals! Who knows what you and Lund are doing inside that room?"

Jack smirked mischievously.

"All sorts of things – but not with dead animals."

As Sanders made a face, I quickly unlocked the door to the dorm room and pulled Jack inside.

"Bye, Sanders."

"Wait a minute – I want to check your bag!"

"You'll have to get a teacher's permission first."

The door swung shut on his face. We waited a few moments until his irritated mumbling and stomping footsteps had receded down the hallway, and then Jack set his bag down and opened it to let Dictionary out. She bolted twice around the room and settled underneath the dresser.

Jack peered at her anxiously.

"Hope she's okay – she's been in there all morning," he said. "I was afraid she'd suffocate."

"Too bad she didn't," I murmured. As he gave me a withering glare, I quickly added, "Just kidding. Your grandmother didn't notice you got a cat?"

"Her eyesight's about as drained and pitiful as her heart, thank God."

"Hear, hear." I sat back on my bed and observed him as he pulled a stack of papers from his bag. "What's all that?"

"Research. Evidence. The works." His eyes lit up maniacally and he ran a hand through his hair feverishly as he began to sort through them. "I've been dying to tell you about the list. You'll never believe –"

He had barely begun to speak when the door reopened and Sanders stepped into the room importantly. My eyes shifted to the dark space beneath his dresser: Dictionary's eyes glowered faintly from the depths.

"Did you really get a warrant to search my bag?" Jack asked, looking up from the mess of papers in front of him.

"Not yet. I'm supposed to tell Lund to go to dinner."

He looked at me pointedly and my jaw clenched.

"Right. Thanks Sanders. I'll go down now," I said.

He fidgeted as though he had expected relaying the command to be a larger role, but then nodded and backed from the room again. When the door shut, Jack turned to look at me.

"What's that all about?"

"Karl. He's ... he wants to make sure I follow his schedule."

"What? He's having you *watched*? Great Christmas present."

"You're telling me."

"I knew he was a control freak, but really – is he going to have someone escort you to classes, too? What happened?"

"Nothing," I said too quickly. "He's worried because of the academic probation. He wants to make sure I stay out of trouble."

"What? Did he finally get tired of writing checks to Barker?"

"I guess so."

Jack continued to complain about Karl as we headed to dinner. I could only catch snippets of what he was saying: the wind had picked up again and was sending a clattering of noises through the dead trees all around. By the time we had ducked into the dining hall, my hands were raw from the intense chill and my teeth were chattering too loudly to hear him at all.

We stepped over to the line and I hastily poured myself a

cup of coffee to warm my hands. No sooner had I cupped it between my frozen fingers, however, than a voice sounded to my left.

"You're going to need more than that, dear."

I glanced up at the owner of the voice with a wary expression. It was one of the kitchen-personnel who generally never spoke to students. Her face was an ugly pout as she looked at me, and the expression was only made more reproachful by how tightly her hair was pulled back to hide beneath a hairnet. I moved the coffee back down from my lips and looked up at her.

"Okay," I said.

I stepped back down the line to retrieve a tray. As I did so, she mirrored my movements behind the counter.

"You'll need to take a main dish and two sides, at least," she told me.

I eyed her guardedly as she dictated the new rules and quickly took the first three choices before anyone could overhear the conversation.

"You weren't kidding," Jack said as I sat down. "Big Brother is watching."

"He certainly is."

"Or, in this case, *little* brother." He took a bite of his food and raised his eyebrows at me. "The kitchen staff looks delighted – this is more power than they've had over students in years."

A faculty member who was circling the hall had come over to stand a few feet from our table. I picked up my fork and looked down at the hastily chosen meal, which appeared to be some sort of casserole. My stomach turned unpleasantly, but I speared a few pieces of pasta and raised the fork to my mouth to nibble it idly: the taste was acrid on my tongue.

"What do you suppose happens if you *don't* eat anything?" Jack asked after a moment. "Karl sends the secret police in after you?"

"More than likely."

"It's just weird that he'd finally start paying attention after all this time," he said. He eyed me carefully. "Did ... I mean, were the holidays alright for you?"

The food in my mouth turned to lead at the question. As I struggled to choke it down, the hand holding my fork began to shake for no reason. I pressed it into the table to still it.

"It was fine."

I feigned indifference as I took another bite, all too aware that Jack was watching me closely. He took another few bites of his dinner and chewed it slowly as he considered something.

"Put it in your milk carton," he said.

"What?"

"The food." He swallowed a mouthful of potato and indicated to my tray. "Quick, before O'Brien comes back. Spoon it into your milk carton – they won't know."

I threw him a grateful look and did as he suggested. The food sank heavily into the white liquid and disappeared from sight.

"This really is awful; it's almost too bad for me to eat," Jack said. He took another bite and gave me an impish smirk. "Almost."

He finished eating and scooped the remains of the dish into a napkin for Dictionary. Upon returning to the dorm room, he locked the door and shoved the desk chair in front of it. When he was certain that Sanders couldn't easily get in, he took out the papers he had hidden about Miss Mercier and began to sort through them. As I moved forward to see what they were, though, he shooed me away.

"Wait – you can't look at it yet. I have to set it up."

He waved me back to my bed and set about laying the papers in their intended order. As I sat down to wait for him to finish, Dictionary began to paw at the scraps of dinner with an offended expression on her face. I felt the slightest bit of fondness for her as she did so: if nothing else, she had some sense.

"Jack," I said after a half-hour had passed and he stepped back again to examine his papers, "I'm sure I'll get the point regardless of the layout ..."

"Shh, I'm thinking."

I rolled my eyes at his back and shook my head. With the amount of time that he had taken, I could have read a chapter of *Jane Eyre* for Doyle's class. Just as I reached for it, though, he stood back and spoke.

"All right – done."

"Finally."

I stood and went to his bed to peer at the papers, which were a combination of maps, newspaper clippings, printouts, and what appeared to be the portraits of several girls.

"What is all this …?"

"Hold on, you can't look at it yet," he said, catching my arm and steering me away again.

"What? I waited all that time for you to lay it out only to not be able to look at it?"

"You'll look at it soon enough," he said. "But you won't understand it until I fill you in on the backstory."

"How long will that take?"

Jack gave me a look and I muttered in agreement. When I had returned to my bed and sat down, he moved to stand in front of me with the same feverish look of excitement on his face that he had whenever he was up to something or introducing one of his wild theories.

"All right, so I spent the last two weeks going over everything," he began, "and I was right."

"About?"

"About this being bigger than what they told us – way bigger."

He came forward to sit on the bed next to me; his expression was one of uninhibited fervor.

"Alright, so Miss Mercier died on October fourteenth," he said. "Now, here's where it gets interesting: she was killed in the middle of the woods, halfway between where she lives and Bickerby."

"There's nothing interesting about that. She was walking home from work."

"But she *wasn't*. The newspapers say that she died on the

190

fourteenth, which was a Friday, but she never made it to class that day. That means that she was killed sometime after midnight. What was she doing walking around after dark, in the woods, and all alone?"

"Taking a walk? Clearing her head?"

"Women don't take walks at night to clear their heads, Nim. They're not men – if something's bothering them they call their friends and talk about it. And they definitely know better than to walk around after dark."

"Well, maybe she didn't. It's a small town, after all, and ..."

"Stop interrupting – there's more to it than that," Jack said. "So she was killed halfway between her house and Bickerby, what does that tell you?"

"That she was walking home," I said. "Really, really late at night."

"But she wasn't," Jack said. "She had already been home – her dinner was on the table, her bag was hanging by the door. Even her shoes were there."

"So ... she was walking back to Bickerby?"

"No – I just said that she was halfway through making dinner when she left the house again. She went out without anything – even her shoes."

"Why would someone run out without their shoes?"

"You just said it: she was *running*."

As I thought of the shoes that we had seen toppled over in her bedroom and how painful it would be to cross the woods with the amount of pine needles on the ground, my teeth began to grind.

"But ..." I began, "what happened between the time school ended and when she got home? I can't imagine she normally ate dinner so late at night."

"No, she had a meeting that ran over," Jack said. "So she got home late and went to make dinner when something happened that drove her back out of the house."

"And do you know what that something was?"

"Not specifically, no. But there was definitely something going on."

He sprung up from the bed and went over to his own. I waited to see if he wanted me to follow or not.

"You know that list of names we found at her house?" he asked. "Well, I looked up all of them. And do you know what I found?"

"No."

"Do you want to guess?"

"Not really."

"Fine. A *pattern*."

I blinked, looking at him with raised eyebrows, and said, "A pattern? What's that mean, they were all part of a quilting circle?"

An image of a group of elderly women swapping fabric crossed my mind, and I was prepared for him to tell me that Miss Mercier was part of a local quilting club that he believed was involved in her murder. I smiled to myself as I realized how much I had missed his conspiracies.

"Of course not, Nim," he said. "A pattern – as in, a bunch of things that all have something in common. The names all belonged to girls in town."

"Unsurprisingly."

"They were all girls, aged fifteen to eighteen – who disappeared."

My expression faltered and I stared at him curiously.

"Disappeared and what?"

"What do you mean, 'and what?' They disappeared *and* they were never seen again."

"But Jack," I said reasonably, "that doesn't make sense. Girls just don't disappear. People would wonder. Their parents would do something –"

"Yeah, that's what I thought, too. Only when I looked all of them up, I found the same story: 'local girl runs away from home, police confident she'll return by Tuesday ...'" He turned to his bed and picked up one of the sheets of paper with a girl's photo printed on it. "Let's see, this one disappeared last March. There's a two-line blurb about her in the weekly, then nothing more is said. This one went in

September – her parents at least sounded worried – this one was in June, this one was –"

"Wait a minute, how many names were on that list?"

Jack scanned the bed and counted them out.

"Eight."

"Eight?" I said outrageously. "Eight girls went missing from the same town, and no one thought there was anything weird going on?"

"No one but Miss Mercier, apparently," he said. "The newspaper labels it as – wait, let me get the quote – 'an epidemic of girls running away from home.' They're putting it down to the explanation that the girls left to chase some unknown and unspoken-of dreams."

"But Jack," I said again as the feeling of unsettlement rose, "it just doesn't make sense. A bunch of girls' disappearances doesn't go unnoticed."

"Why not?"

"Because – somebody can't just disappear: people would notice!"

A slow smile stretched across his face despite the fact that there was nothing amusing about what he was saying.

"That's just it, Nim," he said. *"Somebody* can't disappear. But nobody ... nobodies can disappear."

"What's that mean?"

"Just what I said. Important people can't fall off the face of the earth – numerous people would wonder where they'd gone. Hell, you can't even skip breakfast without Karl sending someone looking for you. But the same doesn't go for the rest of us. There are plenty of people in the world who are as good as nobody – who have little existence and even less importance as far as anyone else is concerned. Who's going to notice if they're not on their couch one afternoon watching their favorite sitcom, or not putting a frozen meal into a microwave? Who really cares?"

I bit my lip; Jack gave me a knowing look.

"Come on, Nim," he said. "You don't get it – it's a foreign concept to you to think that somebody might actually be able to disappear and not be missed. But for a lot of people – and especially a lot of people around here – it's not."

"Yeah, but we're not talking about sixty-something-year-old hermits, here, we're talking about teenagers. Ones who live with their parents and go to school with plenty of people who would miss them."

"That doesn't mean anything. Just because someone is surrounded by people doesn't mean that they'll be missed. Look at me: I could get up and leave right now, and who do you think would care? Barker? Sanders? My lab partner? They wouldn't give me a second thought, and they certainly wouldn't go out looking for me. No one would."

"I would," I said.

"Yeah, but one person's not going to compel a search party. In all the time we've been here – while these disappearances took place – there's only been one search party. And that was for Miss Mercier."

We fell silent. As I thought of the search party that we had watched with interest from the dorm room window, it felt very far away. The holidays had severed a breach between the two semesters impossible to bridge.

"So a bunch of girls go missing and Miss Mercier's the only one who thinks something might have happened to them," I said. "And then she gets killed."

"Yep. Seemingly for no reason, as far as the police are concerned. And then ..."

He trailed off and waved me over to his bed to look at the expanse of papers that he had collected. There were a few maps of the area, several photos, and dozens of newspaper articles. My eyes scanned over the pictures of the missing girls' faces: they smiled up at the camera happily.

I turned to look over the newspaper clippings that he had gathered on Miss Mercier. There was more information on her than all the other girls combined. He had researched and compiled every event from her entire time at Bickerby and set them up in chronological order, even though most of them were undoubtedly not related to her death in any way.

My eyes paused on one of the pictures of the girls who had been separated from the rest of the group and who had a few extra newspaper clippings attached to her.

"That's Sarah Hayes, the one from October."

The girl smiled up at me with a flushed, enthused look on her face. She was holding a ribbon that she had won at a sporting event, and there was an arm around her shoulder that belonged to a proud coach or parent.

"She went missing like the rest of them, only her father refused to believe that she'd run away," Jack said. "Apparently she was really excited about placing in a state track meet and was hoping to get a scholarship. Anyway, he said that she'd gone for a run after school and never returned. He thought that maybe she'd gotten hurt and wanted a search party sent out."

"But?"

"But the police didn't take him very seriously, so he went out looking for her with some of his friends and other fathers in the area. They didn't find her, but a few days later she washed up on the Bickerby shore." He paused and looked at me. "I wouldn't read their statement if I were you. It's pretty detailed."

I felt a knot twisting in my stomach and put the photograph back down.

"But that must have done something," I said. "I mean, they found one of the girls, so why haven't they started looking for the other ones?"

"You didn't let me finish," Jack said, raising his eyebrows. "They confirmed that her death was from a mixture of blunt-force trauma and drowning. They think that she went jogging too close to the cliffs, slipped down the side and fell into the ocean."

"What?"

"Her father's pretty upset. Apparently he warned her all the time not to go jogging on uneven ground, but he was never sure if she listened."

"So he believes that that's what happened?"

"Apparently."

"And what do you think?"

He gave me a dark look.

"I think that she was thrown off of the cliffs. I think all *eight* of them were thrown off, really, only hers was the only body that floated back to shore."

I sat down on the floor next to his bed. My legs tingled on the verge of numbness and my head was buzzing with white noise. I slowly thought over everything he had just told me.

"So eight girls are murdered here on the island," I started slowly, "which means ..."

"That someone around here is murdering them. Exactly."

"And Miss Mercier realized it ...?" I said. "But how? It's not like Bickerby students were going missing. How would she have made a connection to them?"

"I think I have that figured out, too," Jack said, plucking up a highlighted clip that he had printed off. "Remember when I told you that the name Alison Hall sounded familiar, and you said Alan Hall lived in our building a few years ago? They were siblings. He was one of the top students here and was given a scholarship for excellence in French."

"So he said something to her."

"And she never forgot it," Jack finished. "He might've gone off to college, but she stayed here and kept up with the local news. She used to read the local paper every day, you know, to improve her English. She said she wanted to learn the native colloquialisms, learn to speak like a Mainer ... can you imagine?"

He frowned, suddenly looking quite far off, and something forlorn passed behind his eyes.

"What do you think?" I asked.

"I think her accent was perfect."

"No ... what do you think about her finding out about the girls?"

"Right. Well, she obviously started compiling the list of names, and either she tracked down who was behind all of this or vice versa."

"Vice versa?"

"Yeah, it's Latin, Nim, you should know what it means."

"I know what *vice versa* means," I said, rolling my eyes. "But what do you mean by it?"

"Well, if she didn't find out who was behind this, then they certainly found out that she knew," he said. "I bet that the discovery of the body really shook the guy up … it wasn't in his plan, you know? He was probably on edge and worried that she was going to say something now that there was some proof that the girls weren't running away, so he just … did away with her."

I shook my head, the contents of my stomach rumbling unhappily with every passing thought. He watched me as I tried to mull it all over, but I only shook my head in bewilderment for several long moments.

"Jack … are you sure?"

"Sure I'm sure, Nim."

"I know, it's just … isn't this a bit far-fetched?"

But even as I said, it, the papers strewn over his bed confirmed that this wasn't one of his usual crazed theories: the pictures that he had drawn arrows on and scrawled dates in the corner of in his messy handwriting, the maps that showed points of where the girls had been last seen, and the newspaper trimmings and articles he had printed off that were highlighted and marked up with notes were all validating something unexplained.

"But if this was so easy to figure out – I mean, you did it into two weeks – why haven't the police thought of this?" I said. "They can't not care that much."

Jack leaned his head back against the wall.

"It all comes down to the same thing, really," he said. "Who would do this?"

"I don't know. Do you?"

"I can't be certain but … I have an idea."

I tried to imagine who was capable of such a thing: a hermit who lived by himself in the woods, a handful of outcast teenagers, a desk clerk who took too much interest in young girls who visited his store ...

"First, let me say something else," Jack said. "All of these girls disappeared between this time last year and up until the last girl whose body was found, but the months, specifically, were February, March, April, May, June, September, and October. What does that tell you?"

I frowned.

"That the killer takes summers off?"

"*Exactly.*" He gave me an intensely energized look. "Now, who takes summers off?"

We stared at each other for a few moments as he waited for me to confirm his theory.

"Everyone at Bickerby," I said. "But ... how does that relate to what you said before? About how the police don't care?"

"Remember when the police came up here to search for Miss Mercier? How they looked around here for a bit and then just took off? That's what got me thinking. If Barker's in control of everything here at Bickerby and on the island, then who could manage to get something like this past him? Who could make all of these strange disappearances just ... disappear?"

I thought about it for a moment before shrugging my shoulders.

"No one."

"You're not thinking hard enough, Nim. Come on: who could get away with anything they want on this island?"

"I don't know – the police?"

"No. Someone here, at Bickerby, who controls everything ..."

"Not ...?"

Jack raised an eyebrow.

"You got it. *Barker.*"

"Barker?" I said. "But that's ... insane."

"Maybe. But so is all this."

"But why would Barker kill all those girls? And Miss Mercier?"

"Why does anyone kill a bunch of girls, Nim? They're sick

in the head. And Miss Mercier was just something that got in the way, so he did away with her, too."

When I only shook my head in disbelief, he picked up a few papers and brought them over for me to see.

"Take a look at this …"

He laid them out in front of me. I glanced over two maps, several printed newspaper articles, and a photograph before picking up the latter. It was a picture of a building situated on the cliffs overlooking the water that I had never seen before. It was larger and grander than the dilapidated homes in the town, with smooth white paint and a tower in the backhand corner. As I looked at it more closely, I realized that the building had been constructed around a lighthouse.

"That's Barker's house," Jack said.

"His *house*? It looks more like small castle."

"Doesn't it? And yet for its size, it's so well-hidden – over on the opposite side of Bickerby, past the town and forest, and up about a mile's hike through rocks and trees."

I tried to picture Barker in his three-piece suit huffing and puffing his way up to the top of the cliffs, a feat that would exhaust me even on one of my most restless days, and shook my head.

"What's he doing all the way up there?"

"What *isn't* he doing, more likely," Jack said darkly. "A nice private area of the mountain that overlooks the water? Seems like a pretty good place to drag a body and dispose of it. He could just throw the girls out his back door and they'd never be found again."

"But … could he?" I said, imagining Barker trying to heave a body over to the edge of the cliffs. "Those girls were young and active, and Barker's –"

"Six times their size," Jack reminded me. "It doesn't matter if he's not up to beating them in a track meet, Nim. All he has to do is grab them around the waist and there'd be no way they could get away from him."

"So you think he lures them in?"

"I'll tell you what I think: I think he has the perfect house for disposing of bodies. A little too perfect, mind you. I understand that he wants his privacy and all, but you'd think he'd want to live a little closer to the school, wouldn't you? Seems like a waste of gas to drive back and forth every day when he could have had any other house that was closer and walked. Not to mention it would be better on his health."

He took the photo out of my hands and pointed me to the newspaper articles. Scanning through them quickly, I saw that they were all about charities that Barker had donated to across the state.

"What're these?"

"Evidence," Jack said. "Sort of counter-alibis, really. All of these articles are about various events that Barker's been to in the past year – since the girls started going missing. Basically, they mention every date that Barker's left the island for any reason at all."

"And?"

"And none of them are on the dates that the girls disappeared. Like I said, they're more of counter-alibis. Barker does quite a bit of traveling. What are the chances that not one of the times a girl disappeared he was off the island?"

I sorted through the papers and noted the dates.

"And what about this?" I said, indicating to the map.

"That's a chart of the areas where the girls disappeared, or at least where they were last seen. Look at this: two of them never made it home after afterschool activities. This would be the road they would take to get back, and this is the road that anyone leaving Bickerby would take."

I followed both and saw what he meant: the two roads intersected at an isolated point in the middle of the forest. Assuming that the killer met up with the girls there, no one would ever see or hear anything as he dragged them away.

"And the last girl, remember, was going for a run," Jack continued. "Her father said that she normally ran through this part of the woods, though the police think that she was nearer to the cliffs and fell off – like that's the case. And this one …"

As he went through the list of names and pointed out the

spot on the map where they had most likely disappeared, I tuned out his voice and stared at the papers numbly. The entire matter seemed as unlikely as a dream, and yet I hadn't felt so awake or invigorated in a long while. The constant thoughts of my mother that had haunted me so persistently had receded to the back of my mind, and the words that Jack was saying were clearer than the lines from the opera that blared in my ears. Despite the gruesomeness of the crime, I was suddenly at ease searching for a riddle that was answerable rather than one that I would never know.

We stayed up well into the night as he continued to explain what he had found. Finally he piled the papers back into a folder, hid them in the crack behind the desk and the wall, and climbed into bed. I sank beneath the covers of my own bed, as well, but before I could think of everything that he had told me, my eyelids began to flicker shut and I fell asleep without pause for the first time in months.

Ch. 12

Whereas most of the snow in Connecticut had been washed away by rain, the Bickerby campus was still covered in white. On the rare occasion that there was a patch of bare earth, it was always a sheet of ice that no amount of rock salt prevented me from slipping on. After falling to the ground for the fourth time that morning, I swore at myself for not asking Karl for another pair of boat shoes and laid on the ice staring up at the bright white sky. There was no way that I would call and make the request now; I would just wait the winter out.

"Are you all right?"

I was shaken from my thoughts at the voice above me and quickly sat up from my spot in the snow to look at the speaker. Cabail Ibbot was standing above me. His dark, too-large attire was silhouetted against the bright winter sun and I had to squint in order to see him properly.

"I'm fine."

No sooner had the words left my mouth than I slipped again. The ground was not quite padded enough by the thick snow to cushion my fall, and a dull pain began to throb against my skull. Cabail watched me with his magnified eyes.

"You should get some better shoes."

"I know."

I crawled shakily to a less icy patch on the ground and carefully rose to my feet again, thankful that Cabail was the only one there. Anyone else would have turned the situation into something unbearably humiliating.

"You don't have to wait for me, Cabail. You'll be late for Physics."

"So will you," he said. "Besides, Volkov doesn't really notice me."

"Lucky you."

We made our way to class and took seats at the back of the lecture hall. Just as Cabail had predicted, Volkov's withering glare was only aimed at me. Cabail's grades were undoubtedly high enough to warrant some lenience from the reproachful teacher.

He waited until after class to give me a long lecture on how my tardiness disrupted his class, which droned on so long that I ended up being late for Latin. Though Albertson nodded in understanding as I apologized, I had missed the beginning of the translation that he had gone over which would make completing the rest for homework all the more difficult. By the end of the day, though, I had so many other assignments that it would be a wonder if I finished any of them at all.

I tore myself away from the library at a reasonable time to go to dinner, scarfed down the remains of food that didn't fit in my napkin or milk carton, and returned to the library to finish my homework. I was halfway through feigning answers about *Jane Eyre*, realizing that I would never have time to actually read the book, when I remembered my appointment with Beringer. Collecting my belongings, I ran across the campus to the Health Center and hurried inside to his office.

"I'm sorry that I'm late, Dr. Beringer."

"That's quite alright, Enim." He indicated for me to sit down and took a moment to survey me. "How have you been?"

"Fine."

"I was thinking of you over the holidays," he said. "How were they?"

His voice was so gentle that it was a wonder I could hear him at all, and it reverberated as though we were standing at opposite ends of a tunnel. Any possibility of telling him what I had done with the medication he had prescribed was lost somewhere in between, and there was no chance of raising my voice loudly enough to tell him what I had been prepared to do.

"They ... they weren't as bad as I thought they'd be."

"No?"

"No."

"How so?"

"I mean, it passed faster than I thought it would."

"Oh? And why do you think that was?"

I shifted as I thought of a way around the truth, all too aware that Beringer's eyes were watching me carefully as I did so.

"I guess because Karl and I spent most of it arguing."

"I see. And arguing with Karl is ... gratifying?"

"Maybe. He makes it so easy."

Beringer frowned thoughtfully.

"Karl is your father's brother, correct?" When I nodded, he added, "Were you two close before he became your guardian?"

"No."

"Were he and your mother close?"

I eyed him carefully as my heartbeat increased beneath my sweater, wondering if he had somehow gained knowledge of their affair just by looking at me.

"No. Why would you think that?"

"I just wondered, given that he was never close to either of you, why he would spend a year taking care of you and your mother."

"A caregiver takes care of my mother."

"Alright. Why he takes care of you, then."

"My father makes him."

"I'm not sure he can make your uncle do anything," Beringer said quietly.

"You've obviously never met my father."

Beringer smiled.

"No, I have not. In fact, I'm not even sure if we've spoken on the phone since he hired me."

"Lucky you."

He smiled again at my remark and stared across the desk at me with light flickering in his eyes. As the exchange eased into silence, a separate thought occurred to me from the conversation that I had overheard between Karl and his colleague.

"Dr. Beringer, do you ..."

"Yes?"

"Did anyone tell you, or is it written in my file ... what my mother's illness was?"

Beringer's expression didn't change, though only because his features froze to prevent a reaction.

"Why do you ask?"

"Because I want to know."

He gave me another intent look as he tried to decipher my meaning.

"I'm not sure that I understand, Enim: do you not know what your mother suffered from?" He waited for me to shake my head before his frown deepened. "I ... was not aware of that."

"I mean, I thought it was depression," I said. "That's ... that's what my father always referred to it as, only something that Karl said over break made me wonder."

"I see."

"So is there something else?" I persisted. "Was it just depression?"

Beringer continued to frown as he looked at me, and it occurred to me that it was the first time that I had ever seen him uncomfortable. It changed his appearance unfavorably.

"Would you mind if I waited until next week to give you an answer, Enim? Only ... I'm not certain of the protocol on this matter. Medical records are private, and ..."

"But she's my mother," I said. "And it's written in my file, isn't it?"

"It's ..." He glanced down at the file lying between us on the desk. "It is mentioned in here, yes."

"So you're not going to tell me? Is it – is it that bad?"

"I'm only hesitating because I have to check procedure, Enim, not because I don't want to."

My heart had begun to beat very quickly; it rose up to pound in my throat and made it difficult to speak.

"So there is something else," I said. "And everyone else knows but me?"

"Your father and uncle know, and I'm aware of it as well. I apologize – I didn't realize you didn't know."

"But ... but you have to tell me, Dr. Beringer. I have to know."

He let out a breath and relaxed again, folding his hands over the file as he observed me, before continuing on in his calm fashion.

"Why do you have to know? What would it change?"

"Everything."

He looked at me as he waited for a better explanation, but I was afraid that I didn't have one. My father's persistence that I see a psychiatrist to fix whatever odd behaviors I was exhibiting and Karl's concern that I was acting far too much like my mother would take on a new meaning if she had suffered from something besides for depression.

"What are you concerned about, Enim? Can you tell me?"

The music that I would never admit to came to the forefront of my mind, and I shook my head quickly.

"No, I just ... I mean, if it's something bad ..."

"If it's something bad, then what? What will it change?"

"It's just ... it's just, sometimes I wonder why you come here, Dr. Beringer."

"What do you mean by that? We've discussed that before."

"I know, it's just ..."

As I trailed off, I found myself wondering who Beringer was outside of the makeshift office: I tried to imagine him in his proper one off of the island, or amongst friends, or at home heating his dinner up on the stove, but the images wouldn't come. It was unsettling to think that someone I felt so comfortable with was also someone I knew nothing about.

"It just seems like such a waste," I said. "Coming all the way out here if I'm ... when I'm ..."

"If you're what?"

"If I won't get better."

The correlations drawn between me and my mother seemed all too apparent, and yet I had never felt more distant from her. I wanted Beringer to tell me that I wasn't like her, and that I wouldn't become her, and to negate every insinuation that Karl and my father had made over the past few months altogether, but I was afraid that if he did so it would also break the last bit of trust that I had for him or anyone else.

"I don't think that you need to get better, Enim," Beringer said quietly. "I think that you have something that you need to move through. But you, as a person, are whole and intact. I don't think there's anything that needs fixing or changing."

"But what if that's not true? What if I'm like her?"

"Why would you think that you're like her?"

"Because," I said. "I'm just not like anyone else is."

"Just because you're not like others doesn't make you like her."

"No, I know, but ..."

Even without mentioning the haunting music or the sleepless nights, or the way that the water waved up at me from on high, it would be impossible to explain the closeness that I felt with my mother. There was something in the way that she understood things about me that even I didn't understand about myself and the way that she knew what I was feeling before I even expressed it that couldn't be put into words coherent in the office air.

"...but I don't feel like anyone else, and she never did either, so ..."

"I see," Beringer said. He stared at me for a long moment, searching for something unspoken in the reflection of my eyes, before adding, "But I don't know that you're as different as you think, Enim. I see quite a bit of myself in you."

"No you don't."

I spoke without thinking, and didn't quite realize the discourtesy of the statement until it had touched the air.

"Sorry, Dr. Beringer – I didn't mean ... I just meant that you're ... you're ..."

"I'm what?"

"Normal."

He smiled as though I had told him a joke, and his eyes lit up even though he was leaning out of range of the lamp.

"I'm glad that you think so, Enim. But, quite honestly, I find myself wondering if we're not very much the same. And that, more than anything, is why I come here."

Though not convinced, I didn't dispute his claim. When the meeting was over and I had paused at the door to the Health Center to lean my head against the glass, my reflection flickered back at me in an outline in the black. As it wavered beneath the artificial lights, it seemed ridiculous to think that Beringer's statement was true, but it seemed more so to believe that he would lie to me.

I was halfway through the Center Garden when I heard a noise behind me. Wrapping my fingers around the straps of my bag, I slowed to a halt as the sound of footsteps crunching in the snow feet from where I stood became audible.

"Who's there?"

I turned around and addressed the darkness in as firm a voice as I could muster, but it shook from the cold regardless. The branches of a low shrub rustled and the footsteps crunched loudly again.

"I know you're there," I called. "Come out."

The sound stopped and for a moment I thought that it had just been a large animal. Then, however, the shrub rustled again and a large shape appeared from behind it. It was barely visible in the darkness, only a huge outline of something three times my size. I stumbled backwards over the ice as it emerged and slipped on the frozen path and fell to the ground. My shoulder broke my fall painfully.

"Hi, Enim," came a familiarly unwelcome voice.

Clutching my arm, I looked up at the other student and narrowed my eyes.

"Thomas? What are you doing?"

The larger boy shrugged in a noncommittal answer. I swore and stumbled to my feet, slipping again under the weight of my bag, and finally managed to stand. My clothes were covered in snow.

"What are you doing?" I repeated. I tried gingerly to move my shoulder back into its usual position only to find that I was unable to. I clenched my teeth in pain and irritation. "Why were you hiding in the bushes? Were you following me?"

"I was *waiting* for you."

"Most people wait out in the open."

I twisted my neck and managed to wriggle my arm out of the strap of my backpack to ease the pressure on my shoulder, but it still throbbed painfully beneath my cold fingers.

"I wouldn't have had to wait out here if Jack wasn't always around," Thomas said. "It's hard to talk to you when he's there."

"And you thought it would be easier to talk in the middle of the garden in the dark? You can't just go sneaking up on people."

"I wasn't sneaking …"

"You were certainly doing a good job pretending, then."

He mumbled something unintelligible and scraped the ground with his toe. The snow parted to show the frozen soil beneath it.

"I can't hear you, Thomas."

"I just wanted to remind you that there's a math test next week," he said.

"I know. I didn't forget – you'll get the answers, just like last semester."

"Well, I – I was just going to say … if you didn't want to write the answers down, you don't have to."

I looked at him warily.

"What's the catch?"

"There's no catch," he said unconvincingly. "I mean, I was just thinking that you could help me study instead."

The strap was cutting into my hand as I did my best to hold it off of my shoulder. The throbbing pain had spread to both my back and my head, and it was only growing worse in the cold. Looking at Thomas, I had never felt quite so weary.

"Help you study?" I asked.

He nodded.

"Right," I said. "Well, no thanks. Copying the answers down is actually a lot easier."

Turning from him, I made my way out of the garden and crossed to my residence building. I heaved myself up the stairs before struggling to get the door open. Still clutching my shoulder, I finally undid the lock and stumbled over the threshold into the room. Jack looked up from a mountain of newspaper clippings as I did so.

"What happened to you?" he asked, his words barely coherent due to the top of a highlighter that was clutched in his teeth.

"Thomas."

"What?"

"Porter."

"Porker? What'd he do, beat you up? I knew I should have come to look for you when you didn't show up a half-hour ago …"

"He was just lurking outside of Beringer's," I said. "I fell on the ice."

"You should really get better shoes."

"I know."

"What'd he want, anyhow? Permission to sit in on your sessions with Beringer? Get a psychiatrist's advice on why he doesn't have any friends?"

"No, he just wanted to remind me that there's a Calculus test next week."

"Oh, how kind of him."

I sighed and dropped down to my bed, carefully pulling my coat off and freeing my hurt arm, and frowned at the already-forming bruise beneath my shirt and sweater. It certainly wasn't broken, but as it was my dominant arm it would make writing my assignments all the more arduous. I looked at my backpack distastefully and tried to think of a way out of doing the assignments piled within it.

"Wish we could just get rid of him," Jack said, flopping back down on his own bed and staring up at the ceiling. The papers swooshed around him and a few floated to the floor.

"I'm open to ideas."

"Short of throwing his body in the ocean, I've got nothing – sorry."

I paused midway through picking up a textbook to finish my homework. The meeting with Beringer had left me with the same unpleasant suspicion that Karl was keeping something vital from me about my mother, and I no longer felt any obligation to adhere to his strict rules.

"What are you up to?" I asked Jack, dropping the book back down.

"Nothing much ... Just looking things over."

I knew that he had undoubtedly spent hours going through the papers in the hopes of finding something more incriminating that would point directly to Barker. In the week that we had been back, I had not been very helpful in his search given the amount of homework I had received. His excitement from discovering the meaning behind the list of girls' names was quickly petering out as the answer to what it all meant came no closer.

"Well, we'll find something," I said. "Barker can't be that intelligent."

I slid off of my bed and went over to his; Dictionary inched over to make a place for me. As I sat down, Jack glanced over at me.

"What – now?" he asked. "Don't you have homework?"

"Does it matter?"

"What about Karl's hyper-vigilance?"

I picked up one of the newspaper clippings and turned it sideways to decipher a note that Jack had scribbled there.

"Well, he *did* say that I should have more hobbies."

"Somehow I don't think that this was what he meant."

"True. He thinks I spend too much time in my room. You know, with you."

"I bet he does," Jack returned wickedly. "I hope you fill his mind with all sorts of ideas of what goes on in here."

"I do my best to keep him in the dark – I figure he can use his imagination."

Jack cackled.

"So what hobbies does he hope you'll pick up?" he asked, leaning back against the window and fishing in his pocket for a cigarette. He stuck it in his teeth and lit it. The light from the flame warmed his face in an orange glow. "Racket ball?"

"Undoubtedly something masculine."

"You should tell him you want to learn ballroom dancing," Jack said delightedly. "Or figure-skating. See what he says."

"He'd have a fit."

"Definitely." Jack turned his head and exhaled a breath of smoke to his other side. "But really, what does he want you to do? What's Karl's idea of a normal hobby?"

"I don't know. He probably wants me to join the Science Club or something. Make some new friends. Talk about girls."

"We talk about girls," Jack said. "Albeit, *dead* ones – but girls all the same."

"He'll be so pleased to hear that."

"You should call him first thing in the morning and let him know."

"Will do."

He grinned momentarily before looking back at his mess of papers, and his expression fell into a troubled frown.

"I wonder if he'd know how to convict someone without proper evidence," he said. "Since Barker's obviously got himself covered."

"Not that kind of lawyer," I reminded him, but when I caught his expression, added, "There has to be something that would prove Barker did it."

"Like what?"

"I don't know – a record saying when he left the school on the nights that the girls disappeared that showed the times matched up."

"But he could probably just forge them."

"Maybe someone saw him leaving late at night? His secretary?"

"Staff members are almost always out of here by seven, unless there's an activity that runs over or something."

"Right. What about how he killed Miss Mercier? He can't have – you know – cut her up without getting blood on himself. Maybe there's still some on his shoes or something ..."

"I doubt it. He'd probably be smart enough to throw the clothes that he was wearing away."

"Something in his house, then? The towel that he dried his hands on after getting home, or some blood on the shower drain, or ..."

"I doubt there's anything in his house."

"He must be hiding something, even if it's not in his house. I mean, *everyone's* hiding something."

I glanced over at my bed where numerous prescription bottles were hiding beneath the mattress and thought of the knife that Jack kept in the spine of a binder and the cigarettes and whiskey he hid in a carved-out textbook. Barker undoubtedly had something to hide: it was just a matter of finding it.

"Maybe you're right," Jack said after a moment. He scratched the side of his face absently and continued to stare blankly ahead of him as he thought. "Even if he's gotten rid of all the evidence, he might still have trophies."

"Trophies?"

"Yeah, you know – trophies. Killers almost always have trophies."

I gave him a blank look that compelled him to explain.

"Locks of hair, pieces of clothing, newspaper clippings of the victims' deaths – that type of thing."

I scrunched up my nose at the thought of Barker's office wall, with its multitude of honors and framed certificates, and imagined another wall dedicated solely to framed locks of hair. My stomach squirmed.

"And you think Barker just left that sort of thing lying around in his living room?"

"Of course not – what would his wife think?"

"Barker has a wife?"

The idea had never even occurred to me. I couldn't imagine what kind of woman had consented to live the rest of her life with the likes of him.

"Of course he does. Pigs are allowed to get married, after all. But what I'm saying is that he's not about to leave incriminating evidence around his house in the case that she stumbles upon it and starts asking questions or if the police do decide to do their job and search his house."

"Then where do you think he'd keep them?"

"I doubt he'd hide anything here," Jack said. "I mean, there are a couple of locked rooms in the school, but the janitors have to check them regularly. Besides, it wouldn't be safe to leave anything incriminating in one of them – they're too easy to break in to."

"What about his office, then?"

"Isn't that too risky? His secretary's there, and everyone comes and goes from it ..."

"Not really," I argued. "His secretary has her own office, and no one's ever invited into Barker's unless they're in trouble – and I doubt they could snoop around while he's yelling at them."

Jack looked thoughtful for a moment.

"Yeah, but ... do you really think he'd hide something there?"

"Why not? That's where he keeps all his other trophies."

The cigarette hanging from the corner of Jack's mouth drooped and a large piece of ash fell onto his pants. It burned through the fabric before he noticed and brushed it away.

"Right – so he might be hiding something in his office," he said after a moment, "but where does that leave us? If there's one place on this island we can't break into, it's there."

"True." As he slipped into a troubled silence, I added, "But you'll think of something. You always do."

Yet though he stayed up for a large portion of the night, he had not come up with anything by the morning or the next several days. I carved out time from my schedule to help him, but I couldn't bring myself to constantly neglect homework assignments just to go over the same information, and by mid-February I had stopped participating in the late-night assessments of newspaper clippings altogether. While his frustration wore thin, my mind did as well: the lining of my skull seemed to be receding as it was eaten away with memories that could never be put to rest. More than once I found myself reaching beneath the mattress for the medication so that I wouldn't have to spend the night awake and letting the pills ease me into an undisturbed sleep.

As I finished an essay on a Saturday morning, Jack returned from replenishing his supply of cigarettes. He stood in the doorway with a foul expression that I attributed to the horridly cold weather, but the shaking of his hands didn't seem to be from the long walk to town.

"What's wrong? Out of Parliaments?"

There would be no chance of the weekend going well if he was nicotine-deprived on top of his already inclement mood. He gritted his teeth and pulled something from his pocket to show me.

"What's this ...?" I began to say, but the section that he had ripped from the newspaper stopped me midsentence. The article was so brief that it was just a strip of paper in my hand. I read it quickly. *Seventeen-year-old Riley Waverly never returned home after school on Thursday. Her parents say that they had argued earlier that morning. Police speculate that she's gone to a friend's house on the mainland and will return in a few days' time ...*

"You see that? He's done it again."

His voice was deadened with anger. I looked up at him cautiously.

"That's ... that's horrible."

"He's just going to keep doing it, too. He'll just keep at it, killing them off like it's nothing, all because I can't figure this out –"

"It's only been a few weeks, Jack. We can't expect to get him so quickly."

"So when can we expect to get him by? Easter? What's the time limit for catching him? Graduation? Are we just going to stop if it's not figured out by then?"

He reached into his pocket for a cigarette but didn't find one. Swearing, he threw the empty box across the room. It clattered on the floor beside the trashcan along with numerous crumpled papers.

"We'll get him, Jack. We just have to figure something out."

"No, we won't," he said. He sighed and sank down on his

bed, covering his face with his hands in a rare display of blatant discouragement. When he spoke again, his voice quivered lowly. "I thought that it was over with her. I thought that after he'd killed her, he'd stop."

The mention of Miss Mercier chilled the room, and the photos of the missing girls scattered around his bed smiled up at us with eyes as blank and unseeing in the photographs as they were in death. I searched for something reassuring to say but he turned away and went back to rereading his scribbled notes. After watching him for several more minutes, I collected my textbooks and went down to the library to finish my homework.

I selected the most secluded table in the far back of the room and took my textbooks out, but after opening each one and reviewing the assignments, I found that I had no desire to complete any of them. I could barely remember a time when I hadn't felt so tired and drained, or when the distant sound of opera music didn't creep up on me through the silence. And, though I could feel myself sitting there under the harsh artificial lights, I didn't feel like myself; it was as though my mind had been disconnected from my body, and I was just walking about in an empty shell that wore my clothes but failed to reach my senses.

And what bothered me more than anything – more than the sleepless nights, or the thought of the girls being thrown from the cliffs, or the images of them lying face-down in the ocean, or the way that those thoughts drew me back to my mother's botched-suicide and left Jack sitting up in the dorm room agonizing over their deaths – was the knowledge that nine girls had drowned right on the edge of Bickerby's campus, and yet no one could even be troubled to care. I thought of my mother lying hidden in the room at the end of the hallway and of how no one, including her husband and son, ever visited her there. We thought of her only to be tormented by what she had become; if she had not survived the fall, perhaps we wouldn't think of her at all. And perhaps if I had taken the right number of pills and not woken up, no one would ever think of me either. Perhaps we were all just doomed to fade from memory.

"Hi, Enim."

A few of my papers fluttered as Julian Wynne sat down beside me at the table. He smiled as he moved my books to the side to make room for his own.

"Julian."

"I saw you sitting over here alone and thought I'd join you," he said pleasantly before leaning over to look at my paper. "What're you working on? English? I put it off until now, too. Doyle's really asking a lot of questions, isn't he?"

He took a few papers out of his bag and set them on the table. I said nothing.

"I mean, in all honesty, I haven't actually read the assigned chapters of *Jane Eyre* yet, have you?" he asked. "It's a bit dull, isn't it? I mean, how many chapters can she be in that school? I thought something might've happened by page two-hundred, but it's still the same old story. How far have you gotten?"

"Not much further."

"Yeah, I don't think anyone has. I'd blow the whole thing off, but Doyle can have a temper. Kyle got sent to his office the other day and Doyle shouted for an hour, at least, and threatened to suspend him."

My eyes flickered over to him slowly.

"He got sent to his office?"

"Yeah. All because he broke Doug Lawson's wrist trying to get his cheat-sheet back before Mrs. Daley saw. Can you believe that?"

"He got sent to his office," I repeated, paying Julian's story no mind.

"Yeah, don't act so surprised, Enim. I bet Jack's been there a dozen times already this year. All the English teachers send students down to Doyle's."

I could hardly believe that it hadn't occurred to us that we could easily get into Barker's office just by getting into trouble: I just had to think of what it would take to warrant a trip to his office rather than one of the other administrators. The stunt that we had pulled the year before had certainly done it, but Karl had warned me that Barker would expel Jack if he caused any trouble; and if I waited to let my grades slip again, it might be too late for Barker's next victim. I frowned as I tried to think up something else.

"Doug deserved it, anyhow. I mean, Kyle would've gotten into loads of trouble, and it's not like he was the only one cheating. And I don't even think his wrist was really broken, it was more like a sprain or fracture or something, and –"

As he continued to speak, completely oblivious to the fact that I wasn't listening, I reached over and picked up my copy of *Jane Eyre*. Though smaller than my textbooks, it was still thick and heavy.

"—Kyle wouldn't've had to do it anyhow if Doug had just given the paper back, but he insisted on being a prick about it. If you ask me, he just got what was coming to him –"

I stood up, raised the book to eye-level, and then slammed it hard against the side of Julian's face. He was thrown sideways off his chair from the impact and clattered to the floor. As he clutched at his jaw, he looked up at me in bewilderment.

"What the fuck was that for –?"

Before he could get the full sentence out, I raised the book and struck him again. His head snapped sideways and blood spurted from his nose to stain the dark-blue carpet with red. As the students from the next table rose to see what was going on, I hit him a third time even though he was making no effort to fight back, and blood shot up to splatter my sleeves in a pattern of streaks and dots.

"What are you doing? Get off of him!"

Someone grabbed me from behind and pulled me away. Julian had curled up on the ground clutching at his face; his pale fingers were covered in blood, but the expression on his face was worse than whatever injury I had inflicted there. The student holding me pulled me back another few steps and someone rushed forward with a handful of tissues for Julian to press his nose in. A moment later, a teacher hurried through the crowd to inspect the scene.

"What's going on here?"

"Lund just attacked him!"

Someone was helping Julian up from the floor. The hands clutching his face prevented him from speaking.

"You did this?" the teacher said, turning to me. "Why?"

The bloodied book was still hanging in my hand. With as much dissonance as I could muster, I shrugged.

"You don't have an answer?" he said, angrily snatching the book from my grasp and tossing it onto the table. "Maybe you can think of one in my office. Come with me."

He indicated for me to follow him, but I planted my feet firmly in place. Going to his office would do me no good. Aware that everyone's eyes were on me and that my voice would echo around the huge room if I spoke, I unclenched my jaw and did so regardless.

"No, I have an answer." He looked at me expectantly, perhaps waiting for an excuse about how Julian had mocked me or provoked me, or about some trivial tiff that we had had that had caused my behavior, but the expression morphed into one of sickened shock when I continued. "I wanted to hurt him. I enjoyed it."

Ch. 13

My impending punishment would have to wait, as Barker had taken the weekend to go to the mainland with his family. I could hear his outraged tone on the other line as a secretary informed him of the situation in the library. As it would take Karl at least five hours to get to the school, the meeting had been set for that night. Barker gave the task of watching me to his secretary and made it clear that I was not allowed to go anywhere in the meantime.

She appeared to be under the impression that she was not allowed to leave the room, either. After planting herself in front of the computer, she didn't even get up to use the bathroom, and I was growing increasingly anxious that my imprudent plan to search Barker's office would result in nothing more than an expulsion. As the hours dragged by and my window for searching for evidence diminished, I straightened in my seat and cleared my throat.

"Yes?"

"Am I allowed to get something to eat?" I asked politely.

"No; you're not allowed to leave."

"Right. It's just ... I missed lunch, and I'll probably miss dinner ..."

"You should have thought about being hungry before you got into trouble."

"Right. It's just ... I'm not supposed to miss any meals. Did Mr. Barker say anything?"

She looked up from her computer with a wary expression.

"No. Why would he?"

"Because I'm not supposed to miss any meals," I repeated. "I ... have a medical condition."

Her eyes flickered over my thin arms and hollowed, pale features, but she didn't look entirely convinced.

"You're not allowed to leave."

"Right. It's just ... it's written in my file."

When she didn't respond, I inched forward a bit on my chair.

"Do you have anything with you?" I asked, craning my neck as though hoping to see a basket of fruit behind the desk. "A piece of gum or something?"

She sighed and pushed her chair out from the desk to look at me straightly.

"It's written in your file?" she said. I nodded solemnly. "Well, I guess I could get something from the staff lounge ... that wouldn't take too long."

I leaned back in my seat in feigned repose and she left the room, but no sooner had the sound of her clomping heels disappeared down the hallway than I hastened to Barker's private office and went inside to feverishly begin searching for something incriminating.

Despite my initial imagining of framed locks of hair, he had no such trophies on display adjacent to Bickerby's many honors. I went to his desk and opened the drawers, pushing aside monogrammed pencils and pens to leaf through the contents, but shut them again upon finding nothing. Going to the bookshelf, I searched the titles for any sign of a journal or album dedicated to his kills. When nothing there looked remotely out of place, I took out the books one by one and flipped through the pages in search of a similar list of the girls' names that we had found in Miss Mercier's house. I flipped through the last book on the shelf and found nothing. Shoving it back into the line, I ran my hand through my hair anxiously and looked at the clock. Though it would undoubtedly take the secretary longer than ten minutes to walk to the teachers' lounge in her ridiculous heels, I didn't have much time.

I looked around the pristine office once again, running my eyes over the large windows overlooking the sporting fields and the houseplants decorating corners of the room, before settling on the framed honors and certificates on the walls. Thinking again of the prescription bottles beneath my mattress and the knife that Jack hid in the binding of a folder, I crossed to the wall and lifted the frames to look behind them; they only revealed the dull, cracked paint behind them, though.

I looked at the clock again. Another seven minutes had

gone by. My heart began to pound beneath my sweater and I glanced at the door: the secretary's office was still empty. Turning in my spot, I looked around the office again. Apart from the desk and bookshelf, there was only an end table, a drop-leaf table, and a file cabinet. Perhaps he had nothing hidden there after all.

I went to the file cabinet and pulled out the bottom drawer, but it was filled with student files. As I started to shut it again the name *Wynne, Julian* caught my eye and I crouched down to pluck it out, letting my curiosity take over. Apart from learning that he got average grades, though, there was nothing of interest inside. I stuffed the file back and opened the drawer above to look for more familiar names, bypassing *Hadler, John* to look for Cabail Ibbot's instead. It wasn't there.

Before I could think of why, my eyes fell on my own name. I removed the file curiously: it was considerably thicker than Julian's had been. As I flipped through the pages past the yearly grades and exam scores, a few yellow pages slipped out from the rest.

I picked it up carefully to discern what it was. The pages were filled with comments that had been written by various teachers and Barker himself: ... *appears to be reacting to the loss of his mother by engaging in senseless activities ... recent act of torturing animals has more-than-likely stemmed from the strong negative influence of another student ... grades have severely dropped as a result of depression ... deprives himself of food in a desire to disappear ... advised to keep an eye out for warning signs of a psychotic break ...*

My hands turned cold. The comments dated back several semesters. The realization that my father had been having me watched long before that year unsettled me, and my apprehension concerning my mother's unknown illness increased. I laid the papers out on the floor and rifled through -them to find any mention of it, turning the pages with such haste that I creased and ripped half of them, but nothing was there. Apart from the crossed-out name on my contact information, she appeared not to exist.

There was a noise from the outer office and I jumped and

slammed my file closed, but it was only the sound of my bag toppling off the chair, not the return of the secretary. I sighed in relief and turned back to the drawer to replace my file.

And then I saw it. Just a few files down from my name, written in blue ink instead of black and in a slightly different manila folder, was the name *Mercier, Émilie*, which had seemingly been misplaced with the student files rather than the teacher's. Immediately upon opening it I knew that it hadn't been put there accidently: behind the standard academic documents were the familiar-looking newspaper articles regarding her death that Jack had also saved.

As I licked my lips and flipped another page, my breathing hitched. There was an in-depth police report that had been personally composed for Barker. I scanned through the paragraphs underlining where and when Miss Mercier had disappeared and how her body had been found, reading intently to discover what the police had not released to the public, when I turned another page and my stomach heaved.

There, tucked away in her organized file, was a series of photographs. It took me a moment to realize what they were, but then I recognized the forest floor and a piece of fabric, and from there I made out the form of what had once been a person – though it certainly wasn't a person anymore. The body had been hacked with such force that the limbs only clung onto it by threads of flesh, and only the chalk-white of bone gleamed up under the bright lights: the rest was a bloody hue that had oxidized to brown. It seemed impossible that that could be the once-beautiful French teacher.

I sat there for what felt like an eternity. The cold room had turned unexpectedly warm and a thin sheen of sweat covered my skin. I wanted to go to the window and lean against the cool glass, but my legs would no longer function, and when I shut my eyes to block out the photos, the reddish insides of the lids only reminded me of them further.

The distinct sound of clomping from the hallway alerted me to the secretary's return. I staggered from the office and shoved the file-folder into my bag, barely managing to zip it closed and sit back down before she opened the door.

She came in without a word. I glanced at the door to Barker's office: I had left it open just a crack and the breeze from the hallway was gently blowing it open wider. As the secretary came over to me I was certain that she would realize what I had done, but she only handed me a sandwich and returned to her desk. I closed my eyes in relief and slid the sandwich into my pocket. My stomach was far too clenched to consider attempting to eat it.

Barker appeared in the office shortly after five, closely followed by Karl. Despite the confirmation of what he had done to Miss Mercier, I couldn't decide which of them was more frightening. Karl's expression was rigid.

"Mr. Lund, back again, are we?" Barker waved me through to his office and sat down at the ornate desk. He pointed for me to sit down, but didn't bother to offer Karl a chair. "Would you care to explain yourself? I've been told that you attacked a fellow student – in the *library*, of all places. What do you have to say for yourself?"

"Nothing. He'll say nothing."

Karl crossed his arms and I closed my mouth without responding, only then realizing the extent of trouble that I was in. I slid my hands beneath my legs to prevent them from shaking.

"You can hardly tell him not to speak, Karl. A crime has been committed in my school – I would like to hear what the reason is."

"I hardly think that you need to throw around the word 'crime.' I was under the impression that there was a slight dispute between classmates."

"*A slight dispute?* Really, Karl – the other boy needs stitches!"

"I spoke to the nurse at the Health Center. She said that he was fine."

"Perhaps she meant that he was fine considering the fact that he was *beaten in the face with a textbook!* This is ridiculous, Karl! I can't have this type of thing going on in my school!"

"It was a novel: that can hardly be considered a weapon."

"It doesn't change the fact that he struck another student!"

"He was provoked."

"He was – no he wasn't!"

"Enim told me what happened."

Karl lied so easily and convincingly that it was both a wonder he was a lawyer who only ever dealt with taxes, and that he lied so poorly about everything else.

"Then perhaps *he* wouldn't mind telling me what provoked him to attack Mr. Wynne?"

"That hardly matters. And as I said, Enim didn't attack anyone. He and Julian got into a fight – these things happen. Unfortunately for Julian, he lost."

"Unfortunately for Enim, he won," Barker countered. "As I said before, Karl, I can't have this type of thing happening at my school. What am I supposed to tell the boy's parents?"

"Perhaps you could suggest enrolling him in a defense class."

"Karl, that's not – you're missing the point! Enim is unstable! He's dangerous! This is the final straw for him, I'm afraid. He's been in too much trouble: he has to go!"

"He's not going anywhere. He's done nothing wrong."

"He attacked –"

"He didn't *attack* anyone –"

"This is ridiculous. We shouldn't even have to discuss this, Karl: I thought that you would be on the same page as me here."

"I thought we would be as well. Evidently that's not the case."

"You thought I would just let this slide? Now I'm just insulted, Karl. You're abusing the terms of our agreement."

"Contrarily, you're failing to hold up your end. We agreed that Enim would finish the year."

"We agreed that he wouldn't be in any more trouble!"

"You know the reason for this behavior, Charles. You know that this is a result of –"

"Enough! *Enough!* You can't blame this one on what

happened to his mother! You can't even blame it on that friend of his – I was told he acted completely on his own this time –"

"As I said, he was simply defending himself …"

"In no way is bashing a book against another student's face *defense*, Karl – please stop insulting my intelligence!" Barker yelled, slamming his fist upon the desk. "I can't continue to house Enim here – this isn't a mental institution! I can't let unstable, violent young men run loose–"

"Hold on," Karl cut in angrily. "He's not unstable. He got into a fight – one fight in his entire career here. Plenty of boys have been given a pass for doing worse."

"Plenty of *normal* boys have. But Enim – he's – he's –" Barker looked at my blank expression and shook his head several times in a row. "He has problems, Karl! I've tried to ignore it, but I don't think I can anymore. My students and staff need to be protected!"

"Protected from what?" Karl asked, glancing sidelong at my withered appearance.

"From his outbursts –"

"He doesn't have outbursts –"

"He does, Karl! He does! He had one in this very office the last time we tried to have a discussion. He's undoubtedly dangerous –"

"That's just ridiculous," Karl scoffed.

"Is it? I don't have to tell you how many school shootings happen because no one stepped in and got the troubled child help, do I?"

"That's hardly what's going to happen. Enim isn't violent!"

"How do you know that?"

"Because – I'm his uncle, for Christ's sakes!"

"Oh, come now, Karl. You've been his guardian for less than a year. I've had dogs for longer periods that've turned violent unsuspectingly –"

"He's not violent!"

"I know that you don't believe me, Karl. Sometimes it's hard for parents – or guardians – to see that their child needs help."

Karl bit his tongue and smoothed down the front of his dress shirt in an effort to compose himself.

"Enim is normal."

"That's your opinion, Karl, but –"

"I can prove it."

"What?" Barker looked him up and down as though waiting to be presented with a board of evidence. "How?"

"I've asked his psychiatrist to join us." He turned to the door and pulled it open. "Erik, would you mind coming in here?"

My neck cracked as I turned my head in surprise that Karl had willingly called Beringer there, but I dropped my eyes back down as he entered the room. I vaguely wondered if he would backtrack on his statement that we were anything alike and that there was nothing wrong with me: I was certain that he had never caused so much trouble.

Barker stared at the psychiatrist with his mouth agape.

"I – what is this? This was supposed to be between the two of us, Karl ..."

"I thought that Dr. Beringer might be able to shed some light on the situation," Karl said. "Don't worry, he's been filled in already."

"Has he?" Barker gave Beringer a cold look. "And what do you make of young men who are dangerous and unstable, *Doctor* Beringer?"

Beringer gave a polite inclination of his head.

"It's my opinion that Enim is neither dangerous nor unstable."

"Really? You think attacking another student is completely normal?"

"Under these circumstances, yes I do."

"These circumstances?" The headmaster's eyes flickered between the two men warily. "This young man attacked another student – he beat another boy to the ground! That's not normal behavior!"

"Actually, Mr. Barker, violence amongst adolescent males is quite the opposite," Beringer said calmly. "I'm sure that as an educator you've seen your fair share of fights here and there between students."

"I – well, yes – but not like this!"

"Like what?"

"Like – well, with this severity! Dr. Beringer, I can't believe that you're giving this boy a pass. He's your responsibility, you know – if he was to hurt anyone –"

"He hasn't hurt anyone; not profoundly. Nor have I been given any indication that he's going to."

"No indication? You sound as bad as Karl, here! He *beat* a student –"

"It was a minor altercation. Have you even spoken to the other student about this? He might very well admit that he was the one in the wrong in this situation."

"Forget this incident, then!" Barker barked. He looked angrier than I had ever seen him, and I could finally see a glimpse of the man who had murdered all of those girls and Miss Mercier. "What about last year's? What about when he and John Hadler ripped down the Bickerby shield and *burned* an opossum on it in some sick, satanic cult offering?"

His loud voice hummed around the silent room long after he was done shouting. Karl had dropped his gaze, evidently at a loss for how to explain the infamous stunt that Jack and I had pulled, but Beringer cleared his throat thoughtfully.

"Like I said," he began quietly, "many adolescent males experiment in these types of situations. It's a way of expressing control over their surroundings ..."

"That's your excuse?" Barker said disbelievingly. "That boys will be boys? Come now, Beringer – the boy's been sick for a long time – why else does he need a psychiatrist?"

"Erik's reasons for seeing Enim have nothing to do with the situation at hand, nor – should I hope – would they have any bearing on his academic standing," Karl cut in. He gave the headmaster a cold look. "If that was the reason for his expulsion, you would have a lawsuit on your hands, Charles."

Barker's face reddened against the dark-green leather chair.

"This boy tortures animals by burning them alive, attacks a

fellow classmate – and you're suggesting that I'm treating him unfairly?"

When Karl made no response, I took the opportunity to say, "I didn't burn it *alive*."

My voice went through the room like a shock of static. The three adults jumped and looked over at me as though surprised that I was still there.

"I suppose you're going to blame it all on Hadler, then?" Barker said upon finding his voice. "It was his idea, was it, to light the animal on fire? That's fine. He showed you how to do it, did he? Gave you a taste for killing?"

I sucked in my cheeks in a hollowed glare at the thought of Barker's own tastes for murder.

"No," I said. "Neither of us killed it: it was already dead. We just found it lying in the woods and thought we'd ... give it a proper burial."

Barker looked disgusted at the idea. Unlike Karl and Beringer, he had seen the aftermath of the proclaimed burial service that we had given to the opossum. The sight of the scorched, blackened corpse lying in the middle of the ruined Bickerby shield had been something of an unforgettable sight, though I rather thought that what appalled him most was the damage to school property. My face twitched as I looked at him. The silence in the room teemed as it waited to be broken.

"Well," Beringer said at last, "I think that that explains quite a bit. The creature was already dead when Enim and Jack ... cremated it."

I saw Karl's eyebrows rise momentarily at the absurdity of the defense that I was receiving, but he nodded in agreement. Barker looked more appalled than ever.

"Is that what you think, Beringer? That the thing being dead already makes it all right?" He looked at each of us in turn with an expression of disbelief. "Should I have my students partake in these sadistic activities weekly, then, seeing as they're evidently healthy for young men? Should I have them scour the forests for dead squirrels and birds so that they can each have the experience of *flambéing* it until it turns to ashes?"

"I'm not saying that what Enim and Jack did was right. You asked me if Enim was a danger to your students. I'm giving you my opinion and telling you that no, I do not believe he is."

"But is that your professional or personal opinion, Beringer?" Barker asked. "Because it sounds to me as though you're willing to overlook his problems because you're keen to continue receiving a hefty paycheck from his father for treating him."

"That's absurd," Beringer said coldly, and the sheer tone of his voice was enough to make Barker's tongue roll back before he shut his mouth.

Karl was gazing at Beringer peculiarly. His eyes lingered on the psychiatrist's face for a moment too long as though waiting to see something different there, though I couldn't think of what.

"Very well, then," Barker said at last. His displeasure was so unmistakable that I was surprised Karl and Beringer continued to look composed. Yet the thought of being sued for dismissing me unjustly appeared to be too much for him, and he said, "If this was truly a one-time occurrence, I suppose that it's ... only fair Enim gets another chance."

He looked over at me, and in the reflection of his irises I could see Miss Mercier's hewed body and the dead girls floating in the water.

"This meeting is over. I trust that you can find the door."

I stood and stepped from the room with Karl and Beringer close behind me. When we paused in the hallway a moment later, both men opened their mouths to speak, but stopped upon realizing that the other was still there. They shared an unreadable look and then Beringer bowed out of the conversation and retreated down the hall.

Karl crossed his arms.

"Enim –"

"I know," I said. "I know you're angry."

He gave me a discontented look and shook his head.

"No, I'm – I'm disappointed," he said. "I thought that you understood what's at stake here and why you couldn't get into any more trouble."

He waited for me to speak, but I only stared at the floor. He sighed and ran a hand through his hair.

"Alright, then. I should go."

Although we were headed in the same direction, he turned from me and walked to the door alone. I stared silently after him. My bag felt heavier on my back with the French teacher's file within it. I stood for another moment, lost somewhere between thought and reality, and then hurried outside as well. The Welcoming Building had never felt less hospitable.

As I walked back to my residence building, not even the cold air on my face could awaken me. My thoughts were distorted by the tangled images of Julian's bloodied face and Miss Mercier's broken body that had been juxtaposed in my mind. Whenever my feet trampled over something, I jumped back in fear that I had stumbled over another girl's lifeless body, and with every noise beyond the trees I expected to find Barker waiting for me upon realizing what I had stolen from him. I glanced around the dead foliage in the Center Garden fearfully, shaking in the falling snow.

Reaching the residence building at last, I disappeared inside and ran up the stairs to the fourth floor. The halls were oddly silent given the hour. I hastened past Julian's closed door and went to my own. My heart had begun to pound again. Fumbling with the keys in my cold, sore hands, I finally managed to open the door and get inside.

"Nim?" Jack sat up as I entered. "What's going on? What happened?"

"It's fine. I didn't get expelled."

"But what happened?" He slid to the edge of the bed and stared over at me. "Trask came up here shouting about how you'd attacked Wynne, and Collins said he saw the whole thing —"

"I did."

I sank down on my mattress and leaned my chin against my hands tiredly. Any momentary delight that I had felt upon seeing Miss Mercier's file hidden in with the students' had long

LAURA GIEBFRIED

since gone, and the realization that I would have to show Jack
what I had found left a hollow weight in my stomach.

"But what happened? Did he say something? Because I'll
break his –"

"He didn't do anything," I said. "I hit him on purpose. I
wanted to get sent to Barker's."

"But – what?"

"I wanted to get sent there – you know, to look around for
evidence and whatnot."

"You smashed Wynne's face so you could snoop through
Barker's things?" Jack looked as though he didn't know
whether to be outraged or impressed. "Nim, we could've
broken in through the *window* way more easily – I just didn't
want you to get expelled if we were caught."

As I let out a groan, he crossed the room to sit next to me
on my bed.

"So how didn't you get expelled?" he said. "What'd Karl do
this time? Buy Barker a private helicopter?"

"Something like that."

"You don't have to double-up sessions with Beringer or
something, do you? Or join the horticulture club?"

"No, it's ... it's not that."

"Then what's wrong?"

I raised my eyes to look over at him. There was only ever
the occasional hint of carefreeness on his face now, and I was
afraid that showing him the file would erase it altogether. Yet
the only chance of giving him any rest would be to have Barker
held responsible for all he had done. I reached down to my bag
for the file.

"I have to show you something."

"What is it?"

"I found this in Barker's office," I said unsteadily. "And I ...
I think it proves it."

"Proves ...?"

"Proves that it was him." I looked at him carefully. "I ... It's
not good, Jack."

He took it cautiously and turned through the pages, slowing

232

as he reached the report to read through it carefully. When he reached the photographs, his breathing turned ragged though he managed to keep his voice even.

"Barker had this?"

"In his office."

As he lowered his head into his hand, Dictionary sidled onto the bed to sit on his lap. She laid her head upon the horrific photographs to shield them from view and gave a soft, lamenting mew for the woman she had once known. I shut my eyes as I listened to it, suddenly aware of how quiet the world had become.

"What are we going to do?" I said. "Give it to the police?"

"What? No." He shook his head firmly. "No, the police are in Barker's control."

"So who then? Do we bring it to another teacher, or the mainland, or ...?"

"No, Nim – we can't bring it to anyone."

He shut the folder and held it in his hands as though afraid that I might run off with it.

"But ... how are we going to get Barker, then?" I asked.

"By ourselves – our own way."

I looked at him cautiously, unsure of what he was suggesting.

"You mean ...?"

"I mean that we'll take care of him ourselves," Jack repeated, though he didn't give any more details. "Look, Nim – if we bring this to anyone, who would believe us? What would we even say? 'Hi, we've been investigating the murder of one of our teachers, and in the process we realized that our headmaster is a serial killer?' It sounds insane."

"But it's true."

"What good's the truth if no one believes it?"

I stared at the smooth ivory-colored finish on the folder. Jack stood and hid it behind the desk.

"Listen to me, Nim: bringing this to the police wouldn't help anyone. Why do you think Miss Mercier kept her mouth shut? She knew that no one would listen to her, and she was a hell-of-a-lot-of more believable than we'll ever be."

"I know, but ..."

"Look, don't worry about it right now, alright? I'll figure out how we'll take care of Barker."

"That's what I'm afraid of."

He acknowledged my concern with a look but didn't respond, choosing instead to take out his original folder of notes and bringing it over to me.

"There's something else that's been bothering me about all this."

He took out the map with the girls' routes highlighted and laid it flat so I could see it.

"The girls' routes make sense," he said. "But Miss Mercier's has been bothering me. Look at where she's going. Why would she run from her house and into the woods?"

"Because Barker showed up at her house."

"I get that. But why does she run through the woods and *back* towards Bickerby?"

"Well, she had just gotten home, hadn't she? So maybe she was running back to see if anyone else was leaving Bickerby."

"Yeah, but that doesn't make sense. I mean, if someone was chasing you with a knife wouldn't you run to the closest person you could? Why would she run into the woods instead of to one of her neighbors' houses?"

I ran my hand through my hair. Karl was right: it was much too long now. It was all I could do to keep it out of my eyes. I was surprised that he hadn't insisted upon taking me to get it trimmed.

"So she's at home, making dinner or whatever, and Barker shows up to kill her," I said. "She runs out of the house and down at least four streets, past a bunch of people who could have helped her, and into the woods. You're right – it doesn't make sense."

"But she definitely went home. He didn't kill her coming out of Bickerby."

"Maybe it was too dark to see anything so she just ran down the road she knew," I suggested. "She walked here every day, she knew the way by heart. Maybe she couldn't find a way to a neighbor's in the dark."

But even as I said it I knew that it didn't make sense. It must have been easier to fumble her way over to the next house than it was to sprint for miles to get to the school.

"So that's the thing," Jack said. "I just can't figure it out. Why would she turn and run all the way back? It was past midnight – there was no one in their office, no one would have been walking back to their car or towards their house; all of us were asleep. The campus police are never any use – she knew that – and the real police station is right on the way to the woods ..."

"So maybe ... maybe he grabbed her and brought her to the woods. Maybe he thought it would be harder to find the body."

"But if he didn't want anyone to find it, he could have thrown her in the ocean like the rest of the girls. This was a statement. It's almost like – almost like he was warning anyone else who thought to get involved."

"Like who?" I said. "You don't think one of the other teachers knew, too, do you?"

He shrugged.

"I don't know. That's what worries me ... But she didn't have any friends, and she wasn't really close to anyone here, so ..."

"So it doesn't make sense."

It felt as though we were back to where we had started. I rubbed my eyes as I willed myself to think. There had to be something else that we were missing – some point in the story that had been left out. I thought of *Turandot's* uncompleted ending and shook my head. I wasn't sure I could stand to have another unfinished mystery occupying my thoughts.

"Nim?"

I looked up to find Jack staring at me. From so close, I could see the indent from where his nose had been broken several times and the various white scars running along his face.

"I appreciate this, you know," he said. "Everything you've done."

I smiled back at him rather than respond; my voice was lost within me.

"You know, when this is all over, I'll make it up to you," he said. He patted Dictionary on the side as she closed her eyes sleepily. "We'll do something completely uneventful and boring, like go to an opera or something."

The snow falling outside had created a huge barrier on the window pane. It divided the window into a box of half white, half black. I imagined Jack's reaction to *Turandot* and distantly wondered if he would think up a better ending than the one I had.

"No," I said, "when this is all over, we're going to France."

Ch. 14

"Mr. Lund, could have a word with you?"

Albertson's voice alerted me to the end of class when the bell did not. Though I had done my best to clear away any remaining thoughts about Miss Mercier's file, I could not keep my thoughts off of my own file, and found myself repeatedly going over what the unspeakable illness was that everyone feared my mother had passed on to me.

"How are you, Enim?" Albertson said when I approached his desk.

"Fine."

"How's your translation coming along?"

"Good. It's good."

"Is it?" Albertson peered at me as though trying to disintegrate my lie. I smiled slightly to ward off his suspicions. "Well, I'm glad to hear that. I was worried that perhaps you needed more time."

"No, it's going well."

"Good, good. Though, if you needed an extension …"

He left the question hanging. I could almost see it dangling in front of me. Given that I was well behind with the assignment, an extension would have helped me greatly, but I didn't want to admit that I had once again barely started the translation.

"No? Well, all right then, Enim. I won't keep you any longer. But if you do ever need anything, all you need to do is ask."

He smiled kindly at me through his old, wrinkled face; I imagined how it would turn to a frown when I failed to turn in the assignment in a few weeks' time.

I was halfway to the door when a separate thought struck me and I turned back to his desk.

"Actually, Mr. Albertson, I did have a question."

"Of course. Yes – what is it?"

My voice caught in my throat as I opened my mouth. Brushing my hair from my eyes, I cleared my throat.

"I ... well, it's – it's about Miss Mercier."

Whatever Albertson had been expecting, it was certainly not that. He was so taken aback that he had to grasp the desk to keep from toppling over as his knees went weak. Fumbling with the desk chair, he lowered himself into it shakily.

"I – all right," he said as he composed himself. His hands remained clutching the edge of the desk; his knuckles were white against the wood.

"I was just wondering ... well, I guess I just ... I wanted to know if ... if you knew anything about what happened to her."

I put my hands in my pockets so that he couldn't tell that they were shaking. It had been ridiculous to ask him, and yet I was desperate to put an end to the pursuit of what had happened to her.

"I'm not sure what you mean, Enim. It was ... it was just a senseless crime. A tragedy."

"Right. Of course," I said. "It's just ... it's just I wonder what she did to make someone kill her."

The words came out in an accusation that I hadn't intended. Albertson's expression darkened.

"I mean –" I said hastily. "Only, she was out so late ..."

"Émilie did nothing wrong. Teachers don't have a curfew: she was allowed to be out as late as she liked. It was the student who was in the wrong."

"A student?"

I looked at him cautiously as his expression hardened, knowing that I should have ended the conversation minutes before, but his tone was so certain that I couldn't let it go.

He sighed as he realized what he had said.

"I didn't mean to worry you, Enim, but ... the police are quite sure that it was a student who ... who killed Émilie."

"But ... if they're so sure, why haven't they arrested someone?"

Albertson lowered his eyes to the desk and ran his hands over the unpolished wood.

"They will, don't worry. It's just a bit problematic. They found a keychain belonging to a Bickerby student near the –

the body." A strange noise came from his throat. "They only recovered half the set, though, before the snow covered the area, so ..."

"What?"

"But there's no need to worry, Enim. We're sure that this was a one-time occurrence. Miss Mercier was ... she was very special to her students. Her death was undoubtedly the result of an infatuation that turned ... wrong."

My voice was stuck in my throat, but I managed a hasty nod of appreciation before leaving the room.

Wandering from the building, I ran my hand through my hair as I considered how the keys tied into what Jack and I knew. Barker must have planted them to ensure that the blame fell on someone else. And yet, as I thought it over, it struck me that what I had seen of Barker didn't match up with such an elaborate and well-orchestrated plan.

My shoes caught a patch of ice and my feet flew out from under me. Smacking the ground, my shoulder was thrown back into spasm and my head throbbed against the ground. A clattering of voices somewhere behind me laughed and, as soon as I stood back up, a shove to the back pushed me back down.

"What the –?"

I landed face-first into the snow. As I moved to get up, someone's foot stepped on my back to pin me down. I turned my head to spit out a mouthful of snow and saw Julian standing above me with crossed arms. The side of his face was an ugly assortment of colors, and his lip was split and swollen. There were a few more students beside him, including the huge lacrosse player from the residence building, indicating that it was Kyle Trask who was holding me down.

"How are you this morning, Lund?" Trask said, pressing his foot down harder. My ribs rammed against the ground and my lungs compressed with the weight. Trask chuckled in amusement. "Good? Feeling all right?"

I choked against the snow and tried to swat at his leg with one of my arms, but it did little good. A few of the others laughed.

"Taking after Hadler, are you, Lund? Think you can jump us whenever you please?"

Trask wiggled his foot to drive me further into the snow, obscuring my vision in white.

"Let me tell you something, Lund: the only reason Hadler gets away with all the stuff he does is because he's got a good back-fist and knows how to turn into a punch. But you?" He stepped off of me and I shakily raised myself up from the snow. "You've got to learn a lesson."

Before I could splutter out an apology, Trask kicked the back of my head to slam it through the snow and my nose broke against the pavement. Blood ran into my mouth and down my throat, and as I raised my hands to my face, it pooled between my fingers. I quickly tried to hold my head up to stop the flow, but Trask grabbed my shoulder and held me down. My hands shook against the ice and snow.

"Chris, hand me your math book," Trask demanded, holding his hand out for it. "Or whichever's the heaviest."

As he reached for it, I tried to scramble away but was immediately stopped by a foot on my arm. Trask adjusted the textbook in his hands as he calculated how to maneuver it. Grasping it by the bottom corners, he gave me a jeering smile before lifting it up.

I automatically raised my arms to block the impact despite knowing that it was heavy enough to crack my skull. Yet before it could collide with any part of me, the sound of it whooshing towards me stopped abruptly and a familiar voice came through the crisp air.

"You little fuck."

I lowered my arms in time to see Jack wrestling the book from Trask's grip. Ripping it away, he swung it back at Trask and cracked it against his jaw. The other boy went flatly down to the ground. As Julian rushed to his roommate's side, the lacrosse player took a few steps back.

"Get up, Trask, I'm going to show you how to break a nose properly," Jack said angrily. "Get out of the way, Wynne. Your boyfriend's fine."

"Yeah? Yours isn't looking so good," Julian said angrily, nodding in my direction. "And you should stay out of it, Jack. This had nothing to do with you."

"Well, like you said, he is my boyfriend and all – I have to defend his honor."

Trask got to his feet. Rubbing his jaw slowly for a moment, he stepped forward so that he was directly in front of Jack. He was much taller and broader, but it was knowing what he was capable of that made him so menacing.

"You think this is funny, Hadler? That's fine. But Lund's not as good at watching his back as you are – he can expect more than a broken nose next time."

He eyed me threateningly and I didn't doubt his claim for a moment. Jack said nothing.

Trask, Julian, and the others dispersed across the campus. I clutched at my face and staggered to my feet, shoes still slipping on the icy ground, and tried to stop the flow of blood with the sleeve of my jacket. It ran down my face and melted the snow. Jack handed me his scarf to use instead.

"Come on, let's go to the nurse," he said.

I shook my head.

"Come on, Nim, I've had enough broken noses to know when you need to see a nurse."

"No – they'll call Karl," I said through a mouthful of blood.

"Yeah, probably. But consider the alternative: you could end up looking like me."

Taking me by the arm, he pulled me across the campus to the Health Center. Though I did my best to hide my face, more than a few students and teachers caught sight of it as we went.

Despite claiming that I had fallen, the nurse who saw to me immediately dismissed the lie and asked me how hard I had been hit. I only shrugged in response. Once the bleeding had been stopped and the swelling went down, she was able to see that the break wasn't so severe the nose had to be repositioned, but it did require a horrible-looking white bandage that was taped over it to prevent it from further injury.

"Did you do this, Mr. Hadler?" she asked, turning to Jack.

Jack rolled his eyes. He knew the staff at the Health Center quite well; I had taken him there on numerous occasions to have his own injuries taken care of.

"I wouldn't punch someone and then bring them in to get treated," he said indignantly, but the nurse only scowled in response.

When she left the room, I gingerly touched the bandage on my nose and leaned my head back against the wall.

"Karl's going to kill me."

"Nah. Just send him a picture of your face. There's no way he could get upset: you look pathetic."

"Thanks."

"No problem."

Filling his pockets with the contents of the candy jar, he wished me well and continued on to his next class.

I sat in the Health Center for the remainder of the afternoon and pretended to sleep to avoid going to dinner. When I returned to the dorm room that night, I locked the door in case Trask was hoping to get me back sooner rather than later. Barely a minute after I had collapsed on the mattress, though, Sanders unlocked the door and entered.

"Lund? Phone call."

He eyed my face repulsively as I sat up and moved past him to the door. My head lurched forward and my vision was tunneled as I walked down the hallway, and it took me an eternity to get down the stairs to the front desk. Josh Brody openly stared at me as I picked up the phone.

"Hello?"

Karl sighed exasperatedly.

"Enim, I really can't believe this."

"I know."

"I *just* came up there to get you out of trouble for fighting – and already you've been at it again? Was it the same student? What is it with you and this boy?"

I leaned my head against the glass cubicle as it pounded more forcefully.

"No, it ..."

"What's going on with you, Enim? Are you trying to get kicked out of school?"

"No."

"What is this? Just another way to torture me for being here instead of your father? Because acting out won't make him come back."

"I know."

"Do you have anything to say for yourself?"

There was a pause in which I considered telling him the truth about what had happened with Julian and Trask, but the words wouldn't come.

"I need more shoes."

"What?"

"I ... I need more shoes. Mine all got ruined in the snow."

He was silent for so long that I thought he might have abandoned the phone in frustration, but then he said, "Which ones?"

"The boat shoes."

"Nine and a half?"

"Yes."

"All right."

Though he made no sound, I knew that he was shaking his head.

"I'll have them sent by the end of the week."

"Thank you."

"Goodbye, Enim."

When the dial tone sounded, I replaced the phone and returned to the dorm room. Jack had returned and was coaxing Dictionary out from beneath the dresser to feed her a miserable-looking dinner. I gave her a look of sympathy before dropping down on my bed.

"Karl?" he asked, seeing the look on my face. "Did he threaten to come and get you?"

"No, he just wanted to lecture me."

"I have to give him credit: he *has* kept you from being expelled."

"Only because he'd hate to have me home."

"True."

As I leaned my head in my hand, careful to avoid touching my nose, Jack sat back on the floor and looked up at me.

"It'll only hurt for a day or two, tops. And it was worth it – look what you found in Barker's."

"I guess."

"Come on, Nim – forget Wynne."

"It's not so easy when he lives right down the hall from us."

"Wynne won't do anything: he's about as tough as a crayfish. And Trask is just pumped up with testosterone. Wait until rowing season starts up again – he'll get out all that aggression in training."

Though I wouldn't say as much to Jack, I was far more concerned with what Julian was planning than I was about Trask breaking any more of my bones: I had heard enough of the stories that he had dug up about other students and passed along to be apprehensive. I shrugged and picked up my bag to start my assignments.

"How do you have homework?" Jack asked. "You missed all of your classes."

"Not Physics and Latin."

"Too bad Trask couldn't have done you the favor of jumping you after breakfast. We might've been able to do something interesting tonight."

"Yeah ..." I paused midway through opening my book. "Actually, I did find out something interesting in Latin."

"I doubt that."

"No – it has to do with Miss Mercier. I asked Albertson about her after class today."

Jack sat up a bit straighter.

"What?" he said. "What if he says something and it gets back to Barker?"

"I don't think he will; he was pretty averse to talking about it." When he continued to look alarmed, I quickly went on. "Anyway, he said that the police think a student did it."

"Right, but that's nothing new. I mean, we initially thought a student did it, too."

"No, but they have proof – or they think they do. Albertson said they found a pair of keys near her body."

"Think Barker planted them?"

"Sounds like it. Only the room key was missing, so they can't identify who they belong to."

"How coincidental."

"Albertson didn't seem to think so. He said they were just waiting for the snow to melt and then they'd find it."

Jack scoffed and shook his head.

"Good luck with that," he said. "Well, it's another reason it would be stupid of us to try and accuse him: he's obviously covered himself pretty thoroughly."

"Yeah." I ran my hand through my hair uncertainly. "And we're sure it's Barker, right?"

"What? Of course we are."

"Right, I know. It's just ... doesn't the plan seem a bit elaborate to you?"

"What'd you mean?"

"First with killing all those girls without anyone noticing, then killing Miss Mercier and getting away with it by planting evidence ..."

"He's got the police in his hands, Nim. We know that."

"I know, it's just ..." It was difficult to explain where my doubt was coming from. Unlike Jack, I had borne witness to Barker's temper on numerous occasions. If he couldn't control his temper over my transgressions, it was hard to believe that he could keep his composure well enough to ward of suspicions of his crimes. "It's *Barker*. He's not that intelligent, is he?"

"He had the file hidden in his office," Jack said. "That's proof enough."

"I guess."

"Besides, it's not like this has to do with intelligence: it has to do with power. Give the police some credit: they know they're being played."

"True. No one loses their keys so easily."

As Jack took another drag from his cigarette, I opened my book to start my translation. I was too busy wondering how I would ever complete it by the deadline to notice how quiet he had become, and it was only when the room filled with smoke that I realized he had zoned out.

"Jack?"

He had paused in the middle of the room with an odd look on his face: the forgotten cigarette in his hand was skimming the side of his pants, and the ember was burning through the fabric.

"What's wrong?"

He didn't seem to hear me. His clenched hands had gone very pale and the knuckles jutted out sharply. I looked around the room for any sign of what had disturbed him.

"Jack?"

Dictionary crossed the room and circled him. Mewing lowly, she swatted at his leg with a paw. His unfocused eyes slowly scanned over her and found me.

"What's wrong?" I said.

"You're right."

"About?"

"Barker. He's not smart enough to plant evidence."

"So you don't think he did it?"

"No, I do." The cigarette scorched his finger and he quickly shook it away before stomping it into the rug. "But he didn't plant they keys as evidence – a student really did lose them."

"How do you know that?"

His face had paled.

"Because – I was the one who lost them."

"What?" I tossed aside the textbook and sat up on the bed. "When?"

"At the Foreign Language Meeting, when Peters and I got into that fight ..."

"Right, but that was in the school. They didn't just fly out

246

into the woods –"

"I dropped them in her room. I remember thinking that they must have fallen out of my pocket when Peters knocked me down, and ..."

"And what?"

"And Miss Mercier cleaned up the room, and she must have found them and pocketed them ..."

"But why was she carrying them that night? Why didn't she return them to you the next day?"

He averted his eyes and didn't answer.

"Jack," I said as I remembered the events that had taken place that night, "that wasn't the night you walked her home, was it? The night she was killed?"

He didn't respond, nor did he need to. A numbness unlike any other set in over my bones and I stared at him in shock.

"*That* was the night she was murdered? But – did you know?"

"About the keys?"

"No! Did you know that the night she was killed was the same night you walked her home?"

"Yes."

"And you didn't say anything all this time?"

"It's bad, Nim, I know."

"It's *bad*? Jack, it's worse than that – what if someone finds out? What if Peters makes the connection? What if he tells Barker?"

"He won't."

"He might! Do you know what this looks like? You walked her home the night she was killed, and the next day you had bruises all over your face –"

"But it's fine: no one will find out. Barker just wants to sweep the whole thing under the rug –"

"He won't need to if you look guilty!" I said angrily. His passivity was wearing on my nerves, and the throbbing pain in my nose was shooting up into my skull and making it impossible to think. I couldn't believe that he had kept something so important from me for all that time when he knew fully-well what it meant. "What if they think it's you?"

"They won't – I didn't do it!"

"Everyone will think you did it – everyone knows you were in love with her!"

I regretted the words as soon as I said them. Jack's face hardened and his expression turned sour, and when he spoke his low voice was venomous.

"Then everyone's wrong."

He turned from me to get another cigarette and took his time lighting it: his hands were shaking and the flame wouldn't catch.

"Listen, Jack ... I didn't mean that. I just ... I just don't want Barker to use you as a scapegoat, that's all."

He stood at the window staring out into the night, and his reflection was just an outline against the black glass.

"You know why I didn't tell you?" he said. I shook my head even though he couldn't see me. "Because once I realized that it was the same night, I realized something else. I just couldn't figure it out completely until now."

"What's that?"

"She was running back to Bickerby. We never figured out why."

"So?"

"So it didn't make sense. I tried to think of any reason why she would've, but then I started placing the events in my head: I walked her home, and then Barker came after her and killed her. He might've been waiting for her in the woods, but didn't make his move because she wasn't alone. So for a long time I thought that she might've run back through the woods to catch up to me – to see if I could help her."

The guilt was heavy in his voice. It pushed us back from one another as it stretched between us, pressing us up against either wall.

"But that didn't make sense, either," he said, "because if someone came after her, the last thing she would ever do was put someone else in danger. So I thought that maybe you were right and he lured her, or dragged her, out there to avoid anyone hearing ... Until now."

"Jack, I ..."

"No, it finally makes sense. I lost my keys, and she picked them up – but she forgot to give them to me until after I'd left, so she ran back to give them to me."

Though he attempted to detach his tone from his emotions, the thought of what he had done cut into his voice with wretchedness.

"But – but Jack," I said, "that's probably not it, either. She ran out without her shoes – she wouldn't have done that if –"

"*She* would have done that, Nim. *She* would've. She'd have been worried when she realized I didn't have my keys and thought that I wouldn't be able to get back inside my building, so she ran out without her shoes to catch up to me. Only she didn't. She ran into Barker."

"Jack, I didn't mean ..."

"No, don't apologize. It's not your fault. It's mine."

"No, it's Barker's. He killed her, not you –"

"I lured her right to him. If they find that key and trace it to me, I'd deserve it. I helped him do it. I killed her."

"Don't say that," I said quietly. "It's not true."

"Yes it is." He smashed the cigarette into the window, snuffing out the ember in the center of his reflection. "I hope they find it sooner rather than later, too."

"No, you don't," I said angrily. "And they won't find it."

"Sure they will. As soon as the snow melts –"

"They won't find it," I repeated, snatching up my jacket and putting it on. "I'm going to find it first."

"Nim, don't –"

"Are you coming?"

"It's pointless."

"Not to me, it isn't."

He sighed and stared at me with a deadened look in his eyes, shaking his head at the thought of all that had been done. When I didn't yield, he heaved himself from his spot to join me at the door, only halfheartedly consenting to come.

Ch. 15

The campus was frigid at night, and the dark that settled over it only heightened it more. We circled around to find the edge of the woods and the feeble beam of light from Jack's flashlight disappeared into the trees. As we hurried down the path, the light began to peter out.

"Great," Jack muttered from somewhere in front of me when it died. He smacked it against his hand and a meager ray came back again. "Come on – let's hurry."

She had been killed in the large clearing on the route to town, but it was more difficult to find in the darkness. In the cold air, my hands felt like metal weights in my pockets and my feet had frozen stiffly in the ruined loafers. By the time that we reached the area, I was so cold that it hurt to move.

"So, how should we do this?"

"You mean, how should we find a key beneath three feet of snow? I'd suggest a snow-blower, but I'm not sure that's an option."

I couldn't see him through the darkness, but given his contemptuous tone I could guess his expression. As I wrapped my arms around myself, it finally occurred to me that the key would be impossible to find, but I crouched down and began to push through the snow regardless. From my right, the sound of branches snapped and Jack swore to himself. The flashlight had gone out again.

"This is stupid, Nim. We'll never find it."

Despite agreeing with him, I continued to squint through the dark for any sign of the key, but the snow was so deep that it was even difficult to reveal the frozen dirt beneath it. The moonlight barely showed through the trees and the ground was darker than ever. As minutes tore by and I was still digging in the same spot, Jack sighed loudly.

"Nim – come on. This is ridiculous."

"We're already out here – we might as well look."

"We might as well just *announce* it to everyone that I killed her."

I ignored him and continued to push through the snow. It only took a moment before my hands began to throb in pain from the cold. From what I could see of them, the skin was bright red and the fingers were rattling against one another like bones. After an hour went by and I had barely covered any ground, I leaned back on my heels and wiped at my face with my sleeve. When I tried to move my hands I found that they were frozen in place. Jack had slumped down on the raised roots of a tree and had his head in his hands.

"Can you just forget it?" he called through the dark. "You're not going to find anything."

"I might if you'd actually help me."

"This was *your* idea, not mine."

"But it's *your* fault for losing the keys in the first place!"

I angrily swiped my hand through the snow in the direction of his voice. His apathy was disconcerting as was his resolve to take the blame for the matter. I wanted to point out that it had been because of his insistence that we had started the ridiculous endeavor to find Miss Mercier's killer, but my teeth were chattering too greatly to do so.

"I know it's my fault! This is all my fault, so can we just accept it and get out of here?"

"No! We can leave when we find the damn key!"

"It doesn't matter!" Jack shouted. "*It doesn't matter* – alright? No one cares about her, or any of the other girls he killed! She's dead, and finding the key won't help anything!"

"It'll help you stay out of prison!"

"I don't care! What don't you get about that? *I don't care.* I just want this to be over – it was stupid to do this! It was stupid to think we could get Barker – he's going to get away with it and everything else!"

"He won't!"

"He already has! So just forget the keys, Nim! Forget everything!"

It was much too cold for either of us to think rationally, and the pain shooting through my head wasn't helping anything. Everything that had happened that year seemed to press down upon us, forcing us into the frozen ground. Jack was right: no one cared about the dead girls, no one cared about Miss Mercier, and there was no way that we were going to find his keys.

He turned and fled through the trees. I shakily got to my feet, cradling my hands to my chest, and moved to go after him. The failing light from the flashlight disappeared from sight. I wished that I had never agreed to help him look for the killer; perhaps if I hadn't, he would have left it alone and moved on.

I was fumbling through a snow-covered branch when something cracked in the branches behind me. Turning around, I stared into the darkness. It sounded as though someone was walking towards me, but I was certain that Jack had gone the other way. I took a step back as I tried to see anything in the blackness.

"Who's – who's there?" I called.

There was no response, but the footsteps had started up again. They were crunching slowly as they came through the snow towards me. I hastened backwards as my mind reeled between rational and baseless thoughts. *It's your imagination. There's no one there, you're just being stupid …*

A figure stood before me in the darkness, barely visible but for the bright outline ignited by the moonlight. It revealed someone very large who was coming towards me –

I turned and fled from the clearing as fast as I could. Drowned in the darkness, I swiped at trees as their branches flung at me and gashed my skin. My running steps were too noisy to be able to hear if the person was following me, but I didn't dare stop to find out. I couldn't fathom how, but I was sure that Barker had somehow found us in the woods. He must have known that we were onto him. I couldn't breathe in the ice-cold air.

I slammed into a tree and fell back, dazed but unhurt, and only then did I hear the sounds of heavily-following footsteps. There was a pinpoint of light coming from a flashlight better than the one Jack and I had been using. Barker would be able to find me in no time if he scanned the area. Scrambling back to my feet, I tried to get back on the main path so that I wouldn't lose my way but everything around me was black and I had no idea which way to run.

A crunch some yards behind me sent me in the other direction. I covered my face with my arms as I went to keep the icicle-spiked branches out of my face. *You can outrun him,* I told myself. *You just have to get to the school. You just have to make it back to the campus and he'll back off.* But my throat stung as I tried to reassure myself: a similar sentiment must have gone through Miss Mercier's head as she ran from him, as well.

I broke out of the thick trees and leapt down an incline. As I landed, my foot sank down on top of something long and sharp: it shot through the sole of my loafer and up through my foot, pooling the shoe with hot blood and throwing me to the ground. I cried out in pain and grabbed my leg, rolling onto my back in the cold snow, and my nose seemed to break once again as my face contorted in pain. The shadow following me appeared in the distant trees. It halted upon seeing me lying there, relieved that I had stopped running, but my eyes rolled back before I could see more. My leg jerked and I convulsed in pain, sure that it was over, sure that I was about to die –

"Nim? Nim!"

I heard Jack's voice from the opposite side of the trees. He scuffled through branches as he left the path to come towards me, dropping to my side as he tried to see what had caused me to cry out. He let out an odd noise as he looked at my foot. The flashlight that he dropped at my side flickered in and out of the dark.

As he reached to help me, I pushed him away.

"No, Jack –"

"Stop it, Nim – I'm trying to help you –"

"No, Jack – Barker!"

He let go of me and wheeled about. The figure in the trees had paused a distance away from us. My eyesight came and went. Barker and Jack were rigid as they faced one another, unsure of how to proceed with the other's presence. As I clutched my leg in agony, I realized that Barker would kill Jack first given that I was injured, but when I opened my mouth to tell him to run, my voice was strangled from pain.

And then, quite suddenly, Barker turned and ran away. For a moment Jack stood in surprise as though considering running after him, but changed his mind as I let out a moan of pain. Stooping down, he picked up the flashlight to shine at my feet.

"What ... happened?" I asked shakily.

"It ... it looks like you stepped on a broken bottle."

"Yeah?"

"I think the glass went through your foot."

I turned to my side and vomited. I was shaking so violently that Jack had to wrap his arms around me to keep me still. When I had settled a bit, he dragged me up into a half-carrying position.

"Come on, I've got you," he said. "Don't – don't worry. I ... it's not so bad. We'll get you to the Health Center. It's not so bad ..."

He managed to pull me down the path, though not without difficulty. I could feel myself going in and out of consciousness all the while.

"Jack ..." I said when I came to minutes later. "I ... I can't ... can't go to ... Health ... the Health Center."

"Don't worry, I'll get you there."

"No, I ... I can't go. We'll get into trouble."

I had slipped down to the ground and Jack paused to heave me back up.

"Nim, that doesn't matter right now. I lied – your foot's bad."

"I ... just wait," I told him, grabbing his arm to get him to stop. He dragged me to one of the cold stone benches in the Center Garden so that he could catch his breath.

"Don't be stupid, Nim. You have to go – the glass is stuck in your foot."

"No, listen ... We ... can't go. I'll be suspended."

"Stop thinking about all that: you just sliced your foot in half – you have to get it bandaged!"

"No, I … I can't get suspended."

"Nim, don't be –"

"Please, Jack. Let's just … go up to the room."

I tried to stand up on my good foot but my leg was shaking too badly. Jack jumped up to help me.

"Nim, please. It's bad."

I shook my head with as much firmness as I could muster.

"If we go, we'll have to admit we were out after curfew. We'll be reported."

"Forget school – you're going to lose more than that if you don't get that glass out of your foot."

"No, Barker saw me fall. If we go to the Health Center, he'll know it was us in the woods."

"Nim …"

"He'll know it was us, Jack. I don't care about being suspended – I just don't want us to end up dead."

"I … Alright."

I blacked out somewhere in the stairwell and only came to when he heaved me up onto my mattress. When he turned on the lights, my eyes shuddered against the brightness and I thought that I would be sick again. He ripped the covers off of his bed and brought them over to wrap around my shoulders to stop me from shaking.

I shifted my leg to a semi-straight position. Despite my blurred vision, I could see the comforter soaking with blood. As Jack edged around to look at the cut, he sucked his cheeks in.

"Well?" I asked groggily.

"Beer bottle – straight through your shoe."

"Can you pull it out?"

He crossed his arms as he surveyed the injury; his expression had turned sickened. He shook his head.

"I can't. I – I just can't. Sorry."

I pulled myself to a sitting position and twisted my leg up so that my foot was in my lap. My vision swayed again as I stared down at the gruesome injury, and my hands were shaking in such a cold sweat that it took me a moment to pinch the glass between my fingers. Jack turned away. I paused to choke back the urge to vomit again and then, before I could lose my nerve, I jerked the piece of glass back: it caught the skin and ripped the flesh from the bottom of the foot, and for a moment I was left staring down at the horrible hole gushing blood all over my lap, but then my eyes rolled back and I blacked out against the mattress.

The warmth of sunlight hit my face sometime later, and I was partially aware of someone brushing the hair back from my forehead. The touch was familiar on my skin. Through half-closed eyes I reached up to take their arm, but my own were too heavy to lift.

"Mom," I said softly.

I hoped that she would sit by me to softly sing the melody from *Turandot*; it had been so long since I had heard her do so. As she moved away from me again, my head lolled to the side and my fingers scraped the mattress in an attempt to reach her.

"I'm sorry. I'm sorry."

She made no indication that she had heard the apology. Instead the comforters were moved off of me and the window was opened to let some cold air into the room. It was only then that I realized how warm I was. Before I could murmur in thanks, my eyes had flickered closed again.

When I woke up fully, the room had darkened and a harsh chill had come over it. My foot still throbbed beneath a thick wrapping, but the pain had decreased considerably. As I hobbled to the window and pushed it closed, I wondered how Jack had managed to bandage the wound so well.

Outside, the sky was a dull mask of gray and the campus was covered in a fresh covering of snow. As I watched a line of students cross through it to get to class, the sinking fear that had escaped me until that moment began to creep over my skin, and I shivered in the cold air: Barker had seen us.

I heaved myself down the hall to the bathroom and stepped into the shower, leaning against the tile wall to keep the pressure and water off of my foot. The water wasn't quite hot enough to dispel the chill in my bones, and as I raked my fingers through my hair, the dried blood from it and my skin washed down to pool at my feet before swarming down the drain. The images of Miss Mercier's body rose before my eyes. I wondered if that was the fate that awaited me and Jack, or if he would simply throw our bodies into the ocean as he had the local girls'.

I returned to the room and fell back on Jack's bed. Mine was such a mess of covers that it hardly looked more comfortable than the floor. As I laid in silence, Dictionary hopped up to sit beside me. Her soft mewing broke into my muddled thoughts.

"Oh good – you're up."

Jack returned to the room and dumped his bag down. I slowly lifted my head from the mattress to face him.

"How long was I out?"

"A while," he said, coming closer. "How do you feel?"

"Pretty bad."

"Yeah, I figured. I had to keep wrapping it; I stole every roll of toilet paper in the building – Sanders suspects someone's going to teepee the campus."

He sat down beside me and pulled his shoes off.

"Anyhow, it wasn't working so I finally just dragged you down to the nurse. She took care of it properly."

"What?" I gave him an alarmed look and sat up straighter, causing the blood to rush to my head. "Jack, I told you not to!"

"Don't worry about it. I told the nurse I left a bottle lying in the dorm room and you stepped on it, and everyone else thinks you have the flu. I got a few detentions – that's it."

"But Jack, Barker's probably just waiting for someone to go to the Health Center with this type of injury – now he'll know it was us!"

To my surprise, Jack smiled. He seemed to have been suppressing the urge to do so since coming into the room. It wasn't the reaction I had been expecting, and I shook my head while wondering if I was still dazed from the injury.

"Why are you so happy?"

His smile, if possible, grew wider. It stretched his face oddly and made him look like a coyote staring out at me through gleaming eyes from the darkness.

"Barker's had a heart attack," he said.

"What?"

The comment dropped from his mouth and hit the floor so quickly that it seemed to shatter in the quiet room. I shook my head, thinking that I must have heard him incorrectly.

"How? When?"

"A few days ago. They didn't give us details, but ... maybe he was stressed."

His gleaming eyes flashed and the maniacal grin grew. It took me another moment to absorb what he had said.

"Wait – Barker's dead?"

"Unfortunately, no. He was airlifted to a hospital on the mainland and deemed 'in critical condition.'"

"So he *will* be dead."

"That's the hope, Nim."

He leaned back against the wall as I sank back to the mattress, the smile still working on his face as he considered our potential involvement in the matter. Though my initial shock had worn off, my heart was still beating erratically. As I toyed with the bandage over my foot, Dictionary stepped over me to sit by him.

"Strange, isn't it?" he said as he patted her head.

"Not really," I said numbly. "He wasn't exactly healthy."

"Not that. I meant – things worked out. It's strange."

"Guess they did."

It was almost too much to consider. I seemed to have fallen asleep and woken up in another place. With Barker gone, it felt as though something should have lifted from my chest, but I felt both heavier and hollower than ever. The feelings created diametric responses within me, and my insides shifted unpleasantly as they tried to even out.

I blinked and shook my head.

"Did I miss anything else?"

"I have the assignments you missed from the week. Sanders shoved them under the door – he didn't want to catch your supposed illness."

"Great."

"It didn't look too bad, actually. Everyone but Volkov gave you extensions, so if you skip tomorrow you'll have the weekend to finish them."

"What? Isn't tomorrow Wednesday?"

"Try again, Nim. Tomorrow's Friday. You were out for a while."

I shut my eyes and leaned my head back against the wall as the feeling of incongruity grew. Karl would be furious enough when he found out how many classes I had missed, but more so when he found out how far behind I had fallen in my work again.

Jack caught my expression and gave me a nudge.

"Don't worry, Nim. It's not so bad. And think of it this way: Barker's done with. What's a little homework compared with watching our backs for him for the next four months?"

"I guess you're right."

"I usually am," he replied with his characteristic smirk.

Before I could return the expression, though, something else occurred to me.

"Wait, so it's Thursday?" I said, quickly turning to look at the clock.

"Yeah – why?"

"I'm supposed to see Beringer."

"Tell him you're sick. He won't argue when he sees you."

"He's a doctor, Jack. I hardly think he could mistake this for the flu."

"He's a psychiatrist," he countered distastefully, "not a surgeon. He probably hasn't seen blood in years."

But despite his best efforts, I shook my head and stood to get dressed, eying my appearance unhappily: my hair had faded and thinned, the bruises on my face stuck out against pale skin, and the circles beneath my eyes were darker than ever. Though I brushed my hair from my eyes and donned my cleanest sweater and pants, I looked wretched.

"Borrow my shoes," Jack said when I reached for the

ruined loafers. "Yours should be burned. Mine are bigger anyway, so you can fit your foot in them."

As I entered the Health Center, one of the nurses asked if I needed the bandage changed. She peered at me with a sorrowfulness that I couldn't quite place, and I quickly shook my head and ducked down the hallway towards the back of the building. She must have had to call to Karl and tell him about the injury; he would undoubtedly call to reprimand me by the weekend. I was still mulling over what I would tell him when I reached the office door.

"Enim."

Beringer's voice faltered upon seeing me. I stepped into the room and sat down.

"Hi, Dr. Beringer."

He eyed me for a moment before moving to adjust the lamp. The light swam out from behind the shade and filled the room with a deeper glow. As he ran his eyes over me again, his expression turned to a frown.

"What happened?"

"Julian sort of ... paid me back."

"I see."

He stared at me for another long moment. I lowered my eyes to the floor, wishing that the light would die out and hide me from view.

"Well, I was hoping that we could discuss what happened with Julian, actually," he said. "I wanted to get your version of it, since I didn't get a chance to over the weekend."

I shifted in my chair. I was all too aware that he had given me his complete defense without even knowing if I had deserved it, and that I had no way of repaying him.

"Well, I ... I'm not sure that I have a reason for what I did, Dr. Beringer."

"No? Could you have been ... upset about something?"

I stared blankly at the bookshelf off to his side, wishing that I could tell him the truth but knowing that it was impossible.

"I ... I don't really want to talk about it, Dr. Beringer."

"Why's that?"

"There are just ... there are just some things I'd rather you didn't know."

I couldn't meet his eyes. I worried that if I did so, he would be able to peel back the skin stretching over my skull and see into my mind, and that he would become aware of the thoughts that swirled around in my head, and of the guilt that I harbored for the things that I had done, and that he would know about the music I heard late at night when the world was otherwise silent. More than anything, I was frightened that he, of all people, would be the one to see me for who I really was; and I knew that once he was able to, he would no longer make the trips to come see me on the island every week.

"Is that because you feel you can't trust me?"

"No, I trust you, just ..."

"Just what?"

His voice was gentle, but I felt as though I had let him down. After all he had done for me, I couldn't even give him a proper response.

"Have I done something to make you wary of my intentions?"

"No," I said quickly. "No, it's nothing like that. I just ..."

I couldn't explain it to him without letting him know that there was something unsettling hidden beneath the neatly-pressed sweater and collared shirt, so I only shook my head in explanation.

"Is there something I could do to make you more comfortable telling me?" he asked. "I want you to be able to trust me, Enim. I want you to know that you can."

I pressed my hand across the bridge of my nose to hide my eyes. He made it sound so simple, as though the words could easily be erased or taken back again if needed, when in fact they were permanent and unforgettable. And I wanted to tell him the truth, but it burned my insides with such an intensity that I couldn't imagine what it would do out in the open air; I was afraid that it would make him turn on me the way that they had all turned on my mother under the pretense of protecting her.

261

"What are you thinking about, Enim?"

"My mother." I looked across the desk at him carefully. "About what happened to her."

"Her attempted suicide, you mean?"

"No. I was thinking of what happened to her after she got ... sick."

The lamp was facing away from him and his face was cast in shadow, but the light in his eyes still cut through in flecks of gold and brown. He leaned forward with a thoughtful frown.

"What do you mean?"

"She ... My father made her stay in the house. She stopped going out, no one came to see her ... She just sat in her room all the time, listening to the soundtrack from that opera."

"Did he explain why?"

"He said that he was helping her, but he was hiding her. He didn't want anyone to know that there was something wrong with her." I fidgeted in my spot for a moment before continuing. "And that's ... that's what he'd do to me, too. Put me away somewhere until he could fix whatever's wrong with me."

Beringer pressed his hands to his mouth as he considered me, and his brow furrowed further.

"I don't think that that's true, Enim. I don't think he'd do that."

"You don't know my father."

"No. But I do know why your mother was ... restricted to the house during the time leading up to her suicide."

"But you can't tell me."

"Your uncle – and father – both feel that it would best if you didn't know. I spoke to your uncle about it after our last session. He was ... quite adamant."

Karl's coldness towards Beringer during the meeting in Barker's office became clearer, and it occurred to me that he assumed Beringer had incited my inquiry about my mother's illness.

"Why is it so important for you to know?" Beringer asked.

"Because." The knowledge that there was something other

than depression that had crept up upon her and consumed her unsettled me just as the ending to the opera did, and I needed to know the answer. Knowing what had affected her meant knowing what affected me.

"Why?"

"It doesn't matter. You can't tell me anyhow, can you?"

"The circumstances are peculiar. I checked the protocol, and there's nothing that gives me permission to." The throbbing that had left my foot had entered my head instead, and my skull pounded at the words. As I slumped further in my seat, Beringer added, "But there's nothing that says I can't, either."

My eyes flickered up again. Beringer sighed before speaking again.

"She had schizophrenia, Enim."

"What?"

"It's an illness where the individual suffers a break from reality. They often hear voices, and suffer from disordered thoughts ..."

"No, I – I know what it is."

My heart hammered beneath the neatly-ironed sweater and I wondered if Beringer could feel its pounding through the air. As I struggled to twist the words in a way that they would make sense, he leaned forward towards me.

"She had had a break from reality," he said. "She had delusions that there was a mystery of some sort that she needed to solve, and since she repeatedly stopped taking her medication, your father kept her housebound so that she wouldn't go looking for the answer. He was ... trying to protect her."

My limbs had gone numb and still. I didn't believe him.

"But that's ... that's nothing. She just wanted to know the end of the opera – that's it."

"She heard voices, Enim. Voices that promised her the answers to her questions, if only she did what they said."

It didn't seem right. I wished that he had known her, and the way that she would brush my hair from my eyes, or hum the tune of her favorite song, or sit by my side as I played the piano, because the label that they had stuck on her seemed to strip away all of it and leave her in a more barren state than the fall from the bridge had.

"Enim?" Beringer searched my expression cautiously. "Are you alright?"

I wanted to rip the folder from his desk and search through the files until I found the real reason neatly printed within, but clutched the arms of the chair to keep myself still instead. It was clear why he hadn't wanted me to know. And though I wished that he was lying, even if it would mean that everything he had ever said had been a lie, as well, I could finally see someone that I could trust staring back at me.

"Yes. I'm fine."

"Is there something you'd like to discuss? Or something I can do?"

I stared at the wood of the desk for a long time, knowing that it was solid but expecting it to melt away and indicate that this had all been a dream, before answering.

"Could you ... could you walk me back to my residence?"

He stared at me for a moment at the odd request, but then pushed his chair back from the desk and showed me out the building without asking for an explanation. His light footsteps barely crunched in the snow as we walked through the silence. When he bid me goodnight and withdrew into the darkness, I turned and went inside. I had only made it halfway up the stairs when my face finally broke from the subdued expression I had been trying so hard to maintain, and I sank down onto the steps to bury my face in my hands.

Everything that she had been that I had so desperately been holding onto had been shattered. The memories of her were tainted and uglied with the words, and the music that came down on me was harsh and uncoordinated like ringing in my ears. Who she had been was someone different than who I had known, and everything that did and didn't make sense slammed against each other to rebound off of me again and again. And yet worse than anything was the knowledge that the only person who had truly understood me was gone, and the only other person who was drawing close was paid to do so, yet otherwise would not have cared about me at all.

Ch. 16

I hobbled to the mailroom to retrieve the package from Karl between classes the next Wednesday and didn't bother to wait before opening it and taking the boat shoes out. Quickly changing into them, I dumped the ruined loafers into the trash before making my way back out into the cold.

Though I had taken Jack's advice to skip my classes on Friday and work through the weekend, I was still behind on all of my assignments. Even after hurriedly doing my history essay during Physics and spending Latin skimming a few chapters of *Jane Eyre*, I was no closer to finishing anything, and the impending lecture that I knew I would be receiving from both my teachers and Karl had provoked a pounding headache in my skull. Despite knowing that my grades couldn't slip any further without a suspension, none of the assignments seemed to matter.

I made my way back across the campus and paused in the Center Garden to rest my foot. The air was so cold beneath the bright white sky that my bones ached beneath my skin, and the stillness all around was only broken by the slight rustling of trees in the wind. The sky seemed to have dropped lower and the air was tight all around me as though the world was squeezing me in. As I shut my eyes, the familiar sound of music drifted over to me from the ocean. I wondered vaguely if it would ever go away.

"Enim."

I opened my eyes at the voice before immediately narrowing them: Porter was standing a few feet from me with a look of surprise on his face.

"What are you doing here?" he said.

"Sitting."

"No, I meant ... here. In school."

"I still go to school here, Thomas." He was evidently under the impression that I had been expelled after the incident with Julian, perhaps misinterpreting my absence the previous week as further confirmation. "Don't worry: you still have someone to write down answers for you."

He gave a slight scoff. I raised my eyebrows questioningly.

"What?" I said. "You'd rather I didn't?"

"I don't really need you to anymore."

"Really? You replaced me that quickly? Who'd you have to blackmail for that?"

"For your information, no one. A *friend* is helping me study."

"A friend?"

I didn't bother to hide the disbelief in my voice. Porter gave a haughty look and shrugged.

"Yeah. Someone who doesn't want anything out of my friendship."

"*We* were never friends, Porter – and *you're* the only one who wanted anything," I said irritably.

"I'd watch your tone, if I was you," he said lowly. "Remember, I still know about your psychiatrist. You wouldn't want me to ... *mention* it to anyone, would you?"

I bit my tongue without responding. Porter smiled more widely.

"Don't you want to know who it is?" he asked.

"Who who is?"

"My friend."

"Not really, so long as it's not me."

I stood to leave the gardens even though my foot was still throbbing. As I limped down the path, Porter called after me.

"It's Julian Wynne."

I stopped abruptly and turned back to him. Quite suddenly I recognized where I knew the smug look on his face from.

"What?"

"Yeah," Porter said casually. "Turns out we have a lot in common: he said you two used to be friends, too, until he learned what a psycho you are."

"And? What'd you tell him?"

"Oh, this and that. He was interested to know how you get out of trouble so easily, so I told him about your mom. He doesn't really buy it, though – and neither do I."

My heart pounded violently against my ribcage as he spoke; I wished that I had hit anyone other than Julian to get sent to Barker's office.

"So how come you didn't get suspended?"

"For hitting him? I told you, my mother –"

"Not for that. For your foot."

"I can't get into trouble for needing stiches," I said.

"You can when you step on a bottle in the middle of the woods! That's breaking curfew *and* being off of school property – so why weren't you suspended?"

"How'd you know I stepped on a bottle?"

Porter shifted.

"I ... I guessed."

His superior expression flickered with sheepishness, and the heat in my chest turned to cold as I realized that it had not been Barker's large form that we had seen following us in the woods. The flood of relief that came over me dissipated almost immediately to be replaced by sheer irritation.

"That was *you*?" I said. "You're *still* following me? Why?"

"I – well – it hardly matters, Enim. The point is that I know that you and Jack are up to something. What're you two doing in the woods so late at night?"

"None of your business, Porter! Just like everything else in my life, it doesn't concern you!"

"You and Jack are up to something – I heard you two talking: he said something about a murder."

"No, he didn't."

"I heard him –"

"You heard him wrong, then," I snapped. "Maybe you should sneak a bit closer next time you eavesdrop on someone so you can actually hear their conversation correctly."

Porter shook his head to brush off the insult.

"Say whatever you want to, Enim, but I know what I heard. And if you think I won't tell Julian about your psychiatrist, you're wrong."

He turned to leave the gardens. My hands were shaking as I watched him go, and it was only when he reached the walkway that I shouted after him.

"The only reason he's pretending to be your friend is so that he can get back at me!"

"Maybe," Porter replied over his shoulder, "but at least he's pretending."

"Wait, Porter –" I said, hastening after him. "Come on – please. I'll do whatever you want. Just – just name your price."

The hint of a smile slowly stretched across his face and he shook his head.

"Too late, Enim. Turns out that you don't have anything I want anymore." He turned back to look at me for a moment, and his eyes were narrowed as he continued to smirk. "You know, for once, I'm glad I'm not you."

"Porter –"

But he had already gone. I stood alone in the garden for a long moment before turning and hurrying to the residence building. My foot throbbed harder as I stomped up the stairs to the fourth floor and down the hall to my room. When I slammed the door behind me, Dictionary leapt off of Jack's bed to hide beneath the dresser. I scowled and collapsed upon my mattress, no longer caring about missing classes or mealtimes: the threat of being sent to Barker's no longer applied.

When the pain in my foot finally died down, it was replaced with the one from the break in my nose. The throbbing hammered into my skull and shook my thoughts too violently to think, and I was left to stare up at the ceiling in anger that Trask hadn't hit me harder to warrant me taking a few weeks off of school.

"You look happy," Jack said upon returning to the room later that afternoon. He made his way into the room and unwrapped his scarf from his neck. As he tossed it aside, he titled his head to get a better look at me. "What's wrong?"

"Nothing. Just Porter."

"Again? You'd think he'd have a hobby by now – or a friend."

"That's the problem: he does."

LAURA GIEBFRIED

"What? Who?"

"Julian."

"Wynne?" Jack scoffed. "Good. They deserve one another."

I sat up and ran my hand through my hair.

"Not really. Porter's threatening to tell him about Beringer."

"Hasn't he been threatening that all year?"

"Yeah, but now Julian's doing his assignments for him, so he has no reason not to tell him." I flopped back on the bed. "I'm screwed."

"No, you're not," Jack countered. "Why do you think he hasn't told Wynne yet? He knows the only reason Wynne's pretending to be his friend is to get information out of him. Once he spills it, he'll be his old friendless self again."

I chewed the side of my mouth as I considered as much, but I didn't feel any better.

"Listen, Nim – forget Porker. If you're that worried, I can go take care of him right now."

"I don't think threatening him will help any."

"I wasn't planning to threaten him. I was thinking I could break his jaw – that'd prevent him from talking to Wynne."

Though the idea was tempting, I shook my head.

"Alright, well, the offer's always open," he said with a disappointed shrug. "But forget him anyhow, and Wynne, too. If they've got nothing better to do than bait you, then they must be even more bored than we are."

"I guess you're right."

"I usually am," he replied with a familiar smirk. "Besides, we'll be out of here in a few months, anyhow."

"Maybe. Unless I fail all of my classes and can't graduate."

"Don't worry – you'll graduate. If Karl has anything to say about it, at least."

"He'll have something to say about it soon enough. I skipped half my classes today."

"I was wondering where you were at lunch. I figured Big Brother gave you permission to eat in the library, though."

"Nope."

"Well, he might not hear about it now that Barker's gone," Jack said, fishing through his pockets for a cigarette. "Or maybe he's got Porter reporting to him now. That'd be something."

I gave an absentminded nod before his statement jogged something in my memory.

"That reminds me – it was Porter in the woods last week, not Barker."

"What?" Jack halted with the lighter raised to his face; the flame danced across his disconcerted expression. "That was Porter?"

Thomas's admission had only increased my uncertainty of Barker's role in Miss Mercier and the local girls' deaths, but I was hesitant to admit as much to Jack, given that he had finally consented to let the whole thing go. He frowned as he thought it through and took a long drag from the cigarette.

"Well, that's unexpected. Here I was thinking that we'd played a part in causing Barker's heart-attack."

My stomach unknotted in relief.

"If only."

He finished smoking and then we headed down to the dining hall for dinner. As the woman behind the counter piled my plate full of an unknown colorless substance, I took a sip of coffee and stared off across the room. Julian was sitting at a table with his usual group of friends and the addition of Porter. I glowered at their backs before finding Jack and sitting down.

He glanced over his shoulder as my gaze drifted back to Julian.

"Who do you think will kill him first: Trask or Thompson?"

"Thompson. Trask's too busy deciding how to kill me."

Across the room, Trask had caught me staring at him. He made a face and moved his hand across his throat menacingly.

"And you're sure you don't want me to take care of them?" Jack asked. "It'll be a lot easier to get them before they get you, not to mention less painful on your part."

I shook my head.

"Alright, have it your way," he said. "But as soon as we graduate, I'm ripping his face off."

"Not worth it. It'd be an improvement on his looks."

"True. In that case, I'll break both his arms."

"That'd work."

"Might as well do his legs while I'm at it," he continued. "Just to cover all my bases."

When we returned to the room sometime later, I pulled up my bag to get started on the assignments that I had missed. Jack watched me idly from across the room for a moment before hopping up beside me and pulling the book from my hands.

"Nim, you do realize that you're never going to need this in real life, don't you?" he asked, staring blankly at the pages of Latin text.

"Yes. But do you realize that if I don't do my homework, I'll be suspended?"

"You keep saying that, but I'm not sure that it's true. Karl seems to have you pretty covered."

"Only because he hasn't heard how many classes I've missed yet."

Jack gave me a look before decisively tossing the book across the room.

"Jack –"

"Nim, come on: all you ever do is study. Can't we do something fun for once?"

"Like what?"

"I don't know. What'd we use to do?"

"In the dead of winter?" I asked as I thought back to previous years. "Hole up in the room, light things on fire, and plan how to not get caught by the building monitor."

"Was that it?"

"Obviously we had low standards."

"True." He took out his lighter and lit the corner of a piece of notebook paper with it. Giving me wry grin, he added, "I'm not sure our standards are any higher now."

"Good to know some things never change."

"That's the spirit."

We watched the page shrink away until only a blackened piece of ash was clutched between his fingers. He dropped it before it burned his hand and stomped it out against the comforter, leaving a black mark on the fabric. From across the room, Dictionary watched us with a less-than-amused expression.

"Wish the snow would melt – then we could go to the boathouse."

"Don't you remember what happened the last time we went there?" I asked. "We nearly froze to death, and Porter caught us."

"At least it was exciting. I might die of boredom before winter's over."

As he flicked open the lighter to ignite something else, the door opened widely and Sanders stepped inside. Jack hastily dropped the paper he was holding and smothered it, and was only saved from being seen because Sanders had halted upon seeing us huddled on the bed together.

"What are you two doing?"

"I'm not aware that it's any of your business, Sanders," Jack said, his feet still positioned over the charcoaled piece of paper. "But if you *must* know, I was spending a little quality time with Nim, here."

Sanders glanced between us again.

"I can only imagine what that means, Hadler. What are you up to? Smoking? Drinking?"

He looked around the room suspiciously, eyes darting in and out of crevices and around the mess strewn on Jack's side of the floor. Finding nothing out of the ordinary, he moved his gaze back to us.

"Does it look like we're smoking and drinking?" Jack asked.

"It looks like you're up to something."

"We *are* up to something. You just interrupted."

He gave the building monitor a pointed look, but Sanders only stepped further into the room.

"What've you got there?"

"Nothing."

"I hardly think that it's nothing, Hadler. You're always up to something – and I think I should know what it is."

He waved his hand to indicate for Jack to move his feet, but Jack remained in place.

"Sanders, let me ask you something: when you barge in on two guys snuggled up together in their room, what do you *think* they're doing?"

Sanders' eyes moved between us again, but this time his expression muddled with distaste. He dropped his hand and stepped back.

"Jesus," he muttered as he turned away from us. "Well, never mind, then – I don't want to know. I just came up here to tell Lund that he has a phone call downstairs."

He hurried from the room and shut the door behind him without another word. As my face fell at the thought of having to listen to Karl lecture me for the rest of the night, Jack grinned triumphantly.

"That's got to be a record. I don't think I've ever gotten him to leave so quickly."

"Yeah, and only at the expense of Sanders' thinking we were in here snuggling."

He shrugged indifferently and hopped off the bed to put on his shoes.

"Come on, I'll walk down with you."

"Why? Just to further the rumors that we're in here cuddling?"

"No, so Trask doesn't jump you in the stairwell. If you die, things will really be dull around here."

"Thanks."

"It's not like everyone doesn't *already* believe those rumors, anyhow," he said as we started from the room. "You know, seeing as we're the only two students who don't play a sport, we're attached at the hip, and we spend loads of time in our room ..."

"What?" I said, turning to see if he was joking. He only raised his eyebrows in disbelief at my ignorance. "I can't wait to tell Karl. Maybe it'll distract him from lecturing me."

"It might. Of course, if he doesn't have his suspicions by now then I'll be surprised: you're well-dressed, absurdly-neat, you do my laundry more often than not, your hair smells like cranberries –"

"My hair doesn't smell like cranberries. Cranberries don't even have a smell!"

"Is that the only defense for your masculinity that you have?"

I shrugged. Jack cackled.

"I can't help it that I'm neat, anyway," I said as we made our way downstairs. "It runs in the family. My grandfather had it, Karl has it, and I have it. It's a genetic predisposition."

"A genetic defect, more like."

As we reached the first floor where the office was and the building secretary caught sight of us, my amusement dissolved: I hadn't thought up anything to say to Karl to prevent him from lecturing me for hours, and I hated the idea of having Brody overhear another uncomfortable conversation between us. Before I could manage an excuse not to take the call, though, Brody had picked up the phone and said, "Here he is, Mr. Lund."

I took the phone and put it to my ear reluctantly. Jack mimed hanging himself across from me.

"Listen, Karl," I began, "I'm sorry about the flu thing. I really couldn't help it, and –"

"Enim …"

"—and I haven't really fallen behind on my work, because I got extensions for most of it, so there's really no need to be concerned –"

"Enim …"

"And about the broken nose, that wasn't a fight, I swear. I just slipped –"

"Enim, just – just wait. I'm not calling about anything like that."

I pressed the phone closer to my ear. Karl's voice was very quiet and still; I couldn't even hear him breathing. He seemed to be holding his breath to prevent any emotion from escaping into his tone.

I glanced up at Jack. He had leaned against the doorframe with crossed arms.

"All right. What's the reason, then?"

"Enim, I … I don't know how to tell you this."

Something fragmented in his voice came through that I had never heard in his tone before. Though I had the urge to slam the phone down before he could speak, I licked my lips instead.

"Just tell me," I said.

"I …"

I shut my eyes and stared at the ground. Snow from my shoes that sat in sad little chunks around my feet had begun to melt, and they pooled at my feet like tears.

"It's your mother."

I swallowed. I knew what he was going to say and yet I didn't believe it. His voice had begun to shake, coming over the line in short, static gulps that betrayed the admission before it came, but when I spoke my own was calm.

"What about her?"

"She's …" Karl seemed to choke on the other line. In the background, I could hear something falling. He might have knocked the receiver off of the desk. "She's – she's dead, Enim."

I felt myself nod but couldn't say anything. The room had gone very quiet and still around me.

"Enim? Are you …?"

"I'm still here."

I was surprised to hear that my voice was quick and unmoved. With the way it sounded, Karl might have just told me that I got a standard bank statement in the mail that morning.

"I … The wake is Thursday, and the funeral will be on Friday. I've … I've made arrangements. Someone will be up to collect you."

"All right," I said, my tone still formal and detached.

"All right," Karl concluded quietly. He couldn't have said more: our emotions were too diametric to hold any sort of conversation.

I hung up the phone and handed it back to Brody. Jack was watching me with the type of empathy that he always gave when I got a reprimand from Karl.

"What was it this time? He didn't find out about the foot, did he? Jesus, he really is having you watched. Maybe he and Porter are in this together –"

"He doesn't know about the foot," I said quietly.

"No? So it was the flu, then?" Jack shook his head. "Honestly, he can't get mad at you for that. I mean, you're allowed to get sick, aren't you? Or is that against the rules, too?"

I looked at Jack blankly. For the slightest of moments, I considered not telling him – or anyone. It was as though if I didn't speak the words aloud, then they wouldn't be made true. We could go on just the way we had been moments before, careless and jubilant as we talked about everything and nothing at all.

"He doesn't care about that, either," I said.

"No? Then …" Jack straightened and peered at my face with an anxiousness that seldom crossed it. "Nim, what is it? What'd he say?"

I was unsure of how to voice it, and I found myself giving him a slight shrug.

"My mother. She's dead."

Jack's arms dropped to his side.

"Fuck," he whispered.

I nodded in response. There seemed to be nothing more to say.

Ch. 17

I made the walk to the port alone. It was far too early for the ferry, but I stood very stilly on the shore and waited out the time until it arrived even so. The view from the dock looked unfamiliar in the morning light: the water was still the deepest shade of blue, but the sky had faded to white, and though the sunlight was touching every surface, all around it was still just as cold.

Karl's colleague had made the drive to pick me up. It was only after I had seated myself in his car that I connected his voice and name with the ones I had overheard in the conversation during the holidays. Before he could express any condolences, I leaned my head against the window and shut my eyes to feign sleep. I didn't dare to open them until the sound of the waves crashing on the shore died down and the smell of salt faded from the air, and by then the silence was too thick to break. I shut my eyes as I listened to its nothingness, all too aware that that was all there was left for her to hear.

And though the trees running alongside the highway were the same as ever – just a blur as the car whizzed by on its way down to Connecticut – they looked emptier in the cold air. The snow had begun to melt as we traveled further south, and the landscape was just a barren stretch of patchwork green-and-white out the window. I wished that I could fling open the door and run alongside the car rather than stay within it – to have the cold air on my face instead of the heat from the vent pressing against me – but my hands laid like stones beside me. She was dead, and yet I was the one who seemed to have left the earth.

"Enim? We're here."

I hadn't realized that the car had stopped moving: my head was swaying as though I was still on the ferry being tossed back and forth by the waves. I fumbled with the handle on the car before getting out. From where the car had been parked on the other side of the street, my grandmother's old house looked emptier and more forsaken than ever.

The wake had already begun. When I entered the house, the swarm of people chattering in low voices hounded my ears and made my head heavier than it already was. They filled the normally barren house, spilling out of the rooms into the hallway and stuffed into every crevice and corner, like a flood of black over the carpet and hardwood floors. It seemed odd that there should be so many of them given that no one had visited the house when she was alive. Their company would do nothing for her now.

As I watched them, it occurred to me how out of place I was in my light-blue sweater and khakis. The feeling wrapped itself around me until a thick barrier pressed between me and the rest of the world. I took the stairs three at a time to escape it, but the hallway was littered with people, as well. My foot throbbed as I paused on the topmost step and took in the sight of them standing in my bedroom and near the room at the end of the hall. When they turned towards me questioningly, I recognized Mrs. Quincy among them. I tried to turn away, but she spotted me and stepped forward.

"Enim." She pulled me into an embrace before I could step away. Over her shoulder, I had a clear view of the guestroom door; it seemed impossible that there was no one lying out of sight behind it anymore. As the old woman continued to pat my back, I had the urge to push her away. "She went peacefully."

"Right."

I nodded as she withdrew to look at me, but the confirmation that I had heard her was not enough for her to look away. As she stared at me with her old, pale eyes, I thought that she was looking past my own and into my head. I opened my mouth to make an excuse to get away, but was saved from doing so by a voice at the bottom of the stairs.

"Enim, you're here."

Karl was dressed as neatly as ever in dark pants and a navy tie, but the lines around his eyes had deepened into cracks on his skin.

I descended the stairs to stand in front of him. As his eyes moved over me disapprovingly, I was more aware than ever that my face was severely bruised and my hair needed to be trimmed, though for once he didn't voice the criticism aloud.

"Your father's in the living room. The – the casket's there, too."

I nodded and turned away with the pretense of going there, but once the crowd separated us I continued down the hall to find an empty room. The only one was the laundry room, and I ducked inside it quickly. As I shut the door on the voices outside, I was aware of how small and cramped it was. I leaned against the washer and tugged at my collar as my throat constricted. I couldn't go into the living room with both my father and mother there – not after not seeing either of them for so long.

I wedged myself down into the space between the washer and dryer. It was warm there pressed between the metal, and I could only hear the faintest of voices from the surrounding rooms. I shut my eyes and tried to block out the image of my mother standing on the beach in her light sundress and bare feet: the diagnosis that Beringer had admitted to was hanging above her head, ready to crush her. Regardless of the hordes of people filling the house, I had never felt quite so alone.

I knew better than to be crammed there between the two appliances hiding when Karl and my father were expecting me to join them, but I couldn't move. I didn't have the strength to feign politeness or maintain stoicism, and I couldn't speak to them when I hadn't even been able to speak to her when she was trapped in that empty room with the horrible whirring and beeping of machines. I bit down in regret until the teeth dug holes into my tongue. I never wanted to speak again.

And as I stared at the clock miserably, I realized that I would have had a meeting with Beringer in a few hours' time if I had been at Bickerby. I wished that I could have been there with him instead of in the house with Karl, who I had not been able to hold a proper conversation with in years, or my father, who hadn't even bothered to try. It was as though something foreign had crept into my veins to replace any genetic material that we might have shared, and I was something far too different from either of them to claim resemblance ever again.

The door opened and I hurriedly pulled my legs back to avoid being seen. My heart hammered with the fear that I would be found and only lessened when the person stepped over to the window instead of approaching me. I stared at the well-polished shoes for a long moment before recognizing them as my father's.

"Daniel –"

The door opened and shut again as Karl stepped into the room after him. He was a bit breathless as though he had been running, but quickly smoothed his hair back and composed himself.

My father didn't turn from the window.

"This isn't the time for this, Karl, and it certainly isn't the place."

"It's never a good time or place."

"Then let's not talk about it at all. It's done – she's gone. Let it die with her."

Karl's arms crossed, but I was too low on the ground to see either of their expressions. My father's voice was as firm as ever, and Karl's was the same tired but exasperated tone that he always took with me.

"I'm sorry," he said. "I've said it a thousand times, but I'll say it again: I'm sorry."

"It doesn't do anything now, Karl."

"It could. You just won't let it."

My father's oxfords squeaked on the floor as he turned in his spot.

"Stop victimizing yourself. I'm not saying that you caused all of this – Evelyn was unwell regardless of what happened between you two – but you certainly played a part."

"I didn't know that she was sick."

"But you knew *better*." He moved to straighten his tie even though it was hardly out of place and smoothed the front of his dress shirt down out of habit. "What did you think when she acted the way she did? Why did you think she wanted to look at the ocean for hours on end, and listen to that damn song over and over again?"

"It wasn't as bad at that point."

"No, you got her at the best point in her life; and when she entered the worst, she was my wife again."

"That's not fair, Daniel."

"No? How do you think it was for me, then? Or Evelyn, when you left her?"

"You told me to stay away."

"I told you to stay away the day you laid eyes on her – you didn't listen then."

He broke off by turning back to the window. Even when he leaned his hands against the frame and hunched over, he was still just as intimidating in stance.

"Where's Enim? I thought you said he'd arrived."

"He did – didn't he come see you?"

"Obviously not."

Karl sighed and ran a hand through his hair.

"What?" my father asked.

"Nothing. I mean, I'm sure he's not far."

"Not far? Jesus, Karl – have you lost him?"

Karl loosened his collar as he looked towards the door.

"No, well – I don't know. He might've taken a walk."

"A walk?"

"Only ... sometimes he ... sometimes he goes to the bridge."

Even if I couldn't see my father's expression, I knew what it read. As he turned to look at his younger brother and his arms dropped to his sides like deadweights, Karl took a long step back from him.

"The bridge? The bridge where she jumped from?" His tone was so loud that the voices outside the door hushed a bit to hear it, and I pulled my legs back tighter to my chest as my heart hammered harder than ever. "Jesus Christ, Karl – you let him go there?"

"It's not like I drive him there – he just takes off!"

"Don't you watch him?"

"Of course I do! But I'm not here every second of every

day, Daniel, and –"

"And nothing! He shouldn't even think that he's allowed out of the house without permission – what kind of guardian are you?"

Karl's hands tightened.

"Oh, that's rich, Daniel – seeing as you haven't seen or spoken to him *in a year.*"

"Don't tell me my faults as a father – I know them already!"

"Apparently not, or else you'd realize that your son doesn't eat or sleep or talk to anyone –"

"That's why I got him a psychiatrist!"

"Beringer's doing nothing for him! It's been months, and he's no better than he was before!"

"He's fine. His grades are up, his schoolwork is good –"

"He's not! He gets into fights, he talks back to his teachers –"

"Don't act as though you know my son better than I do, Karl!"

"*Everyone* knows your son better than you do, Daniel."

The silence that followed was shattered as a mound of snow fell from the roof and crashed onto the ground. Both my father and Karl had gone very still, but the latter's hands were shaking behind his back. I sucked in a breath for fear that if I let it out they would hear me, though the room seemed to have drained of air and made it impossible to breathe anyhow. Finally, when the silence pressed so hard against me that my back seemed to break against the wall, my father spoke again.

"You're out of line, Karl."

He left the room without another word. After a moment, Karl straightened his collar and did the same. I waited a moment for both of them to return to separate parts of the house before making a break from the room. Shooting past the line of mourners, I hurried up the stairs and down the hall to the bathroom and locked myself inside.

My reflection was even less forgiving under the fluorescent lights, but I splashed hot water over my face to return some color to it. I combed my hair back from my eyes with my fingers, though it didn't hide the fact that it had become dull and brittle. Even my eyes had lost their color: the blue was nothing more than a glassy shade of gray. I blinked at the mirror as I tried to recognize myself, but the person standing hunched over the sink was unfamiliar.

Outside the door, the voices changed from mismatched chattering to low, humble tones that murmured their respects. My father must have come up the stairs. I pressed my ear to the door as his footsteps paused in the hallway and heard his deep voice as he thanked one of them for coming. When I opened the door, he halted midway through the conversation to stare at me.

"Enim."

He crossed over to me and pulled me aside into Karl's bedroom, shutting the door behind him. As I stood in front of him, he took my head in his hands and turned my face up to look at me properly. The lighting in the room was poor, and he had to squint to see the bruises running beneath my eyes and across my nose.

"What happened?"

"I fell on the ice," I said as he released me, careful to turn my head away with the lie.

"I've heard it's been a harsh winter here."

"Yes."

He nodded upon realizing that he had nothing more to say, and we stood in silence for a long moment. I stared at Karl's neatly made bed without needing to look at him. He was the same as ever with his dark brown eyes and iron-gray hair; even the frown lines on his forehead were the same. It was only me who had changed.

"Well, I ... Your mother was ..." He fumbled over his words as he tried to salvage the nonexistent exchange. "It's for the best, really."

"Right."

"The caregiver said she went peacefully. At any rate, she wasn't alone."

He waited for me to speak, but it was all that I could do to hold myself upright in front of him. Another move and he might notice everything wrong with me, and another word and he would realize who I had become.

"You've ... you've been here?" he asked.

"Sorry?"

"In the house?" He searched my face for a moment before determining that Karl had been wrong in his assumption that I had gone to the bridge. "No, of course you have. Only ... I hadn't seen you. Have you seen the casket yet?"

I sucked my cheeks in as I shook my head. He nodded.

"Well, why don't we go down now? They'll be bringing it over to the funeral home soon, so this will be your last chance ..."

He took my shoulder and steered me from the room before I could tell him that I didn't want to go: the image of her was too muddled already. Another damaged one would take up too much space and push the pleasant ones out of my mind. But he led me down the stairs and over to the living room before I could pull myself from my reverie, and the waning crowd with unknown faces parted to let us through.

The casket lay open at the back of the room. As my legs weakened, my father's firm hand on my shoulder pushed me forward towards it instead. My eyes rose very slowly up over the shined black exterior and across the soft white lining before I found her arm, still and folded up over her chest, and then finally moved to look at her face. For a moment I faltered in incomprehension: she looked so beautiful.

The pale, hollowed face was soft and glowing again, the dull hair that had grown matted was now golden and lightly wavy as it fell upon her shoulders, and the bones that had protruded from thin skin were no longer visible. She looked so healthy and well in death that I thought that if I were to reach forward and peel open her eyelid, the irises would be sea-green again and flecked with gentle light. A feeling like a blunt object slammed against my stomach as I looked at her. She looked more alive than she had in years.

And I knew that it was just makeup and prosthetics that

had been used to manipulate her frail appearance, and yet I couldn't get the twisting sensation in my gut to stop. I wanted to reach forward and shake her until she opened her eyes and smiled at me, but the knowledge that she was unwakeable stinging behind my eyes and burning in my throat prevented me from doing so.

"Mr. Lund? Sorry, did you need another moment?"

The staff from the funeral home had come to take her away. My father pulled me back from the casket so that they could close it, and I dug my eyes into her face as I tried to burn the image into my skull. I continued to stare at the black case as they wheeled it from the room, and the want for them to bring it back again and open it up to reveal that it had all been a mistake took hold of me in a childish hope that I couldn't let go of.

The door shut behind them and she was gone. My father had left my side to show the remaining guests out; their pleasantries flittered through the walls, but couldn't mask the unmistakable reserve that had come over the house. I listened hard through it, searching for any sign of life within the walls, but it was as though the entire house had died along with its last resident. I strained to hear the sound of piano music, but for once it had not resumed. Though it had always haunted me, it was unbearably empty without it. It was unbearably empty without her.

I shut my eyes on the place where the casket had lain and tried to picture something other than the emptiness it had left behind. The house grew quieter and quieter as more people flitted through the front door, and the chill from the outside came over the furniture and seeped into my skin. I wished that it would burn the flesh off and leave me with nothing but bones so that I could disintegrate like she would, feet beneath the earth and alone in the frozen, dark ground.

"Enim?"

My father's question was somewhere outside of my thoughts, and I didn't process that he was beside me again until he reached up to take my shoulders. The touch startled me and I flinched without meaning to. He gave me a strange look with his hand still poised in the air.

"What's wrong?"

He was eyeing me with such incomprehension that I felt myself shrink away from his gaze. My head jerked to the side and my limbs shook, but I forced myself to reply, "Nothing."

"You're not upset, are you?" he asked. "Enim, we knew that this day would come. She held on for longer than any of us imagined ... It's good that she's not suffering anymore."

"No, I know."

I nodded in an attempt to salvage my reaction, but he could hardly believe me. I wished that I could tie myself up inside tightly enough to ensure that I would never come undone, but the knot in my stomach was still squirming and threatening to unravel.

"Then what's wrong?"

There were a thousand things, but they had all become so tangled in my mind that it was hard to pick the one that was making me shake so badly. I wished that he would look away from me so that I could compose myself, but his eyes were digging further and further into my façade.

"Why didn't you tell me?" I said.

"Tell you what?"

"What she was sick with."

His befuddled expression hardened. Straightening his shoulders, he put his hands into his pockets as he looked down at me.

"What are you talking about?"

"She wasn't just depressed, she was – you know. Why didn't you tell me?"

"Who told you that?"

I shook my head; I couldn't put the blame on Beringer.

"Someone told you, Enim – who was it?"

"No one. I ... I overheard it."

My father sighed irritably and ran a hand through his hair.

"Jesus, this is – this is why I didn't want you to know," he said. "I knew you'd take it badly."

"I'm not – I just wanted to know why no one told me."

"Because it doesn't matter, Enim. It's over: what happened happened. Let's not talk about it anymore."

"But –"

"Let's not talk about it anymore, Enim."

His tone rose and shook the room. In the silence that followed, footsteps creaked near the doorway. Karl was standing just outside in the hall.

My father turned and strode away from me. As he reached Karl, he turned to him with a withering glare but brushed past him wordlessly. It wasn't lost on either of them who I had alluded to overhearing the information from.

He left shortly afterwards under the pretense of checking into his hotel before he lost the reservation; the house was evidently too small to fit the three of us. When he was gone, I slowly made my way up the stairs. At the top I paused and looked at the guestroom door. It was still shut. Had I not known any better, I might have thought that she was still behind it. It felt as though she was. It felt as though the world hadn't changed at all, and that the houseful of mourners had been mistaken. Because she couldn't be gone – not yet. There were still things that we had to say to one another, and riddles we had to solve.

I crossed the hall and twisted the doorknob with cold fingers. When the door broke open, I scanned over the floorboards and walls: the machines that had whirred and beeped so continuously had been cleared away, and the bed where she had laid was stripped down to a bare mattress. As I searched the room again, my eyes pooled over each inch of floor and into every corner, certain that I would find her somewhere else instead, sitting and waiting for me to find her. But she wasn't there. She was gone.

Ch. 18

I heard a car pull into the driveway the next morning but didn't move from my bed. The sun scattered light over the room through the half-closed curtains and patterned the walls with shapeless streaks. I shut my eyes and longed to fall back asleep so that the day would revert back into nonexistence again, but the world refused to move on without me.

"Enim, get dressed. We're leaving in ten minutes."

My father opened and closed the door so swiftly that only his voice entered the room. I dragged my eyes over to the door too slowly to catch sight of him. My back was stiff from lying in place, and my arms were crossed over my chest as though I, too, would be buried in the ground that day. But though the idea of being shut inside the darkness and made to sleep forever was welcoming, I didn't deserve the peacefulness that she would soon have.

"Enim – what are you doing? I told you to get dressed."

He stepped into the room several minutes later at the sight of me still in bed. From the corner of my eye, I could see the pitch-black of his suit hidden beneath his wool overcoat. He leaned over me questioningly.

"Are you tired? Get up."

"I don't feel right."

"Well, that's hardly unfathomable. Come and have breakfast and we'll go. You'll feel better when this is all over."

I slowly sat up and leaned my arms against my knees. My shoulders shook to keep my head upright.

"No, I ... I don't feel right about this. About going."

"It's your mother's funeral, Enim. You have to go."

"But I – I don't feel right. I don't want to."

As his dark eyes fixed on my face, I lowered it to my hands. His expression was both unreadable and unfavorable.

"Enim, this isn't a choice. I know that this isn't easy, but you can't just skip it because you're upset."

"But I can't – I don't want to go."

My voice cracked as I spoke, and I turned my head to the

wall to hide my face more fully. He couldn't understand why I couldn't watch her be lowered into the ground: he didn't know that I had put her there.

"Enim, please don't be difficult. Put your suit on."

"I can't. I can't go."

"Put your suit on. I won't ask you again."

He pulled away to go to the door. With his back to me, I could finally look over at him.

"Please, Dad," I said. "Don't ... don't make me go."

"Enim," he sighed, "don't. Don't be difficult – not right now. Not today. I can't deal with it."

"But I can't –"

"You *can*. You can go, and you will go!" He slammed his hand against the doorframe as he spoke, enunciating the words with each blow. "Now get up and put your suit on, and come downstairs!"

The anger radiated off of him and boiled onto the floor, and had my feet not been pulled up on the bed it surely would have scorched them as well. But for once his frustration with me wasn't enough to move me from my spot, if only because it didn't compare to the resentment I felt at myself for what I had done.

I shook my head.

"No."

He stared at me in astonishment for a long moment before turning and storming down the hall. His shoes clattered on the stairs as he descended them, and his voice broke through the house angrily as he called to Karl.

"Get him up – I can't deal with him."

"What?"

"Get him up, dressed, and over to the church. I won't be late to my own wife's funeral."

The front door slammed before Karl could say anything more. In the silence that followed the shaking hinges and falling snow from the roof, there was the slightest of creaks on the floor below as Karl shifted his weight in uncertainty.

He waited several minutes before coming up to find me. As

he took in the sight of me curled up on the mattress, still in my t-shirt and pajama pants, he let out a breath that he seemed to have been holding for a long time.

"Enim ..."

"I can't go."

He looked at me closely.

"Alright."

He left before I realized what he has said, and even when his footsteps disappeared down the stairs I wasn't certain of the reprieve. I waited for him to reappear to argue or plead with me to go, but he didn't return. The numbers on the clock flitted through the hour and onto the next, and finally I descended the stairs and stood in the empty hallway. The funeral would be well under way by then, and I wasn't there.

I moved through the house quietly. Now that it was empty, the feeling of my mother's absence was even more apparent. The beeping that didn't sound was just as wrecking as the emptiness of the guestroom, and the piano pushed up in the corner of the living room left a soreness in my chest. I sat down on the bench and stared at the keys. They were covered in dust, just as she would soon be.

Something creaked behind me and I half-turned my head to find Karl standing in the doorframe. Though he was still in his dark suit, he had taken the jacket and tie off.

"You're not at the funeral?"

"No."

"Why not?"

He stepped further into the room so that he was halfway between me and the door. It wasn't lost on him how furious my father would be at our absences.

"I didn't want you to be here alone."

I looked back down at the piano keys. His fear that I would attempt to kill myself again seemed to have overridden the one of his older brother's reaction. But even if I had brought another bottle of medication from the stash beneath my mattress, I wouldn't have taken it. My mother had gone someplace where I couldn't catch up to her, and what I had done was something I could never escape from.

"I wasn't going to kill myself, Karl."

"I know." He put his hands into his pockets and stared across the dark room at the window. The white winter light was too harsh for the day, and the curtains had been pulled shut to block it out. "But I didn't want you to be alone."

I nodded without a proper response. I thought I might have thanked him, but the words were heavy in the base of my throat and I couldn't lift them up to my tongue. I waited for a long time for him to leave again, but he was rooted in his spot behind me.

"I could ... I could call Beringer, if you'd like. So you have someone to talk to."

"No." I stared down at the keys as another wave of silence pushed between us; with just a movement from my hand, and the house would no longer be so silent. "Don't call him. What you said was true: he only listens to me because he's paid to."

Karl's troubled sigh sank into the air as he recalled telling me as much, but he didn't bother to negate the statement. A hollowness seemed to have burrowed around my heart at the thought that it was true.

After a lengthy pause, he let out another heavy breath. I turned toward him, but from the piano bench I could only see the blurred outline of his form from the corner of my eye.

"You were right, too," he said.

"About what?"

"What you said over Christmas. You were right – it was my fault that she jumped." He seemed to chew the insides of his mouth as he stood there, and he teetered a bit as though he might blow over if I so much as touched him. "And I – I'm sorry, Enim. I'm – I'm so sorry."

My breathing wouldn't come. I had waited so long for someone else to admit to the blame that had been crushing me, but now that he had I felt no lighter. We were harboring two very separate streams of guilt – opposite in our responsibility just as we were opposite in everything else – and it pushed between us without allowing either of us any relief.

And though I stared at his broken expression and I knew what my mother had meant to him, it wasn't enough to admit my own blame out loud. The words wouldn't come, just as they never would come, and my secret was lost within me.

"Beringer told me," I said.

"What?"

"About the schizophrenia. I asked him, and he told me. I didn't overhear it."

He nodded. Perhaps he had already assumed as much.

"Well, he ... I guess it's best that you know."

"Did she ever tell you?"

"That she had it?" Karl asked. "No. I don't think she believed it herself. Or maybe she did, but she just didn't want me to know."

"No, I meant ... Did she ever tell you about the riddle?"

"From *Turandot*?"

I nodded, and he mirrored the action with a clouded expression.

"Do you ever think about ... how it would have ended?"

He sighed as he took in my question and ran his hand through his light hair. The smile that came to his face was more of a grimace, and the mention of the opera brought a familiar pain to his eyes.

"I've thought about it."

"What do you think would've happened?"

"After the prince tells Turandot to guess his name, and she threatens to kill everyone to find out what it is?" he said. As I was nodding, he added, "And the servant girl kills herself to save his secret?"

He took a step closer and returned his hands to his pockets. In the proximity and without the usual argument to distract us, I was aware that with his light hair and blue eyes he looked just as I would in twenty-five years. But with a strange sadness, I wondered if I would ever see myself as he was then.

"I think ... I think that the prince realized that he had made a mistake, and that he had fallen in love with the wrong person, but that it was too late," he said quietly. His tone was still as shaken as it had been when he had called me to tell me the news. "But ... but the story couldn't have gone any further with that, so it can't be right."

I turned back to the piano. My palms were moist with sweat, and I rubbed them against my pants to dry them.

"Did you ever tell her that?" I asked.

"No; I didn't realize it until it was too late." The ground creaked beneath him again as he took a step closer, and despite the closeness his low voice seemed very far away. "Don't haunt yourself with the answer, Enim. There is none."

But there was. She had found it before she had gone, and if I had reached out to stop her then I would have known it, too. And we wouldn't have been there in the cold, empty house at that moment: we would've been on a beach somewhere beneath the warm sun, a thousand miles away from the cold, and the snow, and from death. She would be all right, and I would be all right, and we would think no more of it.

I lifted my hands above the keys and held them there for a long, drawing moment. She had taught the song to me so long ago, and it felt both distant and close all at once. I let my hands drop and play the aria in a broken lamentation, and the notes rose up incorrectly only because the piano was out of tune, for I remembered it perfectly. And I remembered her perfectly, too, and she wasn't at all what they said she was. At least not to me.

I was still sitting at the piano when my father returned home. He wordlessly told Karl to leave the room; I could hear his footsteps fade away to the other side of the house as he retreated. I hung my head over the keys so that my hair fell forward and shielded my eyes, but I could see him shaking his head at me even so.

"I can't believe you," he said quietly.

"I'm sorry."

"Your own mother's funeral – and you wouldn't even go."

I swallowed rather than attempt to explain it to him. His expression folded.

"Why would you do this?" he said. "Are you trying to

punish her for what she did?"

"No."

"Is it me, then?" He stepped over to the piano and threw his gloves down atop it: the leather smacked the wood with a sharp noise and I flinched away from it. "Is that what this is? You're trying to get back at me for taking a job away from home?"

"No, that's not it."

"Then what is it, Enim? What is all of this?"

"All of what?"

"This!" He threw his hands down to indicate to me, and I instinctively slid further down the bench away from him. "This – you! You've been pulling these stunts for months now to try and get my attention: first with not eating, then that thing you lit on fire, then the grades, and the fights – I hardly recognize you anymore!"

"I'm not doing it on purpose," I said. My voice was low in contrast to his.

"You are! That's the only explanation, and I won't have it! I can't take it!"

"I'm sorry."

"Don't apologize – just change!"

The words rang harshly through the old house. He didn't understand that I would have been different – that I had tried. If it was possible, I would have stopped the thoughts in my head, and the hollowness in my chest, and the aching in my bones. I would have stopped the music from playing so consistently, and the images that rose behind my eyes when I tried to sleep. I would have been different. I would have been anything.

"Jesus, Enim – I can't put up with this! I can't watch you do this to yourself!" He pulled my arms down so that he could look at me, and my wrists were thin and weak in his grasp. "You were perfectly normal before this!"

I looked away from him so he couldn't see behind my eyes. There had always been something unsettled lying just beneath my well-ironed clothes, and even now that it was hidden so poorly, he still couldn't see it.

"What's this about really?" he said. "Is it because you know about the illness? Is it because I didn't tell you?"

"No."

"Then why are you acting this way? What is it?"

"I don't feel right. I just – I just don't feel right."

"You're out of sorts, that's why. You haven't eaten all day, you're stressed –"

"No, I don't feel right. I don't ..."

My hand skimmed my skull with short, jerky movements as I tried to explain it to him. I couldn't let him know, but I couldn't let him not know, either, and the diametric pleas screaming inside my head made it impossible to speak.

He released my arms and took a step back from me.

"You're not sick, Enim. There's nothing wrong with you."

He forced the words to be calm as though that would make them true. My eyes were sore and my shoulders ached from shaking, and I propped my arm up so that I could lean my head against it. The keys threw out notes at random beneath my elbows.

"You won't be like her, Enim. You won't."

I wished that I could tell him the truth, or anyone the truth. I wished that I had the type of regard for him that I had had for my mother, or for Jack, or for Beringer, but the ability to trust him wouldn't rise high enough to let me take hold of it. I was someone else than who he saw, and he would never be able to help me.

"You're just very stressed, Enim. I don't blame you – this has been a hard year, and I know the situation wasn't ideal. But I've already spoken with my company and they've agreed to have me transferred back by the end of the month. This is all over now: you don't have to worry anymore."

He stepped forward again and took me by the shoulders to right me. As he looked at me with carefully-placed concern and straightened my head, it was as though in the hopes of sliding something back into place.

"I'm sorry," I said quietly. The room was so disquieted that it quivered all around us, but I forced myself to be still. "You're right – I'm just stressed. I'll be better."

He squeezed my arm and gave a tight-lipped smile.

"Good. That's good. We'll put this all behind us, and everything will be just fine."

He clapped my shoulder and stepped away from the broken piano. As he left the room, I felt as though I was watching him go through a thick expanse of water. It was murky as I stared up through it, like I was standing on the ocean floor watching him linger close by on the surface; and though he was so close to me and I could hear him, it was still too far away to reach and too muted to understand. And he could have reached down to me to pull me up, if only he knew that I was hidden there just out of sight.

I watched him pull away from the house in a taxi the next morning with a mixture of sadness and relief. I had waited so long for him to return, and yet now that he had promised to do so I felt no different. If anything, the thought of returning to someplace other than the old house that had haunted me so greatly was just as suffocating as ever, if only because it meant that my mother was truly gone from the place and would never return again.

"Ready to go?" Karl asked, his voice pulling me away from the window. The bright white of the snow stung my eyes, and I had to blink several times to adjust to where he stood in the shadow of the staircase.

"Yes."

As it was a weekend, there was no hurry to get back to Bickerby; yet the idea of either of us spending a moment longer in the house seemed too unbearable to consider waiting for the weekend to pass in silence, so we made the drive up the coast at the usual hurried pace. I watched the house fade away into the backdrop of wintry snow with the knowledge that it would be the last time I did so, and my chest pressed harder against my ribs until I was sure that they would break. The long stretches of ground still partially covered in snow was a constant reminder that she was lying beneath it somewhere dark and cold, and that she was all alone.

By the time Karl pulled into the port hours later, my face was throbbing with the effort to keep my expression intact. I swung open the door before he had fully stopped and grabbed my bag with a hurriedly spewed goodbye to prevent anything that he would or wouldn't say and made my way to the ticket booth. The next ferry wouldn't be in for an hour or so, and my already cold hands were rattling like bones in the chill.

From my spot on the shore, the ocean swelled all around me. It was a horrible sight and yet I couldn't take my eyes off of it. It was such a deep, dark blue beneath the white sky that it looked as though the world had been cut into two: one where I was, and one where she would remain. And even if I were to cross the ocean towards the horizon in the hopes of reaching the spot where her world began, I knew that I could never get to it. I could never get to her, because she was gone. Yet no matter how many times I told myself as much, it didn't become any more real.

When the ferry pulled into port, I wrenched myself from the shore and curled myself up in a low seat by the side. The wound puncturing my chest was stinging in the air; if it didn't close, it would infect every part of me. With my face pressed into my arm, I drew up the image of her in her white dress and focused on it so intently that when I opened my eyes again she was imprinted before me in the sky. I gazed at her with a yearning unmatched by anything that had ever been felt, but the sentiment was unrequited: she couldn't feel me – not anymore. And yet, as the ferry reached the island and the horizon faded into earth, I knew I would feel her there forever.

Ch. 19

I made my way up the stairs to the residence building with slow, heavy steps. The bag on my back seemed much too heavy for what it contained, and my head throbbed from either a lack of sleep or coffee. As I reached the third floor and started towards the fourth, the door above me opened and a clattering of footsteps rang out through the stairwell.

"Perfect timing."

I halted at the voice and raised my eyes from my feet. Trask was standing at the top of the stairs staring down at me with a strange mixture of glee and revulsion.

"I saw you from the window," he informed me as he started down the stairs. "Thought I'd take the opportunity to have a little chat before your boyfriend showed up. Do you have a minute?"

I had barely opened my mouth to respond when he reached out and grabbed me. Twisting my arm so that I couldn't escape, he forced me around so that I was hanging half-over the banister. Only his grip on my forearm and his grasp at the back of my head yanking at my hair kept me from falling four flights below. As my ribs hit the metal and the breath was knocked from my lungs, my vision swayed in and out of blackness.

He leaned down to speak lowly in my ear, pressing my head further down until my toes began to lift off of the floor.

"If you know what's good for you, you'll keep out of everyone's way. Got it?"

My lungs were too compressed to speak and I could only choke in response. Trask tightened his grip on the back of my hair until it felt as though it was ripping from my scalp and then gave me a rough shake; the cement floor below bounded in my line of sight and my boat shoes scraped the step as I tried to keep from flipping over the railing.

"I asked you a question," he said forcefully.

"I – got – it."

The door to the floor below us opened and someone came

out into the stairwell. Trask released me and disappeared up the stairs. I had barely managed to push myself backwards to keep from falling four flights below when I lost my footing and tumbled down onto the landing. As my head hit the cement, the sound of the other student's footsteps receded down to the ground floor and left me in a ringing silence.

I waited a long moment before slowly getting to my feet. My bag had fallen somewhere close by and I struggled to take hold of it in my blurred vision. Then, careful not to lose balance again, I crawled up the stairs and down the hall towards my room.

"You're back." Jack looked up as I entered and gave a partial smile that dissolved into a frown. "Are you alright?"

"Fine. Just ran into Trask on the stairs."

"What?"

"It's nothing," I said, though the persistent pounding in my skull suggested otherwise. "He just wanted to remind me how much he and Julian hate me."

"Again? You could report him for sexual harassment if he keeps this up." He paused to give me another look. "You'd think he'd give you a break, considering ..."

The statement was lost in the air and he cleared his throat awkwardly. He unfolded his legs and swung them over the side of the bed as he watched me unpack my belongings and put them away, but my mother's death still hung uncomfortably between us.

"I told everyone that it was complications from an autoimmune disease that she'd had for a while," he said. "I thought it sounded fairly convincing myself."

"It does."

The lie was strangely easing. As far as anyone else had known, my mother had died the previous year. I was grateful that Jack failed to relay their inquiries as to how she had died for a second time.

"Anyhow, Sanders dropped off some more homework for you," he said. "Between the new assignments and the ones from when you supposedly had the flu, it was getting hard to see the desk."

I sighed and sat down on the bed to lean my head against the wall. Had Barker been fit and well, he would have surely suspended me by now. I was even more thankful for his poor health.

Jack took a stack of papers from the desk to bring over to me.

"Physics looks pretty daunting," he said. "And so does Calculus, but you seem to enjoy that half the time, so …"

"Only comparatively."

He gave a sympathetic grimace as he tossed the assignments next to me.

"Well, I figured if you started them now then you might be able to get them done by tomorrow – then we could actually do something interesting this weekend."

The folder was so heavy that it made an indent in the mattress next to me.

"Jack, there's no way I can get a week's worth of assignments done by the end of the weekend, let alone the beginning."

"You might."

"Five classes times six days of work? Try again. I'll be lucky if they're done by graduation."

"Nah, only two classes. I did the rest."

"You – what?" I stopped midway through sorting through the papers to stare at him in disbelief. "You did my homework?"

"Everything but Physics and Calculus."

"But – but that's impossible."

"Why?"

"Because you don't do homework. Ever."

He shrugged.

"Yeah, well, I was excessively bored and I figured we'd never leave the room if you had to do it all by yourself, so …"

He shrugged again in a very good portrayal of careless nonchalance, though I knew that he was perfectly capable of entertaining himself. As I found the essay that he had written for English and pulled it out, my frown deepened.

"How'd you write this? We're reading *Jane Eyre*."

"I read it."

"No, you didn't."

"I did, Nim. Not to ruin the ending or anything, but she and Rochester end up together."

"But – what?"

"You're surprised? I thought it was pretty expected ..."

"No, not that," I said. I stared at him with the type of bewilderment that only came as a result of his actions alone and shook my head with a loss for words. After scanning through the other assignments and multiple papers he had written, I managed, "You really did all of my work for English and History?"

"And Latin."

"Sorry?"

"Latin. I did those assignments, too."

I gave him a look.

"But Jack: you don't take Latin."

"Nope."

"And you don't *know* Latin."

"True."

"So how did you do my assignments?"

"With difficulty," he said lightly. "And my entire stash of cigarettes. Now I know what you're always so depressed – those were not happy people. You should have taken French: ils sont centrés sur l'amour."

"But how could you do the assignments? They're *in Latin*."

"They were, yes. Then I translated them."

"But how?"

"I used the Latin-to-English dictionary," he said with a shrug, and Dictionary poked her head out from beneath the bed at the sound of her name. As I opened my mouth to protest, he cut me off. "And I used the table in the back of the book so that I could mark all the accusatives as direct objects, and all the verbs in the right tense and whatnot. Relax, Nim. I did a good job. Well –" he backtracked, "—it's passable."

"But ..."

"Nim, the time you're spending obsessing over this could be used to get the rest of your homework done," he said, rolling his eyes. "Just read them through if you don't believe me."

I looked down at the assignments that he had done but didn't bother to read the translation. My throat was tight with gratitude.

"I ... I don't know what to say, Jack."

"Say you'll replenish my cigarettes first thing tomorrow," he said with the usual devious glint in his eye, and I nodded.

I set to work on the remaining assignments as he headed down to dinner. The hurry to get them done was a welcome distraction from the time spent away from school, and by the time I had gotten through the majority of the equations I was so tired and sleep-deprived that I drifted off without lingering on any unpleasant thoughts.

As promised, I made the walk into town the next morning with him. The cold had not let up beneath the white winter sky, and we kept our heads ducked low into our scarves to ward off the chill on our faces. As we crossed through the deserted town to the corner store, the glint of dark blue in the corner of my vision alerted my thoughts back to the ocean, and I unknowingly stopped to stare at it.

"Nim?" Jack had paused several paces ahead of me. "Everything okay?"

"Yeah. No – of course."

I hurried to catch up with him and we continued on. Though we had been relatively silent for the entire walk, it was suddenly much more uncomfortable. I dug my hands further into my pockets as I tried to block out the image of my mother lying in the casket and the way her bright blue-green eyes would have shimmered beneath the closed lids in the exact shade of the ocean.

I ran my eyes over the forsaken island, the muddied snow unsightly beneath the winter light, and took in the sight of the place that we had grown accustomed to living despite hating it, and all at once I wondered what we were doing there. Neither of us had any plans to use Bickerby on a college application, or to walk in line with the rest of the graduates in a few months' time: we seemed to simply be waiting for a change that would never come.

I poked my head out from beneath my collar.

"I'll be eighteen in two weeks."

Jack looked over at me as I spoke.

"What? Yeah, you will."

We stepped over a large mound of snow on the side of the road to get to the sidewalk. I waited until we were on even ground before speaking again.

"I'll get an inheritance from my mother."

Jack glanced over at me inquiringly but quickly looked away again. His brow had furrowed in uncertainty of how to proceed.

"We could use it, Jack," I said. "We could get away from here."

We paused on the corner outside of the store. Jack stared at me with his hands in his pockets but still didn't speak.

"We could just pack up and leave," I said. "Go to France. Barker's done for, there's nothing to worry about ... We could finally do it."

His expression was unreadable. It occurred to me that after what had happened to Miss Mercier he might have no longer harbored the same excitement to go. Still, as we stood in the cold air, the idea of staying in New England seemed unbearable at best, and going anywhere that was far enough away seemed to be the answer.

"What do you think?" I said. "I mean, I know it won't be the same, but ... do you still want to go with me? Despite everything?"

He stood in shock momentarily, but then his expression broke into a smile.

"You're the only one I'd go with, Nim," he said. "In fact, I can count the other people I'd go with on Rochester's amputated hand."

"Good to know."

We flitted into the corner store and he indicated to the Parliaments behind the counter. As I pulled out some money to pay for them, the man behind the register sighed.

"Prep school boys, are you?"

"I'm old enough to smoke," Jack said, reaching for his ID.

"Nah, that's not what I meant," the man said, waving the card away. "Only, I hoped you'd of been in here to fill out the application for the job."

He indicated to the *Help Wanted* sign in the window as he rang up the charge. As I slid the money towards him, I quickly murmured, "Right. Sorry."

"Nah, it's alright. Just the last girl's gone and run off on me, without so much as giving her notice, and I've been working both shifts all week."

I stopped midway through reaching for the change; beside me, Jack's hand had frozen where he was pocketing the cigarettes.

"What do you mean, she 'ran off?'" he asked.

"Just that: she ran off. Called her house and her parents said she never came home. Hardly a surprise. Seems to be a new trend with kids these days ..."

He shook his head in irritation, but neither Jack nor I copied the sentiment. My hand had gone very cold and the metal of the coins seemed to burn against the skin.

"When did this happen?" Jack asked quickly. "Was this – was this weeks ago?"

"Nope. Just last Friday."

"But ..."

He bit down on his jaw to keep from saying anything more, though I knew every word that was crossing his mind from the look in his eyes. We exited the store wordlessly and he veered off down the street. I had to hurry to keep up with him, and struggled to hear his voice over the wind pooling into my ears.

"How could that be?" he said restlessly. "Barker had the heart-attack the week before that – he couldn't've gone and killed someone else!"

"Maybe it's ... maybe it's something else. Maybe she actually ran away."

"What – like the other girls *actually* ran away? That doesn't make sense, Nim!"

"No, I mean ... maybe she really thought her friends ran away, so she decided to, too ..."

But even as I said it, I knew that it wasn't true. My heart was pounding as I realized what the store-keeper's statement meant, and my face was hot despite the cold air. Jack slowed as we reached the woods and turned to face me through the trees.

"How could we have gotten it wrong?" he said, running a hand through his hair in frustration. "How could it not be Barker?"

We had stopped in a clearing and a light wind fell down upon us to rattle the surrounding trees. As I shivered in the chill, it occurred to me that we were standing where Miss Mercier had been killed. Jack was looking at me for an explanation, but the only one I had to give was the same one that he had already figured out.

I shut my eyes in defeat.

"But we found the file!" he said. "And it made sense – it all made sense! It had to have been Barker – it was *supposed* to be him –"

As he broke off and turned away, I dropped my eyes to the snow-covered ground. The piddling suspicions that I had ignored warning me that Barker had not been the one to commit such crimes came back to me with full-force, and it occurred to me that we had both wanted it to be him so badly that we had ignored the explanations of why it was not.

And it weighed down over us and closed in around us with the surrounding trees so strongly that it was a wonder we didn't suffocate. Every aspiration that we had rediscovered after Barker's hospitalization had been sucked from the air along with any hope of fulfilling our plans to get away from the island. I couldn't have breathed even if I wanted to.

"I just wanted it to be done," Jack said. "You told me that it didn't seem right, but I wanted it to be over, so I just ignored it."

"It seemed like it was Barker. Everything pointed to him – we had the cause, the routes he took, the file …"

"I should have known about that file: it was just the documents on the investigation. The police gave it to him to pretend like they were doing something, and he probably shoved it away and never looked at it again …"

The wind subsided and we were left to stand in the frigid air. All around us the island looked dead and cold, and without the thought of escaping to someplace else, it seemed to latch around our ankles.

"We're never going to figure it out," Jack said.

I shut my eyes. The soft sound of piano music had begun to flit through the trees, and it clogged my ears disturbingly. As I shook my head to try and clear it, I knew that I couldn't take having another unsolved riddle twisting through my thoughts.

"We'll figure it out. We have to."

"How?" Jack said. "We just spent months chasing nothing – we wasted all that time looking for something that wasn't there."

"That's not true; we still have all the research and evidence. We just have to go over it again and figure it out."

It took the entire walk back to Bickerby to convince him of as much, and even then his expression was cluttered with disheartenment. When we returned to the room, I pushed away the remaining assignments that I had to do to clear a space on my bed and he dug out the file folder. He took a long breath before opening it and then laid the information back out on the bed.

The familiar sight of the maps with dozens of pen marks scribbled over them and the various newspaper articles dug into my stomach, and when I looked at the pictures of the girls' faces again, the imprint of their smiles burned across my eyes.

"Alright, so it's got to be someone at the school," Jack said as we stared down at the notes, "since we've already confirmed that it's no one in town."

"But can we really be sure?"

He took a seat next to me and rubbed tiredly at his eyes. Any enthusiasm that he had had for the unsolved crime was long gone by now.

"Towns weed out weirdoes, but boarding schools are breeding grounds for all sorts of trouble." He gave me a look. "If you'd read *Jane Eyre*, you'd realize that."

"Did someone get murdered in her boarding school?"

"No, but that's beside the point. What I'm saying is that it has to be someone at this school – student or faculty."

"Right, but does it? I mean, look at it this way: the killings started with girls on the island. They had nothing to do with Bickerby at all until Miss Mercier got involved. And she only got involved because one of her students said something – and he was from the town. So maybe it is a townsperson."

"But it's not."

"It could be – it makes sense."

Jack shook his head and Dictionary hopped up into his lap. She mewed as he scratched behind her ears, happy that we had not completely forgotten her in our fascination with her previous owner's murderer.

"You're forgetting something," he said. "The killings follow a school schedule. I read through the census, and I've looked around town – there's no one who leaves the island on summers except for the students and half the faculty and staff."

"Right. But ... maybe there's another explanation for that, too."

"Such as?"

"I don't know – maybe he purposefully takes summers off to divert suspicion."

"Maybe he *purposefully takes summers off to divert suspicion*?" Jack repeated, his voice heavy with skepticism. "First of all, Nim, what suspicion are you talking about? As far as anyone's concerned, only one crime has been committed on this island – and no one's very concerned about that, even. Secondly, if there's someone out there who's smart enough to commit a dozen crimes without raising suspicion and who would go so far as to cover his tracks by taking summers off to point the police – who aren't even looking for him – in another direction altogether, why in the world would he be living on this island? A guy like that has to have more aspirations in life than to be *here*."

I sighed.

"Good point." My eyes dropped down to the student files in my hands. "I just don't get how it can be someone here."

"Why not?"

"I don't know ... Don't you think it's weird that someone's killed a bunch of people? I mean, it could be someone that we know. A lab partner, even."

"It's not my lab partner," Jack said dryly. "He couldn't even figure mitosis out."

"You know what I mean."

Jack shrugged.

"It's not so hard for me to believe," he said. "I mean, think of it this way: they're hundreds of boys here, all away from their parents, who've put completely unrealistic expectations on them; they've got no outlet for their problems or anger, because Barker runs this place with authoritarianism; and the only women around are – allegedly – unreachable. I'm surprised there's only *one* person running around killing people."

"Alright, I guess you're right ..."

"I usually am."

He gave me his usual smirk, though it was only a halfhearted attempt. As we stretched out to split up the various papers that we had compiled weeks beforehand to go over any information that we might have missed, he let out a long sigh.

"We'll figure it out, Jack," I said.

"And if we don't?"

I didn't respond. In the silence the piano music returned to filter through my ears and fill my head. As it crept into my thoughts with memories of my mother, I noisily flipped through pages to try and mask the sound. All that I knew was that if we didn't find the answer, I would forever be in search of the answer, just like her.

Ch. 20

I stepped down the row of desks to get to Albertson's and gently laid the makeup exam from the one I had missed on his desk. He smiled as he looked up from his work and adjusted his glasses to look it over.

"Did it go well?" he asked.

"Yes."

"No questions?"

I shook my head and hesitantly took a step back, hoping that I could return to the residence building before it got too late, when Albertson spoke again.

"I was just going over your homework assignments," he said. "I applaud you for getting them done so quickly."

I forced a smile but dropped my eyes to the floor. The assignments that Jack had done were undoubtedly filled with mistakes, and I was certain that Albertson could tell that I had not been the one to complete them.

"Right, well ... I may have done them a bit too quickly, Mr. Albertson. I ... I know they're not my best work."

"No, not your best. But given the circumstances ..." He offered another kind smile and put the paper he was holding down. "I'm very pleased with the time and effort you put in, Enim. It shows me how hard you're trying, even when I know there are other things on your mind."

"Right."

The flatness in my voice was evident; Albertson cleared his throat before going on.

"I did want to point out just a few things that were wrong, given the importance of the subject matter. Do you have another minute or so?"

Despite my desire to leave, I could hardly act as though I had to rush off to class given that it was the end of the day. I withheld a grimace and gave a stiff nod, and Albertson moved the graded assignment to lie on the desk between us.

"You seemed to get the gist of the beginning section, but right around the midway mark the translation got a bit muddled. The issues begin with your translation of 'damnatio memoriae' as 'damned memories.' It's not accusative, remember, so it's not the memories themselves that are undesirable, it's the lack of remembrance that is. Does that make sense?"

"Not ... not really, Mr. Albertson."

"To the Romans, the worst thing was not death: it was having their life erased from history. This practice was the ultimate punishment — worse than torture or humiliation or death — because it meant that the victim would never be known throughout history, or remembered, or even thought of again. He wasn't just gone from life: he was gone from the world."

He paused to look at me with his old, pale eyes, and suddenly the room seemed very dry. I stared at the line that he was indicating to but the words were blurred with sorrow.

"So 'damnatio memoriae' truly means 'condemnation of memory.' It's not just dismissing someone, it's the act of wiping away every memory of them until they can never be thought of again." He paused again when I made no indication that I had heard him, and his eyes had gone very still and silent. "No one wants to be forgotten, Enim."

"Right."

The word came out as barely more than a breath. I quickly thanked Albertson and slipped away out the door, tugging at my shirt collar as I went to try and breathe more deeply. Once outside, I crossed to the Center Garden and took a seat on one of the stone benches. The cold could barely shock my senses as my mind finally turned to thoughts that I had tried so hard to keep away.

She was gone. I had told myself it over and over again, even before her life had fully finished, and yet it still didn't seem real. She would never walk along the beach again, or sit beside me at the piano, or open her eyes and look over at me with a smile. Already I could barely remember the way she would brush my hair from my eyes when it got too long, or the way her laugh sounded gently over the phone, or of how we could say things to one another that no one else understood.

And soon enough, the last imprints of her would fade from my memory, too. The room at the end of the hallway would be cleared out and made into something different when the house was sold, and the broken piano would be donated to someone who would never play the aria upon it again, and the tombstone that no one would visit would weather, and she, too, would fade from the world with everything she had ever and never done.

The grounds were nearly empty, and the sun had begun to set behind the trees. I stared at it even though the vivid orange burned against my eyes until it sunk into the ocean, and all at once I wondered what had happened to the girls who had done the same. They had sunk beneath the waves, as well, though they would not resurface in the morning, and no one would wait for them to reappear in the days to come. They were gone without being mourned, thought to have run away when they had been killed, and so their memory would be tainted with the type of displeasure that they didn't deserve; they would be thought of in passing, perhaps, with a type of irritation reserved for those who could be so thoughtless as to run away and never so much as send word back home. They would be lifeless and grave-less all at once, and their memories would be lost like their lives out at sea.

And Miss Mercier would be forgotten in the same way. Her memory clung as tightly as it could to the classroom that had once been hers, and the notice board in the hallway in the Foreign Language Building where her memorial was still pinned up in pictures and farewells, but its grip was slowly releasing. By the next semester there would be a permanent replacement occupying her room, and the board would be covered with more present concerns. The clearing where she had been killed would camouflage back into the rest of the forest, the ground indistinguishable beneath the trees. Her memory was being condemned due to her horrid death. The thoughts of her were marred by the way that she had been killed, and it was easier to forget her than to try and think of her without the brutality of the crime that had struck the campus.

That was what had happened to them, and that was what would happen to us all. We would die and the world would carry on without us. There was no other way that it could be – to hold onto the deceased's memory was like distributing poison throughout the soul. The memory haunted every unused space within the mind, filling it up with laughter that would never be heard again and words that would never be spoken. It dragged the heart down beneath the ground where the decomposing body laid, and once there, there was no way to pull it back up again. It was a choice between forgetting and moving on, or remembering and staying still. The world would continue regardless of whether or not I went with it.

"You shouldn't think about it."

I jumped at the voice and nearly fell off the bench: Cabail Ibbot was seated next to me. He was so small that his legs hung above the ground, and his little feet made no imprint in the snow.

"How long have you been there?" I asked, righting myself and smoothing down the creases in my pants.

"A while."

"Why?"

"I thought you might need help figuring it out."

"Figuring what out?"

"What's on your mind."

He turned his magnified, bug-like eyes towards me, but I couldn't see my reflection in the darks of his eyes.

"You're looking at the wrong part," he said. "And you're looking at it the wrong way."

"Wrong part of what?"

"Of what's bothering you."

"You don't know what bothers me, Cabail," I said irritably.

"Not completely. But I don't think you know that, either."

His eyes were much too still, and I stood to leave before the conversation could go further. For all I knew, Cabail was acting on some plot of Julian's to extract information on me, and I wouldn't give him any more opportunities to do so. I started down the path out of the garden.

"I know you want to know who killed Miss Mercier."

As the statement struck the air, so close that it sounded as though he was still speaking into my ear, I slowly turned back to him. My expression was carefully neutral.

"Who told you that? Porter?" I anxiously pushed back the sleeves of my jacket despite it being so cold. There was no telling what Thomas could do if he had pieced together the conversation with Jack in the woods. "Well, it's not true."

Cabail bypassed the blatant lie.

"You're missing something."

"No, I'm not," I said. "I – I don't even know what you're talking about."

"You know how Miss Mercier was killed."

"So does everyone; it was in the paper."

"You know how she was killed, but you're looking at it the wrong way."

"I don't –"

Before I could get the words out, someone brushed past me on the path and I moved back to let him by. When I turned back to where Cabail had been sitting, I found the bench was empty. Though I stared through the mess of dead foliage for any sign of him, he was gone.

Still hesitant that I was being tricked, I returned to the dorm room and pulled out the folder on Miss Mercier and the dead girls. Cabail had no way of knowing what we were up to or what we knew about the murders, and his advice would undoubtedly prove to be useless. Regardless, I opened the folder and turned to the photographs of the crime scene, ignoring the clenching in my stomach as I did so. Dictionary watched me steadily from the bed.

The pictures were no-less gruesome than they had been the first time that I had seen them. Miss Mercier was lying on the dirt floor of the forest, her brown hair darkened and matted with blood and splayed out around her, and her body was hacked to pieces.

I shut my eyes towards the wall, ready to berate myself for letting Cabail toy with me. The smell of blood seemed to fill the air, and the sight of her lying there, arms and legs detached from the torso, was too horrifying to comprehend. My mind fumbled as it tried to find an alternate explanation as to why there were blank stretches of ground between where her waist ended and her legs began.

"What are you doing?"

Jack had entered the room and moved to stand behind me, peering over my shoulder curiously. As soon as he caught sight of what he was looking at, he pulled away again.

"Why're you looking at those?"

"I don't know, I thought –" I was careful not to mention anything of the conversation with Cabail, nor my concerns that Porter might know what we were up to. "I was just thinking that maybe we missed something in how Miss Mercier was killed."

"Missed something? That's the only part that's clear, Nim: she was hacked to pieces."

He shrugged off his bag and set it beside the bed. As he took a seat on the mattress to pull off his shoes, Dictionary sidled over to sit on his lap.

I made to put the photos away again when one of them caught my attention. It had been taken from afar to include her whole form: her torso lay in the middle and her limbs were spread out around her. In the following shots, the camera had taken the individual pieces separately, and the final ones were of sections of the surrounding forest that held fragments of clothing or places where footprints had been found. My eyes traced the outline of a leg and then the other, and then went up to do the same for both the arms. She looked like a doll whose parts had been snapped from the sockets.

"But she wasn't hacked," I said, my eyes narrowing beneath a frown. "She was cut up."

"Same thing."

"But is it?" I turned to him as the thoughts began to filter through my head, and my heart pounded more quickly against

my chest. "I mean, 'hacked' kind of implies that it was messy –
"

"And you think *that* looks neat?"

"No, well – sort of. I mean, look at her arms and legs: they look like they were just broken off from the rest. If someone had axed her, it would be jagged or uneven, or something, wouldn't it?"

Jack stood back up to look at the photos. His knuckles were white as he clutched the edge of the desk. "Nim, you're right."

"But who would cut her up carefully?"

"Who *could* cut her up carefully, more importantly?"

"What do you mean?"

"Come on, Nim. It's not like anyone could do something so ... meticulous. I mean, you remember doing dissections – how many people were actually good at them?"

"I wasn't."

"No, neither was I. My sheep's eye exploded all over my favorite sweatshirt, and don't even get me started on the cat – that was a nightmare."

"But was anyone good at it? One student in particular?"

"Not that I remember," he said with a frown. "But what about in your class? You were in the advanced ones. Was there someone good at it?"

"No. We were so awful that the teacher wouldn't even let us participate in the cat dissection – he just had us watch."

Jack ran his hand through his hair as he thought.

"Alright, so maybe it's not a student after all. I mean, disarticulating a person is a bit different from finding the stomach in a frog, isn't it? This had to have been someone who knows their anatomy."

"One of the science teachers, you think?" I said. "There's only a dozen or so of them – it shouldn't be hard to check out. Who teaches anatomy?"

"Something-ski. Almunski or Crusunski ..."

"Right. Something Polish."

"All right," Jack said, grabbing up a pen to begin jotting

things down. "Or it could be someone in a science club. Is there a dissection club?"

"You're asking the wrong person."

"Good point. We can look at the event board in the department later, but first –" He ripped the page he had been scribbling on from the notebook and shoved it into his pocket. "—let's check out the science teachers to see if any of them look suspicious."

We turned out of the room and started down the hall, neither of us daring to get too excited. Halfway down the stairs, though, Jack paused.

"I forgot my keys," he said. "Do you have yours?"

"I left them on the desk," I said, patting down my jacket as I spoke. "Why?"

"Labs are locked after class."

"Right."

We turned and hurried back up the stairs. As we approached the dorm room again, I could see that the door was open several inches, though I was certain that I had closed it behind us. Jack took a step forward and pushed it open. The room was empty apart for Dictionary, who was hovering beneath the bed.

"That's weird. Didn't you close it?"

"Yes ..."

We had barely stepped into the room when we realized our mistake. It was midway through dining hours and I had not yet gone to dinner; Sanders must have come into the room to get me. It was clear why he had chosen not to stay: the file folder was still open on the desk, and the photos of Miss Mercier's dismembered body were scattered everywhere.

"Fuck."

Jack had barely gotten the word out when something sounded behind us. We turned simultaneously to the door in time to see Sanders leading his roommate into the room. He was spluttering something incoherent as he tried to explain what his upset was about, but halted upon finding us standing there.

"Hadler – Lund."

"Sanders."

Jack sucked in his cheeks as he eyed the building monitor; both were at a loss for what to say. Sanders' roommate looked between them carefully before he moved into the room.

"What's all the fuss about?" he said.

"Nothing." Jack moved to block his path. The other student eyed him impatiently.

"Get out of the way, Hadler."

"Sorry, Britten. Can't do that."

"You can and you will. Matt says you've got something incriminating in here – something to do with Miss Mercier."

"Well, he's mistaken."

"I'm not," Sanders said firmly, finally taking a step into the room. "He's got something – something sick, right there!"

He pointed to the desk behind Jack, and Jack made another move to block their line of sight. As Britten looked between us to decide how to proceed, another set of footsteps sounded in the hall and an intrigued voice entered the room.

"What's going on in here?"

Julian peered into the room; his eyes were alight at the thought of a spectacle.

"Nothing," Jack said.

"Hadler's hiding something about Miss Mercier."

"Really?" Julian's eyes flickered even brighter. "Don't want to share, Jack?"

"He won't get out of the way," Britten said.

Julian smirked.

"I can help with that," he said. He took a step back and ducked his head into the hallway. "Hey, Kyle – come over here."

Trask was in the room so quickly it was as though he had been waiting for the invitation. He eyed the room hungrily as though deciding who to threaten first.

"Matt and Tristan are having some trouble getting Jack to move," Julian told him easily. "I thought you could help."

"I'd *love* to."

"Hold on –" Sanders said, flinging out an arm as Trask advanced on Jack. "We can't go getting into a fight. There's something more serious going on here."

"Well, tell us what it is, then, Matt – because you've been blubbering for the past ten minutes."

"I – I really think that I should go get the administrators. They need to hear this."

"Hear what?" Britten asked. "What's on that desk?"

He moved to shove past Jack, but Jack blocked him once again.

"I wasn't aware that my room was some sort of forum open for discussion."

"No, talking things out isn't really how you do things, is it, Hadler?" Trask said. "You'd rather just solve your problems through force?"

"Is that an invitation?" Jack asked. He glared at the other students in the room with such animosity that everyone but Trask took a step back.

"You think you can get all of us, do you?" he said. "Is that your plan? Is that what you do when you're holed up in here? Think up the best way to do away with anyone who bothers you?"

"It's crossed my mind a few times."

Sanders made another movement by the door as his attention was torn away by someone in the hallway.

"Oh, good, Jacobson," he said, waving the huge lacrosse player into the room. "I need you to go downstairs and call in some administrators. We've got a situation here. Better yet, have Brody do it: he knows the protocol –"

"Chris, just in time," Trask cut in. "I was just about to teach Jack a little lesson ... care to join?"

The lacrosse player looked around the room with a frown, and Sanders quickly attempted to divert his attention back to his set of rules.

"That's certainly not necessary," he said. "This is not some opportunity for your childish revenge, Trask – this is much bigger than that –"

"I'd like to know what's so big, exactly," Julian interrupted. "Since you're so concerned, Matt, it's only right that we all know, right?"

Sanders blubbered in response. In the momentary distraction, Trask seized Jack and shoved him out of the way. Though he quickly scrambled up again, Trask had already reached the desk and seized the folder.

"What the fuck ...?" He lifted the photos in front of his face in pure shock, and Julian pushed through the others to see what they were of. Jack made a move as though to rip it out of their hands, but the damage was already done. He threw me a panicky look that I could only mirror in response.

"Is this ...?" Julian looked up from the photos after a long moment. "Is this ... Miss Mercier?"

He gaped at Jack in sickened revulsion before looking at me.

"Did you know about this?" he asked.

"It's not what you think," I said.

"So you're *both* in on it?" He bore his eyes into me with such intent that I thought a hole might burrow through my skin. I slowly turned so that I was half-hidden by Jack. "Fuck. I mean – *fuck.*"

The others were at a further loss for words than he was, and he shook his head for several moments of silence as he looked between us.

"I mean, I guess I should have known," he said at last. "After that whole thing with lighting the opossum on fire ... We thought that was all Jack's idea, but I guess it really was both of you. You're *both* fucked."

"It's not what you think," I said again. "I mean, it's nothing bad – we've done nothing wrong."

"You can't mean that," Julian said flatly. "Come on, Enim. You seriously can't mean that."

"No, he does," Trask said. "I told you, Julian. One's as bad as the other. You can't have expected him to live in the same room and not know about all this."

"Just get out," Jack snapped, unable to contain his

321

resentment of the other two any longer. "Go on – get out. Before I make you."

"I think that we should all leave," Sanders said. "Wynne, hand over the folder. I'll get it to the administrators, and they'll sort this whole thing out –"

"No," Trask said angrily. "What're they going to do? Everyone knows."

"Exactly," Sanders said. "So let's just get out of here and let them take care of it –"

"I think we should take care of it – properly," Trask said. "We've all seen what type of stuff they get away with. They killed Miss Mercier, and all they might get is a slap on the wrist –!"

"We didn't kill her!"

"It certainly *looks* like you did."

"Why?" Jack said furiously. "Why would we do that?"

"It's obvious, isn't it?" Julian said. "You were always obsessed with her – everyone knew it. You'd wait for her after class, follow her around, walk her home …"

"That's called liking someone, Julian," I said. "He wouldn't kill someone he actually liked!"

"Course he would. She probably got tired of it … told him to back off. Or maybe he just got jealous. Either way, he snapped and …"

He didn't need to finish the sentence. A collective shiver ran over the group, but Jack remained very still. His expression was hard and set. I couldn't read what was going on behind his eyes: they were so dark that the irises were indistinguishable from the pupils.

"I didn't kill anyone," he said quietly.

"Maybe … maybe you didn't mean to, Hadler," Sanders said as he took a step back. "Maybe it was a mistake, or it went too far …"

"It wasn't an accident," Julian said. "We all know Jack's violent – we've always known. I know tons of people who could attest to that. Me included."

"Getting into fights isn't the same as killing someone," I

said. "And having the file doesn't prove anything, either!"

"But you know what does, Enim?" Julian said. "The fact that everyone knows you two were sneaking about looking for something. Porter told me how you two went into the woods a few weeks back, and he heard you talking about it, too."

"Porter's a joke. He'd say anything to get back at me –"

"Funny, it seems like a lot of people feel that way," Julian said. "Is that how you two were planning to get out of this? Having everyone too afraid to say anything? I can see how you'd think that would work. You're each as unstable as the next."

An impenetrable silence came over the room, and the last of the hope that I had been holding onto drained from me as the disbelieving expressions became definite. Jack's cheeks slowly sucked in as he bit down on the insides of them, and I shut my eyes in incredulity of what they were all so eager to believe.

"Hadler," Sanders said after a long moment. "Do you ... want to say anything?"

Jack slowly lowered his eyes away from Julian's face. They gazed at a blank spot on the floor instead.

"Get out," he said quietly.

"Excuse me?" Sanders said.

"Get out of my room." His eyes snapped back up to the building monitor's face. "Get out. Now."

His voice broke the quiet with a shattering speed. Several of the students jumped, but no one moved away from the door. Trask took a step forward and looked down at Jack, his nose an inch away from Jack's hairline, as he continued to stare at him with contempt.

"I say we don't wait for the police," Trask said lowly. "I say we take care of this right now."

Sanders put his hands between them and tried to break them apart.

"No, Trask – we're not going to do anything. We need to contact the administrators, and they'll need to search the premise –"

"Let's search it ourselves," Trask said, throwing off Sanders' arm. "I bet there's tons more proof right here in this room – starting with the murder weapon!"

He shoved Jack out of the way and started further into the room. Jack reacted immediately: grabbing Trask by the forearms, he swung him back in the direction of the door where he collided with Julian. Sanders cowered back as the two of them stumbled back into the wall.

"So you are hiding something!" Trask said, a malicious glint in his eyes as he straightened back up. "Where is it, Hadler? Where's the knife?"

He shoved through us and went to my bed, a look of deranged hunger on his face. His hands pulled out the drawers to my bedside table and dresser and overturned the contents, sending the neatly organized books and clothing to the floor in a stream of movements. Finding nothing, he stared down at the neatly made bed for a good few seconds before reaching down and overturning it. The mattress gave way and smacked against the wall, sending a stream of orange medication bottles to the floor as it went. Several of the bottles broke and pills cascaded to the floor, and my stomach plummeted as I pressed myself up against the opposite wall to get away from them.

"What the fuck?" Julian said, running his eyes over the mess of powder-blue.

"Where is it, Hadler? Where is it?" Trask said without acknowledging the medication. He emptied Jack's drawers as well, adding to the mess that his side of the room already displayed. When he went to look beneath Jack's bed, though, he had barely lowered his head to the floor when he bolted back with a shout of pain.

Flinging himself backwards and slipping over the orange pill bottles, he writhed on his back as Dictionary shot out from beneath the bed and clamped herself onto his face, digging her claws into the skin with a hiss of anger. Trask grabbed her about the abdomen and flung her back violently, and she flipped over the floor in a tangle of fur before landing back on her feet.

"Hey!" Jack rushed forward and scooped her up. As Trask shakily stood up and looked at Jack through his bloodied face, his expression was more infuriated than ever.

"What the fuck is that thing?" he demanded, wiping at his mouth. He turned to Jacobson and gave him a firm nod. "Let's get him."

It only took me a moment to register what he had said, but by then it was too late. Trask and the huge lacrosse player moved towards Jack, closely followed by several other boys from the floor who had come in during the excitement. They glowered at him with a deep hunger in their eyes for something that resembled – but was not quite – justice. Jack had barely turned away when the first punch caught the side of his face, and he dropped Dictionary from his arms. As he stumbled sideways, Trask aimed a kick at his stomach that sent him bowling over onto the floor.

"Wait –" I tried to say as the group closed in on him and began to hit and kick every part of him that they could, but my voice sounded strangled in my throat and my shoulder blades were latched to the wall. "Wait – stop – you've got it wrong –"

Julian crossed his arms as the boys continued their assault on Jack, occasionally breaking his gaze to look across at me, and Sanders had backed up to the threshold as though uncertain if he should stay or go. They both watched wordlessly as Trask's foot smashed against Jack's jaw, and a bright red tooth clattered across the hardwood and rolled to a stop beneath the dresser. He raised his arms to try and shield the blows to his head, but the constant stream of kicks to his ribs lowered them down again as he sought to protect himself, and his face was masked with pain.

"Wait – stop!" I shouted, using all of my effort to pry myself from my spot. "Sanders – make them stop! They're going to kill him!"

Sanders didn't appear to hear me. He continued to stare down at where Jack was lying on the floor. After a long moment, he said admissibly, "He killed Miss Mercier."

"No, he didn't! Sanders, please, he didn't – I can explain!

It's not like that!"

But no one paid me any mind. As half the boys continued to beat Jack into the floor, the other half watched on; their expressions held the same type of eagerness that they displayed at the Bickerby sporting events as they cheered on their team. And despite the look of agony on Jack's face, I couldn't bring myself to move.

With a flash of dark fur, Dictionary darted back out from beneath the bed and leapt onto Trask's leg. She clung to it as he aimed another kick at Jack, tearing her claws down his skin and drawing another cry of pain from him, and successfully offered Jack a moment of reprieve as the boys jumped back to watch Trask thrash and shake to get her off again.

"You little shit!" he said angrily, seizing her by the scruff of the neck and tearing her away from him.

She hissed vehemently and latched onto his arm instead. With another shout of pain, Trask shook his arm to release her but had no success. Growling in anger and looking far more animalistic than she did, he dropped to his knees and slammed the arm with her on it to the floor, beating her into the wood with all of his might. She made a terrible sound as she finally let go, but as she turned to dart away from him, he grabbed her by the tail and stomped her to the ground. A shattering crack sounded through the room as her neck broke, and she slumped down with eyes open to the far wall where I stood, finally unmoving.

For a long moment the only sound in the room was of Trask's heavy breathing as everyone stared at the twisted, distorted body of the dead creature, and then the eyes began to move up to Trask's face. He showed no concern for what he had done, too preoccupied with his scratched and bitten arm to notice the wary looks of the other boys, at last disconcerted by his stream of violence.

And then Jack's horrified cry broke through the room, and he rolled onto his knees and elbows as he tried to reach the spot where Dictionary lay, and the blood covering his face could not hide the pain that was clearly printed there that had nothing to do with his physical injuries. He crawled to the dead creature, his bloody hands shaking as they picked up the limp form, and the fur matted in his hands as the moisture tangled it.

"No," he said into the fur, petting it back to stare into her glassy eyes. "No, Dictionary ..."

"Kyle, what'd you do that for?" Jacobson said. There was an uncertainty in his voice as he eyed Trask that seemed to collect amongst the group.

"It attacked me!" Trask said. "And he would've killed it anyhow – it was probably going to be part of one of his satanic rituals like last year!"

Jacobson looked over at Julian in the hope that he would offer him guidance on what to believe, but Julian had turned his face away to stare at the mess of pills upon the ground. Only Jack moved to shake as he held Dictionary in his arms.

"That's ... that's enough," Sanders said at last. "We – we should wait for the administrators. I should – I should tell Brody to make that call ..."

Several of the boys slipped out of the door, but Trask stayed in place.

"We can't just leave him here – what if he destroys the evidence? What if he escapes?"

Sanders turned his eyes to him nervously.

"I don't think he'll be going anywhere, Trask."

"He might. I know Hadler's type: he'll want to get away. We should at least hold him down until the police get here –"

"He doesn't need to be held down," Sanders said, looking at where Jack's crumpled form knelt between them.

"Well, I think I'll stay," Trask continued. "I think someone should do *something*, at least –"

"I think you've done enough," Sanders said. He straightened his stance at last and looked at the remaining students in the room. "All of you – back to your rooms. Come on. Right now."

Julian twitched as they brushed past him. His breathing was jagged beneath his crumpled collared-shirt.

"But –" Trask said, "we can't just leave him here –"

"I think we should," Julian said, though he was unable to meet anyone's eyes. "Before the cops show up."

"But we should take care of this before they get here," Trask said lowly. "We don't want him to get away with this!"

Julian's face was still sickened, but it was no longer clear what the cause of it was. He swallowed as he looked from where Jack knelt to where Trask stood.

"Matt's right, Kyle. We've done enough, and – and I don't want to get into trouble."

With no one to back him up, Trask finally consented to leave the room. Sanders followed quickly behind them. At the door he paused to look back on where we shook in the destroyed room. The overturned beds, the drawers pulled from the dresser, and the pill bottles scattering the floor somehow looked whole in comparison to the way Jack looked as he clutched the cat that Miss Mercier had brought in from the cold. And as he shut the door on the sight of us, I was aware that every splinter and crack that had scraped into our skin had finally broken to shatter the bones and burn away the flesh, and that the wreck they left behind was something well beyond repair.

Ch. 21

The ridges of my nails slowly stained with red as I gently pried Jack's grip from Dictionary and blanketed her form in a pillowcase. Jack and I stared at the neat white square in the center of the room for several minutes, the only orderly thing amongst the chaos, before I finally pulled myself away to take a sweater from an overturned drawer and handed it to him. He pressed his face heavily into it, and it grew thick and dark with blood.

He could barely stand. I clutched his arms to pull him up, hardly managing to hold him until he could find his footing, and then helped him over to his mattress to sit down. The silence in the room seemed unshakable, and the dark from the clouded sky made his shadowed face nearly impossible to see. Realizing how badly my legs were shaking, I sank down beside him.

"Jack, they're going to call the police."

He slowly shut his eyes and bowed his head. Then, with careful consideration, he shrugged.

"Jack, we can't let them do that! They'll think it's true – they'll think it was you!"

"It doesn't matter."

"Of course it does! They'll arrest you, you'll go to jail –"

"Nim, it doesn't matter." He turned his head to stare at me, and there was nothing left in the darks of his eyes despite how deeply I stared into them. "There's no point in pretending otherwise: no one will believe it wasn't me. It looks like me."

But even as I opened my mouth to protest, I felt the disheartening reality of the situation sinking into me: Jack's infatuation with Miss Mercier, the mischance walking her home the night of her murder, the key that had fallen from his pocket, the conversation that Porter had overheard between us, and the file folder lying right out in the open on the desk were all too much to ignore. He was guilty by every account but the truth that no one would believe.

"You can't go to jail. You can't – you can't just let them

blame you–"

"Why not? It was my fault anyhow; maybe this is for the best."

"Don't start that again!" I said angrily. "It wasn't your fault – it was whoever did this!"

"Whoever did this was smart enough not to get caught, so it doesn't matter anyhow."

"That's not true, we've almost got him! We can just bring all the information to the police and they'll –"

"And they'll look into it just as well as they did last time," Jack said. "They don't care about Miss Mercier, Nim: they never did. They just wanted it to go away."

"But those girls – we can tell them what happened to them –"

"And they'll think we're insane. Everyone's happy enough to believe they ran away, and no one wants to mess up their lives by changing things around."

"But –"

"*Nim.*" Jack leaned towards me until his face was just an inch from mine, and the bloodied hand that grasped my arm left a purplish stain upon the fabric. "Please stop. Please. There's nothing we can do to make them believe us. Nothing."

The silence pressed down on us harder still and Jack's grip became tighter to clench at my arm, and the skin beneath the shirt and sweater pinched beneath his fingers, but I made no move to pull away from him. I had the urge to latch onto him and never let go, but pushed it away as a separate realization came to my mind.

"You have to go, Jack."

"I can't."

"Yes, you can," I said, my mind humming feverishly as I laid out the plan within it. "You'll take one of the boats from the boathouse and row to shore, then – then you'll take one of the buses up to Canada –"

"Nim, that's impossible."

"No, it's not – just listen. You'll ... you'll take Karl's bank card and get as much money out as you can, then take my passport. No one will be looking out for my name, just yours. And then, once you're over the border, you can book a flight anywhere, then –"

"Nim, stop. I can't."

"But you can!" I said, grabbing his arm as he let go of mine and turned away. "Come on, Jack – it'll work! If we can't convince them that it wasn't you, then you have to get out of here before they get you!"

"But I can't." He ran his tongue over his dry lips and stared at me with an unreadable expression. "I don't want to go without you."

"I'll meet you there."

"Where? I don't even know where I'm going – you'll have no idea where I'll be."

"Sure I do," I said, with an expression flitting somewhere between a smile and a frown. "Provence."

He gave a soft chuckle, but it was wrecked with hopelessness for what would never be.

"I might not get there, Nim. I might not get anywhere."

"I'll find you," I said. "I will – just trust me. But I won't be able to do anything if they stick you in jail."

He looked over his shoulder out the window: the campus was heavily shadowed by dark clouds and the half-melted snow was pooling over the pathways and down the windowpane, but the barren sight was nothing compared with the room around us. After what felt like an eternity, he bowed his head in a nod.

"I ... I guess you're right," he said. "I'll ... I'll go."

Wiping the blood from his face and hands, he stood and made to change into cleaner clothes. A noise sounded from down the hall and I started, but quieted a moment later. As he reached for a cleaner sweatshirt, I stopped him.

"Wait, wear mine."

"What?"

"Wear my clothes," I said, "so you can sneak out of the building. Sanders is probably watching the door, and they'll be looking out for you. No one will recognize you in my clothes."

He gave me a look before dropping the sweatshirt to pick

up the clothes from the overturned drawers and pull them on. Though the khakis and dress-shirt had been wrinkled from the way they had been thrown, they still looked oddly neat and orderly on his normally disheveled form. He pulled on my winter hat to cover his dark hair and wrapped my scarf about him to cover half of his face. As he donned my jacket as well, I squinted at him to carefully scrutinize if he would be recognizable as he left the building. Without the dark, worn clothing, he looked quite unlike himself.

He shoved the passport and bank card into his inner pocket and zipped the jacket up to his neck. As he turned to look at me, there was a tightness in his expression that masked whatever he was thinking. And I thought of saying everything that I had always wanted to tell him – the unspoken things that were in the back of my mind that I could never push closer – but the knowledge that the administrators and police would be at the residence building in moments made me clench my jaw shut again. And even if I had had the time to say what I wanted to, the knowledge that they might be the last words I spoke to him for a long while made me falter with every word that lingered on the back of my tongue.

"Jack, I ..." I began, but the words wouldn't come.

He bowed his head accordingly.

"I know," he said. He took my arm momentarily before pulling away, fingers scraping through mine, and slipped out the door. As it shut quietly behind him and I strained through the silence to make sure that no one stopped him in the hall, my arms fell back to my sides and my hands unclenched to the feeling of the cold air, and I realized just how much I didn't want to let him go.

I sat down numbly on his bed and stared at the pillowcase covering Dictionary's broken body. The room was quiet, and outside the walls the building and campus were quiet as well. I was waiting to hear any noise that would indicate that something had gone wrong and that I had made a mistake in sending him out there alone, but the quiet just continued on its way, tormenting me with time that seemed to move too quickly and too slowly all at once. Perhaps if it had been louder then it could have silenced the thoughts in my head; but the words stringing themselves together were ringing in my ears like voices screaming at me from every side.

"Here, he's right in –"

Sanders fumbled through the door and nearly tripped over pills scattering the threshold. As he straightened to look around the room, his expression paled with the realization of what was missing.

"He's – he's –" He looked fully around the room four times before looking to me. "Lund, where is he? Where's Hadler?"

He had brought several administrators with him, along with Josh Brody, who was standing in the background with a perplexed expression. The sight of them in the doorway was an odd one, and it felt as though they were at the end of a musty tunnel, or at the top of a well that I had fallen down. I stared over at them lifelessly.

"He's gone."

"He's –?" Sanders ran his hands through his hair and glanced anxiously over his shoulder. "But he – he was right here, and I told everyone to make sure that he didn't leave –"

The administrators came further into the room. They dripped water onto the floor from their soaked jackets and waterlogged boots as they searched-over the already destroyed place for the person who would never be there again. When they saw the file folder on the desk, there was a collective intake of breath followed by another ringing silence.

"Mr. Lund, where did he go? Did he say? Did you see him?"

I shook my head to the questions.

"He must have seen him," the man said to his colleague. "*Someone* must have seen him. Go get the boys out of their rooms – I want to talk to all of them before the cops show up. It's all we need to have another scandal this year."

When the room had cleared but for the two of us, he lightly shut the door and crouched down to my eye level.

"Mr. Lund, I need to know where Hadler is. You won't get into any trouble ... if you tell me." He paused as he waited for my response and leaned in further, but my only desire was to push him away. "You must be in a great deal of shock. Maybe ... maybe you'd like to come up to the Welcoming Building, and we can talk about it there ...?"

"I want to call my uncle."

The sharpness in my tone made him turn his head as though it had cut clear across the skin.

"What?"

"My uncle. I want to call him. I'm a minor, and I don't have to talk to you."

"Mr. Lund, you're not in any trouble here, so long as you cooperate –"

"He's a lawyer, and I want to call him," I said, despite being uncertain if the statement was true. "Now."

He scratched anxiously at the back of his head, but then gave a stiff nod.

"I ... all right. That's ... that's fine. You can call your uncle; of course."

He stood to go to the door and said something to his colleague before leading me from the room. A myriad of gazes followed me from the surrounding rooms as I went, but the walk to the stairwell seemed more solitary than ever. As we walked to the ground floor and crossed the campus, I suddenly thought of Dictionary. I wasn't sure what they would do with her upon discovering her; I should have taken her and buried her someplace safe out of the snow.

"Here."

He handed me the phone in the main office and I punched in Karl's number with lead-like fingers. It took me several tries to get it right; my mind was so fogged that I could barely remember the area code.

"Hello?"

His voice came over the line crisply and shook me slightly from my haze. As I opened my mouth to speak to him, the overwhelming realization of what had happened came over me all at once, and my face broke into a painful grimace as I tried to coax the words from my throat. The administrator watched on from the corner of the room.

"Karl, I –"

"Enim?" His tone altered as he asked, and he seemed to strain to hear what the unfamiliar note in my own was. "Are you – what's wrong?"

"Karl, I – I need you to come get me."

"What?"

"Come get me. Please."

"What's happened? Why?"

There was no way that I could say it: the words were sharp against my chest, and if they moved to come to my mouth they would surely cut my throat open on the way. I struggled to find an excuse to give to him, but my mouth only quivered as I thought of all that had happened and I repeated the phrase again and again.

"Come get me. Please. Please, just come get me."

"Enim, alright – don't worry. I'll ... I'll come get you. But ... what's wrong?"

I shook my head even though he couldn't see me, and he breathed a worried sigh that came over the line as static.

"Enim, are you alright? Is it ... Is there someone there with you?"

"No."

"No one's there?"

"No – just come get me, Karl. Please."

"I'll come and get you, Enim, don't worry. I just need to know that you'll be alright," he said, and the worry in his voice wasn't hidden inside the forced-calm of his tone. "You don't sound well. I need to know that there's someone with you."

"There's – there's no one."

"What about Jack? Is he there with you?"

My voice caught and I pushed the phone to the administrator so that I could hide my face behind my hands. He took it and put it to his ear, but the half-conversation was barely noticeable because of the burning in my throat and the throbbing in my ears.

"Hello? Yes, I'm with him ... No, there's been a situation of sorts, I ... I see. No, I didn't realize, I just thought ... I see. Yes, I can do that. I ... Alright. I'll make sure of it. Yes, I understand ..."

He hung up a moment later and wordlessly indicated for me to follow him. We crossed through the snow to the Health Center and he led me inside with a firm grip on one of my shoulders. After saying something lowly to one of the nurses, she brought me in to sit upon one of the white-lined cots in the side room. As her eyes traveled over my clenched white hands and wrecked expression, her face fell into a frown. She stared at me for a moment before retreating from the room. In the silence that followed her dying footsteps, I let my head drop to my hands. The white room felt like a prison, and the campus had never felt so empty.

I shut my eyes. Everything was ruined. If only Jack and I had left the island months ago, then we wouldn't have ever gotten involved with Miss Mercier and the dead girls' deaths, and I wouldn't have had to sit with my mother's death and the tormenting song and thoughts that had taken her place. We could have been someplace warm and covered over with the soft glow of the sun, not sunken beneath cold snow and down-poured with rain and sleet.

I tried to keep myself focused, but my mind couldn't begin to make up where it should settle. Jack would be rowing across the ocean at that very moment while the police began to search the island for him. As I pictured him somewhere out in the blue, I had the urge to jump down from the cot and run after him before he got away, certain that it had been a mistake to let him go. But even if I made it to the shore in record time, he would never see me flailing my arms from so far away.

And the world was ending. I could feel it closing in, could feel the dark, dense, dead sky sinking down and weighing down the ceiling until it broke and collapsed atop of me. I could feel it pressing against me and breaking every bone inside, liquefying the muscles and squeezing the blood from the flesh, and yet I hadn't died. I was just the same as ever: unfeeling, unmoving, undead. And if I could have just put it all back together – to rip the world apart and rearrange it so that it was right again – then everything would be alright again. Then Jack wouldn't be there, and I wouldn't be here, and everything could be fine again.

And I thought, for the most fleeting of moments, that if the world had turned on me, then perhaps it would also consent to turn back around as well. I thought that maybe I would wake up and the time would have reversed itself, or that I would be allowed a second chance to redo things. I pulled myself back to the moment when my mother had turned to walk through the door, but this time I reached out and grabbed her before she went to the snow-covered bridge. And when my head shook with the rationality that that couldn't be, the image was marred by the one of Jack standing by the dorm room door, and I reached out to grab him instead –

I hunched forward on the cot and teetered on the edge of the thin mattress, staring at the floor intently until the image broke, and squeezed my skull between my hands. I wanted it to make sense again, because it wasn't supposed to be like this: it was supposed to add up. I felt as though I was trapped in the final act in the opera, the part when everything beautiful and rich and meaningful to be said had been expressed, and now there was nothing else to say or be done that was worthwhile to watch unfold. I had waited all that time to realize that there was no meaning at all; I had been running and running only to find that I had run out of places to go.

The curtain that served as a door to the room rustled slightly before opening. A shadow fell over the side of the bed and laid across me in a patch of cold darkness.

"Enim?"

Beringer maneuvered through the tight space to get over to me. Snow that still clung to his feet trickled to the floor and pooled around his ruined shoes. I stared at the flood with empty eyes and wished that it would rise to drown me.

"Enim – are you all right?"

He was standing close to me though his voice was far away. A thousand things had happened since I had last seen him, but I was quite unable to make a sound.

"Your uncle called me and asked me to come," he said, stepping closer. "He said that you were upset; he didn't want you to be alone."

I shut my eyes again to block out the harsh fluorescent lights overhead, but the bright blue-white still pierced through the lids at my eyes. It occurred to me that Karl had assumed I was upset about my mother, and had sent Beringer to stay with me until he could get there. I stayed silent for a long while, wishing that the cold would leave the room to make room for the things that needed to be said.

His bare hands clutched at the counter as he waited for me to speak. He was poorly dressed for the weather: he must have run out in too much of a hurry to collect up his scarf and gloves. It reminded me far too much of how Miss Mercier had run out of her house without her shoes to give Jack his keys back, and of how my mother, too, had left without bothering to put something proper on. Perhaps they all knew that it was the end of something unseen, and the trivialities of life were no longer of any concern.

"Enim, can you tell me what's wrong?"

And though I could feel that everything was coming to a close, too, it didn't feel as though it was the end. I pressed my head further into my hands as I realized that I was being cheated out of a proper finale in the same way that I had been with *Turandot*. The part of the story with me in it was over despite it not being finished, and I would never know the answer to the riddle. Someone else would write an unfitting ending in an attempt to tie up the loose ends of Miss Mercier's murder.

"Everything. Everything's wrong."

"Why do you say that?"

"Because now everyone knows, but they've got it all wrong."

"What have they got wrong?" Beringer asked, frowning

down at me in concern.

"They think ... they think that Jack ..." I shook my head until the words would come. "They think he killed Miss Mercier."

Beringer's head moved to the side strangely as though the statement had bypassed his ears, questioning the reason he had been summoned to my side.

"Jack did what?"

"He didn't do anything," I said forcefully. As Beringer raised his eyebrows, I slid to the edge of the cot and corrected my tone. "He – Jack and I – we found something out after Miss Mercier died about something on the island, only we didn't tell anyone, and now he's in trouble, and everyone thinks he killed her, and –"

"Enim, Enim: wait. What's this about? Karl said you were upset about your mother –"

"I'm not. I am – but that's not why I called. I –" It was clear that I was making no sense to him, but he strained to understand. I gripped the edge of the cot as I forced myself to speak rationally. "Dr. Beringer, if I tell you something and swear that it's the truth, will ... will you believe me?"

He righted his head so that he was looking straight at me, and his expression alone would have answered the question fully enough.

"Of course I will, Enim."

And at last the words spilled from me without hesitation: I told him about how Jack's desire to find Miss Mercier's killer had led us to her house where we had found the list of names, and how they corresponded to girls on the island who had seemingly run away from home never to be seen again; and I told him about how we had assumed it was Barker, and of how I had hit Julian just to be sent to his office so that I could steal the file, and of what was inside that solidified our suspicions; and I told him about the girl who had gone missing after Barker's heart-attack, and of how we realized that the killer must have a knowledge of science, and of how close we had been to finding the answer when everything had been ruined.

I told him even though I knew it sounded ridiculous, and he listened without laughing or making any snide comments about the childishness of our actions. He looked at me raptly as though he had never been more serious in his life, but given how ridiculous the entirety of the story sounded, I wondered if his expression was hiding pity.

"Do you ... do you think I'm crazy, Dr. Beringer?"

He looked at me closely for a moment before giving the softest of smiles.

"No, Enim, I don't. In fact I'm ... I'm rather impressed, really, that you and Jack managed to figure all of that out."

"Really?" My heart twitched mid-beat. "So – so you believe me then? You'll tell everyone that it wasn't Jack?"

He adjusted his stance so that he could lean up against the counter. Crossing his arms behind his back, he gave a thoughtful expression before responding.

"Do you two still have the list of names?"

"I – yeah. It's up in the dorm room ... somewhere."

"And all this information on the girls is there, too?"

"Yeah. It's mainly pictures and whatnot ... there's nothing too specific. We only just figured out the last part."

Beringer nodded.

"The last part," he repeated quietly to himself. "And ... how *did* you figure out the last part?"

I turned my head slightly as I regarded him. Despite my elation that he believed me, a damp cold was creeping over my skin.

"I ... I don't know. We just sort of ... put it all together, I guess."

He nodded slowly.

"And what do you know about the ... killer ... again?" he asked. His hands slid on the edge of the desk as though readying to straighten and leave. "You thought he might be a science teacher?"

"Right." I glanced away from him as I spoke. His intent stare was beginning to become disconcerting, and the air in the room seemed to have tightened. "Because he's young, and he takes summers off, and he's scientific enough to know how to dismember someone ..."

Beringer was still nodding, but as he continued to look at me, his face was an expression that I didn't recognize. I chewed the side of my mouth at the fear that he would think that everything I had said was an insane concoction of lies that I had strung together to cover up my friend's wrongdoings.

"You ... you do believe me, don't you, Dr. Beringer?" I said quietly.

"Of course I believe you, Enim. I know you didn't kill anyone. I know that Jack didn't, either."

As I let out a breath, he straightened and stepped closer to me.

"Your uncle was very upset when he called me, Enim," he said seriously. "Nearly frantic, actually. He wanted me to get here as soon as I could. He was afraid that you might harm yourself."

"I know. I'm sorry to've bothered you – I thought that someone would tell him I was upset over Jack. I didn't think he'd call you."

Beringer slid his hands into his pockets and surveyed me.

"No, no, that's alright. I'm glad he did."

His face twitched on the last word as though he was going to smile, and the slight alteration in his features flashed to a face quite unlike the one that I knew. I raised my chin very slightly as I stared up at him, and my fingers clenched the thin sheets on the cot as my mind slowed and repeated the words that I had just said aloud moments before: the killer was someone young, who took summers off, and who had a firm knowledge of science ...

"Right," I said quietly.

He smiled again, a short, terse smile that didn't touch his eyes, and his frozen face had never looked so unfamiliar.

"Of course it is."

"I ... you ..."

"Tell me, Enim, what exactly did you and Jack have written down about this murderer?" he asked softly, taking another step forward towards me.

"I ... it was ... it was mainly newspaper clippings," I said. "And ... and photos and stuff. I mean, we ... we didn't really write much down ..."

"No? Are you certain about that?"

I shook my head, no longer able to speak, and dropped my eyes to the floor. My chest refused to rise and fall as I put it all together: the girls had all been reported missing on Fridays, and Miss Mercier had been killed late Thursday night or early Friday morning. The killings had been going on for a year and only paused during the summertime. The killer was intelligent enough to pass off the disappearances as unhappy teenagers who had run away from home, and knowledgeable of science and knew how to disarticulate a body ...

"Enim ..."

All that time that Jack and I had wasted looking for someone who worked at Bickerby, and the killer hadn't resided on the island at all: Beringer came to the island on Thursdays and stayed into Friday; he came during the school year but stopped for the summer holidays; he was a doctor and knew how to dismember a human body ...

"...why don't we take a walk?"

"I ..."

I glanced at the curtain shutting the room off from the rest of the Health Center, willing the nurse to come back and check on me to see if there was anything that I needed, but no movement came from behind the curtain.

"Eight o'clock," Beringer whispered. "Her shift's over."

"But ..."

I looked at Beringer's unrecognizable face again and didn't believe what my mind was telling me was true. It *couldn't* be him: he was the one person that had gone out of his way to help me, and to treat me like a person rather than some warped, unstable creature. He had cared about me and understood me when I didn't do the same for myself. He couldn't have been a killer – I trusted him.

He leaned down to look at me straight in the face.

"Believe me when I say, Enim, that I truly wish you hadn't found out about this."

I opened my mouth to speak, but only a hollow noise escaped from within me; there was nothing that I could say that would express what was spearing through my skull.

"I ... but you ..." My voice and mind were running parallel to one another, forming and being spoken separately. "You killed those girls? You – you killed Miss Mercier? But – why?"

Beringer contemplated me sadly. The golden flecks in his irises had faded to brown, and the artificial light reflected in his pupils.

"I had hoped that you, of all people, would understand."

"Understand what?" I breathed. "Killing?"

"No." He shut his eyes quickly against the word. "Understand what it's like – to be *different*."

He straightened and pulled his collar up to shield his neck in lieu of a scarf and motioned for me to stand as well. My legs locked as I did so, leaden and dead beneath me. I stared up at Beringer, shaking violently in the deep cold in the room, and silently begged myself to wake up from what must have been the worst yet of my dreams.

"What are you ... what are you going to do?"

"We're going to take a little walk," he said simply.

"I ... Are you going to kill me?"

Beringer exhaled through his nose in the remnants of a chuckle. The smile was still playing softly on his face as he shook his head, and for a moment I felt relieved, as though I had been completely mistaken and that he was not the killer, and that this was all really a misunderstanding that I still couldn't quite grasp –

"No, Enim. I'm not going to kill you," he said. He reached over to take my arm and gently guided me to the door. His eyes flickered in the white light. "You're going to kill yourself."

Ch. 22

The sky was a dark, dirty gray that spread over the horizon and mixed into the half-washed away snow, and the air was thick with an unrelenting chill brought on by the wind and the ground beneath my feet was covered in a sludge that seeped down into my shoes and stung coldly against my skin. In the failing light, I could just see the group of people cluttered in the center of the campus who had returned from searching the island for Jack. My face twitched as Beringer steered me in the direction opposite them and lowered my head beneath a tree branch to shield us from view. Even if they had looked our way, they would never see me through the tree branches crisscrossing in a wall between us.

As the trees grew thicker around us, some of the wind was softened and I was able to walk without my head bent low into my collar. The silence was far too quiet, and I had no distraction from the thoughts running through my head. He was leading me up the familiar path to the cliffs where I had often sat and looked down at the water; it was undoubtedly the same place he had thrown the girls from. I wondered if I would disappear into the water as they had done, or if they would find my body crumpled on the jagged rocks below. Either way, they would all believe the same thing: that I had jumped to my death, just like my mother.

As another wave of cold closed in around me, I wondered if they would bury me in the plot next to her. I could picture my father walking through the cemetery and ruining his good shoes to stand in the space between the two graves, looking down wordlessly and shaking his head as he imagined what might have been if things had just gone the way that he had planned. And at the funeral Karl might apologize for not getting up to the island quickly enough, just like he hadn't gotten to the bridge quickly enough, and perhaps Beringer would comfort him as he pressed his face into quivering hands and tell him that it was not his fault: that I had been sick, and devastated by the events that had unfolded so rapidly, and that there was no way that any of them could have stopped me ...

"Were the girls alive when you threw them off?"

The wind beyond the trees was screeching loudly. Beringer had to lean in to hear what I said.

"Sorry?"

"The girls," I repeated. "Were they alive when you threw them off the cliff?"

He leaned back again.

"Yes."

"What about Miss Mercier?"

I imagined her running barefoot through the woods on the opposite side of the campus again, her espresso-colored hair whipping into her face as she tried to glance behind to see if she was going fast enough, and her colorful skirt staining with mud as she fell to the ground.

"What about her?"

"Did she say anything?" I asked quietly. My mind had flickered back to Jack. He had stayed up for nights on end wondering if the reason that she had been killed that night had been because he had left his keys with her. I wondered if he would ever know who had killed her. I wondered if he would ever know who had killed me, either.

"Before I killed her?" he asked. When I nodded, he paused in thoughtful silence to remember, and I was struck that he was still every bit as considerate as before. It was a wonder that he could be every bit the same and so shockingly different all at once. "She said, 'Je vous en supplie, je vous en supplie.' She was begging me not to kill her."

"But you did."

"I didn't want to, Enim. I'm not a cruel man – you know that."

"You cut her to pieces."

"I disarticulated her, yes. I admit that I got carried away; she wasn't part of the plan."

"But you killed those girls, too."

"Yes ... but that was different. There was nothing malicious in my actions."

"Then why did you do it?"

He waited to answer as the wind raked through the trees around us and rattled the dead branches like bones; a glimpse of blue was visible ahead.

"It was an experiment," he said. His voice had gone quieter; he appeared to be talking to himself as much as he was to me. "I was curious. I wanted to know who they would blame when there was no one *to* blame – if they would turn on one another, or weed out the outcasts among them."

"But they didn't."

"No, they did nothing. And I admit that I hadn't been expecting it – I never thought that they would simply turn their heads and resign that the girls had run away, and not look for them or bother to report them out of anger and spite. But it was good; it taught me what I wanted to know about people. Other people, rather."

The ground beneath our feet changed from frozen pine needles to rocks as we stepped onto the cliffs. The scenery below was a vast expanse of blue, cold and foreboding for as far as I could see, and the sky had never looked so tormented above.

"Damnatio memoriae," I said.

Beringer hummed lowly in my ear. His grip on my arm was the only thing keeping me from dropping down below. I stared down at the rocks beneath my feet, my eyes unwilling to look any further and see the dark blue waving at me from the ocean, and my clothing whipped against my skin as I shook more violently, yet whether it was from cold or from fear I could no longer tell.

"It's despicable," he whispered. "Unprecedented. They all go through their lives alone in the worst way. They surround themselves with others and yet have no idea who the person standing by their side truly is."

He took a step forward, but I kept my feet planted on the ground for fear of getting any closer to the edge. In doing so, his form shielded me from the cold wind and steadied some of my shaking.

"And people like us – people who care so deeply about others – are forced to live our lives alone. We're separate from them, Enim. We see the world in a different way. We see each other in a different way." His fingers relaxed a bit and the grip turned gentle. "I was so happy to have met you, Enim, and I meant it when told you that we're alike."

"That's not true." His proposal was just as unbelievable as it had been the first time that he had offered it to me, yet this time I rejected it out of aversion rather than bleakness. "You're – you're –"

"I'm what, Enim?"

I couldn't settle on a word. They jumbled over one another in my head, pushing to get to the front and describe what I thought of him.

"*Sick*," I said at last.

Beringer's jaw tightened and I could hear the low grinding of his teeth.

"We're all sick, in one way or another."

He leaned his head down next to mine to stare into my face, his grip on my arm turning strong enough to shatter the bones beneath it, and his face was so familiar and unknown all at once that I couldn't look away.

"I searched for years for an answer to what this was – to what *I* was," he said. "I looked through articles and books on disorders that have been thought up and explained by men who all think the same way – who've never had the thoughts that befall the seeming-victims of their diagnoses. And after all of that, after sorting through all of these children, trying to find something remotely similar to what I was as a child, do you know what I found? Nothing. I found that they'll never understand us, or even give it a moment's thought to try."

The wind rattled around us again, and in the dark only the glint from the moonlight told me where his eyes were. I shook my head at him, unbelieving, and my feet slid on the wet rocks as the gusting air blew us about.

"But you and I, Enim, we're the same. We understand."

I shook my head as I struggled to answer.

"No, I'm not – I'm not like you."

Beringer bowed his head.

"No, I suppose you're not. But if I had had more time, and if you had trusted me fully ... you might have been."

He straightened and pushed me forward: my feet skidded across the rocks and I lurched ahead to stare over the cliffs. The ocean below took over my sight as I stared down at it, a dark blue that swayed and circled about as though opening its arms to me, and I clung onto Beringer's arm to keep from falling. He gripped me back for a moment as we stared at one another, both wishing that the other would change his mind, and our expressions mirrored our regret that neither of us would.

And as he gently eased my fingers to loosen my grip, it was such a different feeling than the one when Jack had grasped my arm before leaving the dorm room. Even though the motions were so similar, there was something completely contrasting in the way that I had wanted neither of them to let go. And as I thought of him disappearing through the door in my clothes, I thought of my mother leaving me as well, only this time it wasn't with the knowledge that I had let her go, it was that it had been her choice to do so, and that, had she wanted, she could have held on to me instead.

And just as Beringer pried the last finger from his arm and let me go, I flung my other arm up and grabbed onto the fabric of his coat. My body twisted about as his weight halted my fall, and I saw his face morph into an expression of shock as I clung to him without falling over. For a moment he teetered on the edge, trying futilely to keep himself upright, but the ground beneath his feet was wet and icy and he slipped, falling forward, and we both tumbled over the edge and down, down towards the rocks below –

My vision turned dark as we dropped. I felt the impact of us hitting the ground in a state of disbelief, sure that I would keep falling until I hit something hard and sharp, but instead I fell forward on all fours into warmth. My arms slammed back into my shoulders as they were thrown from their sockets, but when I crashed forward it was onto Beringer's body rather than the jagged ground. His weight had shifted below me as we fell and his body had cushioned my fall. I was oddly aware of the sound of his skull crushing inwards against the stone, and then of the blood rising from his form and smothering over my shaking hands and skin, and then we continued to topple down over the last of the rocks and plummeted onwards into the water.

The cold hit me worse than the fall had. For a moment I was in shock, thinking that I had been given a reprieve, but then the water came up and swallowed me down into it and every part of me screamed to tell me to raise my arms and heave myself back out, but my body had stopped functioning. I was stuck in place – every inch of me frozen as I sank lower and lower down – motionless and heavy as I drowned.

Beneath the surface, face towards the sky and arms outstretched, the season was so deep into winter that even the salt water had frozen into crystals in places, cutting against the skin in crucifixion. Through the surface, the barely-visible sky was simultaneously as dark and bright as ever, and the image was blurred and changing as the waves shifted overhead. And from where I was suspended somewhere between the top and the bottom, cold and broken and bleeding into the blue, I finally felt as though I could see the world for what it truly was.

Ch. 23

Muted noises were coming from afar, like the distant sounds of people chattering on the beach in springtime. I had stopped sinking and was suspended somewhere in the darkness, cold but numb and conscious but unmoving, and all of my senses felt weighted down by the cold and solitude. Time seemed to have shifted forward without touching me at all, and somehow I had been stuck beneath the ocean for years without ever needing to breathe, and there was no chance of being found.

As I attempted to open my eyes, one of my shoulders jerked back into something cushioned and soft, and I was half-aware that my breathing was coming in low, regular intervals. My mouth was somewhat agape and something had wormed down inside of my esophagus, scratching and scraping at the skin, yet no water flooded down into my lungs to drown me. I tried to raise my arms and pull it from my throat, but the heaviness was too much to overcome and I only squirmed in place instead.

The sounds above me drew closer as though the crowd on the beach had leaned over the water to watch me struggling on the ocean floor. Their voices were deep and muted through the thick expanse of liquid, and though I knew that they couldn't see or hear me fully, I opened my mouth wide to let out a shout before remembering the object that had taken a place in my mouth. My head fell back as I choked against it, and in my struggle to spit it out, something like glass shattered in my ears and all the noise from the world became audible again all at once.

I jolted to my side and made to clutch my hands against my ears to quiet it again, but my limbs were barely functioning. The echoes of people speaking much too loudly and the crashes of metal and wood all around were impossibly hard to bear: it tore at the insides of my eardrums and ripped them apart. And just when the ringing set in and sent a sharp pain shooting through my skull, the familiar sound of beeping rose up through the rest as though I was pressed up against the room at the end of the hall in my grandmother's old house.

"Enim? Enim, calm down. It's all right."

Something warm pressed against my shoulder and held me still, and I froze in place to listen to the broken-silence. The voice was a distantly familiar one that implored me to do as it asked, yet I couldn't focus on it long enough to know who it belonged to. As I laid motionless with ragged breathing, my mind went into overdrive to place who it could be, and the only thought that came to mind was the last that I wanted as an answer.

Beringer.

I traced back through the memories that had shoved themselves into every far corner of my head and tried to remember all that had happened: he was the killer, he had murdered Miss Mercier and the local girls, and he had tried to kill me. I felt an overwhelming shakiness come over my skin as I replayed the image of him leading me up to the cliffs, and of how he had tried to throw me off but I had pulled him down with me –

"Can someone help him? He's sick – I think he's seizing –"

The object in my throat was expanding and barring every last bit of oxygen from my lungs. My back arched as I failed to lift my arms or legs to pull it away, and my head jerked to the side to spit it out instead –

Someone pulled the tube from my throat. As it came up, several large mouthfuls of salt-water followed and splattered on the tile floor as I heaved over the side of the bed. The hands holding my arms to keep me upright were far too reminiscent of how Beringer had suspended me over the edge of the cliffs, but it took me several moments of blinking before I could see against the bright fluorescent lights overhead to feel well enough to speak.

"Beringer –" I choked out, but the sound was hardly comprehensible. The hands over my arms clenched momentarily before helping me to lie back down and loosening.

"No, Enim, he's ... he's not here."

"Beringer."

The figure above me was blurred against the white lights, and his fuzzy outline seemed to unmistakably be the one of the psychiatrist before sharpening into my uncle. As Karl's face came into view, he raised his hand to run through his hair and briefly shut his eyes. When they reopened, they were the same dark blue of the ocean.

"No, Enim, it's me. It's Karl."

He had taken a step back with the words. My seeming disappointment that it was him there could not be rectified because of the quick, sharp breaths racking my lungs. Someone lifted a mask over my mouth to ease the discomfort; my breathing calmed as I wheezed into the plastic.

"He should be fine, now," the nurse said, and Karl nodded absently and looked away until she left the room. It was only as I watched her go through the door that I realized fully that I was in a hospital, but the realization did nothing to ease the blankness of the white walls or the humming and beeping of machines.

Unable to speak, I made to wave my hand to get Karl's attention but my arm only flopped to my side. Something was pinching against one finger and wires were running in crisscrosses across my body. The movements in my limbs were forced and heavy as though my bloodstream was drained and filled with sand, and my head throbbed against the pillow worse as though it was split against the jagged rocks.

Karl looked down at me uneasily.

"Do you ... remember what happened?"

My head lulled to the side in an attempt to shake it; though the memories were clear, they were more fractured and disjointed than ever.

"You ... you don't remember?" he asked. He glanced at the door as though hoping for an interruption, but it was solidly closed. "You ... you called me to come get you."

Jack. I shut my eyes as his departure washed over me again, and the horrible sensation in my gut would have risen to my mouth if I had not just emptied the contents of it moments before. He had gone; everyone thought that he had killed Miss Mercier. And I had called Karl to come and get me, but that was before I had worked out the riddle. I knew the answer now: everything would be all right again –

"You remember?"

When I nodded, he sighed and slid his hands into his pockets, choosing to stare out the window to his other side rather than at me. I watched the crease in his brow deepen on his profile as he stood there in silence, and only when several moments had stretched between us did he speak again.

"You ... I ... I'm sorry, Enim. I should have been there faster; I should have done things differently."

The words sounded vaguely reminiscent of the ones he had given my father fourteen months earlier. I blinked up at him, not quite sure that I understood.

"I should have said something months ago when you –" He broke off and ran his hand over his face to collect himself. "I knew that something wasn't right; it was my responsibility. You wouldn't be here if I had done things right, and Beringer ..."

I moved the mask off of my face with an aching arm so that I could wheeze, "What ... happened ... to ... him?"

Karl's expression darkened and the hand poised on his face halted to hide his eyes from view.

"You ... don't remember?" he asked. "I ... I ... Just remember, Enim, that what happened was my fault. I called him to get you because I was worried, and you – we all know that you didn't mean for it to happen –"

I glanced around the room, half-expecting to find Beringer lying in wait in the bed beside me as my apprehension grew, and my heart pounded so violently that I was sure my ribcage would crack and break against the strike of it.

"Beringer – Erik – he – he –" Karl stopped himself again and made another attempt to compose himself, but there was no mistaking the uneasiness in his eyes. He ran a hand down the front of his usually-ironed shirt that had been unbuttoned at both the collar and sleeves and crumpled up on his arms.

"Beringer – Beringer has died, Enim."

The pounding in my chest stopped abruptly; the machine beside me made a high-pitched noise as it noted the sudden change.

"He's ... dead?"

I shut my eyes in stunned relief. He had crashed against the rocks, breaking my fall, and succumbed to the death that he had inflicted upon all of those local girls. It could finally be over: I had figured the riddle out at last, and now that it was solved, Jack could come back and we would never have to think of it again.

"Yes," Karl whispered. He seemed to be waiting for something more to escape my mouth, but the calmness that had overcome me had eased me into silence. "I ... I'm sorry, Enim."

The door to the room opened again; the nurse had returned to check on me. Karl sank back into the shadow of the open door and pressed his thumb and forefinger into his eyes, looking wearier than ever.

"Don't take this off," the nurse instructed, replacing the oxygen mask over my mouth. She turned back to Karl. "Have you told him yet –?"

His quick shake of the head cut her off midsentence, and she closed her mouth into a tight-lipped smile as she adjusted the pillow beneath my head.

"Well, I'll come back a little later, then, to see if you have any questions or concerns ..."

"Thank you," Karl said, but the statement was an imploration for her to leave rather than a sincere note of appreciation. When the door shut behind her, I reached up to pull the mask off of my face once again.

"What ... does ... she ... mean?"

"Nothing, it's nothing." He gave me an odd look before continuing. "I'm not sure that you heard what I said before, Enim ... Dr. Beringer is dead."

I blinked up at him. He was waiting for a reaction that wasn't coming to my features, though I couldn't think of what it could be. Beringer was a murderer – he had proven that when he tried to kill me. Perhaps Karl thought that I should be taking it more heavily, but my concerns were elsewhere.

"What ... about ... Jack?"

"I – what?" Karl spluttered. "Jack's – Jack's – they haven't caught him yet."

My relief was mixed with uncertainty at the word choice, and I turned my head questioningly as I tried to decipher why he hadn't realized that Jack had done nothing wrong.

"But ... why ... not ...?"

"He's run away, Enim. We don't know how – they've searched the state for him, but he's gone. But ... but don't worry. I'm sure they'll get him."

"He ... should have ... come back ... by now."

Karl paused as he took in the sight of me, and his frown deepened into a V-shape on his brow.

"Come back? Enim ... I don't understand. Do you ... Are you sure you remember what happened?"

My breaths had reduced to wheezes again, and Karl reached over to replace the mask on my face. As I tried to steady the inhalations, the sudden image of Jack huddled somewhere cold and miserable came to mind. My throat scorched as I tried to swallow.

"Everyone ... thinks ... he killed ... Miss ..."

"Enim, Enim, keep the mask on," Karl said, adjusting it again and glancing at the door. "We shouldn't even be talking about this. You only just woke up ..."

"I ... need ... to find ... him ..."

"Enim, please, keep the mask on." He held his hand over it to prevent me from pulling it away again. From so close, I could see every line creasing around his eyes. "Please, I don't think you remember ... at least not fully. Jack ... he attacked one of the teachers a few months ago. You ... you couldn't have known – I've already made sure that they know that, and they can't question you about it anyhow. But ... they think ... they think that when the others found out, and you realized what he had done ... they think it caused some sort of break, maybe, and that you – given that you'd just lost your mother, and now your best friend – they think that's what caused you to ... to go up to the cliffs ..."

I jolted and tried to push his hand away so that I could correct the horrible fault he had made of the story, but he wouldn't allow it.

"And it's like I said, Enim, they don't blame you. They're willing to put it down as an accident, because I know – we know – how you felt about Erik. We know you would have never tried to hurt him, only ... when you tried to kill yourself, and he tried to stop you, and you both fell, he – he just didn't make it."

The sound in the room crumpled out again as though plastic-wrap had filled up my ears. I stared at Karl in my wordless state for several moments as I tried to discern if I had heard him correctly, and only when I was certain that I had did I allow my hopefulness to deflate fully. They had gotten it wrong, just like always: they still thought that Jack was the killer, and that Beringer was innocent, and that I ...

"I ... didn't ... try ... to kill ..."

It was even more difficult to speak with the suffocating realization. It pressed against my chest and crushed the air in my lungs until my eyes burned with dryness, and I blinked rapidly to moisten them again.

"Here, keep the mask on," Karl said, replacing it once again. "And I know, Enim. I know you didn't mean to kill him."

"No ..." I pulled it off no sooner than it had laid over my mouth. "I didn't ... try ... to kill ... myself."

Karl looked down at me with a familiar expression behind his frown. It was one that he wore all too often when he looked upon me, knowing that I was lying to him and trying to decide whether or not he should confront me or let it go.

"Enim ..."

"No, Karl –" My breathing hitched and I allowed him to replace the mask again, taking several deep breaths of oxygen before my chest resumed a somewhat steady rhythm. "I didn't

... try ... to kill ... myself."

"Enim, you were up on the cliffs. You jumped."

"I ... didn't," I breathed. "Beringer ... brought ... me up ... there ..."

"Enim, don't. Don't be ridiculous. Erik wouldn't have done that."

"But ... he ... did. He's ... the ... one. He's ... who ... killed ... Miss ... Mercier. Not ... Jack."

Karl strapped the mask back over my mouth and turned away before I could say another word. From the way that he shook his head repeatedly and the drained light darkening his eyes, I knew that it was lost on him and that he couldn't believe me.

"Don't say that, Enim. Don't. I don't – I don't want to hear it again." He ran a hand through his hair and returned to stare out the window at the sunless sky. "They already think that you're confused. Don't give them another reason. Please."

"But ... I'm ... not. I'm not ... confused."

"Enim ..."

"He ... tried ... to kill me. He ... killed ... local ... girls ..."

"Enim ..."

"No, Karl ... listen. Beringer ... killed ... Miss ... Mercier. He's ... been ... killing ... girls ... for ... months. Miss ... Mercier ... found out ... so ... he ... killed her. And Jack ... was trying ... to find out ... who did it ..."

Karl continued to shake his head, as though doing so would somehow keep the words from entering his ears.

"And then ... the others ... found the evidence ... we'd compiled. And they thought ... that Jack had done it. But ... he didn't. It ... was ... Beringer."

"Enim, stop. Stop right now. This is – you have to know how absurd this sounds. You have to realize that it's not true."

He stared firmly into my eyes in an attempt to see past them, but it was my turn to shake my head.

"But ... it ... is ... true."

He looked at me fully for perhaps the first time. In the nothingness that passed between us, the only sounds in the

357

room came from the deep, artificial breathing and the beeping and whirring of machines. If I closed my eyes and focused on it all, I could have very well been back in the guestroom at the room at the end of the hall, leaning up against my mother's form as she pulled away from the last tormented moments of her life. I widened my eyes to keep myself away.

"Enim, who is Cabail Ibbot?"

The question took me off guard, and for a moment I didn't understand him.

"He's ... in ... my ..."

"No, Enim. Who is he really?"

My breath caught in my lungs and gurgled in the base of my throat. Karl was staring at me with eyes that twitched back and forth between my own.

"He's ... a ... tenth-grader ... in my ..."

"Enim, cut it out!" Karl snapped suddenly. "Cut it out – tell me who he is, *who he is really*, right this instant!"

I shook my head and glanced at the door, half-hoping that his raised voice had alerted one of the nurses to come back and check on me, but the door was shut on the two of us.

"I ... don't ... understand ..."

"Cabail Ibbot," Karl repeated. "You told me he was a friend of yours over the holidays. Why?"

"Because ... you asked ..."

"But where did you get his name? Why did you tell it to me?"

"He was ... the only ... one ... I could think of."

"So you made it up?"

"That we're friends?" I shook my head again, unaware of why it mattered so greatly to him at that moment. "We're ... on ... alright ... terms."

Karl sank down to the mattress. From where he was perched on the edge, his profile looked jagged and unkempt beneath the unforgiving light. He stared at the window for a long while without speaking.

"What's ... Cabail ... got ... to do ... with ... this?"

He didn't look at me as he answered; his eyes were dark

and unseeing as the sun sank lower outside.

"There's no such person as Cabail Ibbot, Enim."

"What?"

"There's no one by that name in your physics class, or at Bickerby at all."

"No ... that's ... not ... true," I said. He must not have realized that Cabail wasn't in the same grade as me, or was spelling it incorrectly. "I'll ... write ... it ... down ..."

"Enim, you don't understand what I'm telling you," Karl said. "There's no Cabail Ibbot – you made him up."

"No ... I ... didn't ..."

"Yes, you did, Enim. You did. Maybe – maybe not on purpose, but –"

"I – didn't – make – him – up!" My breath ripped in my throat as I expelled it, but it was not enough to keep me from speaking too quickly. What he was saying wasn't true. "He's – real. He's – in – my – Physics –"

"He's not, Enim – he's not!" Karl said, struggling to keep his voice from rising again. "I called the school to inquire about him; I wanted to know what sort of people you were hanging around. And when I spoke to Barker, he said his secretary couldn't find the name in her files –"

"His ... file ... is ... missing." I had discovered the same thing when I had broken into Barker's office; someone must have misplaced it. "But ... he's ..."

"No, Enim, *no*. It's not missing – it doesn't exist! I spoke to Barker, I assured him that that was the name that you had said. We tried every spelling and every year – he finally called Volkov to his office to set the record straight: there's no Cabail Ibbot. Not in Physics, not anywhere."

He stared at me with an unruliness in his eyes, daring me to counter his claim again, before plowing on.

"Volkov told me that you sit in the back of his class, alone," he said. "He said ... he said that he's caught you muttering to yourself, and that sometimes you ... you act as though there's someone back there with you."

I wanted to shake my head, but I was too numb to move.

My throat had tightened to such an extent that my voice couldn't squeeze through it if I tried.

"Enim, I'm sorry. I'm sorry that I had to tell you like this, it's – it's not what I wanted. But I – I just didn't know how else ... You wouldn't believe me. You weren't getting it."

"Weren't ... getting ... what ...?"

"You're schizophrenic, Enim."

The gentleness in his voice was scattered with shakiness; it fell over me in pieces rather than wholeness.

"No."

I pulled away from him as though he had struck me again, instinctively curling up to cover myself from his lies. The suggestion was unprecedented: I wasn't insane. He was only saying so because he couldn't find an answer to fit what he didn't understand, just as the locals had concluded that the missing girls had run away and the other boys thought that Jack had killed Miss Mercier. None of them were willing to look past the murkiness of it all to find the real meaning, and so they had simply written it off as something unclean that they no longer wished to deal with.

But I knew the truth, and so did Beringer, and so did Jack. Yet even before the slightness of hopefulness could rise within me, it sank back down to the bottom of my stomach: Jack was gone, and Beringer was dead, and no one would ever believe me.

"Enim?" Karl said, quietly crouching down beside the bed in an attempt to see my turned-away face. "Enim, I know that this is difficult for you. I know that this has been a great ... shock, what with your mother dying and finding out about Jack, and what happened to Dr. Beringer. But I ... I want you to know that we're going to get help for you. We're going to fix this."

I stared at the blank wall across the way unseeingly.

"I don't need to be fixed."

"Enim ... you're ill. You've been ill for ... for a very long time."

I shook my head again, this time with so much force that

the contents seemed to rattle within the skull. The words pressed against me from every angle, and the lies dug beneath my skin before I could brush them away. I wasn't confused, and I wasn't insane: I was positive. It was the rest of them who were so intent to make me into another version of my mother who were ruining anything and everything that they had never understood about me.

But as I laid there on the cold sheets with the horrible sound of the incessant beeping and the wires running in lattices over my form, something began to trickle down from my certainty. And though I knew that I wasn't the person who searched the ocean for the answer to an unsolvable puzzle, or who sought something comforting in the depths of an iced-over river, I also knew that there was something odd in the way that no one else knew who Cabail was, or that his name hadn't appeared in the filing cabinet in Barker's office, or by the sheer coincidence that he had only ever showed up to tell me as much as I already knew at the precise moment when I needed his help.

But if it was true – and if he wasn't really real – that didn't make me insane. Cabail's existence in my head and lack thereof in the world meant nothing: he was just an extension of myself that I hadn't been present-enough to see. It was the same as the music that floated to me from afar: it was a way of knowing when the world got too quiet and needed something back that was no longer there. It was a memory that only I could remember and a part of the world that would be lost if I let it go.

I made a sudden movement to get off the bed, but only half of my body moved: my arms and torso half-flung over the edge of the mattress as my legs remained firmly positioned in their place.

"Enim –"

Karl hurried back to right me before I flopped fully to the floor. Heaving me up, he replaced me gently against the pillows before quickly checking that none of the wires or tubes had been dislodged from my actions.

"Try to stay still, Enim ... You're already injured enough."

I stared down at where my legs were lying uselessly beneath a stark-white sheet, and for a terrible moment I thought that the fall had rendered them paralyzed, but a sharp pain went through my chest and prevented me from voicing the fear aloud.

"You've suffered a serious fall," Karl said. "When you fell, the bones in your legs ... shattered. They don't know the extent of the damage. They've been more focused on ... other things. But considering everything, you were extremely lucky. It's a wonder that you didn't drown; somehow you were carried back to shore ..."

I reached down to pull the sheet off of my legs so that I could see them properly. They were lying as stilly as ever across the white bedcovering, seemingly undamaged and normal as ever but for the fact that I couldn't move them. As I stared at them, a sudden wave of anger came over me: first at the ocean for tormenting my mother the way that it had, then at Beringer for doing this to me, and then at Karl for not believing me – for *never* believing me –

"Enim ..."

"Get out!" I shouted, thrashing at him as he reached out to me. "Get out! Get away from me! Get out!"

"Enim, please calm down – you don't want them to think – "

"Get out!"

The noise ripped from my throat with such force that I was sure the vocal cords had been shredded to pieces, but it hardly mattered. I would never need to speak again.

Karl stared at me in incomprehension for a moment, slightly shaken from the sudden outburst, but then pulled himself away and retreated to the door. Only the beeping and whirring of machines remained with me in the room.

And it struck me that whether or not what he had said was true didn't matter. Regardless of whether I had lost touch with reality wouldn't change the way that they had always looked at me. They would have never believed the story about the local girls or Miss Mercier, or of what Jack and I had been trying to do. They had already convicted each of us to our states and nothing could change their minds.

And it wouldn't matter if they believed me or not, because I would never speak again. I would never utter another useless word that would go unheard, or try to reason with what they could never understand. Whether real or imagined or right or wrong, I was something different, just as Beringer had or hadn't said, and there would always be something barring me from the rest of the world and leaving me out.

And it occurred to me that the only person I wanted to speak to was Beringer, but that that was impossible. He was dead, and even if he hadn't been, he hadn't been who I thought he was. And the loss of him was so strong that I felt something crack beneath the skin stretching over my chest, and it shattered within me and let loose the shards into my bloodstream to rip at every part of me from the inside, and there was no explanation for the pain that I could give to the nurse when she asked me where it hurt.

He was gone. They were all gone – Beringer, Jack, my mother, Cabail. And the others whom I should have harbored some affection for had only ever been concerned about a part of me that wasn't any more real than the aria that sounded in the dark campus at nighttime. And I couldn't blame them for it, because it had been my fault. I had failed to find the answer to the riddle in time to save my mother, or to discover the killer in time to save Jack, or to see Beringer for who he really was, and now that I knew all the answers there was no one to tell who would ever believe me.

I didn't know what had happened. I seemed to have stepped away from the world for just a moment too long, and upon returning found everything fragmented and reversed. They all believed that Jack was a killer and that I was insane, and neither of us could save the other as long as they thought so. The rest of the world was holed up in a reality separate from mine, and we were doomed to run parallel without ever touching. Jack's world had been severed from mine and thrown in pieces away from me, scattered somewhere across border lines and oceans, and I had no idea where it was.

And it wasn't the ending that I had been searching for. It wasn't the final act that I had been waiting for, but rather the poorly thought-up one that had been composed by another writer with a different story in mind. It suddenly occurred to me why *Turandot* had never been finished: it was because it couldn't be finished. The characters were doomed to remain stuck in place forevermore with no chance of finding a way onward. The opera was doomed from the moment that *Nessun Dorma* began to play. The beauty of it was wasted as it gave way to the pain of being unresolved.

And maybe no one would sleep ever again. Maybe the forced un-brokenness that had stretched over the world like ice had frozen every living soul awake, and we would lie as still as the dead as we were made to contemplate the mysteries that could never be solved. Maybe the world would go on without me now that I had no place in it, and I would lie in the hospital bed unmoving and unnoticed just as my mother had for all those months.

As the night fell over the room, I rolled onto my back and stared up at the ceiling. It was the same sight that I had had every night for over a year as I failed to fall asleep, and yet there was no comfort in the familiarity. The snow had changed to rain, screeching against the glass as it slid down the side of the building, and the blackened sky radiated down on me with its emptiness.

And my longing to be in the dorm room and turn to the side to see Jack across the room grew so great that it hurt to breathe, and the oxygen mask hissed until the nurse came to check it. And I missed him so badly that it felt as though I would never breathe again, and it was the type of agony that only Beringer had ever been able to soothe. And despite what I knew, the person whom I had known and who he had turned out to be was still oddly misplaced in my head, and I wished intensely that he was there, because he would have listened to me when I spoke to him. He would have brought me back into the world and kept me from feeling so alone.

But he was dead. And he wasn't that person. I shut my eyes as I reiterated it to myself, letting the understanding echo inside my head endlessly in an attempt to make it more real, but it only seemed to bound back and forth off of my skull. My mind went unwillingly to how Cabail Ibbot had sat next to me on a bench, his short legs hanging over the side and feet not disturbing the snow, and how sure I had been that he had been there, and of how sure I had been of everything else, too.

And the sudden fear that I could be schizophrenic came over me with such desolation that it left me shaking, because it seemed impossible that I had formed the entire idea of Beringer being a killer in my head, because then it would mean that I had been deceived by my own mind into killing the person who had done more for me than anyone purely to cope with the questions that I had so desperately wanted answers to.

And as I thought of how it might have been – how they said it had been – the inconsistent memories untangled to play back in my head. I watched what had happened in the Health Center as though it was a film captured from the ceiling: I was sitting on the white cot in the empty room with a dead expression played upon my face, and then a look like realization came over my eyes, and I stood up and left the room and exited the building, completely alone –

And Beringer entered just moments afterward, but upon finding the room that the nurse indicated to empty, he went back to the desk and frantically inquired as to where I was. And when she only shook her head at my absence, he took off out the door after me and ran up the path to the forest, following me as I wandered through the trees to the cliffs ...

And when he found me teetering on the edge there, he ran after me to pull me back, but I struggled against him so violently that he couldn't keep his feet from sliding on the icy ground, and we plowed over the edge and down towards the rocks, and he was crushed against them as he broke my fall, and I tumbled into the water to sink, but not drown, before the waves carried me back to safety. And I was alive, and he was dead, and I had done it. I had killed him, the only person who had cared for me so deeply and undemandingly, and he had done nothing wrong.

And as I thought it, I was struck by an intolerable disbelief that emptied me of will. I squirmed where I lay, my face shattering as I thought of what I might have done, and the entirety of the world crashed down upon me and broke everything within me all at once.

Tearing the oxygen mask off, I threw it to the side of the bed and let out a piercing cry that ripped from my throat as though slicing jaggedly through it. I seized the IV in my arm and tore it out violently, wishing that it would bleed me of my mistakes, and then ripped every other wire and tube from my skin as well. I wished that I could feel it the way that I could feel the pain in my mind. I wished that I could hurt like I had hurt so many other people who had done nothing wrong: my mother, Jack, *Beringer* –

"Mr. Lund –"

Someone wrapped their arms around me and tried to hold me down, but I had gained an unprecedented strength that fought against their grip and threw them off again. I rolled off of the bed and onto the floor, knees smacking the tile painfully as my legs re-broke beneath me, and continued to scream into the glossy white as I waited for something, *anything*, to come and change what I felt –

"Let me die!" I shouted as the arms reappeared around me, fighting to keep me still. "Let me die! *I want to die!*"

"Hold him down – just keep him still –"

Something pricked against my skin, but it was hardly noticeable amongst the other rips and tears there. I continued to struggle, to scream as loudly as my voice had never risen before, so that I could rid myself of anything and everything that made me feel this way – that made me *be* this way –

"Just hold him down. It'll work in a minute."

And I wished that I could tear myself free of them, that I could run through the doors and walls and glass until I had sliced myself to pieces, and then out into the snow and cold and dark to collapse and die alone – because I did want to die. I had wanted it. If only I had done it then, had swallowed just one more of the powder blue pills and curled up to rest forever next to the fragile, broken form in the room at the end of the hall, then none of this would have happened. I could have left the world to an unknown ending, a *better* ending, and no one would have gotten hurt. No one would be gone or dead – no one but me.

The tranquilizer buzzed in my ears and took over my head, wrapping it in a fog too thick to see through, and my arms fell heavily at my sides and my legs grew tired and numb beneath me. I felt my body slump to the floor, my face pressed against one of the wires that I had ripped from my skin, and the trickling of fluid from the various tubes was like water beneath me – water that should have drowned me, time and time again, but that only ever submerged me for a moment too long, and everything blurred around me to the bright whites of fluorescent lights that had taken the spot of the sun.

Ch. 24

They let me sit by the window.

The view from it was dull and unchanging, like the soft pounding that had come over my head, but the touch of sun was welcome. I leaned my forehead against the glass as I stared out at the remaining snow that the rain had not yet washed away, now just a white blanket filled with holes over the earth, and let the condensation seep into my skin. My skull thudded rhythmically against the glass, but the mind underneath it had gone very still, neither concerned nor content as it settled in place. I could barely hear the voices outside the door from where I sat, but couldn't bring myself to move back underneath the artificial lights in order to hear them better. I was resolved to stay in the ephemeral daylight.

"... calm now. We'll keep him here for observations for a few more days, but then we hope to move him somewhere more suitable."

"You mean that he can come home?"

"No, no, Mr. Lund. That would be a bit premature, I'm afraid. He still needs extended care."

"Can't I give that to him? I've had a patient in my home before. A nurse looked after her."

"I'm afraid that at this point that won't be an option. Enim has demonstrated some violence when he's having an episode."

"Yes, but he's medicated now. You've drugged him – he's calm. You said so yourself."

"Yes, yes I did. But you have to understand the situation that we're dealing with here. The boy killed a man."

"That was an accident. Enim would never – he's not – the entire thing's been ruled an accident already. They're not holding him responsible for what happened."

"Even so, he's a danger to himself. He's tried to kill himself multiple times now. We can't overlook that. He'll have to stay here with us, just for a while."

"Yes, but ... I don't live here. Enim only goes to school

here – and he's still a minor ... at least for a short time."

"I'm aware of that. In fact, I've already spoken to your brother about it. We would be able to transfer Enim to Connecticut; we can get the paperwork all ready for you. But ... he still has to stay in a psychiatric care facility."

As they grew silent, I rested my head on another spot of glass to allow my skin to soak up the cool condensation there. It pressed against my closed eyes and numbed some of the throbbing in my skull. I wished that I could tilt my head to the side to shift the layer of fog that had come over it into the bottom corner; then at least I could regain a hold on part of my thoughts again.

"I ... but ... what will they do with him?"

"They're just going to get him adjusted, Mr. Lund."

"Adjusted to what? You've already given him the medication – he should be fine now."

"I'm afraid that it's not that simple. These things take time. We've given him a preliminary dose of antipsychotics, but it's unlikely that they'll be the perfect match for him. Schizophrenia affects individuals differently – medications and dosages aren't an exact science."

"But you said that he's fine – you said that."

"No, I said that he was calm. There's a difference."

"Meaning?"

"The medication that we've administered has greatly reduced the positive symptoms of schizophrenia – meaning that he no longer shows signs of experiencing hallucinations or delusions or disorganized behavior. But he's still showing the negative symptoms of the illness: emotionlessness, social withdrawal, little motivation, lack of enjoyment ..."

I let their voices drift into the background. In the newfound stillness, I could hear the quiet in my head settling in to stay for a long while. It cozied up to me and pressed itself against my heart like a cat would rub up against my legs: I could feel the fur on my skin and hear the soft hissing. I could have been back in the dorm room at Bickerby with Dictionary and Jack. I shut my eyes and listened for his laugh, and breathed in the smell of his cigarettes, and felt the bed next to me sink down as he hopped upon it to talk to me, to tell me his plan of how we would get away from this place ...

"He'll be all right, Mr. Lund. Give it time. He'll be all right again."

"But ... what if he's not? What if he never moves past this?"

"Don't linger on what your son looks like right now. We know much more about schizophrenia than we did ten years ago. It can be better treated now."

"But not cured."

"No, not cured."

My father murmured something too quiet to hear and the conversation died. I shut my eyes and raised my head to the warmth behind the glass. The lids turned an orangey-red against the sunlight, and the thoughts swirling behind them were muddled and confused. I tried to pick them apart to remember, but the fog that had grasped them wouldn't shift. Everything was either too hard to recall or too painfully clear in my memory. I wished that I could pick and choose which memories stayed and which went, but I had no control over them anymore. I could feel the ones that I was searching for sinking to the bottom of my mind as I tried to bring them up, drowning into the blackness of an empty consciousness.

It was too hard to decide what was real and what was imagined. The things that I had felt so strongly once were now just whispers against my skin, barely touching and hardly noticeable, and I was still unsure of it all. The medication didn't make past events any clearer, and it was still too difficult to pull apart what had happened at the cliffs. The two separate memories of Beringer leading me and following me to the cliffs replayed at random and without explanation, and neither made more sense than the other. It was too difficult to decide what was worse: that I had wrongly killed the person who had cared most for me in the world, or that he was someone so starkly different from the person that I had thought I'd known.

Only Jack would know the truth and be able to confirm it to me, but he was as good as a thousand miles away from me now. We were stuck in different worlds with no way of reaching one another, and I could feel the pain of his absence even through the thickness of detachment that the medication had set over me.

And if this was all that the real world was, then I didn't want to be a part of it. I wanted to be sitting beside Cabail Ibbot in Volkov's class, for once feeling as though I wasn't the strangest person in the room, or with my mother on the beach, with the aria looping repetitively from the car for hours on end, or, best of all, with Jack, standing on a different beach beneath the sun, someplace far away from here and so close together.

The door to the room opened and slow, heavy footsteps sounded on the floor. They paused a foot or so behind me, and a shadow cut into the sunlight as it fell over my form. My father's reflection glimmered behind mine in the window. In the outline that the glass gave of each of us, we had never looked less alike. He was so tall and firm, and I was just something small and warped beside him. He stood behind me for a long while, his hesitation so unlike him, before finally raising his hand to my shoulder as if to grasp it. He let it hover there for a full minute, his eyes staring down at the back of my head with unfamiliarity, before pulling it back to his side again. The movement sent a gust of air down my spine and I shivered. He couldn't touch me.

I pressed my face closer to the window. I could hear someone laughing from the parking lot and scanned my eyes yearningly to search the pavement below. The laugh was familiarly lighthearted and untroubled, with just the hint of crackling from smoking. The person getting into his car was not Jack, though. I watched him for a long while, wishfully thinking that the orderly's uniform and light-brown hair might just be a part of a disguise that my friend had adopted, but then the man got into his car and drove away. I stared after him as he went, still wishing that it was Jack and that I could go with him.

But I was going somewhere else: back to Connecticut. My

father would sign the papers and have me transferred to someplace in the city where I would sit in a cold room day after day, both the staff and my injuries preventing me from leaving to stretch my legs in a long, much-needed walk through the woods. My days would be empty of the chattered-ideas and plans that Jack's absence had left behind, and filled instead with the meaningless conversations that my father tried to hold during the set visiting hours in the psychiatric care facility. He would come to visit as often as they suggested and say the things that they thought would aid my treatment because he wanted me to get better. He wanted me to be cured. He wanted it so badly, and yet he couldn't even touch me.

And I realized that I didn't want him to. I didn't want him to come home anymore, and I didn't want him to look at me the way that he had years ago. I didn't want him to take the family portraits out of storage boxes and line them up on the mantel again. I didn't want to go home with him and eat dinner with him at a quiet table, or to have him stand in the audience and clap when I graduated at the top of my class. I didn't want it – not any of it – anymore.

But I would have given anything to have Jack there with me, or my mother, or the Beringer that I had thought I'd known. I would have clutched onto any of their hands when they laid them upon my shoulder, and looked intently into their faces for a smile. I would have stayed there peacefully forever if any one of them could be there beside me, instead, without the aid of medicine to keep me calm. Because it was them who had kept me calm all that time, I knew. It was them who had kept me sane.

"Enim, I ..." My father's voice petered out in an uncharacteristic uncertainness, and he cleared his throat before trying again. "I came as soon as I heard, son."

I shut my eyes on the window; the light from the sun had gone cold.

"They ... well, they've told you everything already, I think, so there's no point in reiterating it now. But I ... I want you to know that we're going to do everything we can to make this as comfortable as possible for you. Karl's taking care of the situation with the Hadler boy and Beringer, so the police won't be harassing you ... You can just focus on getting better."

He waited a long moment for a response that would never come.

"Enim, I ... I'm sorry, son. I should have come home sooner. I should have – should have realized that you weren't well."

I moved so that I was staring straight at him but found myself looking right through him instead. He was only a few inches from my face, and his hand laid close to mine on the seat, and yet somehow he was very far away. I didn't feel close to him at all, and it occurred to me that perhaps I never had.

I turned away and returned my gaze to the window. The parking lot below was just the desolate sight of a stretch of dark pavement scattered with cars. I missed the window overlooking the horizon in the dorm room at Bickerby, and I missed the way that Jack cracked it open even in the middle of winter to let the smoke from his cigarette out of the room. I missed the way his carelessness rubbed off onto me when he convinced me to do something exciting and unfounded, and the way his scent rubbed off onto my clothes and didn't come out in the wash. I missed him. I missed him so badly.

And they would never understand. They would never look any further than what they already believed that they had seen, and Jack and I would slowly slip further into the roles that they had cut out for us. He would outrun his innocence, and I would be overcome by guilt. If we could meet somewhere in the middle of it all, though, then we could balance one another like we always had. I shut my eyes more tightly as I thought of it, and I tried to imagine where he was at that moment. The idea that he might not have made it out of the ocean was too much to bear, and I shook my head before the thought could enter my mind.

"Enim, they want to transfer you to another part of the hospital now that you're more stable. It won't be permanent – we've already begun to look for arrangements closer to home."

He had to be in Canada by now, I thought desperately. I let the idea fall over me and settle behind my eyes, pushing out the less hopeful ones as it came. He would have shoved the rowing boat back out into the ocean once he had made it to land, and then he would have taken the bus from the ferry dock to the largest town. From there he would have boarded a bus heading north, undoubtedly filled with older women and their knitting projects who had come down for some post-holiday shopping. I could see him sitting next to one, leaning his head against the window to avoid making conversation, his head still ducked low into my scarf to hide his broken face as he pretended to sleep.

And he would act nonchalant at the border when they pulled him off for questioning, perhaps with a ready-made excuse as to why he was going up to Canada for a few days. I imagined what he would say to the guard checking my passport: perhaps something in French about visiting Quebec for the weekend and catching part of the winter carnival. I wasn't worried about what excuses he would make, for I knew that it wouldn't be a problem for him, and I wasn't worried about him trying to impersonate me because he knew me better than anyone. I forced myself to smile at the thought of him trekking through the snow as he sought out a place to buy cigarettes near the rest-stop. He would be all right. He had to be.

"Enim, I know that you don't understand all of this right now, and so I don't blame you for being confused. But if you just trust me, then I promise it will all make sense very soon."

I opened my eyes slowly. The sunlight struck them and my vision of Jack taking a long drag turned to white as though he had been caught in a sudden gust of snow.

"No, I understand," I said quietly.

"You ... you do?"

"I'll go. I'll go wherever you want."

He opened his mouth to respond, but – for what might have been the first time in his life – he didn't know what to say. It was odd that our roles had been reversed, and he had become the one to stumble and fret over his word choice. At another time it might have been a shock to me, but the world had changed so much that it hardly seemed surprising that we might have changed with it. Now I was the one who was deceiving him with empty sentiments and long-awaited promises that I never intended to fulfill, for my only intention of complying with their demands was to wait out the time before I could slip away again.

"Good, that's good then. I'm glad that you're taking this in stride, son. It'll be – it'll be good, I think. It'll work out alright, so long as you take the medication and adhere to the treatments. You don't have to be ... like her."

He smiled encouragingly, but the view was broken as I blinked up at him.

"Who should I be?"

"I – what?" He stammered at the words, having expected a polite smile or nod in return to his own. "You can be anyone, Enim. You can be anything, just like always. Anything but this."

"But I am like this."

He faltered and gave way to a frown before deciding that we had said enough, and he left the room as empty as he had come upon it. When the door had closed behind him, I stood and turned towards it. It was just a piece of wood, and yet it separated me from the outside, and from the cold air, and from the ability to disappear into the familiarity of the woods. It separated me from my mother, and from knowing my own thoughts and hearing the aria one last time. It separated me from Jack, and from carelessness, and from devising a plan to meet up with him somewhere where we could hide right out in the open.

And sometime later, after they had wheeled me down the hallway and into a sparsely-furnished room and tipped a handful of assorted pills into my hand, I realized that I didn't know where he was, or where I was, or what would become of either of us. I had the answers to my questions and nothing else, and they weighed down heavily upon me, and the brokenness of the world shined in pieces before my eyesight, too jagged and misplaced to be put back together. And as I watched the door shut on the image of Karl and my father in the hallway outside, standing together but separately as they watched what would become of me, it occurred to me that I was now the secreted, evaded patient in the room at the end of the hall.

Made in the USA
Las Vegas, NV
19 October 2023

ABOUT THE AUTHOR

Laura Giebfried was born in Bangor, Maine in June of 1992. She is the youngest child of Joseph and Rosemary Giebfried, a surgeon and a nurse, who moved to Maine from New York to raise their family.

Giebfried earned her degree in Psychology and Technical Writing from the University of Maine, as well as screenwriting certificates from The National Film and Television School in the UK, The Film School in Seattle, and the University of California, Los Angeles.

Giebfried has been married to Stan Wells, an actor, director, screenwriter and improv teacher, since 2016. They currently live in Bangor, Maine.